DYING EMBERS

DYING EMBERS

An Art Hardin Mystery

—— Robert E. Bailey ——

M. Evans
Lanham • New York • Boulder • Toronto • Plymouth, UK

Dec. 8, 2012

This M. Evans paperback edition of *Dying Embers* is an original publication. It is published by arrangement with the author.

Published by M. Evans
An imprint of The Rowman & Littlefield Publishing Group, Inc.
4501 Forbes Boulevard, Suite 200, Lanham, Maryland 20706

Estover Road, Plymouth PL6 7PY, United Kingdom

Distributed by NATIONAL BOOK NETWORK

Library of Congress Cataloging-in-Publication Data

The hardback edition of this book was previously catalogued by the Library of Congress as follows:

Bailey, Robert E., 1947–
    Dying embers / Robert E. Bailey.
      p. cm.
      I. Title.
    PS3602.A55 D95 2003
    813'.6—dc21

                                                          2003042132

ISBN-10: 0-87131-997-7 (cloth : alk. paper)
ISBN-13: 978-1-59077-123-5 (pbk. : alk. paper)
ISBN-10: 1-59077-123-0 (pbk. : alk. paper)

This novel is for Linda—my wife, my love, and my best friend.

Linda Diane Bailey
8-16-48 to 11-07-02

She was a Child and I was a child,
In this kingdom by the sea
But we loved with a love that was more than a love—
I and my Annabel Lee—
With a love that the winged seraphs of Heaven
Coveted her and me.

"Annabel Lee," Edgar Allen Poe

ACKNOWLEDGEMENTS

Thank you to Heather McLees, my line editor, who hung in with me when time was short and the pages long.

Thank you to Darby Grover who gave the manuscript the final critique, and helped me keep focused. Special thanks to Darby's wife JoAnn who tolerated and encouraged us both.

Thank you to the Bard Society members for their critique, especially all who made the Exhumas sailing trip: Frank Green, Darby Grover, Tyler Payne, Jeffrey Phillips, David Poyer, and Captain Steven Kerry Brown.

Thank you to Joe Erhardt, the chairman of my writer's group and the members—Gordon Andrews, Meredith Campbell, Kaye Carrithers, John P. Carter, Cathy Hill, Gertrude Howland, Pamela K. Kinney, Linda Lyons, Heather McLees, Mark Pruett, Maurice Reveley, David Swift, and Richard Thomas.

Thank you to Sergeant McLoed for updating me on form numbers.

Thank you to my wife Linda for her unflagging support; my son Sean for his enthusiasm, my son Eric for his encouragement, and my son Adam for his wit.

Thank you to my sister Mary Sue for her faith and support, even when it was needed on short notice.

Thank you to my brother Bill and sister Gloria for their joyous enthusiasm.

God bless my parents.

PEOPLE CAN BE TRUSTED TO LIE. They lie in the bedroom, the boardroom, and the courtroom. The biggest lies are told the loudest. The worst lies are the ones they whisper to themselves.

Tracy Ayers was tall, tan, thin, and blond. She had porcelain skin and a pouty little mouth, ripe with lies. Folks like Tracy lie to me, a lot. I never take it personally. I'm a detective—when people quit lying, I'll be out of business.

Tracy breezed into the office of Howard Butler, dressed for success, wearing a string of pearls and a navy blue shirtwaist dress with white piping and a pleated skirt. She sported perky and unfettered breasts that swayed in unison like a pair of fat puppies doing a vaudeville soft-shoe with their noses pressed into the curtain.

Howard Butler owned Butler's Prestige Import Automobiles. I sat enthroned on Howard's custom recliner chair behind two acres of leather-topped mahogany. I stood as Tracy sashayed from the door to the desk, across an oriental rug that protected the parquet floor. My suit pants had crept up my backside. I resisted the temptation to give a discreet tug on the seat of my trousers.

"Hi, my name is Art Hardin," I said. "This is my associate, Lorna Kemp."

Lorna sat to my right in an office chair we'd wheeled in for that purpose. These days it doesn't do for a male investigator to interview a lady without a female chaperon.

Lorna wore a charcoal business suit over a white silk blouse with a collar that made a ruffle around her neck, a costume I believe she considered camp. She was twenty-two—eight years younger than Tracy—and also tall, tan, thin, and blond. Unlike Tracy, who was a thief, Lorna had a degree in law enforcement and a job with the DEA that started in the fall.

"Mr. Butler said I should come and talk to you," said Tracy. She spoke to me first and then nodded to Lorna.

The desk was too wide to reach across and offer her my hand. I said, "Please have a seat," and motioned to the straight-backed chair I'd placed across the desk from me. Tracy made a swish and flounce of her skirt as she sat, filling the room with the scent of jasmine.

"I think it would be best if we kept this private," I said. "Do you mind if we close the door?"

Tracy shook her head. "What's this about?"

Lorna stood and stepped over to the door. She wore flat-heeled shoes that revealed a lithe and athletic gait.

"I'll try to be brief," I said, and opened the manila file folder in front of me. Tracy's work application was the first item in the fat file, which also contained her bond application, a background investigation, and a list of her financial assets—including those she shared with her husband Ken. Under the top sheets I had enclosed case notes and added a wad of miscellaneous crap to give the file an ominous bulk. Tracy leaned forward and twisted her head to look at the file. I closed the folder. Lorna returned to her seat.

"Just so there's an accurate record for all of us I'd like to record our interview," I said. "Is that all right with you, Tracy?"

"Sure," she said, all smiles.

I took the recorder out of the top right hand drawer—where I'd stashed it after the previous interview—set it on the desk, and pushed the play/record button. After a quick glance at my watch I said, "It is nine fifty-two A.M. The date is May thirty-first. Present are Tracy Ayers, Lorna Kemp, and myself, Art Hardin. Tracy, do we have your permission to record this meeting?"

Tracy leaned toward the recorder and spoke. "Yes," she said in a smoldering alto. Lorna rolled her eyes.

"Please state your name."

"Tracy Ayers."

"Thank you," I said. "You're a cashier. Is that correct?"

"Yes."

"It's your job to handle the work orders, add up the charges, and take payment from the customers?"

"Basically," she said. "I also answer the telephone, direct the calls, and take messages."

"A man brought his car back for warranty work on a repair. The service manager had no record of the sale. The customer had an attitude and a canceled check. Do you have any idea how that could have happened?"

Tracy shrugged. "I just take the money," she said.

I studied her silently. She was good—not a fidget, not a flutter, just the truth that was a lie with a fresh coat of paint—and all innocence incarnate.

"Do you know Mary Ellen Straten?"

"Sure," said Tracy. "She's the day shift cashier. They called me in early because she went home sick."

"Her responsibilities are the same as yours?"

"I don't know. Mostly, I just work nights."

"But you have worked as the day shift cashier before?"

"When Mary Ellen was on vacation," she said.

"Was your job different when you worked the day shift?"

"You have to wrap the deposit for the previous day's receipts when you come in. The armored car company picks it up around ten."

"So, when you work nights all of the daytime work orders and receipts are in the cashier's booth?"

"Sure," she said with a little toss of her blond head.

I said, "We finally found the mechanic's hard copy back in the parts department, but the invoice copy didn't turn up until this morning. It was in Mary Ellen's purse along with seventeen other invoices. Do you know anything about that?"

Tracy gave me the owl eyes and shook her head. "Why would she put them in her purse?"

"She said that she did that to keep track of the money she stole, so that she could pay it back."

Tracy folded her hands in her lap and squared her shoulders. "What does that have to do with me?" The tone of her voice was accusatory.

"Mary Ellen said that she wasn't the only one doing it." Okay, right there

I lied to Tracy. In court I'd swear that it wasn't a lie. I'd say it was a pretext—a tool used to reveal information that might otherwise be concealed.

As to Mary Ellen, I'd installed a pinhole camera in the ceiling of the cashier's booth and we had watched her take an invoice and stuff it in her purse with the money. She wet her pants when we arrested her. We kept the interview short. After she signed her confession and a promissory note she was in such a state I had to send her home in a cab.

"I don't know anything about this, and if you're accusing me, you're going to be sorry. My husband is the shop steward—"

"At Accredited Avionics," I said.

"Yes—and he knows a lot of labor attorneys."

"He's also the sergeant-at-arms for the local chapter of the Road Rats Motorcycle Club. I've got his rap sheet here. I'm sure he also knows a lot of criminal attorneys, but I don't think that you want to embarrass your husband or involve his business associates in this matter." I opened the file and turned past the personnel forms to a sheet from a yellow legal pad that listed an invoice number, a date, and a list of bills and coins.

Tracy glanced at it, made a stern face, and started tapping her foot on the parquet floor. Her whole body jounced in the chair like she'd left her motor running.

"Yesterday was May thirtieth?" I said.

"Yes. Maybe. So what?"

"You worked yesterday?"

"Yes."

"You wore a white blouse and black A-line skirt?"

"I don't recall."

"You were carrying a white leather handbag?"

"So? What has all of this got to do with me or my husband?"

"We'll get to that—but first I want to know, did you steal invoice number 1-7-8-5-2-9 and a one hundred dollar bill, seven twenty dollar bills, a ten dollar bill, a five dollar bill, two one dollar bills, three quarters, a dime, and three pennies?"

At this point, I'd have been a quivering pile of gelatin. Not so for Ms. Tracy. She stood up, made fists of her hands, and crushed her bosom with her folded arms. "No, I certainly did not," she said. "And if you persist in this, I am leaving."

"I thought you'd want to see the videotape before you left."

Tracy sat back down, perched on the front edge of the chair. Her eyes had gone from narrow to quite round, which, along with her parted lips, made her face telegraph a silent, "Oh-oh."

I pushed my chair back. I'd hidden the monitor and tape player under the desk in front of my feet.

"The camera is in the ceiling, over the white table, behind the cash drawer where you wrap the deposits." I set the monitor on the desk and turned it so that we could all see it. "It's called a pinhole camera because it takes the pictures through a tiny hole in the ceiling."

I bent back over to get the tape player from under the desk, and that's when it happened—a long, baritone rip. I felt my trousers go slack across my fanny. I sat back up with a start, but without the machine.

Lorna, her face red, held a hand over her mouth. I looked at Tracy. A smirk had settled on her face.

"How bad is it?" I asked.

"You have little yellow smiley faces on your boxer shorts," said Lorna as she sat and giggled behind her hand.

I looked back at Tracy. Her smirk had turned smug.

"Be that as it may," I said, "the damage is done and I think that we should press on." I bent over again but stopped when the size of the draft area reached panic proportions, opting to hook the player with my foot and skid it within easy reach. I set the player on the desk and scooted my butt back on the chair. The leather felt chilly.

Lorna had turned away and sagged down in her chair. She held her side and gasped for air. Tracy planted her face in her hands and collapsed onto the desk. She wheezed out laughs in groups of three or so, separated by gulps for air.

I closed my eyes and shook my head. I had to laugh.

Tracy sat up, folded her hands on the desk, and affected a serious face. When our eyes met, she slid off the chair and out of sight. I could hear her pulsing and gasping on the floor. Lorna's jaws were tight as she tried to cap off the heaving in the rest of her body.

"Could you help Tracy back into her chair?" I asked.

"Art, I don't think I can walk yet," Lorna said in a faint voice, then slumped back down in the chair and lost it again.

The door opened, and Harold Butler's head and shoulders appeared through the opening. His hair and moustache were both steel gray and he wore a black pinstriped suit. He looked around his office. "Is everything all right?" he asked.

"Yes," I said.

"We can hear you all over the dealership."

"Sorry."

Harold looked at Tracy and said, "Oh my god." He brushed in the door and bent down to lift her from the floor. "What's the matter?"

"Nothing," I said.

"I wanted to make sure that Tracy wasn't as mortified as Mary Ellen," he said and piled her in the chair like a rag doll.

"She's not."

"She's laughing?" he said.

"Maybe I over-corrected." I punched the play button on the recorder. "Tracy, Tracy," I said, "Tracy! Try to focus here!"

Tracy wiped her eyes with her forearm and looked at the screen. She fell silent but not quite sober as the tape played and she watched herself stuff the money and the invoice in her purse. Finally she said, "I guess I stole *that* money."

Harold Butler pushed the door closed behind him and made an astonished face. "Is it all right if I stay?"

I looked at Tracy. She shrugged and giggled.

"On Friday last did you steal . . ." Tracy started sliding down her chair, and I flipped the next half-dozen sheets of yellow legal pad paper into the middle of the desk one at a time. "Tracy, when you stole the first hundred dollars you made this a felony. On each of these incidents you stole over a hundred dollars, making every incident a separate felony."

"Tracy," said Harold Butler, "I know how much money you stole, and I expect you to pay it back."

"I didn't steal anything Mr. Smiley Face doesn't have pictures of," she told him.

I pushed the stop button on the player and then the rewind. While the player hummed away, I fished a spreadsheet out of the file, circled the total, folded the paper, and stashed it in the breast pocket of my jacket. The player clicked to a stop.

"This is the second of two tapes concerning your thefts," I said, "but I suppose we can play this one first." I pushed the play button. Tracy watched, entranced.

I picked up the telephone and dialed.

"Who are you calling?" asked Tracy. Panic replaced the mirth in her face.

"My wife," I said. "This is a two-hour tape and I've already seen it."

Tracy deflated back in her chair and Wendy answered the telephone, "Silk City Surveys."

"Hi," I said, "I have a little problem. We have to back off my meeting with your client."

Wendy ran a detective agency from the house that specialized in industrial undercover work. Her client, Scott Lambert, had a personal matter that he wanted looked into, and Wendy had recommended me for the job.

"I told you about this last week," said Wendy.

"And I called."

"Yeah, to tell me you weren't going to make it. Like always. Like last week you missed Daniel's football game."

"I called."

"So what?

"Honey!"

"Scott is flying out at three and wants the work done before he gets back. This is business. I thought I could at least count on you for that."

"I split my trousers." Now Harold gave me the wide eyes, and the ladies started giggling again.

"So pull your jacket down and don't turn your back to Scott," said Wendy.

The door exploded open, and Tracy's husband crashed into the office. Ken Ayers stood just under six feet tall, weighed a lean one-eighty, and sported a Fu Manchu moustache that drooped around the corners of his mouth to hang an inch and a half below his chin. He wore a black leather vest over a black T-shirt and jeans. A folded red bandanna wrapped his forehead, tied at the back; he'd left the loose ends to trail down with his ponytail.

"The sales manager called me. He told me Tracy was hysterical," he said, his face red with anger. He looked from Harold to me and then back to Harold. "What the hell is going on?"

Harold backed up behind Lorna and pointed at me. Lorna had her black leather purse in her lap like she was digging for her cigarettes or a lipstick—that's where she kept her Walther PPKS. Ken looked at me and I pointed to the screen of the monitor on the desk.

"You okay, baby?" he said as he stepped up behind Tracy's chair and settled his hands on her shoulders. "Hey, that's you on the TV."

"Right hon," said Tracy, "and I'm in big shit."

"It's worse than that, kiddo," I said into the telephone, "the curtain is open like a Broadway play."

Both the ladies giggled. The lights came on in Ken's eyes. He looked at me, leaned over the desk, and pushed the stop/eject button on the player.

"Just a sec," I said and whacked Ken's patty with the telephone.

Ken straightened up and snapped his hand back. He stared at me with his mouth open while he rubbed his right hand with his left.

"Think 'obstruction,'" I said. I put the telephone back to my ear.

"What on earth are you pounding on?" said Wendy.

"Sorry," I said. "There must be some way to reschedule."

Ken dove onto the desk and grabbed my tie. I bopped him on the nose with the telephone. Lorna stood with her right hand inside her purse. Ken let go of my tie and grabbed his face with both hands. I switched the telephone to my left hand and put it back up to my ear.

Harold started for the door. "I'm calling the police!"

I held up my hand. "Wait!"

Harold stopped, his face drained of color. "Have you lost your mind?"

"How soon do you want your money back?"

Ken's right hand went back to his hip pocket. By the time he got his butterfly knife up to my throat Lorna's purse crashed to the floor, she had a double handful of Walther, and I had the front sight of my Detonics .45 inside Ken's left nostril.

"What is going on, and what's all that pounding?" asked Wendy.

"A man is holding a knife to my throat."

"Don't shoot him," said Wendy. "If you shoot him you'll miss the meeting with Scott."

"Here, you talk to him," I said. I held out the telephone for Ken to take. His face was less than a foot from mine, and he looked like he had just discovered a cabbage in his bowling bag.

I waggled the telephone a little. "It's my wife," I said and nodded affirmatively.

He took the telephone with his left hand and raised it to take a swipe at me. I thumbed the hammer on my lead launcher, and he lowered the telephone to his ear in short jerks.

He listened for a few beats. "Yeah," he said. "Yeah, a brown check suit."

"Oh, shit," I said. "Now I'm in trouble."

"Maybe you can bury him in it," he said.

I couldn't hear what Wendy said, but Ken was done talking. His eyes went from narrow slits to saucer circles, and his face flushed. The knife rolled out of his hand and clunked onto the desk. He handed the telephone back and showed me his empty hands.

I took the telephone. "Thanks, doll," I said, "Looks like we have that cleared up. Just a sec." I took the handset off my ear and pressed it to my chest.

"You're crowding the desk, pard," I said. "You want to get back over on your side?" I arched my eyebrows, twitched his nose with the muzzle, and added, "Pretty please?"

Ken's moustache started to pulse, and his eyes crossed. I kicked my chair back. Ken snatched the bandanna off his head, clamped it over his face and sneezed.

"Bless you," I said.

"Thanks," he said through the bandanna. He rolled over on his back, sat up facing away from me, and wiped his nose. I snapped up the safety on the pistol. He stashed the hanky in his hip pocket and scooted off the desk.

I used the muzzle to slap shot the butterfly knife across the desk top. "Put that in your pocket." I returned the telephone to my ear. Wendy was already talking.

"—your fault. You wore that damn suit. I put it out for the clothing drive."

"Yeah," I said, "but I like this suit."

"It's ugly."

Ken cast Lorna a sidelong glance while she studied him over the sights of the Walther. "Just nothing sudden," she said.

"It was ugly when you bought it and the pants are too tight," said Wendy.

"Not anymore," I said. Wendy didn't answer.

With his index fingers Ken folded the halves of the handle around the blade of the knife as it lay on the desk. "I'm going to pick it up now," he said. He put it in his hip pocket with his right hand.

"Okay Hon," I said into the telephone. "Where do I meet him?"

"Yesterdog's on Wealthy," said Wendy. "I told him that you'd be there at one. Try not to be too late. Scott pays his invoices in ten days."

"I'll be there."

"Good," she said. She hung up.

I set the handset back in the cradle.

"Lorna," I said, "please give the gentleman your chair. I'm going to put my pistol away but I think you should keep yours out."

Harold Butler took Lorna's chair by the backrest and rolled it over next to Tracy. Ken sat. Harold backed over to the corner away from the door and across from me. He folded his arms, his face stern and accusing.

"We're almost done," I said, but it didn't improve Butler's face. Ken made a tight-lipped smile at Lorna and folded his hands in his lap. Lorna lowered the pistol but kept her shoulders square and her stare icy.

"Tracy, I know that this is all new for you—the getting caught part I mean. You've been stealing from Mr. Butler since the week you were hired."

"You can't prove that," she said.

"You're busted and you're good for it," I said. "Wouldn't you say that was about right, Ken?"

"Yeah," he said. He rolled his eyes up.

"So here's how it goes when you're busted and you're good for it," I said, but I had to wait for Tracy to stop glowering at Ken and look back at me. "You cop to it all. I mean everything. If you filched a tuna sandwich from the lunch truck—you tell us now. That way you make your best deal." When I said the word "deal," Ken straightened up in his chair and his face snapped over to meet mine. "That way nothing creeps up to bite you on the backside."

I nodded once at Ken, and he nodded back. Tracy let her mouth fall open as she directed a horrified gape to Ken, then to me, and back to Ken again. Harold Butler's stern countenance softened.

I took the folded ledger sheet out of the breast pocket of my jacket and slid it across the desk to Tracy. "Twenty-one thousand, eight hundred thirty-three dollars," I said. "That's all I can prove. If you got any more, I guess you got over."

Ken looked at Tracy with merry eyes. "Babe," he said and tucked in his chin.

Tracy backhanded the paper without looking at it. "That doesn't prove anything."

I pushed the play button on the video deck. "That proves everything," I said. I left it running.

"I don't have that kind of money."

"Of course you do," I said and leafed through the file to the financial work-up. "In the bank next door you have eleven thousand, six hundred and twenty-two dollars in a savings account. You haven't made a deposit in three months, but the days and amounts of your deposits coincide with days that you worked and the amounts of missing invoices. Ken here," I nodded and smiled, "just registered a brand new Harley Davidson with no lien."

"If the Glide has to go," said Ken, leaning back in his chair, "the bitch can go to jail."

"Then there's the white Jag convertible that you drive to work," I said. "You only financed half the book value."

Tracy deposited a cobra stare on Ken. "All Billy got for a down payment was a blowjob," she said.

Ken swiveled his chair toward Tracy, put his elbow on the desk, and rested his chin in his hand. "You don't think, maybe you could suck one out of him for me, do you, dear?" said Ken. "The black Targa GT on the front line kind of caught my eye." His face turned malevolent as he sat back in the chair. He folded his hands in his lap and squared his shoulders. "And I'm going to need a ride if I have to give up my scooter."

"Clements?" asked Harold Butler, scratching a note into his pocket secretary with a gold fountain pen.

"Yeah," said Tracy, still staring at Ken, "fat, bald, wrinkled-ass Billy Clements—the sales manager." She turned her face to Butler. "You can take that and stick it because that's all I'm giving you. I want to see an attorney."

"That's your right," I said, and Tracy looked at me. "But if this problem leaves this room, right now, here, and today, it gets turned over to the bonding company. They'll pay the entire claim and come after you like the cavalry. They always insist on prosecution because they want the court to order restitution plus interest. You get to pay an attorney four or five grand for a deal that makes you pay back what you stole and includes jail time."

"That's blackmail!"

"Call it what you like," I said. "The judge is going to call it three to five on each count."

"Bitch, bitch, bitch," said Kim Goldberg. "I tell you what,"—he waved his tape measure at me—"Jews are God's chosen people. The Irish?" He shrugged and backhanded the air. "Never more than a hobby. We got Egypt and Babylon. We got the Roman Empire and the Third Reich. What'd you get? Lousy potato famine! Still, you come stand around my shop in you unnapants and bitch about lucka-da-Irish."

He draped the tape around his neck and inspected the seat of my trousers at arm's length. "Boy, you got some gas, eh?" he said and laughed. Kim glanced at me and winked. "A little Jewish-Korean tailor joke."

He'd parked his wire rimmed-glasses atop his bald head with the legs anchored in the short gray fuzz that his fifty-plus years had spared him. Maybe five feet tall on his tiptoes, he had a chest that was more like a divot between his shoulders. He wore a white shirt and used suspenders to level his tan wool slacks around a belly weaned on too much pot roast.

"What'd you do, buy this for Dutch Schultz's funeral?"

"It's the belt loops," I said. "All the new suits, you know, the loops are too narrow for my gun belt."

"That's because you shopping off da rack," he said in a low voice, with downcast eyes—as if buying ready-to-wear was something furtive that people did in dark places. "Tell you what, you go get a cheap suit, bring back, and I'll open up the jacket to hide a shoulder rig. I got good at dat in Chicago. Buy something double breasted; maybe I be homesick."

"I've been carrying on my hip for twenty-five years," I said. "If I go to a shoulder rig I'm gonna die grabbing my ass."

"Art, I know exactly how to help you," he said. He ripped the trousers in half and handed them back to me. "Next time you want something done, have it laundered before you bring here."

"Jesus, Kim," I said, "I gotta meet a client in twenty minutes and I'm standing here in my boxer shorts."

"And cowboy boots. Most fetching, if you put da gunbelt back on. The little happy faces very chic."

"Maybe you got something to match the jacket?"

Kim stuck his hand out and waggled his fingers. I dropped the trousers and shrugged out of the jacket.

"I did dis lining for you," he said.

"Yeah. Pistol tears up the lining."

"Lining very handsome, but brown plaid make ugly suit."

"It's very muted."

Kim took the glasses off the top of his head and settled them on the end of his nose. "Dis muted—I'm Air Jordan," he said. He took a seam ripper out of his shirt pocket, made one quick fleck at the collar, and tore the jacket in half. "There, now matches pants."

"Are you nuts? My God! My suit!" My brain churned up the image of me standing in front of a judge who says, "Let's see if I have this right, Mr. Hardin. You strangled this man because he tore your suit," and me saying, "Well, Your Honor, it seemed like the thing to do at the time."

"Not to worry," said Kim. He dropped the halves of my jacket on top of my divided trousers, tilted a tall gray waste can out from under the table, and swept my suit away like fish guts into a bucket. "Hold arms a little higher, please," he said and whipped the tape measure off his neck and around my waist so quick and precise there should have been an audible crack. "Thirty-six," he said.

"Thirty-four," I said.

"You wish."

"The only thing I'm wishing for is pants."

"Maybe I got just the thing, match you shoes anyway. I think your belt fits da loops." He turned and walked back toward the line of garments hung from a rod along the back wall of the shop. "You remember da country singer, da one with the big hair—was down at da Van Andle Arena?"

I hadn't the foggiest notion. "Sure," I said.

"His security guy come down here—slim hips and a lot of beef, just like you."

"Don't know him."

"Conroy—he brought in some jeans to be hem and ordered a jacket." He pulled a hanger of garments covered in dry cleaning plastic out of the line. "Said I cut da jeans too short, so he left it all."

Kim hauled up the plastic and showed me a single-breasted, Western-cut, gray herringbone jacket as he walked back to the table. From underneath the jacket he dragged out a pair of black stonewashed denim trousers. I stepped out of my boots.

The jeans were starched and pressed. The pants legs had been hemmed on the bias. The waist was loose enough for a big pasta dinner and the legs wrinkled a little on the tops of my boots when I stepped back into them. "Just right," I said.

"I guess he taller than you, dey hung straight on him."

"That was the problem."

"So, how you mean?"

"That's right, you said 'Chicago'; you're not from Texas." I laughed. The jacket fit a little snug under the arms but I generally wear them open anyway. I started my belt around the trousers. The magazine pouches and holster had to be threaded onto the belt between the loops.

"What so funny—I like to know?"

"The jeans are supposed to wrinkle up when you're afoot so that they'll hang straight when you sit on a horse."

"He came in a limousine—no horse trailer."

"Doesn't matter. Trust me."

Kim shrugged.

"How much?" I said.

"Don't worry, you regular customer, I'll send you bill."

"How much, Kim?"

"Special for you—just because we're friends—five hundred dollars."

"I'll give you a yard and a half—the rest I'm going to need for bandages and ice packs because I gotta walk around looking like Roy Rogers."

"Two and a half—you write me check."

I started the belt back out of the loops.

"What are you gonna do? You can't walk out of here in your shorts."

"Bet me."

"Two hundred—and I'm taking a beating here."

I stopped hauling on the belt. "You don't sell these to me—they hang on the rod back there until Halloween."

Kim rolled his eyes. "You're killing me. I gotta have cash."

"What tax bracket are you in, Kim? Twenty-eight percent? I'll split it with you. A hundred and seventy-two dollars. Cash."

"Deal, and I hope you step in horse poop—*Roy.*"

• • •

Lorna sat at the wheel of her yellow Olds Cutlass, her eyes closed and her head nodding to something on the radio. When I opened the passenger door and climbed in, she gave me a glance, then snapped her head around for a double take.

"Howdy, Tex."

"Don't start," I said. "We're late."

"What's the matter—Kim out of matador outfits?"

"Gimme a break," I said. Lorna pulled out of the lot and turned west toward Division Avenue. "Closer to take Breton up to Lake Drive."

"Traffic is a zoo," she said.

"How are you fixed for dough?"

"I got parking money."

"Better hit a teller machine," I said. "Kim skinned me for this outfit." Lorna tightened her jaw but her eyes made merry slits under arched eyebrows.

"I like this jacket," I said.

"Really?"

"Paid a hundred and seventy-two bucks for the jacket and jeans. Anything I pay that much for, I like."

"Sorry," she said, "I just got used to you looking like one of those guys in the old Raymond Chandler flicks."

"This is more casual. You know. They even dress casual in the insurance offices now."

She laughed. "In Texas."

"No, really," I said. "This is an All-American outfit. Go to Europe—business suits. Go to Tokyo—business suits. Only in America do you get an outfit like this."

"In Germany they wear leather shorts, and in Scotland the men wear skirts."

"Yeah, and Dutchmen wear wooden shoes, but not to business meetings."

• • •

There's nothing like a Detroit Coney Island Hot Dog, especially in western Michigan. All you can get out here is a chili dog—which is not even close to the same thing. North and east of the city, in Rockford, the Corner Bar sells a lot of chili dogs—the blue-collar version with mustard, cheese, and onions—and holds pig-out contests. The winners take home a T-shirt and a box of Bromo Seltzer.

In Grand Rapids there's the Yesterdog Restaurant, located along the red brick pavers portion of Wealthy Street and nestled among yuppie-puppie used book shops and picture frame emporiums. Yesterdog features a wider variety of toppings for the stately frankfurter, including broccoli, pineapple, and yogurt. It even has a vegetarian chili dog, which strikes me as an oxymoron on the order of "committed political moderate."

The warm late May day had filled the half-dozen wrought iron tables on the sidewalk in front of Yesterdog's with office types leaning over paper trays, trying not to return to work wearing their lunch. Scott Lambert, my wife's client, was not among them, thank God—too much sun ruins my barroom pallor.

"Get us some chow," I told Lorna, handing her a double sawbuck, "I'll find our client."

I headed past the serving counter toward the back room but stopped and turned around after a couple of steps. Lorna had a mischievous face. I shook a finger at her. "Nothing clever for me."

"No jalapeños?"

"No."

The darkly paneled back room had a half-dozen mix-and-match tables attended by an assortment of garage-sale kitchen chairs. An old-style wooden telephone booth graced the near corner. Since it lacked a telephone, I suppose that its purpose was to accent the antique Coca-Cola signs on the walls or to accommodate Clark Kent if he happened to stop by.

All the tables were occupied. No one wore a red cape and blue tights, but a Fidel Castro-looking dude sat alone sipping coffee and reading a newspaper. In the far corner a man in a blue knit shirt, with his hair neatly combed to conceal a tonsure, sat with his back to me. On the table lay several large stacks of fanfold computer paper pushed aside to make room for the laptop computer he bent over. I walked around to the back of the table.

"Scott Lambert?" I asked.

"Yes," he said and looked up. "You're Wendy's husband?" Mr. Lambert was clean shaven and wore dark horn-rimmed glasses. A diet of work for lunch had netted him a thin body, gaunt face, and pronounced Adam's apple. He looked at his watch.

"Art Hardin," I said, and offered my hand.

He looked to be in his mid-thirties but he took his glasses off and set them aside before he reached across the table to take my hand. Maybe he was older than I thought.

"Please call me Scott," he said. "We've got about twenty minutes and my driver will be out front."

I pulled out my chair and sat down. "How may I be of service?"

"I want you to find someone for me," he said, turning his attention back to his laptop.

"Why?"

He quit fingering the computer, sat bolt upright in his chair, and looked at me with an astonished face. "That's what you do, isn't it? Wendy said that you could find anybody."

"Of course I can find people. I need to know why."

"Is that the law?"

"My rules."

"This is a private matter."

Lorna strolled up carrying a cardboard tray loaded with drinks in paper cups and a couple of bags of chips piled on top of chili dogs in paper boats. Scott eyed the load suspiciously, folded his computer, and slid it off the table.

"This is my associate, Lorna Kemp. Lorna, this is Scott Lambert."

"Saw you on the news, Mr. Lambert," said Lorna. "It's a pleasure to meet you." She set the tray on the table. Scott pushed his chair back and started to rise. Lorna patted him on the shoulder.

"Sit," she said, "but thank you for being a gentleman." Scott settled back into his chair. Lorna passed me a comic sneer and sat down.

"Wait," I said, "I'll get your chair."

"Why? You made . . . *moi* . . . go get the food."

"And a good job you did, too."

"I don't know if this is going to work out," said Scott.

"Scott, I respect privacy. I respect yours, and I'm not going to intrude on someone else's without a good reason."

"My reason is valid," said Scott.

"One-eight-hundred-find-somebody—something like that?" I said. "I see it on TV all the time. I don't think they ask any questions, and it's cheap too."

Scott picked up one of his stacks of tractor paper, reached over the lunch tray and plopped it in front of me. "Already tried that," he said. "Every time I call one of those outfits it costs a hundred dollars and I get another stack like this."

I looked at the stack—four folded inches of single-spaced Anne Jones—from Anne Jones in Anyplace, Alaska, to Anne Jones in No-Place-in-Particular, Wyoming. "Guess you're looking for Anne Jones," I said. "Why?"

"I know her from Michigan State. We were friends. I just got to thinking about her."

Lorna made a small mock cough, turned her head toward me, and shaded the side of her face with her napkin. She mouthed, "Is there a wife?" She put the napkin over her mouth, coughed again and said, "Sorry, gentlemen, I have to make a trip to the *casa de pye-pye*." She scooted her chair back, and Scott was on his feet again.

"You should take notes," Lorna said, casting me an innocent face with a little tilt of her head.

"When you get to the DEA and they're sitting around passing wind, scratching themselves, and talking about your 'headlights,' you're going to think I was Prince Charming."

"*Ribbet, ribbet*," she said as she walked off.

"Bring mustard packets on the way back," I said.

Scott sat down. I took my drink out of the tray and tapped the end of the straw on the table to strip the paper cover loose.

"I take it things didn't work out—what is it, fifteen years ago?"

"Twenty. I went to college when I was fifteen. She was four years older. I don't think the age difference would be such a big deal now."

"Scott," I said, and stabbed the straw through the lid on the drink, "maybe the best thing to do is cherish your memories and get on with the here and now."

"What we had was very special, and it's important to me to get in touch with her."

I took a sip of my drink—oh God, the devious wench had gotten me unsweetened iced tea—and studied Mr. Lambert's face. Here was a man, an engineer with a hundred patents, one of which was about to make him a billionaire, mooning over an adolescent crush. He had lost his wife to cancer. Wendy told me that the loss had devastated him, and in the two years since, he had poured himself into his business. Maybe it was easier for him to fantasize about this Anne Jones person because he had known her before he had met his wife, and maybe that way it didn't seem like cheating. Anyway, he looked like a man holding a busted straight.

"Scott, she's probably married to a welder, weighs three hundred pounds, and has six mean-ass kids and an ugly mongrel dog named after you."

"You don't know that."

"No, I don't."

"I want you to find out. I'll pay whatever you ask."

"I'll find her, but if she's married, I won't talk to her and I won't tell you where I found her. If she is socially available, I'll tell her that you'd like to get together, but it will be up to her to make the first contact."

"I could hire someone else."

"If you don't care enough about this Anne person to leave her in peace, then you most assuredly should hire someone else."

Scott slouched back into his chair. "All right," he said. "How much?"

"A thousand shares of Light and Energy Applications."

Scott looked up, and smiled for the first time. "We're still a year away from going public," he said. "I can just give you cash. What do you need to get started?"

"A dream. You have yours and I have mine."

"The current value of a share is about ten cents."

"So it's a bargain."

"Done," he said, and offered his hand across the table.

I took his hand. "I need some information."

He took his hand back and looked at his watch. "I have six minutes," he said.

I took out my pen. "What was her name when you went to school with her?"

"Anne Jones."

"I was afraid you'd say that. What was her date of birth?"

Scott pointed at the stack of tractor paper printout. "Those are the same questions they ask me."

"Tick-tock."

"Her birthday was in June. It was the third or maybe the sixth."

I scribbled that on the top of the stack in front of me. "What year?"

"I was born in sixty-one. Anne was four years older."

"Social Security number?"

"God, I have no way of knowing."

"Where was she from—her family I mean?"

"Ypsilanti or maybe north of there. She mentioned Whitmore Lake, like maybe they had a cottage there."

"Father's name? Mother's name? And don't tell me Mr. and Mrs. Jones."

"I don't know. She mentioned a brother named Leonard. Sometimes she called him Junior, but it was derisive. He was older, and in the Navy. She didn't approve of that."

"Sisters?"

"No."

"What about her major?"

"Fine Arts."

"She graduate?"

"I don't know. It's a big campus. I lost track of her."

I looked up at Scott with what I guess must not have been my best poker face. He squirmed in his chair and turned his face down to the table.

"She was in my physics lab. She was embarrassed to walk around campus with me because people asked if I was her little brother. Sometimes we met at the library or had a burger together. She got real active in the women's rights movement, and I never saw her after that."

"Did she have a boyfriend? Maybe you could remember his last name."

"She always said that she planned to keep her name, even if she got married. I don't remember her going with anyone."

"Maybe that's a plus. Did she belong to any campus organizations or sports teams? A sorority?"

"I don't think so."

"What did her parents do?"

"Her mother was a teacher. Her dad worked at the gear and axle plant at Willow Run," he said and looked at his watch. "I have to go." He scooped his laptop from the floor and stood as Lorna returned to the table.

"Sorry you have to rush off," said Lorna. She offered her hand and he took it. "It was a pleasure to meet you."

"The pleasure was all mine," he said. He looked Lorna full in the face and smiled. "I'm sure that lunch with you will have been the highlight of my day."

Scott was tall. Lorna liked 'em tall, and I could tell that she was charmed. He took his hand back.

"I'll leave you the printouts," he said. "Maybe they'll be of more use to you than they were to me." He turned and took a step but stopped and turned back to wag a finger at me. A black Lincoln limousine pulled to a stop at the curb.

"Tell Wendy," he said with a stroke of his finger for each word, "that her operative in Wisconsin hasn't showed at work for a week." The low buzz of conversation in the restaurant stopped and everyone stared at Scott and then at me and Lorna.

I nodded. Scott's face went blank and he looked around the room. When he looked back, he had colored. "I have to go," he said. "I'll be back Wednesday, early." He walked out.

Everyone turned their heads to watch him leave. Or maybe it was the Castro clone that folded his newspaper and walked out just a few steps behind Scott. Lorna and I sat down. She took her drink out of the tray.

"Iced tea?" I asked.

"No, lemonade," she said. "I don't like iced tea."

"I was afraid I got your drink."

"Nope," she said. "Try your chili dog yet?"

"Nope, I lack the courage."

"So, is he married? We going to do this one?"

"His wife died of cancer."

"Sorry to hear that," said Lorna.

"We're taking the case with some provisos. First, if I find her, she'll have to make the first contact, and second, Lambert doesn't get the address."

"He was flirting with me."

"He's eligible," I said.

"And charming."

"And nearly twice your age."

"And rich as a Rajah," said Lorna, with a Cheshire Cat face.

I studied Lorna's face until she tilted her head and narrowed her eyes. "So why are we looking for an old heartthrob?"

CHIEF PETTY OFFICER LEONARD JONES, Junior, U.S.N. Retired, mowed his lawn astride a green and yellow lawn tractor as Lorna and I pulled up into his drive. He wore khaki shorts and blue deck shoes without socks. White block letters on the back of his dark blue T-shirt announced something about "iron men and wooden ships." A blue ball cap—crimped at the crown with the edges of the bill folded down like fenders—perched over his dark aviator sunglasses.

"Matty told me you had low friends in high places," said Lorna as she pushed the shift lever into park.

"Sounds like an accusation," I said.

"You found this guy in one phone call."

"A shot in the dark," I said. "I called the VFW in Whitmore Lake. He turned out to be a member."

"Oh?" she said, with a little arch of her eyebrows and tilt of her head.

"So why are you and Special Agent Matty Svenson chinning about some old fart PI?"

"She did my National Agency check and I told her that I was going to work for you until my class date came up."

"She have anything nice to say?"

"Told me to get rid of the Walther and buy a nine millimeter." Lorna twisted her keys out of the ignition.

Jones's gray brick ranch included an attached two-car garage. The garage door stood open, revealing two stalls with everything in its place. Several sets of scuba tanks hung on the back wall, and a folded hang glider hung from the rafters. An electric-green crotch rocket lurked next to a "write-me-a-ticket red" Humvee—the kind with canvas doors and zip-out plastic windows.

"Your lucky day," I said, "another eligible guy."

"What makes you think so?"

"Psychic impression," I said.

The retired Navy type pulled up and shut off the tractor. I opened the car door and stepped out.

"Leonard Jones?" I asked.

He pulled off his sunglasses and drilled suspicion into my face with cold, slate-gray eyes. "Yeah, and you?"

I stuck my hand out. He took it and held on. "Art Hardin," I said. I relaxed my hand and arm. Leonard brushed back my jacket with the leg of his sunglasses and exposed my auto loader.

"You look like a cop," he said and scanned my Western livery. "But not from around here. You with Naval Investigative Service?"

"Nope."

"You were in the military," he said.

"Yep."

"Marines?"

"Army. I couldn't suck my face into the mayonnaise jar."

He laughed, let go of my hand, and knocked up the bill of his cap with his knuckle. Lines at the corners of his eyes and a little gray at the temples punctuated an otherwise young and clean shaven face.

"Some kind of trouble?" I asked.

"I said some ugly things about the chain of command."

"Oh."

"In the *Navy Times*."

"You're retired," I said.

"I was with the teams. They still come steal my trash twice a year."

"If what you said was ugly enough, we can go have a beer."

"I don't drink anymore," he said. "What the hell do you want?"

"I'm a private investigator. I'm looking for Anne Jones."

"I don't have a sister."

I looked him in the eyes and nodded once. "Thanks, Chief," I said. "Pleasure to meet you. I gotta go." I kept my hand to myself and turned back toward the car.

"If I had this sister, why would you be looking for her?"

I turned back. "An old flame from her college days wants to know if she'd like to do lunch."

He looked at Lorna.

"That's my partner, Lorna Kemp."

He laughed. "How is she at watching your back?"

"So far, so good."

"You find this sister I don't have and you just give up her whereabouts?" he asked.

"I give her the name and address. Any contact is up to her."

"How do I know you're telling the truth?"

I took the "Ben Wright, Mid-West Casualty" pretext business card out of my breast pocket and handed it to him. "I haven't lied to you yet," I said.

He chuckled. "This phone number any good?"

"Answering service."

"How come you didn't use it?"

"Pretty sure it wouldn't work."

"Come on in the house," he said. He stepped off the tractor and walked toward the open garage door—five foot ten or so of kiln-fired brick with double-fist calf muscles. Lorna got out of the car and followed me up to the house. He held the door open, and we stepped into his kitchen. The walls were pale yellow, the kitchen table and chairs white wicker. The table had a glass top. He waved us toward the table.

"I was expecting a field table with jerry cans for stools," I said.

"My ex did the decorating," he said. "Have a seat."

He took the telephone off the wall, wedged it between his chin and shoulder, and punched in the number off my pretext card. "Yeah, I want to speak with Ben Wright." He opened the refrigerator door and crouched to look inside. "He is? . . . Sorry I missed him. . . . No. . . . I'll call back later."

He reached into the refrigerator and produced three bottles of Vernor's Ginger Ale racked between his fingers, bumped the door shut with his hip, and set the drinks on the table. Back on the telephone, he drilled in another number and returned to the table.

"This is one of the things I missed most," he said. "Only place in the world you can. . . . Yeah, this is Leonard, I want to talk to Anne. . . . Her brother. . . . I want to leave her a number for an old college friend who wants to get in touch."

He picked up one of the bottles, twisted off the cap, and set it in front of Lorna. Lorna stared at the lip of the bottle and then at me—the top was not the twist-off variety.

"Look, just leave her the message. . . . Then just tell her to call me." His face went blank, and he took the handset off his shoulder and stared at it like Lorna had stared at her drink. He went over and hung up the telephone.

"Houseman," he said on his way back to the table. He sat and opened the other two bottles. "One of these days I'm going to drive out there so that we can discuss his manners."

"I'm a little confused," said Lorna.

"So am I," said Leonard, "and I know the whole story." He turned to look at me. "Tell you what," he stuck his hand out, "give me one of your cards—a real one—and write the name and number of this person. I'll see that she gets it."

I fished a card out of my ID case. Leonard watched me write the name and number on the back of the card.

"That's the guy?" he said.

I clicked the pen and put it away. "That's the guy," I said and handed him the card.

"I saw him on TV. The guy with the electric paint—turn the dial and make your car any color you want."

"Light and Energy Applications."

Leonard took a big slug of his Vernor's, washed it around his palate, and chewed it like a piece of steak. His eyes went narrow. Finally, he swallowed and looked at me.

"There was some whiz-kid who followed her around like a lovesick puppy at State."

"That's the one."

"Fancy that! I'm sure she'd remember him. Don't know if she'd want to talk to him."

"If she's married, my client feels that it would be best not to intrude."

He gave me a wry smile. "Not married. I'll give you her address."

"I'll tell her you said hello."

"Tell her she has a niece and two nephews who'd love to hear from her."

Leonard leaned back in his chair. "Tell her my door is always open. She doesn't need an invitation. She doesn't need to knock." Lorna started to squirm in her chair.

"Write her a note. I'll give it to her."

"I've written several times," he said, "the letters came back unopened." He looked at his watch. "Not like it's really that far. Want to go for a ride?"

"Sure." I said. "Where are we going?"

"South Haven."

"Let's go," I said and swilled the rest of my Vernor's. Lorna left hers half full.

"We can take mine," he said. "I don't think either one of us will fit in the back seat of that little yellow thing you drove up in."

"Great," I said, "I always wanted a ride in one of those. They came into service after I left active duty."

"Great," Lorna said, but her tone wasn't what I would call joyful. She took the shotgun seat to avoid the gale from Leonard's unzipped window. The noise from the diesel engine would have drowned out the radio if Leonard had thought one was necessary. The suspension was tight and after every jolt Lorna turned to look evil at me. The Humvee filled the lane and lumbered around on the expressway as we headed west toward the eastern shore of Lake Michigan.

"So why did you say that Anne wasn't your sister?" asked Lorna. She had to raise her voice to be heard.

"She was adopted," he yelled back. "Broke my parents' heart. Dad's gone now and my mother moved out to the cottage at Whitmore."

Lorna looked at me and then back at Leonard. "Well, even if she were adopted," said Lorna, "she was still, you know, like your sister. You certainly seem to care a great deal about her."

"Oh, she was my parents' natural child. She just decided to be adopted." He drove on in silence for a moment and went on, "My ex says that I have to respect her choices. My mother says that she decided not to be my sister."

Lorna closed her eyes and shook her head. She looked at me. I shrugged. She turned her attention back to Jones and patted the wide console between the front seats. "I haven't got a clue," she said.

"Mr. Jones," I said, "it really doesn't matter to us. We wanted to speak with Anne. If the rest is—personal?" I fixed Lorna with a hard stare. "There's no need to pry."

"Look over there," he said, and pointed to a lake surrounded with million-dollar homes. "Frampton Lake. It's only eight or nine hundred acres. The housing development around it is called Frampton Lake Estates, used to be the Frampton family farm, but it made a pretty poor farm—mostly sand and gravel. When they built this expressway, old man Frampton made a fortune selling sand and gravel to the government. When they finished the road, most of his farm was a hole filled with water. He subdivided the part that wasn't underwater and made a bigger fortune. Most of the Framptons are gone now, just two heirs to the fortune—Anne and Shelly Frampton."

"Your sister is a lesbian?" Lorna asked, making it sound like a statement.

Leonard shrugged. "Anne's an artist, Shelly claims to be a patron of the arts. They met up at State. Shelly taught veterinary science. They were both active in politics."

No one could call the ride silent, but nothing more was said until we arrived in the city of South Haven. Leonard pulled into a supermarket and parked.

Lorna said. "Your sister is Anne Frampton, the sculptor? Anne Frampton, who did the stainless steel sphinx in front of the Amway Pyramid."

Leonard said, "I'll be right back."

Lorna staggered out into the parking lot and took stock of the vehicle. I fled for the gas station next door to use their facilities. Twenty ounces of iced tea with a ginger ale chaser doesn't ride well on a stiff suspension.

As I passed Lorna, she said, "I'm never buying one of these."

"You're going to love them in the jungles when you're tracking down smugglers and dope growers."

"That's just in the movies."

I didn't stop to argue. When I got back, Leonard had already returned. He'd placed a paper sack on the rear seat opposite mine. I looked inside and found a smoked picnic ham.

"Soup bones for the soup hounds," he said.

"I guess this isn't your first trip."

"Nope." He shook his head.

"What's going on?" asked Lorna.

"It appears that the Framptons are less than cordial hosts."

"Wouldn't a bottle of wine be a little more appropriate?"

"Not if you're a dog," I said.

"Oh," she said, but the lights didn't come on.

"Under the passenger seat, there's a tackle box," said Leonard. "There's a knife inside. I think we should unwrap our yard warming gift."

Nestled among some road flares, a compass, and some freeze-dried meal packages I found a Marine-issue reconnaissance knife in a metal sheath. Razor sharp. I liberated the ham from the shrink wrap and dropped it back in the bag. The scent of hickory smoke wafted through the truck. Considering my lunch, I was envious of the dogs.

The Frampton residence turned out to be a rambling stone mansion located on a bluff overlooking Lake Michigan. A twelve-foot stone wall surrounded the property, and an iron gate guarded the entrance to a quarter mile of blacktop drive.

Eight acres of neatly trimmed grass and carefully tended shrubbery surrounded the house. Just inside the gate stood a small stone house. Between the wall and the house a little girl with shining raven hair and dark cautious eyes studied us from her swing as we pushed the call button on the intercom mounted on the fence. She was barefoot and wore red cotton shorts and a floral cotton blouse. She pumped away on her swing and summoned her "Papa" in sing-song Spanish. A gruff male voice crackled out of the intercom.

"Who is it and what do you want?"

"Interstate Express," I said, "I have a package for Anne Jones."

"Just leave it with the gardener at the gate house."

"It has to be signed for."

"The gardener will sign for it."

"Anne Jones has to sign for it."

"He'll write whatever you want."

We heard a click, a hum, and then silence until a telephone rang inside the house near the gate. A small man—Hispanic with a sparse moustache, carrying an eight- or nine-month-old baby with a finger in her mouth and a pink T-shirt that didn't quite make it all the way to her diaper—exited the house and walked out to the gate.

"You have a package?" he said as he surveyed the three of us and took stock of the now-greasy paper grocery bag in my hand.

"I want to see Anne Jones," said Leonard.

"You should go. In the house they don't like visitors."

"Anne is my sister, and I need to see her."

"They can see the gate from the house. You should go. This can only be some trouble. They don't want no visitors." Up near the house a motor started. "Go now, and hurry."

He turned away like we were insane. Fright in his eyes, he hurried over to the child on the swing and seized her by the hand. A black and silver Dodge Ramcharger gunned away from the house and headed down the drive toward the gate. The gardener hustled into the house with his brood.

"That's probably Hemmings," said Leonard. "Best back off the gate a step or two."

Hemmings loomed over the steering wheel. The top of the windshield obscured his face above the eyebrows. He pulled up to the gate and jammed the shift lever into park with an angry uppercut. Three one-hundred-pound brindle mastiffs with spiked collars preceded him out of the truck and charged the gate set on full nasty. They managed to get their heads a full foot and a half on our side before the bars stopped their massive chests and shoulders. The wrought-iron barrier groaned in its tracks as the dogs drove against it.

I HELD THE BAG OPEN. Leonard Jones pulled out the ham and waved it back and forth in front of the pulsing nostrils of the mastiffs until their snarls gave way to expectant eyes and dripping jowls.

Six and a half feet and two hundred seventy hard and square pounds of Hemmings stepped out of the truck wearing jeans and canvas combat boots. He carried a satin nickel Desert Eagle in a tan leather shoulder rig, over a black T-shirt that revealed every ripple in his massive build. "Hey, knock it off," he said.

Hemmings's shaved head revealed a mastoid scar behind his left ear and he wore the remnants of a black moustache that started just above the corners of his mouth and drooped to his chin with the consistency of braided rope. He glowered at Leonard. "I told you not to come around here anymore."

"Jesus, a cyclops," said Lorna Kemp. Hemmings took it as a compliment and smiled at her.

"Has two eyes," I said.

"A minor detail," said Lorna. "He looks like he could snack on sheep like popcorn."

Leonard held the ham just close enough to the center mastiff for the creature to get a lick and try to snatch it with his stubby snout. The other two keened and strained quaking muscles against the fence.

"I told you I wanted to see my sister," said Leonard. "The people with me are detectives. They need to talk to Anne."

"I don't care if they're Santa's little helpers. If you don't get out of here, I'm going to rip off your head and shit down your neck."

Leonard threw the ham high over the gate, and the dogs bounded after it, snarling and tearing at the ham and each other.

Hemmings looked at the dogs and then at Leonard. "Suit yourself, squid," he said.

Leonard said, "Can't do a thing from in there, jarhead." He smiled.

Hemmings took a small black box out of his pocket and squeezed it with his thumb. The gate slid slowly sideways and in three steps Hemmings loomed over Leonard. Drilling his index finger into Leonard's chest, he said, "Make your peace with God while you can still talk!"

Leonard wrapped his fist around the finger and bent it back toward Hemmings's wrist until I heard it snap. Hemmings went to his knees. He opened his mouth to speak and got out the word, "You—" The rest was a scream as Leonard twisted the broken digit.

"Hup-up-up, not your turn to talk," said Leonard. "You'd just say some more of that rude crap you learned in boot camp."

Hemmings started his left hand up to his pistol and earned another twist of the finger.

"I sure wouldn't do that," said Leonard, his voice taking the even tone of friendly advice.

Hemmings, his face contorted, eased his hand back down to his side.

"Mr. Hardin," said Leonard, "would you please relieve Mr. Hemmings of his hardware?"

I took Hemmings's Desert Eagle and patted him down. In his left pant leg, just above his boot, I found a six-inch dirk with a black textured rubber handle. I showed it to Leonard and gave it to Lorna to stash in the Humvee.

"Here's the problem you can help me with, Mr. Hemmings," said Leonard. "Members of the Frampton family seem to keel over dead, drown, or die on the highway and I've not heard from my sister in two years. My letters are returned unopened and you're rude on the telephone. Think maybe you can help me with that? Just nod your head."

. . .

The fireplace was big enough to roast a spitted ox. Above the teak mantle, *The Dutchman*—a brass square-rigged sailing ship—took a starboard tack, emerging from the red brick as if it were a fog bank. An interesting decorator piece, I thought, but hardly the *Lyin* she'd parked out in front of the Amway Pyramid.

The maid, Juanita—a young Mexican woman in full black livery, including a ruffled apron—had answered the door and showed us to the parlor. When she returned with Shelly Frampton the right side of the her face displayed a red handprint. She fled clutching her face and sobbing into her hands.

"You-have-in-vay-ded-my-home," said Shelly Frampton, holding a voice synthesizer to her throat. She had almond-shaped nails lacquered a pearlescent white and gave the appearance of being larger than her one hundred and sixty pounds. Could have been the spike heels, or maybe it was her double-D bosom strapped firm and high against the effects of gravity. She wore enough make-up to be the wife of a televangelist. Clad in a white silk blouse with black pearl buttons over a black leather A-line skirt, she had elegantly permed hair some shade of Lady Clairol auburn. Whatever the damage to her throat, the scars lay beneath a black scarf wrapped several turns around her neck.

"And-you-have. In-jured. My-em-ploy-ee." she said.

Hard to guess her age, most of the clues being dyed, painted, or hidden. Late fifties, maybe—and that based solely on the slackness of the skin on the back of otherwise muscular hands.

"Your employee got injured because he sicked a pack of dogs on us for announcing ourselves at the gate," said Leonard.

"I'm-cal-ling. The-po-lease."

"We already did—on the gardener's telephone," I said. "Mr. Hemmings assaulted Mr. Jones just prior to getting injured."

"Get-out-of-my-house."

"Last I heard," said Leonard, "it was also my sister's house and I'm not leaving until *she* tells us to go."

"You-are-tres-pass-ing."

"Your maid, Juanita, let us in and brought us here to wait for you," I said.

"Our-biz-ness. Is-con-clu-ded. Get-out."

"I'm afraid our business isn't quite done, Ma'am," I said. "Mr. Hemmings is handcuffed to the gate and my associate is waiting with him for the police to arrive. The police will take their statements, and then they'll want to talk to us. I expect they will ask Mr. Jones to sign a complaint. I intend to have them speak to your maid. If Mr. Hemmings has any open warrants or unpaid child support you may both be guests of the county."

Shelly turned to Leonard; the muscles in her cheeks twitched as she prepared to speak. "Anne-does-not-live. In-this-house. She-has-a-suite. And-stu-dee-oh. In-the-boat-house."

"You don't mind if we go down there?" I asked.

"She-gets-angry. If-you-int-er-rupt. Her-work."

"So have Juanita give her a call," I said. "Maybe Anne's watching a talk show today."

"There-is-no-phone."

"Given Mr. Jones's concerns, I'm sure that the police will ask you to take them down there. If you refuse, they might come back with a warrant."

Shelly constructed a malevolent smile. "Go-to-the-God-damn-boat-house. Go-to-hell. If-you-come-back. My-broth-er. Will-deal-with-you."

Out of the corner of my eye *The Dutchman* caught my attention again. The edge of the ship, where it emerged from the fog, described the inside line of a three-quarter profile of a bearded man wearing a nautical cap. The bricks seemed to be sculpted into subtle suggestions of planks and waves. The facial features appeared as a shadow cast by the ship—the images opaquely laid one upon the other. I walked up to examine the piece more closely and the image disappeared. The bricks were neither sculpted nor painted. I shook my head and we left.

We went out the veranda doors and across a marble patio to the edge of the bluff, where we found a weathered wooden stairwell. Halfway down, a deck provided a resting place and a view of the lake over the roof of the stone boathouse, which had been built on a cement pier out into the lake. The boathouse had a dock and was as big as a four-bedroom home. A foot pedal boat, a catamaran day sailer, and a fifty-foot Donzi with a canvas cockpit rested against fenders, tied up at the dock.

I knocked on the door. No answer. I knocked loud and hard until I got an answer.

"Get the fuck out of here!" said a woman's voice from inside the boat-house. "Leave me the hell alone."

"There's someone here to see you," I said. "This'll just take a minute."

"What language would you like to do this in, asshole? You don't understand English? Get fucking lost!"

"Please! This is important," I said.

Inside the house someone touched off a large hand cannon. The bullet
ripped through the top of the door above our heads and gave us a shower of
splinters and paint chips. Leonard and I stood for a frozen moment and
examined a half-dozen similar ragged holes in the top of the door.

"The next one won't be as kind!" The voice seemed closer to the door.
"I'm working, asshole. Leave me the fuck alone!"

"Annie?" asked Leonard.

We got silence for a reply. Then someone, inside, snapped off the latch.

Leonard turned the doorknob and gave it a shove. The door creaked
slowly open and revealed a woman standing in an unlit hallway. She wore
tan coveralls under a black welder's apron. On her head was a welder's
helmet with the face shield turned up to reveal an angelic face. She wore a
heavy gray gauntlet on her left hand and a large frame revolver on her
right. Her eyes were dark watery pools.

"Why have you come here?" she asked.

"To see you, Annie-fannie," said Leonard. He smiled and spread his arms.

It happened in a flash. She pitched the helmet aside, took maybe three
steps, and leapt on Leonard—her arms around his neck and her legs
around his waist. Luckily for Leonard she was only about five feet tall and
a shade over a hundred pounds—gear and pistol included. Leonard staggered back a step but kept his feet.

"I missed you," she said, the only part I could make out. The rest was
sobs. She settled her face into Leonard's neck.

"You missed Dad's funeral," he said, patting her back.

"I was in Europe. I didn't find out until I got back." She wiped her face
on the sleeve of her coveralls. "I called Mom. She said I had broken Dad's
heart and hung up."

"After Dad died," said Leonard, "I retired to be here for her. She's
moved out to the cottage. Sometimes she says mean things when she's
hurt or frightened."

"I know," said Anne. She snuggled her head back to Leonard's neck and
tightened her hug. She made a sob and retched out, "So do I."

I left them, walked down the hall and turned right. I found myself in
the well of a two-story studio. The west wall and roof were made of glass
like a greenhouse. The room should have been an inferno, but a cool

breeze off the lake was drawn in through a series of screens on the bottom row of windows and blown out through exhaust fans in the ceiling. The studio comprised fully half of the building and held a jumble of construction materials. In one corner a kiln and casting furnace glowed cherry red.

A gas welding rig with long, coiled hoses on a small cart sat parked at the base of a stone and metal spiral—a double helix—topped with a burst of bright metal balls that swayed on the ends of thin metal rods. Drawings cast about on the floor were titled, *Reach for the Stars.*

"I wrote you every couple of months," said Leonard as he and Anne walked arm-in-arm into the studio, "but I always got them back unopened and marked 'Return to Sender.'"

"I really don't understand that," said Anne.

"I called, but I got the houseman. He was always rude. He said you didn't want to talk to anyone."

"Brian?" she asked. "He is usually such a sweetheart."

"Yes, ma'am," I said. "He is such a sweetie that he sicked a pack of dogs on us when we came to the gate today."

"This is Mr. Hardin," said Leonard. He gave her the card I had written Lambert's telephone number on. "That's his card."

Anne set her pistol on a wooden crate that had been pressed into service as a table for a newspaper and a half-eaten Danish roll. She examined the front of my card and then the back.

"Scotty Lambert?"

"Yes, ma'am."

"What does he want?"

"He's not fifteen anymore. I think he wants to do lunch."

"What if he's a nutcase?"

"He owns a large manufacturing firm dealing in cutting-edge technology. His wife passed away a couple of years ago and he said that he just got to thinking about you. On the up side I can tell you that he, for one, hasn't shot at me lately."

Anne laughed. "No one bothers me while I'm working, and no one sees a work in progress. But since you brought Lenny, I'll let you slide—this time."

"That's nice."

"So you're just going to tell him where I am?"

"No, ma'am. I give you his name and number, and if you want to talk to him it's up to you to make the contact. I do need you to give me some little tidbit of information that only you and he would know so that he will feel assured that I contacted you."

Anne made a mischievous face.

"It doesn't have to be personal," I said. "Something about school, maybe."

"We were in the same physics lab. The professor didn't like either one of us so he put us together. Scotty was like this computer geek and I was a fine arts major, so the professor thought we were wasting a bench."

"He said that sometimes you met at the library or you had a burger together."

"And that was it?"

"Yes, ma'am."

Anne laughed. "Tell him, 'Tacos—no onions.' He'll know you talked to me."

"Thank you," I said. "I have one more question—not about Mr. Lambert—if you don't mind."

"Sure."

"*The Dutchman.*"

"You were in the main house?"

"Yeah," I said, "we met Shelly, not very—"

"—Really? Shelly's been gone for a while."

"Out of town?"

Anne shrugged. "Wherever Shelly goes, she's the real work of art."

"What do you mean?"

Anne laughed and waved her hand at her face. "Takes a lot of paint," she said. "A piece of work, the bard would say."

"What happened to her voice?"

"Car accident."

"Sorry to hear that. Tell me about *The Dutchman.*"

"That's about Scotty."

"How so?"

"You want to know how the ship captain appears?"

"Absolutely."

"It was our physics project. There's a photoelectric cell under the main-sail. When the light enters from the side it puts a positive charge on the paint pigment and causes the ghost to appear. It looks like a shadow but it's not."

"On brick?"

"It's not brick. The wall behind the artwork is cast out of a ceramic mud that's electrically conductive, even after it dries. Scotty invented it."

A knock exploded onto the door. "Don't shoot," I said. "I think that's the police."

It was—a county sheriff's deputy with a brown uniform and a Smokey Bear hat. He escorted us back to the gate where an ambulance, the county animal control truck, and two patrol cars showing red and blue rollers crowded around Leonard's Humvee.

Hemmings sat in the back of the ambulance with his hand wrapped with an ice pack. His knife and gun had been laid out on the front deck of a patrol car.

Shelly stood in front of one of the deputies and made monotone threats and demands. The deputy stared benignly down at her. Lorna stood next to the cruiser and showed me a mean face over folded arms.

"What's up?" I asked.

"You didn't close the gate," she said. "When the dogs finished the hors d'oeuvres, I had to climb on top of the truck to get away from them."

"Why didn't you just get inside the truck?"

"Canvas doors."

"Uh," I said. "Sorry we didn't think to lock the gate."

"It worked out. They're going to charge Mr. Hemmings with 'felonious assault by doggie.' But they want to talk to Mr. Jones about Hemmings's broken finger."

Anne steamed up to Shelly. "Listen," she said over a pointed finger, "unlike you, I have a family. Where do you get off returning my brother's letters?" Shelly turned from the deputy. Anne added a sarcastic smile and the word, "Bitch."

Shelly caught Anne with a roundhouse open-handed slap. Leonard wedged himself between Shelly and Anne.

The deputy smiled, and I saw him mouth the words, "Hot damn." He grappled Shelly to the patrol car and bent her over the front deck. "You're under arrest," he said, reaching for his handcuffs.

LORNA KEMP DROPPED ME in the parking lot behind my office a little after nine. The sun hung low, leaving just a sliver of red-orange to filter through the trees. I shut her car door and she motored off with a wave and a toot.

My car, a nondescript dark sedan—all dash and no flash—had the parking lot to itself. I dug out the keys, opened the door, and found the steering wheel dangling by the ignition wires. A cement block nestled in the driver's seat. The windshield lay sprinkled about on the dash, seats, and floor.

Lorna loitered at the stop sign, waiting for traffic to clear on Forty-fourth Street. I thought about running over to catch her before she pulled out, but on the way up from Whitmore Lake we had discussed her open cases and decided that one of them needed a morning surveillance. Better to let her get some rest. I could have the car towed and write up the Lambert/Jones case while I waited for a ride from home.

My office is in Kentwood, the first suburb south of Grand Rapids, in a row of brick three-story office buildings on Forty-fourth Street. I rent a corner office off the common area on the first floor, which is down a flight of steps from the main door—the office being sort of half-assed in the basement. "Peter A. Ladin Associates" was painted on the window, facing the common area—black letters shadowed in red.

I unlocked the door and turned on the lights. Marg, my late partner's widow, had left a note taped to my office door. "I NEED YOUR EXPENSE REPORT!"

After Pete died, Marg sold me her half of the business for a dollar and accounts receivable. She stayed on to work as the secretary, typing my reports and invoices, and operates her own accounting business from the reception desk. The name painted on the window makes Marg feel at home.

I left her note on the door. If I took it down, it was going to be hard to deny that I'd seen it. I flopped into the chair at my desk and dialed up Wendy on the telephone.

"Silk City Surveys," she said. She sounded chipper, but then, she didn't know it was me yet.

"Hi, Sweets," I said, "this is your one and only." I rocked the chair back and stacked my heels on the corner of the desktop.

"If you're not in jail, how come you're not home?"

"How do you know I'm not in jail?"

"You didn't call collect," she said.

"I'm at the office. I found your client's old flame."

"Really. What do you think?"

"I think he's not her type but she's not married and—after today—maybe not attached. I gave her his number."

"So you're on your way home? Bring milk and bread."

"I need a ride."

Less than commiserate, she said, "Now what?"

"Fan club disabled my car again."

"I'm watching something."

"Enjoy. I gotta call the police and write the report on Scotty's gal pal."

"He doesn't like 'Scotty,' and I'm watching the last part of a miniseries that's on until eleven."

"Give it an hour and send one of the boys. Scott gave me a message for you. He says that your operative in Wisconsin hasn't been to work in a week."

"Must be why I haven't had any daily reports. I e-mailed the Dixon Agency this morning but so far, no answer. Don't forget the milk and bread," she said, and hung up.

I put my feet back on the floor and dialed up the Kentwood Police administrative number. Due to the lateness of the hour I got Kent County Dispatch.

The dispatcher said her name was Deputy Paxton—a voice like honeyed almond. I complained about my windshield while I wondered if she looked as sultry as she sounded. She said that if the damage was less than a hundred dollars I'd have to come in to make the report. I told her the car was "deadlined." She said they'd take a report as soon as someone was available.

I put the phone back in the cradle and stirred the clutter on the top of my desk until a yellow pad surfaced. I scrawled "New file series—new client, Light and Energy Applications."

By the time I'd scratched out the details of the Lambert/Jones file, I heard the front door open. I looked up at the video monitor that hung from the ceiling diagonally across from my desk and watched Gerald Van Huis, the Chief of Detectives from Kentwood, scan the office like Bo-Peep looking for her sheep.

"Back here, Jerry," I called out, clipping a memo on the front of my report to cover Lorna's time.

Detective Van Huis, six feet and some change and well over two hundred pounds, had a fair complexion and a full shock of sandy hair despite his five-plus decades.

"What are you, psychic now?" he said. He strolled into my office with his hands in the pants pockets of a black suit. He wore a white shirt with the collar unbuttoned, and his tie loose.

I pointed at the monitor. "Chip-cam in the smoke detector on the back wall of the front office."

His face bloomed into a toothy smile. "Hey, Tex, what happened to your hoss?"

"Somebody fed it a cement hay bale," I said, "but I sure am flattered by this kind of attention."

"We have a jackknifed semi up on Broadmoor, and the patrol sergeant is taking a dump. I was on my way home, so I told them I'd take the call to spare everybody your usual bullshit."

The left side of my credenza is a small refrigerator. I opened the door. "I got cola and orange. Sorry, no sarsaparilla in here, Kemo Sabe."

"Orange. You doing a cowboy divorce case or did you take up community theater?"

"I have a Jewish Korean tailor," I said, casually, as if that explained everything, and handed him the soda. I took out a cola for myself.

Van Huis tapped the top of the can twice and sat in the wing-back chair across from my desk. "And?"

"You had to be there."

"I don't want to hear it. If you shook this up I'm going to go put that cement block in your back seat." He flinched as he opened the can and said, "So who'd you piss off today?"

I popped open my can. "I'd have to work up a list," I said. "It's been a long day."

"So how are you going to get home?"

"I called my wife. She's sending one of the boys."

He reached into the breast pocket of his suit coat and dropped a pad of white raffle tickets on my desk. "My church is having a raffle. You live on the lake. We're giving away a bass boat, and the dealer will make you a good deal on the trailer."

I picked up the pad. He hadn't sold any yet.

"Hole in the water impossible to fill with money," I said. "Besides, I hate fish."

"Tickets are a buck apiece. How many you want?"

"Five," I said. Van Huis looked happy. I peeled off five tickets and started filling out the stubs. "You still driving that ratty minivan with the fake wood siding?"

"It's got a windshield," he said and took a slug of soda.

I finished the stubs and handed back the pad. I took a similar pad from my jacket. "My son's football team is having a summer raffle for new equipment. The Chevy dealer donated a Silverado Suburban. It's a couple years old, but the tires come with it."

He laughed. "Hardin, you're a pain in the ass," he said. He took the pad, peeled out five tickets, and tore them off.

I asked, "At what point did you delude yourself into thinking that you weren't going to buy the church raffle tickets yourself?"

He set the soda on my desk and leaned forward to fill out the stubs. "Some guys really sell these things."

"Sure they do," I said.

"One of the ushers already sold two hundred."

"Does he fish or has he just got a gambling problem?"

"I think he fishes."

I watched him fill out the stubs while I finished my soda. I crumpled my can and dropped it in the wastebasket at the end of my desk.

"Hey, there's a deposit," he said.

"Not on those. I bought 'em down in Indiana when I went to get Wendy's cigarettes."

"Kay-ryst, Hardin! I come over here and you feed me bootleg soda?"

"You could always run me in."

He rolled his eyes up to look at me directly. "No," he said. "I'm waiting for something good."

"You busted me for murder once."

"That was a hummer," he said and flipped the pad back in front of me as he clicked his pen and put it away. "But it had its moments." He smiled.

Headlights flashed across the short window high on the back wall of my office.

"That's probably my ride," I said. Van Huis finished his soda and dropped the can into the wastebasket.

I locked up, and we went out to the lot. We found my son Ben leaning against the front of his brother's Camaro with his arms folded and one heel racked on the bumper.

A month short of his seventeenth birthday, Ben stood six feet tall, was lean at the waist and wide at the shoulders. He wore a black denim jacket over white jeans and a black T-shirt. He had my brown eyes and—I told him—his mother's hair. Far too long to suit me. Wendy liked it. When he was out with me he tied it in a ponytail and hid it under a baseball cap.

"I would have donated my left testicle to science to have a car like that when I was a teenager," said Van Huis.

The Camaro was a black T-top with a four speed, Corvette rims and tires, and a sport suspension. Eye candy. Ben had turned off the ignition and Van Huis could not hear the part that I would have sacrificed significant appendages for—two-and-a-half-inch dual-exhaust pipes relieving a big block V-8 that loped like a three-legged dog until you cranked it on.

"So would I," I said as I turned to look at Ben and told him, "and your brother would blow a gasket if he saw you sitting on it."

Ben made an embarrassed smile that included a roll of his eyes. He stood up, hooked his thumbs in the pockets of his jeans and walked over to look in my car. He had driven on a dawn-to-dusk "farm license" since he was fourteen. Working for local farmers, he'd piloted everything from harvesters to five-ton straight trucks. He proudly displayed his newly acquired "real driver's license" to anyone who cared to look. But how Ben got out of the driveway in his brother's car was a story I could hardly wait to hear.

"Hey, Pop," he said, "you're supposed to put that kind of stuff in the trunk."

"Let me get my flashlight," said Van Huis. "Maybe they keyed the paint too." He reached into the open window of his minivan and extracted a flashlight that was a "two stroker" on the scale of the "twelve cell rule."

Kent County District Courts guarded the twelve cell rule jealously. Unarmed desperados who resisted arrest could be subdued within the twelve cell rule. The amount of force was calculated as follows: two strokes with a six cell, three strokes with a four cell, et cetera. I expected that Van Huis could probably subdue an ox with his six cell and stay within the budget. He flashed it up and down the side of my car.

"What the hell make is this thing, anyway?" he asked. "There's no emblem."

"Buick body, Olds engine, Chevy transmission." I said. "Pick a brand you like and go with that. When they made this one, they all looked alike except for the bumpers and tail lights."

"Where do you get off ragging on my van and driving a dinosaur like this?"

"It's got five hundred horsepower."

"It's got bullet holes, for God's sake," said Van Huis.

"I was a little slow making the jump to light speed."

"But not in Kentwood?"

"'Course not," I said.

"I think the windshield job probably totaled it," said Van Huis. "You still want a report for the insurance company?"

"I want you to catch the perpetrators and bring them to justice."

Ben laughed.

"Might have been eco-terrorists trying to get this thing off the road," said Van Huis.

I caught a glint of light off a puddle next to Van Huis's foot. I pointed. "I think you got a clue, right next to you on the ground."

He searched out the puddle—really just a dribble—with his light. I stooped over, stuck my fingers in the liquid, and stood back up to inspect my fingers in the light of his torch. They shimmered pale green.

"Antifreeze," he said. "Probably yours."

I rubbed the liquid between my thumb and fingertips and held it under my nose. "No," I said. "Hydraulic fluid."

"Hydraulic fluid is red," said Van Huis.

"When it's green, what does that mean?"

Van Huis guessed. "Foreign car?"

"In this case a Jag, I think."

"DANNY HAD A DOUBLE DATE so he took Mom's car," said Ben. We lined up at the stop sign with Detective Van Huis's fake-woody minivan. He went left and Ben turned right onto Forty-fourth Street.

"It's a school night," I said.

"Danny would've been in college if he hadn't broke his leg and been in traction for six weeks."

"Coulda, shoulda, woulda," I said. "Take the next . . ."

I flopped down the visor and focused the vanity mirror out the rear window, we had three sets of headlights behind us.

Ben flipped up the turn signal. "It's a school play," he said. He took his foot off the gas and pushed in the clutch.

"Oh yeah? What are they doing?"

"*Oklahoma*," he said, and eased into the turn—onto a residential street.

"Sorry I missed it."

"It's on again tomorrow and Friday," said Ben. "What are we doing? Do we know somebody down here?"

"Nope. Checking for a tail."

"Cool."

The car directly behind us passed the intersection, but the second one turned in after us. I watched for it to flash under the street light—a small white car with a dark top.

"Maybe your mother and I will go see it on Friday," I said. "Take the next right."

"Friday is sold out. We have somebody?"

"Maybe."

"Cool."

"Signal a left turn but turn right." I watched the car in the mirror. Ben flipped down the turn indicator and got on the clutch and brake for the turn. The car behind us signaled a left turn. We made the right.

At this point the casual observer would think we were nuts, but a pro would know he was toasted or that I was cleaning myself. He'd pass the intersection, scoot up to the next parallel street and make his turn. A cop would come ahead around but would close up fast and touch off his rollers. Only an idiot or a shooter would stay behind us. The car behind us made the turn with his headlights off.

"He's still there," said Ben. He got his foot into the gas. The torque raised the right front fender.

"Ease off," I said. "This is a residential area. Just lock the doors and head for the bright lights." My pistol started to itch, but it's one of those things you just can't scratch in polite company—or in front of your impressionable, almost seventeen-year-old son. "If this guy is dumb enough to think he's still covered, let's let him follow us down to the Kentwood Police Department."

The driver of the car following us waited until we were on Forty-fourth and he had a cover car before he pulled on his headlights. It had to be embarrassing for him because the oncoming cars kept flashing their lights. The stiff suspension on the Camaro made it hard to ID the make of our trail car in the vanity mirror.

The parking lot of the Kentwood Police Department was an island of bright light in a sea of vacant land. To the west and the north apartment complexes stood silhouetted in the night-time glow of Grand Rapids. To the west and south fallow farm lands and feral orchards waited for the city to consume them. Kentwood dispatches through the county at night, so the doors were locked. I picked up the red telephone by the door.

"Emergency operator," said a sweet but mechanical female voice.

"My name is Art Hardin. My vehicle was vandalized in the parking lot at my office, and now I am being followed."

"Where are you?"

"At the front door of the Kentwood Police Department."

"Are you alone?"

"My son's with me," I said.

"How old is your son?"

"Nearly seventeen."

"What kind of car was following you?"

"Kind of a small white car with a dark top. I'm not certain of the make or model."

She asked, "How many people were in the vehicle?"

"Don't know."

"Did you have some kind of altercation in traffic?"

"Nope," I said.

"How do you know this car was following you?"

"It followed us through a half-dozen turns and made some of them with the headlights off."

"Well, if the car isn't there now, perhaps you were mistaken," she said.

"I'm a detective, ma'am. There's no mistake."

"What department are you with?"

"I'm private."

"Are you armed?"

"Yes, ma'am," I said.

"Do you have a permit?"

"Yes, ma'am."

"What's your day job?"

"I'm a detective—all day and all night."

"If there's no car there now, I can't send a police officer. Perhaps you could come to the office in the morning and make a report."

"Sure," I said. She hung up while I was saying. "Thank you." I went back to the car, climbed in, and hooked up my seat belt.

"What did they say?" asked Ben.

"Told me to take two aspirin and phone them in the morning. Let's go home."

"They didn't say that," said Ben. He turned on the radio—head-banger music. I turned it off.

"No way I'm listening to that," I said.

"I don't want to listen to them 'doo-wop' oldies you always put on. What did they really say?"

"They wanted to know if the guy was here now. How about country?"

"You can listen to that while you're riding with Daniel. That's all he has on the buttons. I don't see why you're always so sarcastic about the police."

"I'm a child of the sixties," I said. "But you're right—that was a reasonable question."

"I got just the thing," said Ben. He took a compact disc out of the console and popped it in the player—somebody doing some very hot licks on "Take the A Train."

"Duke Ellington?"

"Cherry Poppin' Daddies."

"That's my father's music."

"It's baaa-ack."

On the way back to Forty-fourth, a small white car with a dark top came out of an apartment complex after us.

"Now what?" asked Ben.

"How much gas have we got?"

"Almost full. You want to head for the Mackinaw Bridge? Maybe our friend hasn't seen the Upper Peninsula lately."

"I don't know," I said. "This beast gets real thirsty on the expressway. If he's running a four or a six banger, we won't be able to shake him that way. Just head for the house. If he's still with us on Cannonsburg Road, turn left on Addison."

"Plan B?"

"You know that long curve with the buttonhook on the end as you go by Grover's Orchard?"

Ben smiled and stopped for all the yellow lights. At Addison Road we still had company. Our friend had his bright lights on but wasn't making any attempt to close it up.

"You want me to do this?" I asked.

"Nope. I got it, Pop," said Ben.

"We bend this Camaro and we're going to have to get out of town," I said.

"I'll just tell Daniel it was your idea."

"Thanks," I said. "After you turn on Addison pull over and we'll do a Chinese fire drill."

"I can do it."

"Your mother will kill me."

"Let's don't tell her," said Ben.

"It's going to be hard to cover up when we're laid out in intensive care under a pile of tubing."

"I got it!"

"You've done this before?"

"No," he said.

"Then you ain't doing it now!"

"So, I did it before."

"What do you mean you did it before? Are you nuts? Where do you get off driving like that—your brother's car—for God's sake!"

"Daniel's good at it, too. He showed me. Now I'm better than him."

I sighed. "That's nice to know."

"It's kind of the local challenge," said Ben, as if he were revealing a secret. "You know, that's why Grover plants corn on the north side of the road."

I knew all about Grover, Grover's chopped 'fifty Mercury, and how, thirty years ago, he'd rolled it through his dad's peach trees that, in those days, had been planted on the north side of the road. The local joke was that Grover's dad asked him if he was hurt. When he said, "No," his dad said, "Good—that way I can hurt you myself."

Grover recovered, his dad retired, and Grover regularly showed up at the township board meetings to bitch about getting the road closed, or straightened, so that the local "hooligans" would "quit running down his corn."

Belding stages a Fourth of July parade every year. Sandwiched between the antique tractors and the high school marching band, the local car buffs show off their chariots. Grover—and his now candy-apple red chopped 'fifty Merc with "Thunder Road" scrawled across the trunk in gold leaf—never misses the parade. I always check to see if he's dragging any cornstalks.

Ben turned off the music and slowed into the turn. I tightened my seat belt.

"Tired of that CD?" I asked.

"No," said Ben, "I need to hear the engine wind, I don't want to take my eyes off the road to look at the tach."

Our friend had added bright yellow fog lights when he turned north onto Addison behind us. Ben power-shifted through the quarter mile measured by wide white stripes that had been painted across the blacktop by the local teenagers.

A yellow warning sign marked the approaching curve with a fifteen mile-per-hour speed limit. Ben mashed the binders and dropped the shifter back to third before he got into the turn. The shoulder belt pressed into my chest, and I planted my hand on the dash. Our friend came on hard.

The curve began gently enough and put you off your guard. Ben accelerated into it, staying low but keeping his wheels off of the gravel shoulder. About halfway through, the curve took a steeper bank. Ben got off the gas and pulled the shifter down to second—allowing the engine to slow the car without showing any brake lights and bucking us both forward. The big rat motor roared up to about four grand. Our friend was already in the middle of the blacktop and charging hard.

The last third of the curve had a sharply banked diminishing radius. The rear tires of the Camaro lost traction and started to slide up the banked asphalt. Ben cranked the steering wheel into the skid and allowed the car to drift up the banked pavement. When the nose of the car got pointed into the straightaway at the end of the curve, he nailed the gas. The positraction rear caught and generated a couple of G's that pushed us back into the seats. Ben banged third gear without losing five hundred RPM, and we bolted onto the straight ribbon of blacktop beyond the curve. I pulled the vanity mirror down again. Our friend's headlights flashed around twice as he took a flat spin into the cornfield.

"Front wheel drive," I said. "Must not have been the Jag. Let's go home." Ben was silent.

"Every time you drive like that," I said, "you risk your life and the life of anyone you might meet in the oncoming lane. Things happen. Small things can make a big difference in your life. A spill on the pavement or a critter crosssing the road could put you in a wheelchair or make you responsible for a tragedy."

• • •

We live on a lake, a dream that Wendy and I discussed on our honeymoon, but one that had not been possible to realize in the suburban Detroit area. In the late seventies, high-tech defense industries moved to Western Michigan and so did my job with the Defense Intelligence Service.

Pete Ladin and I had been "sheep-dipped"—discharged from the military to work as civilians on the economy, where more latitude was available to make discrete inquiries and run surveillance operations—sorting the wheat from the chaff—before disturbing the rest of the federal alphabet.

The Berlin Wall fell directly onto the DIS, crushing the counterintelligence program into a slide show and a one hour lecture, and squirting guys like Pete and me onto the economy for real. We retired, but kept the PI business. A couple of snotty bureaucrats bitched, but—not wanting to discuss the matter publicly—went away. Wendy and I stayed on to enjoy our dream house, but Marg lost Pete to a stroke.

We crunched up the gravel drive, and motion sensor lights on the garage and corners of the house came on. Rusty, my Frisbee-getter chocolate Lab, was out on his chain and greeted us with a motor tail. Wendy walked up to the window to look out, holding the telephone up to her ear. We have one of those long telephone cords—you never know who might be listening to a cordless phone.

I gave Rusty a brisk two-handed rub on the head and unhooked him. I pulled the chain up to the porch and opened the screen door. Rusty thundered up the stairs to the great room.

The house is one of those bi-levels that was popular back in the decade of shag carpets and leisure suits. As you come in the door it's a choice—eight steps down to the "walk-out" lower level or eight steps up to the all-in-one kitchen, living room, and dining room, with bedrooms down the hall.

Before I could get up the steps Rusty stood at the head of the stairs with a battered green Frisbee in his mouth. He dropped the toy so that it tumbled down the stairs, then studied me with expectant eyes, his tongue lolling in and out as he danced from paw to paw.

"Dark outside," I said. His tongue stalled and his tail drooped. I picked up the Frisbee and gave it back to him. He took it and skulked off to climb into the ratty recliner that was "his" chair, and cast sullen eyes on me.

"We are getting stonewalled," Wendy said into the telephone. "There's no way we're going to send the Dixon Agency a retainer to go and find their own employee."

She sat parked on a tall stool with her back resting against the island counter that divided the kitchen from the dining room. She gestured with her free hand as if whoever she was talking to stood right in front of her.

Wendy, not quite a year younger than me, had never spread into the sturdy body style of middle age. Her summertime attire was a daily pilgrim's progress. For the cool of the morning she was in sweats or slacks and long sleeves with her light brown hair on her shoulders. By noon she wore shorts and a tank top with her hair tied on top of her head. This evening was a flannel-shirt-worn-open-over-a-tank-top-and-shorts-with-her-hair-down kind of night.

"Not a chance," she said into the telephone. "We need to find him ourselves."

"Come on, Rusty," said Ben from the foyer behind me. He pushed the screen door open and held it. Rusty erupted from the chair and rattled china with the two bounds it took him to get to the head of the stairs. I had climbed to the top of the steps and had to get out of the way or ride eighty pounds of canine enthusiasm down the stairwell.

I walked out in front of Wendy, spread my arms and did a slow twirl for her to inspect my Western get up. Wendy put her hand over the telephone, arched her eyebrows and said in a horse whisper, "So where's the milk and bread?" Outside I could hear Ben console Rusty about "Dem mean old guys," and the gallop of Rusty's paws on the gravel. I don't know what was on my face but I could see the steam rise in Wendy's.

"No," she said, "Art just walked in. Was he wearing that silly outfit when he talked to you? You do. . . . I have no idea. . . . You'll have to ask him." She handed me the telephone, snatched Danny's keys off the counter and stalked down the steps.

With my hand over the telephone I said, "You're going to miss the end of your show."

Wendy slammed the door as she left.

"Howdy, pard," I said, racking the telephone between my ear and shoulder while shrugging out of my jacket.

"You found Anne!" said Scott Lambert. "Wendy told me."

"Yes, sir, I did."

"How is she?"

"She's well and surprised that you asked about her."

"Where is she?"

"That wasn't the deal," I said, and hung my jacket in the hall closet.

"This is important to me," said Scott.

"Yes, sir," I said, and listened to a few long moments of silence.

"How do I know you really found her?"

"She said to tell you, 'Tacos, no onions.'"

He said, "Oh God! She told you about that?"

"Just what I said. What did you do, order your dinner without onions and have to wait at the counter?"

"Sure!" he said.

"She has your number. She may call. The rest is up to you."

"I'll give you ten thousand shares. I have to know where she is. She can't be far if you've found her already."

"Good grief, Scott, I just gave her your number today!" I took the pistol off my hip and set it on top of the refrigerator. "Give her a chance."

"I have to know how to contact Anne."

"Where are you now?"

"Washington, D.C."

"How long are you going to be there?"

"A couple of days," he said.

"So wait until you get back and see if she's called. You can't meet with her now, and it's way past the hour for a polite opening chat on the telephone."

"It's just, you don't understand! It would be very helpful if I could talk to her now, while I'm in Washington."

"Her own family hasn't been able to reach her on the telephone." I put my spare magazines next to the pistol.

"Let me talk to them—her family, I mean," he said. "I could explain it to them. I could give them my telephone number for her to reach me here. They could go and talk to her."

"Bad idea," I said. "I can't explain why because of our original deal."

"Why?"

"Scott, you're a little shrill right now. If you talk to Anne or her family like you're talking to me, you'll poison the well for sure."

"You don't get it!"

"What is it that you didn't tell me?" I listened to a pause.

"Nothing," he said.

"Okay," I said. "So we're exactly where we started."

"Except . . . Wendy has done a lot of business with me and there's going to be a lot of business you could do. I need you to go and find Wendy's operative. He was more than a janitor. He had keys for all the offices and production facilities in Wisconsin."

"Change the locks," I said, and looked in the fridge.

"He picked up our mail at the post office and then disappeared. Some computer discs are missing from the plant manager's office."

"Call the police," I said. No soda.

"We did. They said that since there was no sign of a break-in, the discs might have been misplaced."

"What was on the discs?"

Silence from Lambert.

I asked, "Proprietary information?"

"Is that important?"

"Very!" I got a coffee cup out of the cupboard.

"Mr. Hardin, I just want you to find the man and ask him about the discs."

"How many discs are we looking for, and how are they labeled?"

"We're not sure. There have to be at least a half-dozen CDs. I don't know what brand they had in the office. The plant manager can help you with that."

"You need to tell me what's on the discs. I mean just generally. Is it text or figures?"

I got more silence from Lambert. This time I didn't interrupt. Finally he said, "I don't know." He paused, then asked, "Mr. Hardin, are you there?"

"Yes," I said and waited.

"The plant manager's workstation was wiped. We don't know if all of the data was taken or just part. The most sensitive material would have fit on six discs."

"Can't you tell what was downloaded? I understand that even deleted information is retrievable, and you certainly must have had some security protocols."

"We have a backup database, but the manager's hard drive was destroyed. They probably had a high-intensity electromagnet. We can't recover anything."

"I'll need you to front the expenses for this job."

"When can you start?"

"Tomorrow, if you like," I said.

"There's a direct flight to Madison that leaves at three-thirty in the afternoon. There'll be a ticket at the airline counter tomorrow. Bill Johnson, my Wisconsin plant manager, will meet you. I'll instruct him to give you whatever you need."

"I'll need to start in Brandonport. The Dixon Agency is based there and I need to review the operative's personnel file."

"Hank Dunphy is the Michigan plant manager. I'll have him set up a flight and meet you at the airport with a company credit card."

"I think that'll cover it."

"In the meantime I need to know how to contact Anne or her family."

"Mr. Lambert," I said. The line went silent on his end. "I appreciate the opportunity to work, but I don't see how you could go on doing business with someone who betrayed the trust of a woman you care so much about."

WENDY WASN'T FEELING WELL—hadn't for a while. She didn't sleep well, mostly she said that she was too warm. I actually got to put the fan in the window before July. I like the cool air off the lake at night, but when I tried to snuggle up, Wendy was all knees and elbows. She said it was like lying next to a furnace, and she did feel warm to the touch. Sometimes she just didn't come to bed. When she did she was up at two or three in the morning for a shower and change of nighties. Wendy thought it was a virus. For my money, it had gone on so long it had to be an allergy.

She had a doctor's appointment in town so things kind of worked out. She could drop me at my office on the way. On the other hand, she had an hour to work me over and started with, "I guess the boys and I are lucky you ignore us."

Just lately I had found it best to let her complete her thought before joining the conversation. I said nothing and got twenty minutes of silence so thick it would have spilled out and splashed down the side of the car if I'd let window down.

Finally, her knuckles white on the steering wheel, she said, "Well?"

"Well," I said, as gently as I could muster, "I'm not real sure what you mean."

"Of course, you think everything's just great. You ignore us. But what do you do to other people? Why do they get so angry they have to smash your windshield or slash your tires? Our car insurance is going through the roof, and it's because you can't learn to be nice to people."

I had a flash in my mind of a Yellow Pages ad. "Pollyanna Detective Agency—We Always Try to Be Nice." I didn't share the thought.

"See, that's the problem," said Wendy. "That smirk on your face."

"It's the business, Hon. People don't hire me to dish up ice cream at birthday parties."

"I'm in the same business you are. I've got a windshield. My tires wear out before I have to replace them."

"You do industrial undercover jobs," I said. "People don't find out about you until Officer Friendly snaps on the bracelets."

"And that's another thing. You keep getting arrested. Your luck's going to run out. You'll end up in jail. And then what about me? You want to put the boys through that?"

I didn't have time to formulate an answer—if there was one—Wendy had only stopped for air.

"Or dead," she said. "Like yesterday! What on earth did you do to make that man so angry he put a knife to your throat?"

"He tried to take the evidence tape and I whacked his hand with the telephone."

"Had to be more than that."

"That's how it started," I said. "Just what was it you told him, anyway?"

"I told him that your .45 had a hair trigger and you had a nervous tic," said Wendy, as she turned onto Forty-fourth from Breton Road. "And if he got his brains all over that ugly suit. I'd have to bury you in something else."

"Damn right," I said. "I expect to be laid out in my dress blues. And I want the hat in the casket. And my low quarters. I'm not marching into eternity barefoot and hatless. One of the boys will want my sabre—no point to burying that."

"Your blues probably don't fit any better than that plaid suit."

"I liked that suit. The belt loops fit my gun belt."

"It made you look like Howdy Doody."

"Now I just look like Buffalo Bob."

"Scott liked your jacket," said Wendy.

"Tell him Kim Goldberg down on Twenty-eighth Street."

We pulled into the parking lot behind the office. June or not, the morning air sliced sharply off the whetstone of a west wind. I didn't loiter at hauling a couple of suitcases and a two-suiter out of the trunk of Wendy's old Cadillac. The smallest bag was a lime-green cardboard number that smelled like granny's attic, into which I had packed rags, a brick, and the Sunday paper. The other was Wendy's hard-sided tan traveling case—with wheels and a handle—that matched the two-suiter.

Wendy let her window down to say that she'd stop by when she was done at the doctor's office. "If you're still here, I'll come up to the airport with you."

"Could save cab fare," I said. I bent over and gave her a kiss through the open window. She had put on a little makeup because she was coming into town. Her lipstick tasted dreadful. I smiled anyway and added, "I'll wrap this up as quick as I can."

"You're going to look silly, you know," she said. Her eyes squinted against the breeze and she reached out to tug at the elbow of my suit jacket. "A wrinkled-up old fart with half a dozen gray hairs and a full head of liver spots, laid out in a dress blue uniform."

"From your lips to God's ear, Wendy, me darlin'," I said and put my arm around her shoulder through the window. I kissed her again and stood up. She waggled her fingers bye-bye as the glass wound up with an electric whine.

I found Marg already at her desk. She wore a gray cashmere suit with a pleated skirt over an ivory silk blouse with a mandarin collar. Her hair, a uniform dark brown despite her fifty-something years, hung to her shoulders with a little flip at the end.

As I shouldered the door open she rolled her eyes up to survey me over the top of the horn-rimmed half glasses perched on the end of her nose. "I want your May expense report before you leave."

I dropped my luggage on the settee in the front office and picked up the three pink message slips that Marg pushed across her desk in my direction. The tow company wanted the keys for my car. The insurance company wanted a police report. The adjuster at Pacific Casualty wanted an update on the Fenton case. "Nothing from Light and Energy Applications?"

"A man called and asked for you about ten minutes ago. He wouldn't leave a name or number. He said he'd call back." Marg turned her gaze down to her work. "I need your expense report," she added without looking up.

"Yes, ma'am," I said. I took the telephone messages into my office and flopped into the chair at my desk. I got the number for Lambert's Ada Plant from information and let them dial it.

"They charge extra to people who are too lazy to dial," said my conscience in Marg's voice. Hank Dunphy was out and not expected to return until the late afternoon, if at all.

I bulldozed the clutter on the top of my desk until I had a clear spot and sorted the contents of my wallet into piles. The first stack for receipts, the next for crap I wanted to keep, and the last for crap that only God knows why I saved in the first place.

I had my wallet put away and held the wad of "God only knows" crap over the trash can with hesitant fingers when Lorna marched into the office with her arms folded, her cheeks luminescent red, and her long blond hair tied in a ponytail. She wore a ratty yellow cardigan sweater buttoned up to her neck. Her tight lips underlined a hot stare.

I cast one last doubtful glance at the wad of crap that I released from between my thumb and forefinger.

"What on earth happened to you?" I asked while I watched the scraps of paper flutter into the trash.

"Do you know how far it is to that Fenton character's house?"

"Seventy, eighty miles?"

"Ninety-three miles, and you told me to be there by six."

I looked at Lorna and said, "It was a morning surveillance."

"I had to leave at three-thirty."

"Sounds about right."

"It was cold. I froze my ass off!"

"Yeah, I heard the furnace come on around two. I had to get up and close the windows at the house. Your heater broke?"

"Heater's fine," she said. "Some asshole broke into my car—broke the driver's window and trashed the inside. They took something sharp and carved 'DIE BITCH' into my windshield."

"Steal your radio?"

"I wish," she said and rolled her eyes. "They emptied my glove box all over the floor and pulled all the trash out from under my seats."

"They take anything?"

"No, but I found those tractor-paper printouts you left in my back seat blowing all over the street."

"Someone blasted the windshield out of my car with a cement block yesterday before you dropped me off."

Lorna leaned forward, her arms still folded, and gave me an ugly, "Why didn't you warn me?" stare.

"Have a seat." I said. "I'll get you a cup of coffee." Lorna climbed into the wing-back chair across from my desk and sat on her feet. I stood up, but Marg was already at the door with a steaming cup of something in her hand.

"Mister, you're confined to this room until I get that expense report." She looked at Lorna and said, "Chicken soup. I keep a couple of packets in my desk."

Marg kept enough provisions in her desk to outlast a nuclear holocaust. "I'm working on it," I said.

Marg walked over to the chair, and Lorna unfolded her arms to take the soup. "You could deduct the expenses next quarter but the FICA is gone forever."

I raised my hands in surrender. "I'm doing it," I said and sat back down.

Lorna held the mug in both hands, blew the steam away from the top of the mug, and took a noisy sip. When she looked up she asked, "So what happened to your car?"

"The windshield was smashed out and the steering wheel left hanging by a couple of wires, but they didn't ransack it like they did yours. I had it towed to the shop this morning. Ben came and picked me up last night. We had to shake a tail before we could go home—somebody in a small white car with a dark vinyl roof or maybe a convertible."

"What's going on?"

"Until you walked in, I thought it was an unhappy camper from the car dealership—still could be, I suppose. You carry comp coverage on your car?"

"Yeah, but there's a hundred-dollar deductible."

"Put it on your expense ledger."

"What case do I bill it to?"

"I'll make it an office expense until we figure that out. What did Mr. Fenton do?"

"Came out of the house around seven-thirty, stood on the porch and drank a cup of coffee. Around eight he drove into town in that ratty pickup truck and bought a newspaper. Then he sat in front of the Dodge dealership and read his newspaper. He was back home around a quarter to ten, and I broke it off."

"Well, he's not working a morning shift," I said, "and if he were working midnights you would have seen him come home."

"All that leaves is an afternoon shift," Lorna said and took another drink of her soup.

"Be there Friday around one o'clock. Friday is usually payday. If he's working—even part-time—you might catch him. You want some work for this afternoon?"

"I've had all the fun I can stand for today, thank you."

"Good. You can drop me at the airport."

"Where are you going?"

"Brandonport. Lambert wants me to go find Wendy's missing undercover operative."

"I could do that!"

"I need you to cover business here while I'm gone. If I'm not back Monday, I've put a couple of local workers' comp cases in your file. The background and neighborhood checks should keep you busy until I get back."

"I need an expense check."

"How much?"

"About a hundred dollars," said Lorna, deadpan but for a slight curl of her lip.

I tried not to laugh. "Just write up your surveillance and give Marg a draw slip and she'll fix you up. I wrote up the Jones/Lambert case last night. I need you to put your mileage on the memo slip on Marg's desk. Better draw enough walking-around money to cover yourself until Wednesday."

Lorna unfolded herself from the chair and walked out, clutching her soup in both hands. The front door opened, and I looked up at the video monitor. I saw a man in a brown messenger service suit with a metal clipboard under his arm.

"G'day Luv," he said. "Got a package for Art Hardin."

"Mr. Hardin isn't here," said Marg. "Can I sign for it?"

"No," he said.

It's hard to guess height off the video monitor—you can't see their feet—but he looked mid-thirties, clean shaven, short hair, and athletically lean. A Smith and Wesson tumor bulged under the left arm of his brown jacket.

He took a brown nine-by-twelve envelope off the clipboard and showed it to Marg. "This envelope is all, just have to hand it to 'em personal like."

"He's not here."

"Well, that's dreadful inconvenient, isn't it?"

"Mr. Hardin's work doesn't really require him to come to the office. Sometimes he just phones in for weeks at a time."

The man unzipped his jacket. I drew my pistol and stepped around the desk. I found Lorna standing with her back to my door with her hand in her purse. I looked back up at the monitor in time to see him take a ballpoint pen out of his inside jacket pocket. Under the jacket he was wearing a white shirt and a mostly red print designer tie at half mast on a loose collar.

"If you could give me his home address, Luv, we could deliver the package to him there." He clicked the pen and looked down at his clipboard.

"Just give me your number," said Marg, "and I'll have him call you."

"City Delivery," he said. "In the book. If you tell me what time you clock off, I might catch him on the flop."

"We close when I get done," said Marg. "Sometimes I don't come back from lunch."

"I could just wait, Luv. That his bindle? Suppose he might be back most ricky-tick."

"The bags are mine," said Lorna. "I won a trip to Las Vegas." She shook a cigarette loose and clamped her lips on it.

"Lucky you," he said.

"You can wait if you like," said Marg. "What's your name?"

He smiled. "Andy," he said. He was good—didn't blink or hesitate. He looked at Lorna and asked, "Need a light for that, do ya, Miss?"

"Nah," she said, and pushed the pack in her purse to close her hand around her Walther. "I think I got a light in the purse here."

Marg picked up the telephone. "Why don't you give me your supervisor's name and number? I'll give him a call and tell him you're here so you don't get in trouble."

"No worry there."

Marg hit a number on the auto-dialer. After a moment she said, "Grand Rapids . . . City Delivery."

Andy pulled a hanky out of his pocket and coughed into it. "Just ring us up, Luv. Pleasure chattin'. G'day." He turned on his heel, was at the door in two long steps, and let himself out using the hanky to pull on the door handle.

Lorna was moving. I got a hand on her shoulder just before she got to the door. She had her teeth clamped on the filter of an unlit cigarette and still had her hand in her purse. Through the window I could see good old Andy on the stairwell headed up to the front door, taking the stairs three at a time.

"Let him go," I said. "Go watch through the window in my office."

Lorna went.

"Thank you," Marg said into the telephone. She banged the handset back in the cradle and looked up at me. "No listing for City Delivery," she said. "Who's suing you now?"

"I haven't got a clue," I said, "but process servers usually don't wipe the door handle on the way out."

"White Lincoln Mark Seven with a blue carriage roof," Lorna announced as she came out through my office door. "I couldn't get the plate because you wouldn't let me go out there."

"I don't think he was a process server."

"You think it was the guy you had to shake last night?"

"Last night they didn't want to get this close. Maybe he didn't think I was in the office. My car isn't in the lot."

"If he's not a process server," asked Marg, "what was he doing here?"

"Smelling us over," I said. "He wanted to know where I lived."

"He could just run your plate," said Lorna.

"All my plates come back to a box number and leasing company in Detroit."

"I wish mine did," said Lorna.

I nodded at Marg.

"I'll take care of it," said Marg. "Is there a lien on your car?"

"Not really, I bought it from my dad."

"You'll have to sell us your car for a dollar," Marg said with a feline smile.

"What?"

"It's all right," I said. "We lease it back to you for a buck, and that's the buy-out price when you leave my employ. You still have to buy your own insurance."

The telephone rang and Marg picked it up. "No," she said. "Mr. Hardin is not here. May I take a message?" She picked up a pen and started writing on a pink call slip. Lorna and I studied her in silence as if she were the lion tamer in the center ring at the circus.

"Flight two-oh-six . . . first class," she spoke as she wrote, "gate eleven . . . two-fifty P.M."

Lorna walked over to the end table next to the settee, parked her purse, and picked up her soup. I holstered my pistol and fished a cigar out of my inside jacket pocket. As I peeled off the cellophane I kept the stairwell in the corner of my eye. Andy was familiar; not the face, the style—he was a shade from my past, had to be a fellow graduate from the house of mirrors.

Marg hung up the telephone and looked up at me as she handed me the call slip. "Avatar Air," she said. "They booked you straight to Brandonport."

"I'm going to miss the wind sprint from one end of O'Hare to the other," I said.

"A Mr. Dunphy will meet you in the departure lounge," said Marg.

"That's the guy from Light and Energy Applications."

"I saw the report in my in-box," said Marg. So how come we're not billing? You found the subject. We have to cover Lorna's time and mileage."

"Light and Energy is Wendy's client. We did it more or less as a favor," I said.

Marg arched her eyebrows like the back of a hissing cat. "If you keep working for nothing you'll be tapping your retirement fund to buy paper clips."

"It worked out," I said. "We're billing Light and Energy prime rates now, and Wendy says they pay in ten days."

Marg smiled and leaned back in her chair. "Well, it's best not to do too many unpaid favors. Like Pete always said, 'No good deed goes unpunished.'"

"I'll get you my expense report," I said. I had seen Marg smile before, but twice in one day was an occasion. Back in my office I pushed the window curtain aside and studied the parking lot. No Wendy. No Andy. I screwed the cigar into the side of my face and stoked it up. Half a cigar later, the expense report was ready and it was time to go.

"If Wendy shows up in time to see me off, give her the gate number," I said to Marg, handing her the report. Lorna took my briefcase and the small green suitcase. I got the rest. She had so much rummage in her trunk that we had to stow the luggage in the back seat. The "DIE BITCH" salutation was scratched in so that it could be read from the inside, but they got the E backwards.

It's a straight shot east down Forty-fourth to the airport. The sun had remembered that it was June, but no driver's window made for a chilly ride. Lorna cranked up the heat and turned down the radio.

"How come you never told me about covering my plates?" asked Lorna.

"Your class at Quantico starts in August," I said. "Seemed like a lot of agitation for couple of months of insurance drill. Besides, your car is still registered in your father's name."

Lorna snapped her eyes over to me and then back on the road. "So how did they find my apartment?"

"Could be unrelated."

"You ran my plate?"

"Just a sec," I said and turned up the radio.

The news reader said, ". . . stolen car was recovered last night from a cornfield in northeastern Kent County. Stuart Grover, a local farmer, called the sheriff's office to complain of drag racing near his home. Sheriff's officers reported that the vehicle had been stolen from the Grand Rapids Public Library parking lot earlier in the day. The license plate had been altered. The perpetrators set fire to the vehicle after an unsuccessful attempt to drive it out of the recently cultivated field. Sheriff's detectives state that the area is well known to local teenagers who frequent the area to race cars. They have promised to increase patrols in the area."

"Damn," I said. "Grover has a first name. Who knew?"

"Not teenagers," said Lorna.

"Not amateurs," I said. "I'm not in the Bresser's Cross Index for Kent County so they filched a car for plan B." I turned the radio down.

"What do you mean, 'could be unrelated?' You think I just piss off people at random—and you ran my plate!"

"I know you don't just piss people off at random. I talked to your high school counselor and two of your college roommates."

"Jesus!"

"I put you on the street with a gun in your hand. What did you expect?"

Lorna shook her head.

"Pull into the short-term lot," I said.

"I can't stay. I've got to go in and file a police report for my insurance company. I'll have to just drop you off."

"You don't have to stay," I said. "I need to pack my hardware and I don't want to do it in front of the terminal."

She pulled up to the arm and a short white kiosk spat a ticket in her direction. "So how did they find my apartment? No one's bothered my car before and nothing was taken." She took the ticket and the arm went up.

"It's probably safe to figure that whoever followed me wouldn't have had time to get to your place and rummage through your car. They most likely followed you from the office, same as me. That means there's at least two guys working us, and somebody is spending a hell of a lot of money. Go to the back of the lot. Look in the mirror and see who comes in behind us."

"Gray Dodge Shadow," she said. "I don't want anybody making trouble for my dad and mom." She pulled into an empty spot.

"Skip Sunday dinner," I said. "Running a plate leaves a paper trail, and if they burned the car, they're determined not to give the cops any easy ones. If you don't lead them out to your parents house they won't know how to find them."

I opened the door, stepped out, and opened the tan hard- sided suitcase on the front seat. Buried in the socks, shirts, and underwear were two metal boxes with combination locks. I unloaded my pistol and put it in one; the ammo and spare magazines went into the other. I stripped my high-ride hip holster and magazine holders from my belt and dropped them in the suitcase as well.

"You can still get out of the business, if you do it now," I said. I locked the suitcase and put it in the back seat. "Drive me up to the terminal."

I got back in and pulled the door shut. Lorna didn't have anything to say. She stuck her hand out for the buck it cost to get out of the lot without looking at me. I watched the gate as we pulled out to circle back to the terminal. Nobody came out after us.

"You should have told me about covering my plates." said Lorna. She nailed the gas pedal until her tires squeaked.

"We've had this conversation before."

"Not about the plates."

"I tried to talk you out of taking this job," I reminded her. "Rotten hours, boredom, pandemonium, and the question of your safety and the safety of the people around you. I'm sure you remember the conversation."

"I thought you were being sexist."

"You wanted to go to work for a sexist?"

"I wanted to show you that you were wrong," she said. She pulled up to the curb in front of the terminal. "I mean, the Feds hired me, so who the hell were you?"

"The man you wanted to work for until you got to be a real detective. So what do you think happens when you go to work for the man?"

"The man?" She wrinkled up her face like she had a sour taste in her mouth.

"Uncle Sam—Prince Charming. You think his playmates are nicer than mine?"

"I guess not."

"So, what're you going to do?"

"Fenton, Friday," she said and looked at me. She arched her eyebrows and added, "Monday I start a couple of comp cases."

I got out of the car and set my luggage on the curb. A skycap, starched, polished, and impeccable, pushed up a cart. I bent over, stuck my head in the car, and waited for Lorna to look at me again.

"Marry a detective," I told her.

"Maybe I'll just buy a cat," she said. "Don't you worry about Wendy?"

"Sure," I said, "but I married a detective and it's still hard. I can't imagine being married to a civilian."

The ticket agent asked for my driver's license. I had to assure him that I had packed my own bags and that they had not been out of my sight.

"No, I wasn't carrying a bag for anyone else," I told him, but he stopped sleepwalking when I said, "Yes, I'm transporting a firearm." The low buzz of conversation around me stopped and the ticket agents on either side of mine stopped and stared at us both.

"It's unloaded and locked in a steel case inside a locked hard sided bag," I said. "That's what they told me to do on the telephone. Do you want me to get it out and show it to you?"

"No," he said, his eyes wide. "Which bag is it in?"

"The green one," I said.

"Do you have any ammunition?"

"Magazine and a couple of spares," I said. "Locked in a steel case separate from the firearm, but in the same suitcase."

He tagged my luggage. The green suitcase got an extra tag; a long red and white paper loop that repeated the word "FIREARM."

"Gate eleven," he said. He assembled my ticket and handed it over. "Your flight is already loading."

I departed, and the low buzz of conversation returned to the counter. I could feel the heavy weight of eyes on my back.

A man stood at the side of the check-in counter, watching the crowd instead of the attendant at the desk. He looked to be in his early forties, decked out in a white cable-knit sweater over a blue broadcloth shirt, gray slacks, and a pair of those black loafers with little tassels like attorneys wear.

"Are you Mr. Dunphy?" I asked as I approached. I switched my briefcase to my left hand and offered him my right.

"Yes," he said as he took my hand and gave it a limp shake. "You must be Mr. Hardin. I was afraid you wouldn't make it."

I took my hand back and gave my ticket to the check-in clerk. "Had to wrap up a few things at the office," I said.

"I was expecting someone in western attire," he said. A smirk washed over his face.

"They wouldn't let me bring my hoss," I said.

"I need to see some identification," he said as he reached through the neck of his sweater to the pocket of his shirt. I showed him my detective license, and he handed me a "Platinum" credit card with my name embossed across the bottom. "Whatever this is must be very important," he said. "That's our corporate account." His face flushed.

"I don't have to worry about some sales clerk cutting this in half?"

"Buy the store and fire them."

"A dream come true."

"What exactly is it that you are doing for us?" he asked.

"I'm sorry if this is awkward," I said, "but I'm to report to Mr. Lambert."

The attendant tore a page out of my ticket, put the rest back in the folder and walked over to the jetway door. "Mr. Hardin, you have to board now," he said and held out my papers.

"Thank you for coming down," I said.

"Yeah," said Dunphy, grim-faced. He added, "Good luck," and strolled off with his hands in his pants pockets.

The door shut behind me as soon as I was in the jetway. I had an aisle seat in the first class cabin. Since no one had the window, the stewardess let me switch. I watched Kent County disappear below the clouds without seeing Wendy's car.

I opened my briefcase and started through photocopies of the missing operative's daily reports. Jacob Anderson, a.k.a. Jack Anders, filed his dailies via e-mail. All were written in the third person. The first report—falsely labeled day fifty-one—began, "A new employee by the name of Jack Anders was observed working as a janitor and company messenger," so that if some absent-minded executive left a report lying about, the operative wouldn't be toasted.

"Jack" had been under for five and a half weeks when his reports stopped. He began roping, gathering information, in the traditional fashion, bowling and drinking after hours with employees. His beginning reports detailed matters of time clock violations, petty thefts, and questions of employee morale. His assigned target was the research and development department and the leak of proprietary information to BuzzBee Batteries, which was challenging Lambert's patents.

Anders had gravitated to an engineer he identified with a cryptonym,

A4PR, by volunteering to help with a roofing job on the engineer's cottage. While doing the weekend chore he learned of the engineer's hobby, collecting old movie posters. Jack hit the library for a little background study and he and the engineer were soon spending off hours scrounging old movie houses in small-town Wisconsin.

Jack's last report revealed that the engineer had been asking if security searched the trash that he carried out at night. Jack characterized the conversation as "cheap talk" over beer and reported that Jack Anders was among the persons observed at a wedding rehearsal party for the engineer's daughter.

I locked the reports back in my briefcase and walked through the curtain to get to the restroom. Seated halfway down the aisle, on the right, his seat reclined and his eyes closed, sat the Fidel Castro–looking dude who'd followed Scott Lambert out of the Yesterdog restaurant.

"Oops! Sorry. Excuse me! Pardon me. You, too, pal!"

I was the first one off the airplane—the first passenger thanked for flying Avatar Air and ordered to have a nice day.

Just past the metal detector I found a shop in a glass cubicle that sold snacks, magazines, and souvenirs. I grabbed a mint green T-shirt off a rack near the door. Looked big enough, no time to check the tag. I flopped it on the counter and handed the clerk my client's Platinum Card.

The name tag on her powder-blue smock read, "Betty." No last name. Just plain Betty was a pear-shaped matron with rouge circles on her cheekbones, hair bleached white around her mouth and chin, and a red wig so frizzy I was afraid to look at her shoes. I pulled off my suit coat, my tie, and my shirt, and dropped them on the floor at my feet. Betty stood with the credit card in her hand and watched me with an open mouth. I pulled the T-shirt over my head.

Passengers from my airplane began walking by the shop toward the baggage carousel. Western-style straw hats teetered in misshapen stacks on the shelf to my right. I grabbed one and plopped it on my head with the brim low over my eyes. Someone patted me lightly on the back. "What?" I asked and turned around—nobody there, but I got tapped again. I reached behind my head and found a fake ponytail sewn to the headband. Through the glass wall, I saw my bearded traveling companion coming down the hall.

I turned my head back and forth, and the ponytail brushed my back and shoulders as it wagged from side to side. The clerk flashed a bonded denture smile.

"Cool hat," I said. "I'll take it. Got a bag?"

"Are you hiding from someone?" she asked. Her smile melted. I made quick glances to the left and right and leaned forward, beckoning her with a finger. She leaned toward me and turned her ear in my direction. I whispered, "I'm a secret agent, Darlin'."

"Betty," she whispered. She straightened up and studied me, her face blank. I gave her a wink and one sly nod of my head. She smiled again. I could see Fidel approaching the crowd collecting at the baggage claim area.

She asked, "Is this like one of those murder mystery tours?"

"Absolutely."

"I went on one of those, too," she said, "but it was a train ride."

"Really? Where's it out of?"

"Ashland," she said. "They do them after the fall color tours." She swiped the Light and Energy card through the reader. "I know just what you need," she said, and produced a pair of clip-on sunglasses from under the counter.

"I'll take 'em," I said. I snapped them onto my wire-rimmed glasses and everything got dim and green.

"Oh, dear," she said studying the credit card reader, "it says your card's invalid."

"Swipe it again," I said. "It's a brand-new card."

She swiped. We waited. Fidel stood with his back to me, watching baggage swirl past him. My baggage was up, but no green suitcase yet.

She shook her head. "I'm sorry." She handed the card back. "It says, 'Try another tender.' Perhaps you have another card."

"How much is this?"

"Forty-two eighty-seven."

"You're putting me on!"

She shrugged. "This is an airport. It's like buying candy at the movies."

"Disposable razors?"

"A dollar-ninety-nine."

"I'll take it." I put the card in my wallet, pulled my money clip out of my pocket, and peeled off two twenties and a five. I thumbed what I had left. Seven bucks. I picked my suit coat, shirt, and tie off the floor and folded them on the counter. Betty gave me my change and stashed my stuff in a big brown plastic bag. I departed, leaving my bearded friend watching the baggage swirl.

In the restroom I wet down my moustache and shaved it off. My upper lip looked as big as a billboard. Wendy would be thrilled. She never liked my cookie duster—said it was too bristly. The T-shirt had "QUAD CITIES" emblazoned in white over a stern-wheel riverboat.

Back in the concourse Fidel loitered near the baggage carousel and pretended to ignore my luggage—which still did not include the green suitcase. I returned to the shop. Betty said, "You look younger."

"Thank you," I said. "Got one of those disposable cameras?"

"Do you have a computer?"

"Sure."

"I've got just the thing," she said, excitement in her voice. She took a carton the size of a pack of cigarettes from under the counter. "It's digital and a bargain too. They make them up in Madison. That's in Wisconsin, but not all that far from here. A good thing, too, because we sell them as fast as we get them in."

She opened the end of the carton and pulled out a foil- wrapped object with rounded edges. Her fingers seized upon a red pull tab, but she stopped and looked up to me from the object. "I love to do this," she said. "Are you going to buy it?"

"Is it a camera?"

"Oh, yes, and lots more. It has a clock with a travel alarm, an AM–FM radio, and it's a flashlight."

"Sort of a Swiss Army camera?"

Betty grinned and said, "Since it doesn't need batteries there's room for the rest, and it's light as a feather, too."

"How does it work without batteries?"

"That's the neat part. Are you sure you want to buy this? I can't open it unless it's sold. Once you open it, it's too big to go back in the box."

"How much is it?"

"Nineteen ninety-five."

A man walked up and stood behind me. His reflection was faint in the glass wall behind Betty—male, white, heavyset, and wearing a windbreaker unzipped over a shirt and tie. He had a magazine and candy bar in his hand.

I gave her my debit card from my wallet. "I'll take it," I said.

She swiped it through the reader and smiled when the cash register spit out a receipt.

"This is the fun part," she said and pulled the tab with all the glee and wonder of a child opening a birthday present. Lying open, the flaps of the wrapper revealed what appeared to be a black bar of soap with a lens and shutter device stuck in it.

"That's a camera?"

"Wait," she said. "It charges up on the light—has a little computer chip to tell it what to do."

The black blob took on a gray patina and began to swell. I thought of the "monster eggs" I'd bought my grandchildren—drop them in water and they expanded into sponge dinosaurs. This thing rose like a muffin in the oven until it was twice the original size and took on a flat blue cast.

"Now watch," she said. The man behind me moved to look over my shoulder. "It goes real fast outside but in here you can watch it happen." A spider web of yellow lines appeared on the camera. The lines widened until the camera was entirely yellow. Luminescent green letters developed forming the message, "SUN POWER DIGITAL and LIGHT AND ENERGY APPLICATIONS, patent pending."

I shot a glance from the camera to Betty.

"Like magic," she said. "The salesman told me the company recruited blind workers because these have to be assembled in complete darkness."

She picked the camera up, turned it over and glanced up at the back wall. I turned to see what had caught her interest, and so did the man behind me. She was studying a clock above the door next to the exit sign. When I turned back, Betty showed me she had set the clock on the back of the camera which shared the same liquid crystal display as the radio tuner.

"The buttons on the back are for the radio and travel alarm. The big one on the top is for the shutter. Isn't that just the neatest thing?"

"Yes, ma'am," I said and picked up my purchase. It had a strange feel: almost no heft, and the texture of a clay pot. "Betty, would you keep my briefcase behind the counter for a couple of minutes while I go try my camera?"

"Sure," she said. "You can leave your bag, too, but I go off shift in an hour. Oh, and don't drop the camera. If it chips or cracks, it doesn't work anymore. You can send it back to the manufacturer, but they just send you a new one and your pictures are lost."

"Plenty of time," I said. "Thanks a ton." I put it all on the counter. She tore the receipt off the cash register, put it in the bag, and then set the rest of my stuff on the floor by her feet. I turned and walked out.

"Gimme one of those cameras," said the man who had been standing behind me.

Fidel junior—he had no gray in his beard and a full head of dark brown hair—picked a single black athletic-style duffle bag off the baggage carousel. It was small enough to have been carried onto the airplane.

In the middle of the terminal floor red velvet theater ropes guarded a stark white Lexus convertible. A placard on the roof of the car announced the name of a local car agency.

I lifted the camera to my face, swallowed some air, and framed up the Lexus in the viewfinder. As my bearded buddy stepped into the frame I belched, Fidel snapped his face toward me, and I touched off the shutter. The flash caused Fidel to make an ugly face. He started toward me with long quick steps.

I leaned to the side as if to shoot around him, but kept him centered in the viewfinder. I got a good three-quarter shot before he planted his hand on his face, pretending to rub his eye.

"What the hell are you doing?" he said in a ripe baritone and midwestern accent. His eyebrows were holding hands.

"Howdy," I said. "Don't it beat all what folks will pay for half an automobile?" I stuck my hand out. "Jubal Jackson, Toop'lo, Miss'sippy."

"What?" he said, his face growing red.

"Well, I sure am sorry if I give y'all a start—just wanted a pitcher of this here car."

Junior stopped short. He looked at the car and then back at me. "Lexus is a fine automobile," he said. "Maybe you ought to rent one and give it a try."

"Sure don't have the money fur that, but it'd be right neighborly for y'all to take my pitcher by it."

"Sure," he said. He put out his right hand palm up.

I snatched his right hand into mine. "What'd y'all say your name wuz?"

"Andy," he said. His eyes narrowed and his grip tightened.

I squeezed back until his eyes widened. "That's what I like," I said, "a feller with a man's grip."

"You wanted a picture?" he asked. The question sounded a little urgent.

I released my grip, planted the camera in his hand, and walked over by the automobile. When I turned around he snapped the shot, lobbed the camera toward me in a high arc, and walked off. I snatched my new straw hat off by the brim and caught the camera in the hat.

"Hey, Andy," I called after him, "d'ever anybody say as how y'all look like that there Castro feller?" Good old Andy made a dismissive wave without looking back.

"Andy," I said to myself and looked at the camera in the hat. "A lot of Andys. Can't tell the players without a program."

I watched Fidel, a.k.a. Andy, wander out the door and walk down the outside of the building to where he could watch the baggage return through the front window. He set his bag on the ground.

I sat at a bank of telephones where I could watch him, set the hat with the camera in it on my lap, and dialed up Wendy, collect. She had it in two rings and said she would accept the charges.

"Hi, Hon," I said.

"Now what?"

"I'm in Brandonport, at the airport."

"Oh, I thought . . ."

"No, I haven't been arrested, not yet. I'm calling because I need to sit here and watch a fellow I saw at Yesterdog when I met with Scott. Now he's in Brandonport. He took the same flight I did."

"Grand Rapids is a small town," said Wendy. "Maybe he wanted a hot dog."

"I thought of that."

"You are supposed to be looking for Jack Anders."

"There's a little glitch here," I said. "Your pal Dunphy gave me a credit card for expenses but didn't authorize the bank to let me use it."

"I've never met Dunphy."

"Don't you report to him?"

"He doesn't know we have people in."

"Ho-lee shit!"

"You didn't tell him, did you?" Wendy's voice took on the edge of panic.

"No! But I could have. How on earth did you get your people in?"

"Through the temp service they use. Scott told me what kind of experience to have them write on their applications. The temp company never does backgrounds."

Alias Andy knelt by his bag. He was still watching the baggage claim area through the window. He unzipped his bag and took out a pack of cigarettes.

"Call Lambert and tell him I've run aground here."

"I left a message at his hotel this morning, but so far he hasn't called back."

"How much money is in our checking account?"

"Around eight hundred, but we have to keep a minimum balance of five hundred to keep our free checking."

Alias Andy shook out a cigarette and stuck it in his face, then dropped the pack back into his bag and extracted a cell phone.

"That'll be enough to hole up, but I don't think that they'll rent me a car on the debit card. Call Marg in the morning and have her deposit something in our personal account."

"How much?"

"Tell her I need a grand; that way I'll get at least five hundred."

"Try the card again in the morning," said Wendy. "Could be that your authorization just hasn't been posted yet. If it doesn't work, then I'll put the money in from Silk City. It's our case anyway."

The unlit cigarette in Alias Andy's face levered up and down in spurts as he spoke into the cellphone. He dipped a wind-proof lighter out of his bag.

"Listen, I'm going to call Dunphy," I said. "I'll let you go." Wendy hung up. I watched Alias Andy, Alias Andy watched the baggage, and Dunphy's secretary wouldn't accept a collect call. I tried to charge the call to my office telephone, but the answering machine picked up. At that point I remembered my calling card and got through to Dunphy's secretary. She said that he was out and not expected to return. I told her I'd call back when I had a local number where I could be reached.

Mine was the only baggage left on the carousel—still no green suitcase. Across the lobby an electronic bank teller advertised one of the wire services that my bank used. I rummaged a used, mostly dry, soft drink cup from the waste can next to the line of telephones, tipped the camera out of my hat into the cup, and snapped on a lid. With my hat back on my head I walked over to the ATM and popped my card into the machine. Alias Andy was at long last lighting his smoke. I punched up three hundred dollars. I could hear the machine cycling my cash when the building heaved a sigh and went dark.

"It's like I told you, Officer! The lights went out. I was trying to get my debit card out of the teller machine. I looked up and saw this guy running toward the door with my luggage."

Deputy Fairchild wore a brown Smokey Bear hat and a khaki uniform. He kept his head tipped down so that I couldn't see his eyes—just a nose nested in a bushy guardsmen's moustache.

"Then what happened?" he asked, his pen poised above his pocket-sized notepad. He'd already written down my name and address and summarized my statement in a sentence or two. This was our third trip through the story.

I rested my butt against the rear bumper of the brown and gold patrol car and folded my arms against the evening chill. "I tried to catch up to him." An ambulance pulled out with its lights rolling and another one backed in to take its place.

"So what did you do when you caught up with him?" asked the deputy.

"That's when someone yelled 'Fire!' The crowd at the door swallowed him up. In the panic and the crush of people I never got near him. I had to struggle to keep my feet while I backed out of the crowd."

"Why didn't you try to get out?"

"I didn't smell any smoke or see any fire. Where's my luggage?"

"Lieutenant Ross took it downtown."

"I don't have a car."

Deputy Fairchild snapped his notepad shut and raised his head to look at me while he clicked his ballpoint pen and put it away. He wore the smug smile of a man who had just filled an inside straight. "As it happens," he said, "that's exactly where I'm going. You can ride with me if you like." He opened the back door of the cruiser.

"If you don't mind," I said, "I'd rather ride in the front."

"Policy," he said.

I climbed in. The car had those hard plastic seats that are cast to look like upholstery, but handy to hose out in the case of a sloppy drunk. The deputy had nothing to say on the way into Brandonport. As we parked he got on the radio and asked the dispatcher to tell Lieutenant Ross that we had arrived. He parked and let me out of the back seat.

"Wait," he said, then he searched the rear compartment of the cruiser.

"Policy?" I asked.

"Yeah," he said and pointed at the side of the car. "Lean on it."

"Am I under arrest?"

"No."

"Then *you* lean on it."

Fairchild shrugged, but his eyes gave away a little heat. "Policy," he said.

"Good," I said, "I have a policy too. It's called the Fourth Amendment."

"The lieutenant wants to talk to you."

"Fine," I said and looked around. The gray dog station was across the street. "Tell him I'll be at the bus terminal at the lunch counter. I need a cup of coffee."

"Don't you want your luggage?"

"Sure," I said. "I'll send my attorney to pick it up." I hadn't taken a step when the deputy clamped a hand on my shoulder. I looked from the hand to the glower on his face.

"Deputy Fairchild," I said, "that much alone is misdemeanor assault."

"The lieutenant just wants to talk to you."

"That's not what's at question here, Deputy." I looked back at his hand. "What's at question here is US 42."

"You some kind of lawyer?"

"No, I'm some kind of detective."

"Then as a professional courtesy?" He made the question sound like a statement and let go of my shoulder.

"I'll be having a cup of coffee across the street here," I said and walked off. I went all the way to the corner and crossed at the light.

I can remember when bus terminals had grand diners—no chandeliers, but lots of chrome and Naugahyde, and the menu featured a daily special like open-faced roast beef or meatloaf sandwiches with loads of mashed potatoes and gravy. This one had a row of pick-your-poison vending machines guarded by a phalanx of sticky benches.

Next to the coffee machine stood a row of gray coin-operated lockers. I fished out a quarter and deposited my cupful of camera. I had to pump in another quarter before the lock would release the key.

The coffee machine dispensed cups printed with poker hands. I got a busted flush. Before the coffee was cool enough to drink, the Lieutenant hard-heeled the boards into the bus terminal with Fairchild and another deputy in lockstep.

Lieutenant Ross was black and slim with one of those ageless, clean shaven faces that, just now, was a mask of determination. He wore a blue serge three-piece suit. His unbuttoned jacket breezed about as he approached, revealing a gold watch chain on his vest, a gold detective shield on his belt, and a fat nine millimeter on his hip. Five or six strides away he started talking. "Mr. Hardin, I'd like you to come over to the sheriff's office."

"Am I under arrest?"

"I'll arrest you if that's what you want."

I stood up. "Well, if I'm under arrest, let's go."

"You're not under arrest," he said.

I sat back down.

"I just want to review your statement," Ross said.

I patted the bench next to me. "Sit. Talk. I explained what happened to Deputy Fairchild, but if there's something you don't understand—I'm your guy."

The lieutenant worked up a serious scowl. "It would be better to do this across the street. More private. Just one detective to another." The detective part came off on the ragged edge of a short ration of civility.

"Lieutenant Ross," I said, and waited a couple of beats while I tried for a sympathetic face. "What you want to do is take me across the street and jerk me around. You want to run a tape recorder while you ask me a lot of questions that you already know the answers to. You hope that I will lie to you, say something stupid—maybe even incriminating. Let me assure you, I haven't broken the law, and I have nothing to hide. I'm just not in the mood. If you have some questions, sit! Ask!"

The lieutenant put his hands in his pants pockets, rose up on his toes and studied me with his lips pressed into a taut line. When he rested his heels back on the floor he said, "All right."

I sipped my coffee. "Buy you a cup?"

"Keeps me up," Ross said. He nodded at the deputies. They left. "I want to know about the gun."

"Detonics .45 caliber auto loader, serial number 6117—belongs to me. But you know that. You already ran the registration."

"Why do you have a gun?"

"Second Amendment."

"Why did you bring a gun to Brandonport, Iowa?"

"I came here to work. I'm a detective."

"You're a detective in Michigan," said Ross.

"I'm pursuing a case that started in Michigan. Iowa has reciprocity with Michigan on both my private ticket and my permit to carry."

"I'm not so sure about that."

"Call the State Police. I did."

"You have to check in with us," said Ross.

"Had a little problem at the airport," I said and took another sip of my coffee.

Ross smiled. "You know a woman by the name of Betty Simmons?"

"There was a lady by the name of Betty at the shop where I bought this hat and shirt. Don't know her last name."

"When did you buy the hat and shirt?"

"When I got off the airplane."

"How long after?"

"Immediately."

Ross sat on the bench across from me, folded his hands in his lap, and studied me. Finally he said, "Here's my problem. I ran the pistol, like you said, then I ordered an NCIC. While I was waiting, I teletyped for your DMV information. I got your date of birth and your height and weight. Now I'm looking at you. I had a different picture in mind."

I took the hat off and showed him the dangling hair piece. "Ponytail comes with the hat."

"I'd like to see your driver's license," said Ross.

I dug out my wallet.

"While you're at it," he said, "let me see your private ticket and your permit to carry."

I gave him the cards, and he did a couple of takes between me and the pictures. He said, "Where's the moustache?"

"In the drain at the airport men's room."

He took out a pad and started to copy the license numbers and expiration dates from my private ticket and my concealed pistols permit. While he wrote he asked, "So what do you do, lift weights or what? I'm in the gym three times a week and can't bulk up like that."

"I work the street. You get soft, you get hurt. I've just been doing it longer than you."

He rolled his eyes up to meet mine and said, "I've been doing it for eighteen years."

"Exactly my point."

He handed the cards back. "So what are you doing in Brandonport?"

"I came here to find someone."

Ross twisted his head and said, "You need a gun to find someone?"

"You need a gun to talk to a man in a bus station?"

"My job," said Ross with a positive nod of his head, "requires me to wear a gun."

I played with my hat and did my best Dennis Weaver, "There you go."

Ross stared at me like he didn't get it, or it wasn't funny if he did. He put his pen away. "You going to tell me who you're looking for or claim privilege?"

"Jacob Anderson. I'd claim privilege, but I want your help."

"Don't know him," said Ross. "This a domestic thing?"

"Mr. Anderson is an undercover operative. He was doing an industrial undercover when he disappeared about a week ago."

"This a drug thing?"

"Industrial espionage. Mr. Anderson worked for the Dixon agency here in Brandonport, but his undercover job was up in Wisconsin."

"I know Dixon," he said. "He's retired from the Bureau. Why don't you just ask him?"

"Did that. Dixon doesn't know where Anderson is and doesn't seem very concerned about it either."

"So how did you get involved?"

"My client ran the operation, Dixon just subcontracted the labor."

"So who's your client?"

"Privileged."

"I thought industrial espionage was against the law."

"It certainly is. We were doing a counter-espionage job."

Ross hauled out his pad and pen again. "Jacob who?"

"Anderson," I said. "a.k.a, Jack Anders, 8-14-76, I don't know his social security number. I was planning to visit Dixon in the morning and review Jack's personnel file for some leads."

Ross wrote it down but kept the pad and pen out. "You told Betty that you were a secret agent," he said and looked up from his pad and grinned.

"A joke," I said. "Sometimes the best cover is the truth, especially if the interviewee isn't likely to believe it. I had to explain why I was removing my shirt, tie, and jacket while she was ringing up this T-shirt and hat."

"You said you were part of a murder mystery tour."

"She suggested the idea so I let her believe it."

Ross thumbed up a couple of pages in his pad. "That was right after you got off the plane."

"Immediately."

"That's what you said before."

"Yes, it is."

"Was the terminal already dark?" asked Ross.

"No."

"Why did you change your clothes?"

"I wanted to change my profile," I said.

"Why?"

"There was a fellow on the airplane with me that I'd seen once too often."

"You were being followed?" asked Ross.

"Maybe."

"What makes you think this man was following you?"

"The little hairs on the back of my neck," I said.

Ross blinked. "So what did you do when he got off the airplane?"

"Watched him."

Ross wrote a short note. "What did he do?"

"He picked up his bag and went outside. He watched the baggage carousel through the window, talked on a cell phone."

"Anything else?"

"He lit up a cigarette."

"So he was outside the terminal."

"Yes, sir."

Ross made another small note. "You felt that this man's actions were threatening to you?"

"I thought he was watching the baggage carousel and waiting for me to pick up my bags."

"How would he know what your luggage looked like?"

"They were the only ones left."

Ross twisted his head and tapped on the pad with the point of his pen. Without looking up he said, "So when did he come back into the terminal?"

"I don't know that he did. I was at the bank machine when the lights went out. I lost track of him. The machine ate my bank card."

"He's not the man who ran off with your baggage?" asked Ross. This time he looked up and fixed hard eyes on me.

"Absolutely not."

"What did you do when you caught the man who stole your bags?" Ross made the question sound like an accusation—a question he should have asked casually. His third mistake, but who's counting?

"Someone yelled, 'Fire!' and there was a panic at the door. I never got near him. I was lucky to keep my feet while I backed out of the crowd."

"That's what you told Deputy Fairchild," said Ross, still with some heat in his voice. Deputy Fairchild brushed in the door and headed for us at a determined gait.

"That's what I told Deputy Fairchild three times. How many more times would *you* like to hear it?" My coffee had cooled. I took a long drink.

"Just one," said Ross. He snapped his pad shut and put it away. "I want you to come over to the sheriff's office and give me a written statement."

"You don't get a written statement unless you read me my rights," I said. "If you read me my rights, you get a very short statement about how you can direct your questions to my attorney."

"Lieutenant!" said Fairchild.

Ross was on his feet and reaching for his handcuffs. He looked at Fairchild. Fairchild wagged his head in the negative.

"What?" asked Ross in a clipped tone, leaning toward Fairchild.

"We got the security tapes from the airport, and we got your NCIC back on Hardin," Fairchild said. "You better look at 'em first."

I heard the cover snap back down on Ross's handcuffs. He turned and looked at me, his hands folded in front of him. "I don't suppose you'd mind being our guest for a few minutes?"

"Nah," I said. "I'll follow you over. I want my property, all of my property, and I want it double quick." I stood up. "And if I *don't* get it, you *will* be in a courtroom—a federal courtroom—and I'll be sitting next to the jury. You'll be the one sitting on your thumb trying to look intelligent."

Ross's eyes went wide and hot. His mouth drooped open slightly as he leaned toward me, inhaled, and said, "Nobody talks to me that way."

"Sure they do," I said. "Your mother did. Your drill sergeant did, and your wife still does."

"My wife is none of your business!"

I smiled and looked from Ross to Fairchild and back. Fairchild's face colored red. Ross looked sideways at Fairchild and then back at me. He straightened back to the vertical. His neck and shoulders relaxed. He pointed at Fairchild.

"Fairchild's wife talks to him that way," Ross said. "My wife doesn't talk to me that way."

"You're a lucky man," I said, "because mine does. Only she points her finger while she's doing it."

We laughed and went across the street. Jaywalked, this time. Folks actually slowed down and changed lanes.

Betty sat on a bench in the waiting room of the sheriff's office. I gave her a wink and a smile, but she looked away as we passed. Ross and the deputy led me down a lime green hallway and I heard footsteps in the waiting room behind us.

"Can I go now?" Betty asked. "They said I could go after he walked by and saw me sitting here."

A male voice answered. "Not yet. Please just wait. The stenographer needs you to sign your statement. She's almost done."

Ross pushed open a wooden door with a frosted glass window and led us into an interview room furnished with a gray metal table and a couple of straight-backed wooden chairs. A stanchion fan guarded the corner next to the barred windows. The table was set with a video recorder and monitor. A manila folder lay abandoned on the top of the recorder.

"This is from the security camera that's aimed at the main door over at the airport," said Fairchild. He flipped on the monitor and the player and hit the play button on the recorder.

Time lapse video, in black and white, wiped a fresh picture across the screen every three seconds. The man with my bags lurched across the screen. A crowd appeared at the door in two wipes. The man with my bags was tall, and you could see his head above the crowd. On the next wipe the head was gone. Fairchild turned off the player.

"I've done this a frame at a time," Fairchild said. "No silly hat and no head with that bald spot in the back."

"It's pretty dim," Ross said.

"I turned the contrast all the way up," Fairchild told him.

"What bald spot?"

"The one on the back of your head," Ross said.

"Oh, that one. I keep the hair combed over that."

Ross gave me a deadpan face. "Are you saying you're on that tape?" he asked.

"I'm saying that if I were on that tape I would already have my luggage. Somebody tune this guy up? What are you trying to finger me with?"

Ross picked up the folder and opened it. "Shit," he said. He threw it back on the table. He pointed a finger at me. "Whatever kind of happy horseshit you people are up to, you don't do it here. You don't do it in Brandonport."

"What are you talking about?" I asked.

Ross handed me the folder. I looked at it and handed it back.

"I'm retired," I said. "I guess my clearance isn't. I'm doing exactly what I told you I was doing. I'm a private investigator working for a private client."

"What about Gus Harris?"

"I don't know anyone by that name."

"He's a local drug informant and petty thief," Ross said. "He's the man who stole your bags."

"And?"

"And someone with a lot of upper body strength—someone who knew exactly what he was doing—got behind him in that crowd and snapped his neck like a chicken."

Go toward the light. I think that's the usual advice. In Brandonport the only light showing was the bus terminal—a veritable Las Vegas in a sea of empty streets, darkened shops, and rolled-up sidewalks. I jaywalked my luggage across the street and hoped that heading for the light worked out better for me than it did for the insects that visited the bug zapper on my deck at home.

"You can't stay here unless you have a ticket," said the clerk from behind the counter. His blue uniform jacket didn't quite make the trip around his belly. He had sleep in his eyes and the map of Ireland on his face.

"Great," I said. "What's the first bus in the morning?"

"Davenport," he said. "Leaves at seven-thirty."

"How much for a ticket to Davenport?"

"Seven bucks."

"Just right," I said, "I'll have a ticket for Davenport."

"Ticket counter opens at six A.M."

"So how come you're open?" I asked.

"Western Union," he said, "and the Omaha bus comes in at two-thirty."

"You don't mind if I use the telephone?"

He pointed a thumb to his left. "Knock yourself out."

I used my card to call home. Ben answered and said Wendy was at the high school to see the play.

"Tell her the ATM ate my debit card and to wire me some money. I'm at the bus terminal in Brandonport."

He reminded me that the only Western Union in Belding was at the Covered Village Mall and that it didn't open until morning. He didn't know what time exactly.

"Not to worry," I said. "I'll be here in the morning. What are you up to?"

"Nothing," he said.

"How's that game you were playing—the one where the guy has to find the horse and the flute?"

"I had to start over. I picked up all the treasure in the present. The trick is to play the flute to get into the future and pick up the treasure—so you can pick it up again in the present and then go into the past and pick it up again."

"Sounds complicated," I said.

"That's the only way you can buy enough bombs and arrows to finish the game. I finally figured out how to beat the guardian at the last gate. I'll show you when you get home."

"Cool. Have you got a pencil?"

"I'll get one," he said.

When he came back to the telephone I gave him the information Wendy needed to wire me some cash and finished with, "Give your mom a big hug and kiss for me."

"I'll tell her you said hello," he said, and hung up.

The big lockers were fifty cents. The two suiter went in because it was scrunchable. The green bag with the firearm tag had disappeared en route—fancy that. And the bag of clothes that Ross had gotten from Betty also fit, but the locker just wasn't deep enough for the suitcase.

I went back to the counter and found a sign that read, "Ring bell for service." I could hear the clerk snoring. He lay stretched out on a baggage cart. I left his bell unrung and found a bench—one where I had my back to the wall. I draped one leg across the luggage and tipped my hat over my face to check my eyelids for pin holes. Any crap from the clerk and I'd tell him I was waiting for a wire. Until then, I'd follow his lead. A good idea doesn't care who has it.

• • •

Three men stood in front of me. The man in the middle had a revolver on his hip. I'm not sure why I opened my eyes but I closed them again. Someone made throat clearing noises. I opened my eyes again. They were still there.

"We want your suitcase," said the man with the gun, his arms folded over a blue security guard shirt with the sleeves rolled up past his elbows. Grizzled but mostly gray hair hung to his shoulders. Lines cut deep into his face and across the bridge of a nose, that from my angle looked as big as Lincoln's on Mt. Rushmore.

"That right?" I said.

"That's right," said the one on my left, pulling at the straps of his bib overalls. Sweat stained the armpits of his white T-shirt and made a vee down from his neck. Wiry yellow hair stood out from his head like it was trying to get away, except for the top part, where it had made good its escape.

"Happens I'm partial to my suitcase," I said.

"Damn fine suitcase," said the man on my right, wearing a black T-shirt featuring a picture of a camel shooting pool with a cigarette dangling from its lips. A man blessed with plenty of hair, which he wore slicked straight back from a pronounced widow's peak—most likely brown hair if he took his head in for an oil change. His stubble beard had gone mostly gray. "Good for playing cards."

"You want to play cards for my suitcase?" I said.

"Want to play cards *on* your suitcase," he said.

"You know how to play euchre?" asked the man with the gun. "Jerry can't play because he's back on days at the mill. His wife had a stroke, and he has to take care of her when he gets home. So he has to sleep now—can't play cards with us no more."

I asked, "Is it a hard game?"

They all smiled.

"Real easy game," said the man with the gun. "Hell, you only use half the deck. How hard can it be?"

"Sure," I said. "I have to wait here until morning anyway."

They pulled up a bench so that we could make a table by setting the suitcase on our knees. The man with the yellow fright-wig hair was named Greg. His partner—in the cigarette shirt—was Ralph. My partner—the one with the gun and guard shirt—said his name was Morning Bear, but mostly he went by Max.

A dime a point and a quarter a euchre?" asked Max. He took the cards out of the breast pocket of his guard shirt.

I shrugged. Greg and Ralph shared a sly grin—but couldn't ante up a full set of teeth between them.

"We just have to keep track," said Max. "We can't put no money out because I'm working."

"You can play cards but you can't gamble?" I said.

"Boss says I just have to stay awake. I think if he knew we were gambling he might get pissed."

"Who cares?" said Ralph. He looked at his cards. "We ain't been paid for three weeks and I ain't going to my post until I get my check."

The smell just sort of crept up on you. Like someone had left vegetable beef soup to go sour in the pan and then accidentally turned on the burner. Could have been one or all of them, but I was betting on Greg because of the yellow half moons that stained his T shirt under his arms. On the upside, it took the edge off my appetite.

"Dixon gonna lose that contract," said Max, "then you ain't gonna have no post to go to."

I let all that slide for the first half hour while I successfully named suit based on having three cards the same color. Finally I asked, just in passing, if they all worked for Dixon.

"I don't work for him no more," said Greg. "I don't get paid; I don't work. Maybe I find something at Pinks or Burns."

"I was looking for something," I said. "I was hoping you guys would put in a word for me, with Dixon."

The Omaha bus showed up, and Max went to wake Jerry so that he could load the express packages. The passengers crowded into the restrooms. I retired to the coffee machine with Greg and Ralph. They said that since Max and I were up a buck and a half, I should stand them to a round of coffee. I obliged and threw in a package of peanut butter crackers from the vending machine. It was a small package but we each got an orange cracker. Greg said that he'd save one for Max, but he ate it anyway.

"So you think I can get a job with this Dixon guy?" I asked.

"Sure," said Ralph. "Just about everybody quit but Max. Most folks won't work where they don't get paid."

"That happen a lot?"

"Just only once'st, last year," said Greg. "Dixon said it was about the Feds taking his bank account and about how it was a mistake. But that was just only a couple of days so I didn't quit that time."

"Yeah, but he keeps a new car and he's got that brick house up on the bluff," said Ralph.

"He keeps that on account of he's retired from the FBI. That's why we get the guard jobs," said Greg.

"I think he ought to sell that damn white Lincoln and gimme my paycheck," said Ralph.

"FBI," I said. I wagged a finger and gave them both the thousand yard stare. "I heard of Dixon. A guy named Jack Anders—up in Wisconsin— said Dixon might have some work, was I to come down here."

Ralph and Greg looked at each other and back at me, their faces blank. "Ain't never heard of him," they said in unison.

"I ain't heard of Dixon doin' nothin' in Wisconsin," said Greg.

"Ask Max," said Ralph. "Him and Dixon is pretty tight. He's like a sergeant for him. I think he still gets paid. He don't let on though—in case we might want a loan."

The Omaha bus departed just before three. Jerry bitched about me hanging around without a ticket and I used my "waiting for money off the wire" line. Max and the boys smiled real big and told Jerry to shut up and go back to sleep.

"Max," said Ralph as we settled my suitcase on our knees, "you know some guy works for Dixon, name of Jack Anders?"

Max got the cards out and looked at them while he shuffled. "Why you ask that?"

"Art here says he run into him up in Wisconsin and this Jack guy says maybe Dixon has some work."

Max looked at me. "Where at in Wisconsin?"

"Madison," I said.

"Don't know him," said Max. "Maybe he worked for Dixon in his janitor business. Dixon don't tell me much about the janitor stuff." Max smiled. "I told him I don't do windows." Ralph and Greg laughed. "Anyway, there's gonna be plenty of work since these two got too self-righteous to cover their posts."

Max and I took the first two points. Greg reneged on Ralph's ace, but it didn't help. Max set hard eyes on me and said, "Maybe there's something you didn't tell us."

"Yeah?" I asked. "Like what?"

"I don't know. Like something! You know what it is."

Greg had turned up the ten of hearts on the deal. I had both bowers, the ace and queen in suit, and the ace of clubs. "Pick it up," I said. "No, really! Like what?"

Max grinned. "Like maybe you played this game before?"

"If that cat's out of the bag," I said, "stay home."

Max folded his hand. I led power and had all the trump in the first three tricks. The queen was a gimme trick, but when I led the black ace, Max smiled and the boys cussed.

"I think you been sharpin' us," said Greg. He tried to sound agitated but his face was sly.

"Sure, he's sharpin' us," said Max. He laid the hard eyes on me again. "But he's my partner, and we're shearing you guys like sheep. Ain't like I'm gonna find fault with that plan."

"You got to give us a chance to get even," said Ralph. He smiled at Max. "Or we got to tar and feather you both."

"I only wear feathers when the tourists pay me," said Max, "and you ain't got no money."

"I guess you guys want to make it more interesting," I said.

You want to make it a dollar a point?" asked Greg.

"Let's keep it friendly," I said. "I can't run too fast dragging a suitcase."

"Fifty cents," said Ralph.

I looked at Max. He shrugged.

"Works for me," I said, "but you got to settle up now."

Ralph had a buck—bitched about it being his gas money, but forked it over. Greg had change, including a nickel stuck in a plug of chewing tobacco flocked with pocket lint. He peeled off the nickel, took a bite from the plug, and then offered it to me.

"My mother beat that particular habit out of me with a switch," I told him. I fished the hard pack of cigars out of my hip pocket. "But I got a smoke here if you don't think Jerry will throw me out."

"That would be my job," said Max. "But I couldn't hardly complain if I was smoking too."

I passed them around. We all lit up except Greg. He put his in the bib pocket of his overalls and said that he was "fixin' to smoke it after he ate the breakfast he bought with my money."

Max suddenly turned into a real lame partner, while the boys started using signals. For clubs they made a fist. Spades was a hand flat on the table. Hearts was a scratch in the middle of the chest. For diamonds Greg spit in his coffee cup—Ralph drummed the fingers of his left hand.

By five I had let them get about twenty bucks up. After that every hand I could play alone without getting euchred I had Max stay home. Some of the loners paid off due to the boys telling me what was in their hands.

By six-thirty I was only down two bucks, the boys were surly, and Max seriously amused. He dealt a hand and turned up the ace of spades. We all passed, and Max looked at me. I took the jack of spades out of my hand, licked the back of it and stuck it to my forehead.

"Jesus!" said Ralph. He threw in his hand.

Max laughed so hard our suitcase table jerked up and down and sent the cards skittering.

Greg splattered his hand on the suitcase and said, "If y'all gonna cheat!"

"He's been reading your signs all night," said Max, and laughed some more.

"There an Art Hardin out there?" asked Jerry from behind the counter.

"That'd be me," I said.

"I need to see some ID," said Jerry. "I got your wire here."

"I'll settle up when I get back, fellas," I said and went up to the counter. Jerry checked my driver's license and asked me what my mother's maiden name was. I told him, and he slid my license back with a check for two hundred dollars.

"Don't you have cash?" I asked.

"Don't keep no cash here at night," he said and then yelled into the lobby, "because all the damn guard does is play cards all night."

"I'da played a damn sight better but for all that snoring going on back there," Max yelled back.

"Mama Rosa down at the Breakfast Nook Café will probably cash that for you if you're in a mind to eat," said Jerry. "If not, the bank down the street will cash it when they open, but they charge five dollars."

I nodded and returned to Max and the boys. I gave Ralph back his gas money, and Greg got his change. "The man said Rosa at the Breakfast Nook would cash this," I showed them the check. Their heads wagged up and down as they tried to read the check. "If you give me a ride down there, breakfast is on me."

"Unless you guys don't eat with no card sharps," said Max. He laughed some more.

"Card sharps is my favorite people," said Greg, "'specially when they're buying. When we're done we can go down to the Crystal Palace for a couple of cold ones."

"You're awful generous with the use of my pickup truck," said Ralph.

"I'll buy you some gas," I said. Ralph seemed pleased. I added, "I'm gonna go in here and take a dump. Then we can head for Mama Rosa's."

I took my suitcase into the men's room and opened it in the stall. I slapped a magazine into the hilt of the Detonics, racked a round into the chamber, and eased the hammer down. The high ride holster would make too big a bulge in my T-shirt, so I took a rubber band out of my shave kit and snapped it a couple of turns around the grips and put pistol in my waist band just behind my right hip.

When I opened the stall door I found Max standing there with his arms folded. I hadn't heard the restroom door open.

"You want me to ask Dixon about that Jack Anders fella?" Max asked, his face blank.

"Suit yourself," I said. "I'll head over to the Dixon Agency after breakfast. I can ask him myself."

"The boys want to go for a beer."

"Too early for me," I said. "Maybe tonight, after I talk to Dixon and get settled. You gonna put in a good word for me?"

"Sure," said Max. "I don't get off here for a while, but I'll meet you at Rosa's. If you want I'll give you a ride over to see Dixon."

"Sounds like a plan," I said. "See you at the Breakfast Nook."

Ralph drove a mix-and-match collection of parts assembled from old Chevy pickup trucks—the doors and fenders all different colors. The gas tank was a red five-gallon jerry can, bungie-strapped into the corner of the truck bed. The fin I had left in my money clip filled the tank with change to spare.

• • •

The Breakfast Nook, a white clapboard affair with a flat roof, stood in the middle of a hard packed dirt parking lot. Folks hadn't parked so much as just pulled up and stopped.

"Don't everybody have a reverse gear," said Ralph, by way of explanation.

Inside, three rows of picnic tables covered in red and white checkered oil cloth seated a crowd of people dressed for the factory or farm labor. A chipped five-foot plaster sailfish, with a red and white "Bud Light" base-ball cap duct taped to its head, decorated the wall behind the buffet serving line.

Mama Rosa collared Ralph and Greg before the screen door could bang twice behind us. Five feet tall and about the same in circumference, she wore a starched white bib apron over a red and white granny dress, her henna-red hair neatly secured in a bun under a hairnet. Greg and Ralph called her "Ma'am." She wanted to see their money.

"This is our good friend, Art Hardin," Greg said. "We brought him cause he said he wanted the best breakfast in town. He got a check from Western Union and he's gonna pay."

"This the only breakfast in town," said Mama Rosa. "And with you vouching for him, I'd say the three of you ought to git, and don't let the door hit ya where the good Lord split ya."

I handed her the check and said, "Jerry up at the bus depot said that you might cash that if we had breakfast here."

She glanced at the check and then studied me from head to foot. "Them boots worth more than this check," she said, "and where's the rest of your suit?"

"In the locker at the bus station."

She gave the boys a sidelong jerk of her head and they bounded off to the serving line.

"Your teeth are too good to be hanging with them two," she said. "If you want to keep 'em you best find someone else to ride with once'st I cash this check."

"You want to see some identification?"

Mama Rosa wagged her head in the negative. "You got cop eyes. Besides, I'll know about this check 'fore you leave. If it ain't right I'll have Junior whup your ass till I tell him to stop." She nodded at a tall, well-built man serving scrambled eggs with a long metal spoon. I'm sure he had to duck to get in the door.

"Yes, ma'am," I said.

"I charge five dollars, same as the bank, but you tell that colored girl spooning grits that I said fix you a steak any way you wants it."

"Don't you need me to sign that?"

"You can sign it after I call Jerry and I bring out your change. Now you go and wade on in," she said and gave me a wink and a smile. "The water ain't too deep."

I found the boys parked at a table and attending to groaning board-loads of scrambled eggs and flapjacks. I set my tray down. "I'm going out-side to make a telephone call. Mamma Rosa says that if you eat my steak when it gets here, she'll have Junior whup your ass until she says stop."

"She give you a steak?" asked Greg.

"Yeah," I said, "I guess because I was buying."

"You in big trouble," said Greg, shaking his head.

"How's that?"

"Mama Rosa done set her cap for you," said Ralph between bites and without looking up. "I hope you like 'em hefty."

I found the pay phone outside, around the corner and near the back, by the doors to the restrooms. On the way I pondered the sly smile the gal serving grits gave me when I ordered the steak.

I dialed up Dunphy with my phone card and got his secretary. She said that he was out in the plant and couldn't be reached.

"Tell him Andy called about that Hardin guy," I said.

"Just a minute," she said.

"Dunphy," he said.

"You put my expense card to sleep," I said. "I need you to wake it up."

"Who is this?"

I said, "Who do you think?"

"My secretary said that it was someone named Andy."

"I'm sorry," I said, "she must have misunderstood. I asked if you were handy. This is Art Hardin. Who's Andy?"

Dunphy didn't answer.

"You still there?" I asked.

"I'm here. I don't know who Andy is, Mr. Hardin. I thought it was one of my suppliers. I'm trying to track down a shipment of pigment. What can I do for you?"

"Like I said, your Platinum Card is a dud."

"Mr. Hardin, I'm a fiduciary for this company. Unless I know what's going on, I'm not turning you loose with our assets."

"I report directly to Scott Lambert."

"Mr. Lambert is out of town. You can report to me."

"Fine, I'll tell you exactly what's going on. I had to spend the night at a bus depot playing cards with some of the local color. I charge extra for that. By my watch you're two thousand dollars into the toilet. If you waste any more of my time, the hourly rate doubles."

"Mr. Hardin," said Dunphy, "you're fired." He hung up.

Something hard poked me in the back of the head. I turned around to find myself looking up the barrel of a revolver in the hands of a man with a ski mask over his face and fire in his eyes.

I FLEXED MY KNEES to lower my head and clamped my fist around the barrel of the revolver in my face—levering the muzzle to my left as I jerked my head to the right—hoping I was fast enough. My hand found the short grip of the Detonics. I heard my thumb rack the hammer as the pistol came off my hip.

"No!" said a familiar voice from behind Mama Rosa's. Max. My assailant let go of his gun. I took my finger out of the trigger guard.

"Back up," I told the man in the mask. He did. Max stood at the rear of the building, at the edge of my field of vision.

"Holy-shit-goddamit, don't shoot!" Max said, and stepped toward me waving his open palms at chest level. His empty holster flapped on his hip.

"What the hell is this?" I said.

My assailant ripped the ski mask off his head to reveal a full shock of black hair over a drained face. "My name is Jack Anders," he said, "and I've never met you in my life."

"So you come and stick a gun in my face! Are you nuts!?"

"I just wanted to scare you enough for you to tell me who you are and why you're asking about me."

"Silk City!" I said. "You remember Wendy Hardin? I'm Art Hardin."

Anders clenched his eyes and rolled his head in a slow circle while he said, "Oh." On the second revolution he said, "Shit!"

"I came here to find you. You disappeared in the middle of an undercover job. We wondered if you were dead."

I looked at Max and shook the revolver. "This is yours?"

"Yeah," he said, and made a long face.

"What is this? Euchre on the short bus?"

Anders closed his eyes and twisted his head.

"I went to see Dixon this morning to tell him about you asking for Jack," said Max, "The cops were all over his office. They said he ate his gun last night. They asked me to identify him."

I handed Max the gun. "Try not to shoot me," I said. "I'm on your side."

Max put the gun in his holster. I kept mine in my hand.

Ander's eyes fix on the muzzle of my Detonics which I kept focused on his ton-ring.

"I knew you had a gun," said Max. "I heard you rack it up in the shitter. Dixon and I were friends since the Bureau."

"You were an agent?"

"I was kind of a go-between on the reservation, you know, at Menominee up on the Wolf River," said Max.

"You were CI for the government in the AIM movement?"

"Not like that," said Max, and looked at the ground. "Someone needed to explain—like a diplomat—both ways, both sides. That's all." He shook his head, "I was never a rat."

Anders started a side step to his right. I put my finger back into the triggerguard. He froze.

"You took the money?"

"I took the money," said Max, eyes hot, looking straight at me. "I *had* to take the money. It wasn't about the money!"

I shrugged, "So?"

"So, I know a lot of cops," said Max. "Indian cops, white cops—all kinda cops—and most of them are assholes but they aren't stupid. They don't shoot themselves in the head. They know what kind of mess it makes. If they get drunk and do it anyway, they do it outside or in the basement or the garage—someplace you can hose the floor."

Anders shrugged and showed me his open hands. I made one negative wag of my head.

"I didn't shoot him," I said. "I was playing cards with you and the brain trust all night. You remember the bus station. The guy you and your pals were trying to hustle."

"That wasn't personal, we were just being social," said Max. "Jerry can't play anymore more because of his wife."

"Sticking a gun in my face is pretty personal."

"Sorry, but who the hell are you?" said Jack Anders. "Ain't like you were up front. All I know is, Dixon is dead, and you're asking about me."

"Lieutenant Ross, with the sheriff," said Max. "He—"

"I know Ross," I said. "I talked to him yesterday and asked him to help me find our friend, Jack here."

"Ross asked where I was last night," said Max. "I mentioned your name and he said bring you over."

"He said come over here and stick a gun in my face?"

"No," said Max. "But, like Jack said, you was maybe too slick—saying Jack sent you. A lot of strange shit is happening. We thought maybe you could give us some answers if we asked the questions right."

I pointed the Detonics at the ground and eased down the hammer. "Come on in. Anders exhaled. I'll buy you breakfast and tell you whatever I know. You can tell me how strange things are. I gotta get my change from Mama Rosa."

"I don't have much appetite," said Max.

"Coffee," I said. I put the pistol back in my waistband and pulled my shirt down over it.

"Ross said he wanted to see you," said Jack.

"Ross can wait. He's paid by the hour," I said. "I'm sorry about Dixon, but he's not in a hurry anymore."

"I guess if you gotta get your change," said Max, "Ross can't bitch about that."

"Mama Rosa promised me a steak," I said. Max and Jack snapped their heads to look at me. "I'm hungry."

"That ain't the question," said Max.

"Question is how much do you like Mama Rosa," said Jack.

"Depends on the steak," I said.

The steak—a T-bone, big as a roast, with the fat grilled crisp—occupied its own plate on a placemat. Coffee, tomato juice, and a pile of home fries on a separate plate finished the setting. Folks had cleared away and gave it space as if it were radioactive.

We sat, and I cut into the steak—purple and cool in the middle. "Just right."

"Jesus," said Jack. "I've seen cows hurt worse than that recover."

Mama Rosa strolled up, draped an arm across my shoulder, and put my change on the table. "Man knows what's good," said Mama Rosa. "Try the tomato juice."

I took a drink and found it included a shot of vodka. "Just right."

"We got some steak sauce, if you want."

"A little salt," I said.

Mama Rosa clamped a vice hold on my shoulder and gave me a side to side shake, kind of the friendly version of a terrier with a rat.

"See," she said, looking at Max and Jack, "Man knows what's good. You gonna stand these two to breakfast, too?"

"Absolutely," I said.

Mama Rosa took four dollars off the table. "You're a good man. Enjoy your breakfast. I like to see a man eat."

Jack shambled off after a tray.

"Just coffee," said Max. I pushed my mug over to him. He shrugged, took a sip, and arched his eyebrows. "Just right."

"Whiskey?"

"Bourbon, I think." He smiled and let the steam bathe his face. "Good Bourbon, maybe Wild Turkey."

I worked on the steak. "You said things have been strange."

"Well, you got to know the whole story."

"This is a big steak."

Max took a good pull on his coffee and set the cup down. He leaned back and measured me with his eyes. After he swallowed, he said, "About a year ago the mill went to contract security. They did an open bid, but everybody knew that Dixon would get it, him being retired FBI and all. He spent a lot of money on radios and equipment. We had an old Ford Escort we painted and put a light bar on to patrol around the parking lot and along the fences. Then some West Coast outfit came in and bid ten cents over minimum wage, just to get the contract. So we're out on our ass, and they run in a bunch of guys that make Greg and Ralph look like Einstein, wearing ball caps and T-shirts for uniforms."

"That's the contract security business. People don't want *good* security; they want *cheap* security."

"The deal is, Dixon spent so much money on the equipment that he was right on the edge with the withholding and social security. When we lost the account he couldn't pay, so he went down and worked out a payment schedule with the feds. He got the contract to clean the restrooms out on the toll road and he did that job himself. He used the money to pay the government and everything was hunky-dory. Then last week the feds seized his bank account, and some guy from the IRS dreamed up this big fine. No court, no lawyer, no judge. They said Dixon just had to pay or they'd seize his house and his pension. Then he got a letter from the state police. They said they might cancel his license."

"Maybe he did go out sideways," I said.

"Dixon was a deacon in his church," said Max, "and one tough cookie, too." Max stared into the steam rising from his cup and shook his head. "No chance he ate his gun."

Jack sat down with a tray full of flapjacks, scrambled eggs, bacon, and biscuits.

"All this for two bucks?" I asked.

"And you can go back for more if you want," said Jack. "Some people, all they get to eat is what they get here. You just can't take any food out. Mama Rosa gets some kind of federal grant."

I sliced a piece of steak and raised the fork like a symphony conductor with a baton. "So, you got tired of the undercover job? What?"

"Dixon came up to Madison and left a note on my door to meet him for lunch. He told me the job was over." Jack forked up a load of flapjacks dripping with syrup and chewed it thoughtfully. He swallowed and added, "Dixon let on like I'd done something wrong. He said there was a difference between getting next to the target and getting personally involved."

I swallowed. "He was getting copies of the reports?"

"Yeah."

"He wasn't supposed to," I said.

"Well, he told me to do it anyway. I wasn't supposed to tell. I don't guess it matters—he's gone now."

I stopped dissecting the steak to look Jack in the eye. "All that aside, I think Dixon had a point. You're supposed to report the target's activities, not make excuses for them. You don't usher at a target's daughter's wedding, stand up as a godparent, or bang his wife. You're looking to testify against the target, not join his family."

"The wedding is next week. I'm an usher. If I don't go, maybe he'll know something is up."

I shook my head. "Doesn't matter," I said. "This case is so hot a guy followed me out here from Michigan. Some dumb bastard stole my bags at the airport, and they snapped his neck like a chicken, maybe because they thought he was me. Dixon turned up dead, maybe because they missed me. It didn't make a lot of sense until you told me that he had copies of the reports."

Jack shrugged and shoveled in a forkload of scrambled eggs.

"You know what Light and Energy is doing," I said. "It's a quantum leap in technology. I don't think the buggy whip manufacturers are going to 'go quietly into that good night.' If you go up to that wedding, you'll be the next one to have a fatal accident."

"I can handle myself."

"I'm sure you can," I said, thinking of the bonehead play he pulled out at the phone booth, "but these people are good, way good, Cold-War good—the kind of guys only the government could afford if they were still in the business."

I heard myself say that. It had been in the back of my mind since I got a load of the "Andy" that visited my office. But the people I'd worked with at the puzzle palace knew where I lived, and they wouldn't have leaned on Lorna Kemp.

"I don't work for you or Dixon anymore," said Jack.

"Do whatever you want," I said. "I'll send flowers. But right now you're on the clock. This is called a debriefing. What happened to the keys, the mail, and the computer discs?"

"Dixon took the keys and the mail," said Jack, using a strip of bacon as a pointer. "I met him in the parking lot at the post office. He put the stuff in his glove box." He turned his head and laid a vacant gaze on his tray, but left the bacon at the ready. When he looked back he said, "I don't know anything about computer discs."

"The discs from the hard drive in the plant manager's office," I said, "what was downloaded?"

"Beats the shit out of me," said Jack. "I wasn't allowed into the plant manager's office. The plant manager's office, the R&D office, and the room with the servers were card access only. They shredded the paper waste and left it in a burn bag outside the door at night."

"So what did you clean?"

"The rest of the place."

"They have in-house or contract security?"

"The place was locked down at night," he said. "They had an alarm system and used some patrol outfit to shake the doors."

"Who had access to the plant manager's office?"

"He did. Nobody else went in there. He met with people in the conference room."

I said, "How about his secretary?"

"He didn't have one. He used the receptionist from the front door. She took his calls."

"What reason did Dixon give you for shutting down the job? How come you just disappeared?"

"Dixon said there was some kind of big trouble. He told me to go home and lay low. I figured he touched all the bases. Sorry if you guys got excited."

"Ross wants to see you," said Max. He looked at his watch. "I need you to vouch for me playing cards. Ross wouldn't believe Greg or Ralph if they swore the sun came up in the morning."

"You gonna hurt my feelings," Greg yelled from two tables down. "'Sides, Art and us is going over to the Crystal Palace."

"Sorry, Greg," I said, "I'm kinda boxed in here. How about I spot you a sawbuck and I'll catch up with you when I'm done with the cops?"

"Works for me," said Greg, all smiles.

"Where's Ralph?"

"In the crapper."

We got up and side-stepped down the row of tables until we were standing next to Greg. I peeled him off two tens and said, "I'll leave Ralph's sawbuck with you. You guys can get the wake started."

"Sure," said Ralph. He folded the bills and put them in the bib pocket of his overalls. "You can trust me."

"Yeah," said Max, "but Ralph can't."

"You're giving a bad impression here," said Greg. "I'll give Ralph the money, sure as hell, and tell him it's a loan—won't charge him no interest neither."

We laughed and worked our way up toward the door. Greg stood up and yelled, "Hey, Junior, Art's fixing to leave."

Junior got to the door before we did. Three axe handles tall and an axe handle wide at the shoulders, he blocked the door—hell, he blocked out the sun.

"We get cleaned up here around one-thirty or two," he said. "Don't be late 'cause Mama needs her rest. And better bring flowers, else you might need some."

I gave him a wink. "You can count on me." We left.

Jack followed me over to get my suitcase out of the back of Ralph's truck. I asked him, "So how'd you land the undercover job? Dixon run an ad?"

"Nah, I was just working as a guard, man. Dixon asked me to do the job because I had a computer and could file the reports."

I dog eyed Jack on the way to Max's car and considered the things on my mind. A big thing: Greg and Ralph didn't know him. And a strange thing: Dixon and Max went back a long way and they knew him.

"You have to get in my door because the passenger's won't open," Max said. Max's blue Ford coupe had sun-faded to gray on the top parts. He opened the driver's door and pulled the seat forward. Discarded fast food wrappers, at high tide in the back seat, tumbled out onto the parking lot.

"Genuine Indian artifacts," said Max.

"Anything alive back here?"

"Just what ate the burgers."

I threw my suitcase across the seat and pushed enough of the litter aside to make room to sit. Jack walked around to the passenger side of the vehicle. Max flopped the seat back in place and slid in behind the wheel. Jack stepped into the passenger seat through the open window. The old Ford left a blue smoke screen as we drove out.

I said, "About your reports. There's one more thing."

"What?" said Jack. "I wrote a report every day. Maybe I got to see them to answer your question."

"This should stick out in your mind. You'll probably remember." I waited for him to look at me. "If all the paper trash was shredded, why do you suppose the engineer asked you if the bags were inspected after you picked them up?"

"We were drinking beer and half in the bag," said Jack.

"Who was working who?"

Jack turned around in the seat to look at me directly. "I've never burned myself," he said.

"Burned?" I asked. "You were playing with matches?"

"Burned, toasted—revealed, you know what the fuck I mean. I never heated the guy up."

"Oh, right. I don't work the street very much anymore." I shrugged. "Tell me about the engineer."

"He was talking about the BuzzBee battery suit and wondering how they got the information they used in their complaint."

"Maybe your target knew damn good and well," I said.

"He didn't come to work until after the suit was filed."

"Who was there before him?"

"Some guy. He mentioned the name. The guy didn't leave the company; he went to Michigan. Something about sand—quartz, silica, mica—I don't know. Funny name like Humpty Dumpty, I don't remember."

"Dunphy?"

"Yeah, that's the guy," said Jack.

"Look, if we send you a ticket, you think you can fly to Michigan for a couple of days? We'll cover your expenses and you'll be on the clock for a week."

"When? I got to find some work."

"Soon," I said. "I need to review your reports again."

Max turned onto a narrow gravel drive guarded by scrub pine on both sides. After a curve to the left, the trees opened to reveal a white mobile home. A magnetic sign on the door announced, DIXON SECURITY AND INVESTIGATIONS. A black station wagon with tinted windows and chrome cabriolet fixtures had been backed up to the steps and shared the gravel parking area with a white Lincoln and a marked county sheriff patrol car.

Leiutenant Ross, wearing jeans and a windbreaker over a yellow pullover shirt, stood at the open passenger door of the white Lincoln and watched us pull into the drive. Deputy Fairchild strode toward us from the cruiser and showed us the palm of his right hand. Max rolled down his window.

"What do you want?" asked Fairchild.

"Ross told me to bring Hardin," said Max.

"Stay here," said Fairchild. He walked over and spoke with Ross.

Ross shook his head and then beckoned to us with a wave. "Just Hardin," he yelled.

I walked over and offered my hand. The contents of the glove box of the Lincoln lay scattered on the passenger seat. Ross peeled the latex glove off his right hand and took mine. "You still here?" he asked.

"You told me not to leave town."

"Yeah, well, now you can go. The sooner the better."

"What about your snitch?"

"Tragic accident. One of the four people hurt in the panic."

"You really think so?"

"The sheriff thinks so," said Ross.

"How come the lights went out?"

"Somebody sprayed graphite silly strings into the main breaker box."

"Happen often?"

"Never heard of it before."

"Max said that he needed me to vouch for his whereabouts last night," I said.

Ross made a dismissive wave. "I never doubted him. This is a suicide. Dixon left a note on his PC."

"How many bullets were left in the gun?"

"Five. He stuck it in his mouth. It's not like he was going to miss."

"Dixon was a cop. You think he'd leave a loaded gun behind?"

"Dixon was a fed. It ain't the same. Lawyers and accountants shouldn't be allowed to carry guns."

"PI's?"

"Two strikes. Listen, I got shit to do here. Why don't you have Max take you to the airport?"

"I'm not quite done here," I said.

"I got an address on that Jacob Anderson," said Ross, "but I'm afraid if I give it to you he'll turn up on my dance card."

"Too late. That's him over there with Max. We had breakfast this morning."

"How did you pull that off?"

"Hardy Boy stuff—when the power went out, the ATM ate my bank card, so I had to spend the night at the bus terminal. Turned out that Dixon had the security account there."

"I'm surprised Max gave up an undercover operative."

"He didn't, really." I said. "He went to Jack and told him someone was asking about him." I waited for Ross to give me a nod. "How old is Jack's address? Jack doesn't seem like he's from around here."

Ross started pulling his glove back on. "Two weeks," he said. "He bought a fishing license—got nothing from the Department of Motor Vehicles."

I said, "Jack came out and introduced himself. My luck runneth over, even Mama Rosa bought me a steak."

Ross laughed and looked at his watch. "You've got about two and a half hours to find an oyster bar."

"Not really?"

"Really! Mama Rosa is a fixture here. She does a lot of good for people. You have to look at it like jury duty or a draft notice. She gets pissed, the breakfast portions get small."

"You're a young stud," I said. "You can fill in for me."

"That's the thing—as sweet as she is I think she still harbors some ugly prejudices," he said with a smile. "I find it deeply troubling."

"Deputy Fairchild?"

"Makes it a point not to eat breakfast."

"Never a cop when you need one," I said. Ross turned back to the Lincoln. I cleared my throat and asked, "What if—"

"You still here?" said Ross without looking up.

"What if your snitch wasn't an accident and Dixon wasn't a suicide? I can tell you for sure that the graphite in the switchbox wasn't a high school prank."

Ross turned and straightened, his face was dour. "I wouldn't push that idea if I were you."

I took out the key for the bus station locker. "You remember the guy I said followed me here on the plane?"

"Yeah, he talked on a cell phone and lit a cigarette. A regular desperado."

I held the key up. "In this locker at the bus station there's a soft drink cup. Take the lid off and you'll find a digital camera. His fingerprints are on the camera and his picture is in the camera."

Ross took the key with his gloved fingers. "How on earth did you do that?" was written on his face, but he said, "More Hardy Boy stuff?"

"Sure," I said. "You went through Dixon's property?"

"Doing it right now." Ross stared at the key.

"My client is looking for a ring of keys and some mail addressed to Light and Energy Applications."

"They looking for the computer discs too?"

"Yes, sir."

"They were lying on the desk in front of Dixon. The mail and the discs were bound together with a big red rubber band."

"How many discs?"

"Seven. If your client wants their stuff, they can have it after the inquest."

"What was on the discs?"

"Dixon's brains," said Ross.

WENDY SAID, "LET ME SEE IF I HAVE THIS RIGHT. You want me to send flowers to a woman for you."

"Not from me, from us."

"Just get on the airplane and come home," said Wendy.

"Exactly what I plan to do. But we may need contacts out here and the woman's like a local Mother Teresa—except for this one little quirk about being horny and luring men with large cuts of beef."

"Just what did you do to attract this woman's attention?"

"I had a full set of teeth and calf skin boots."

"Why didn't you say, 'I'm married?'"

"It's not like she came on to me. She gave me steak and eggs for breakfast. Turns out to be a public announcement of her intentions."

"Well, what were you doing at her house."

"I wasn't at her house. It's a restaurant. Breakfast Nook, something like that. She runs some kind of subsidized government food program. It's the only place open in the morning and they said she'd cash the Western Union check."

"How was the steak?" said Wendy, with crouched feline menace.

"Terrible, tough, ack-poohy—wouldn't have eaten it if I hadn't been starving."

"That good?"

"Wasn't bad."

"Look, this has to be a joke," said Wendy. "Some guys pulling your leg."

"That's what I thought until her son met me at the door and told me to bring flowers and come early because his mother needed her sleep."

"Why didn't you tell him you were married?"

"My basic plan was to get the hell out of the restaurant."

"How about a wine and cheese basket?"

"Sounds about right," I said.

"Good. You got your check cashed," said Wendy, deadpan. "Go buy her one."

"No way I'm going around there. I don't have a ride. And in the afternoon, for entertainment, she and her son go out and maim elephants with a stick."

"Fine," said Wendy. "I really would like to have this woman's address."

"I have little doubt that Mama Rosa, Brandonport, Iowa, is all the address you need."

"Sure. What would you like on the card? Thanks for the memories?"

"How about, 'Thank you for being so kind—Art, Wendy, and the boys. I think she'll respect that."

"This is stupid."

"No, this is being nice. I think we just talked about being nice."

"Maybe there's something else we need to talk about." Wendy banged the telephone in my ear.

• • •

I got the hell out of Dodge—or tried. Mechanical difficulties delayed my flight out of Quad Cities Airport. I had four hours to kill and used the time to write up the Jack Anders report. The sun was already teed up on the eastern horizon when my flight rumbled onto the runway at Kent County International Airport. Wendy read while I drove. It's an hour drive to get to the house. She had little to say—after years of carping about my moustache—not a word.

My ominous dark sedan lurked in the drive, in front of the garage. "Hey," I said. "You got my car fixed."

"Ben picked it up for you," she said. She marched into the house while I got the bags.

Rusty's nails clicked on the foyer tile as he pranced and waggled through his "welcome home" dance. Dogs are always glad to see you. A night spent on a chair in the airport wouldn't make *them* cranky.

I dropped my suit in a pile at the foot of the bed, but Wendy hustled to claim the shower. Rusty trotted into the bedroom with his battered Frisbee and dropped it at my feet. He backed into his "let's play" crouch and fixed me in the glare of joyous eyes.

"Well, I suppose," I said. Rusty closed his mouth around the pink sliver of tongue and perked his ears up. "But if I went out dressed like this, it would be a scandal, dog."

Rusty let his fanny collapse onto the floor and watched me eagerly. I pulled on a pair of gray sweat pants—cut off to make shorts—and a matching sweatshirt with the sleeves cut off at the shoulder and the neck cut into an air-conditioned vee.

"Check this out," I said as I threw my suitcase onto the bed. Rusty turned his head to follow me with his eyes. He gave me a couple of furtive tail wags but dropped his chin onto his paws. I opened the suitcase, pulled out my new hat—not too misshapen from the trip, I punched it up a little—and plopped it on my head. "What do you think?"

Rusty bounded to his feet and pushed the Frisbee over to me with his nose. He backed up and stared at me with his chin high and his tail fanning.

"All right," I said and picked up the Frisbee. Rusty bounded down the hall, and I could hear him nosing the screen door as I stepped into a pair of blue deck shoes. I knocked on the bathroom door and told Wendy I was taking the dog out. No answer. She probably didn't hear me over the sound of the shower.

A twist of the screen door handle launched Rusty into the yard like a rocket. The sun promised a warm day despite a lingering morning chill. Rusty did his ground-to-air doggy number, leaving loopy trails cut in the glistening dew that frosted the lawn. He caught a long floater near the end of the drive and trotted across the road to a fence post where he checked his mail.

We made our way the half mile to the corner at Ashley in short jogs, with Rusty occasionally stopping to study a message and pen a short reply. On the way back, Rusty—out of ink but unperturbed—left several blank missives.

As we returned to the end of the drive I saw the porch light flash a summons. We hustled up the drive. I opened the door, and Rusty nosed into his water bucket to fill his fountain pen.

Wendy met me at the top of the stairs, wearing her fluffy white bathrobe and a turban made of a red bath towel. She smelled of talcum powder and herbal shampoo.

"There was a break-in at your office," she said, handing me my pistol, keys, and wallet. "Marg's in a terrible state. She said she was afraid to go back into the office and afraid to wait for the police. Go!"

• • •

I found Van Huis's fake woody van and a Kentwood patrol car guarding the lot behind my building. The yellow curtains Wendy had hung on the window next to my desk spanked in the breeze from my office window. A pane of glass leaned against the side of the building, near the window frame.

I left my silly hat on the seat, locked my gun in the glove box, and walked over to inspect the window. Fingerprint powder coated the glass, but no prints had been revealed. I shoved the curtain aside to look in and found Van Huis wearing his game face and a tan suit looking out. "They came in your window," he said.

"Ya think?"

"Are you Arthur Hardin?"

"I'm the evil twin, Jerry."

"Do you rent this space?" he asked.

"Why, yes I do."

"This is a crime scene, Mr. Hardin. We'd like to take your statement. I can have a patrol officer drive you to headquarters if you like."

"Headquarters, Jerry? You have one building and you share it with the District Court and the Fire Department. What I'd like is to know what's going on."

"It's Detective Van Huis, and you may come down as far as the door."

The News 9 van lurched up the apron into the lot. Generally speaking, a penny-ante burglary doesn't rate that kind of attention. I ran for the front door and down the stairs. Van Huis met me at the entrance to my office.

"Where's Marg?" I asked, surprised to hear the edge of panic in my voice.

"She's in the top floor lounge giving her statement to the patrol sergeant."

The contents of Marg's desk drawers and file cabinets littered the floor. The chip-camera had been ferreted out of the smoke detector and smashed into a lump on her desk. Video cable, jerked out of the suspended ceiling had left the floor cluttered with acoustical tiles.

Through the door of my office I could see the broad beam of someone in blue police trousers bent over at the waist. "When did this happen?" I asked.

"Marg called it in at seven forty-four this morning. She said that everything was fine when she locked up at around three yesterday afternoon. Can you tell me what her duties are?"

"Mostly, she tries to keep me in line." Van Huis gave me his business face so I said, "She spends the rest of her time doing taxes and accounting. Strictly her business. We split the rent but she gets a break for acting as my secretary."

Van Huis asked, "Was there a recorder on that video line?" He took out his pad and clicked his pen.

"No, I'm sad to say—just used that to sort the cusses from the customers."

The bent-over trousers straightened, and I recognized Patty Oates, the Kentwood Evidence Tech. She wore her light auburn hair short and brushed back from her face. A furious case of teenage acne had left her with a stippled complexion. I waved but she looked away.

"We need to find Lorna," I said. "Sometimes she comes in to write up her stuff when she's done on the street."

"Lorna has a key to the office?"

No, she usually comes in the window. "Sure," I said.

Van Huis wrote in his pad and then asked, "She have a key to your private office?"

"No lock on the door."

"How about your desk and the storage closet in your office?"

"Come on," I said. "Lorna didn't do this."

Van Huis gave me the blank and expectant face cops are so good at.

"Yes, she had a key for the closet," I said. "The radios and battery chargers are in there. I bought the desk used—never had a key. I keep her job assignments in a file folder in my lower desk drawer. If I'm not here she picks up her work from the file."

Van Huis scribbled away. "When do you expect her in?"

"I don't know. I've been out of town. I can page her if you like."

"I don't want you to touch anything in here," said Van Huis. "Just give me the number."

I gave him the number. "This is my office," I said. "My fingerprints are all over this place."

Van Huis looked up from his pad, paused, and studied my face. Finally he said, "Maybe not."

"Okay, Jerry," I said, "Cut the crap!" I could feel my jaws tighten. "What the hell is up here?"

Van Huis looked at my office door and called out, "Patty, you done in there?"

"Not even close," she said. "I'm still working on the surfaces. I have to bag and tag the rest of this vomit. I'll do the prints in the lab."

"We'll wait," said Van Huis, then looked back at me. "What have you been working on?"

"You know better than that," I said.

Van Huis made that expectant face again. I didn't add anything. He asked, "Some widow have you looking into the contents of her late husband's estate?"

"Vomit, Jerry. I do vomit! Just like the lady said."

"Mr. Hardin, I'm sure that wasn't a comment directed at you, personally or professionally."

"'Mr. Hardin?'" I said.

"The hell it wasn't," said the lab tech.

"God sakes, Patty!" Van Huis snapped, then looked back at me. "Are you storing or investigating anyone else's property, Mr Hardin?"

"Nothing like that. What's in my office?"

Van Huis wrote in his pad. When he looked up he asked, "What then?"

"I don't discuss my clients and you know damn good and well the kind of work I do."

"I need to hear it from you," he said, without looking up from his pad.

"Screw you, Jerry." I found myself watching—praying for—a squint, a flinch, the pause just before the move. Nothing. "Read the license on the goddam wall."

"It's Detective Van Huis," he said, in a monotone.

"Asshole!"

Van Huis squared his shoulders and raised his head. The move was in his eyes—then gone. "Mr. Hardin," he said, all public servant, "I know this is upsetting. I have to ask some questions. You may feel they are personal, but I assure you they are important."

"Okay, Detective Van Huis. I'm not surprised this is all a mystery to you."

He looked back at his pad. I watched him close his eyes and stifle a head shake. "I do insurance defense, product liability, liability loss, and a lot of surveillance. I try to avoid domestic work. My favorite is criminal defense. I get appointed by the court, lose money doing the work, but I get to catch a lot of cops with their procedures on hold and their heads stuck up their asses."

"Maybe you have a side business," he said, looking up now, his face malevolent. "Maybe something like mail order."

"I'm a detective—a good one," I said. "My customers pay me because I'm good. I don't have a city to pay me to stumble around and shrug my shoulders while I wait for an informant to save me breaking a sweat."

"Hey, Patty," Van Huis called out, looking toward my office door.

"Yeah."

"Bag something for me, will ya—pick something nice." He turned back to me and said, "Stay here."

Van Huis walked over to the door of my office and reached through. Whatever he was given he held behind his back while he returned to where I stood. "I haven't said anything, Mr. Hardin," he said, and the "Mr. Hardin" came off with a lot of venom, "because of your reputation for lockjaw. I need you to listen carefully. You have the right to remain silent. You have the right to an attorney—"

I said. "You think I broke into my own office? Are you nuts?"

"I don't want to get caught with my procedures on hold."

I folded my hands. I deserved that one.

"Now," he said, "this belong to you?" He held a clear plastic evidence bag in front of my face with a magazine inside. The color picture on the cover was of two prepubescent boys engaged in blatant sexual activity.

"Oh, my God," I said. I backed up and turned my head. "It sure as hell does not!"

Marg came down the stairs with the patrol sergeant a step or two behind her, her face as white as her blouse.

Van Huis pushed the package back in front of my face. "Take another look, Hardin," he said. "Make real goddam sure."

I snatched the bag out of his hand and threw it past him back onto the floor. He grabbed my wrist and I pushed my face up to his. Nose to nose I said, "Goddamit, Jerry, you know me better than that!"

Van Huis is taller than I am. He pushed his forehead down on mine. "And maybe I just *thought* I knew you," he said, his eyes narrow, and what I could see of his face, red.

"Detective!" said the patrol sergeant, making it sound like an admonition. Van Huis backed up a step and looked past me. "What?"

"A word," said the patrol sergeant.

Van Huis produced his handcuffs and snapped a cuff around my right wrist. He left the other dangling and stuck a pointed finger in my face. "Hold that thought," he said.

Marg stepped up and threw her arms around me. I hugged back. In the fifteen years I had known her, this was the second hug. The first was at Pete's funeral.

Van Huis and the sergeant walked down to the end of the hall and opened the fire door to the stairwell. Van Huis held the door ajar and, now and again, passed me a furtive glance while he and the sergeant conferred in low tones.

"Who would have done this?" asked Marg. Her voice quaked. "He said they're sending a copy of the report to the licensing agency in Lansing. I told him I'd never seen that trash. He said that if I testified against you I might not be charged."

I patted her on the back. "Sounds like you're home free."

Marg backed up, and gave my shoulders a shake. "That's not funny, Art. I told the son-of-a-bitch to snap the cuffs on."

"Potty mouth, Marg!" I said. "That's the first time I've ever heard you resort to the Anglo-Saxon."

"This is the first time that I've ever been accused of peddling depravity!"

"Since you're not under arrest, maybe you should go home. I'll call you when I get this cleaned up."

"My clients' books and files are all over the floor," said Marg. "I can't leave it to you. Whoever did this spread that filth all over your office. They put it in the storage closet and in your desk."

"Lucky for me, Van Huis and Oates will bag it all up and take it away."

"They drilled the locks on the file cabinets in the investigators' room," said Marg. "The files are ankle deep on the floor." The sergeant walked by in long strides, without a word or a nod.

"Do you use a cleaning service?" asked Van Huis as he stopped beside us.

I held up my right wrist. "You need to take this off or hook up the other wrist," I said.

He made a face and jangled a ring of keys out of his pants pocket. "How about it?" he asked as he unlocked the cuff.

"Jerry, you had to remind me that you were a police officer doing your job. And I apologize for being a jerk."

Van Huis smiled.

"A big jerk. I'm sorry," I said. "But now I need to remind you that you accused me of a disgusting felony and read me my rights."

"Let's start over."

"Interesting technique," I said, "but I can't think of any case law that says the phrase, 'let's start over,' negates the fact that you read me my rights."

Van Huis closed his eyes and shook his head while he made a noisy inhale. When he opened his eyes he said, "Look, the sergeant is going to page your investigator and have her meet him at the station for an interview, but she works for you. If you have a cleaning service and they've never seen any of this crap, then that goes good for you."

"Detective," I said, "the only thing that's 'going good' for me is you actually brought in a technician and have a chance of catching the people who did this. Now, I can call my attorney from my telephone, or I can go across the hall. You can go with me if you think I'm going to crawl out the window."

"Wait a minute, Art," said Van Huis. "First, just look through your office and tell me if anything is missing."

I threw my hands up. "Sure," I said.

We stepped around the clutter and up to the door of my office. The picture tube of my surveillance monitor had been hammered out with the base of one of my shooting trophies and the trophy left inserted into the void. The rest of my trophies had been reduced to a pile of rubble.

"Patty," said Van Huis, "maybe you got a spare pair of gloves?"

"Who for?" she asked.

"Me," Van Huis said.

We stepped into my office and Patty produced a pair of latex gloves from her print kit. The top of my desk had been swiped vacant, the usual clutter now a pile on the floor at the end of the desk. "PERVERT" had been carved into the desk top.

"You take a picture of the art work?" I asked.

"Why?" asked Oates as Van Huis snapped his gloves on. "Seems appropriate!"

"Because a couple of nights ago someone trashed one of my investigator's cars and scribed the words "Die Bitch" into her windshield. The handwriting looks the same to me."

"We don't have the windshield," said Van Huis.

"Ask Lorna when she gets to the station. She probably took pictures for her insurance company."

"Dust some of the magazines in the desk," said Van Huis to Oates.

"I really need to do that in the lab," said Oates.

"Humor me," said Van Huis, "You know, maybe just the covers."

Oates made a face. "Fine."

I stuck my hands in my pockets and walked over to the storage closet. The door stood open, the doorjamb split. Shards of wood lay on the floor.

"They took it all," I said.

"Your library's in there," said Oates as she laid out magazines on the top of my desk.

"What's missing?" asked Van Huis.

"Four FM radios along with the batteries and chargers, are gone. A half-dozen kevlar vests are gone. A couple of video rigs, blank tapes, and a tripod."

"There were video tapes?" asked Van Huis, already writing in his note-book.

Marg walked up to the office door. "Are you done out here?"

"Done out there," said Oates as she ran white dust over the magazines with a small feather brush.

"Can Marg clean up out there?" I asked.

"You get pictures?" asked Van Huis.

"Not out there," said Oates. She blew the dust off a magazine, made a face, and then moved to the next.

"Better wait," said Van Huis.

"I got a camera in my purse," said Marg.

"Jesus Christ!" said Oates. "Will you get these people out of here until I'm done?"

"A quick walk-through and we're out of here," said Van Huis.

"This guy's mouthpiece is going to beat me to death with this walk through," said Oates with her hands on her hip. "There are no fingerprints on the covers of these magazines."

Van Huis turned his face to mine. I gave him arched eyebrows. "Anything else missing?" he asked.

"I kept a big gym bag in the closet," I said. "They probably used it to carry the stuff out."

Marg started taking flash pictures in the front office. Oates rolled her eyes and bent over to dig in her kit.

"Any firearms?" asked Van Huis.

"No," I said. "I kept a cleaning kit and a box of ammo in my desk."

"Not here," said Oates. She hustled by us with a camera in her hand and went out into the reception area.

"So you're telling me that someone broke in here to plant this crap in your office," said Van Huis.

"Sounds like a good question to ask my attorney," I said. "Let's go have a look at the investigators' room."

A dozen file cabinets lined one wall of the investigators' room. The long wooden table the street investigators used as a desk had been turned over and the legs broken off. We had to step over file drawers to get into the middle of the room. Scattered files covered the floor. On the top of one cabinet a ginger ale can stood—displayed as if enshrined.

"I guess they were here for a while," said Van Huis.

"Had to be looking for a particular file," I said. "This is way too much work for vandalism. They could have just poured paint or ink in the files."

"Why would they have to open *all* the files?"

"The file titles are encrypted," I said. "You can't just look up something alphabetically."

"Isn't there a list or key?" asked Van Huis.

"In my head. Marg also knows, but the investigators have to ask for files."

"So this took hours."

"Yes, even if there were several of them," I said and pointed at the soft drink can. "Looks like somebody got thirsty."

"These guys raid the refrigerator all the time."

"That one is a Michigan deposit can," I said. "I don't have that brand. I bought all my sodas in Indiana, remember? You bitched about bootleg sodas. They brought that can with them."

Van Huis's face lit up. He picked it up with his gloved hand and wagged it gently to see if it was empty. Something rattled about inside the can. He turned the can toward the light and looked inside.

"Cigar butt," he said.

"This is a crime scene," Oates growled from the reception office. "You need to back out of here and take that cameraman with you."

Van Huis and I hustled for the front office but we had to pick our way through the clutter.

"Delia Dumas, Live News at Five," said the voice in a smoky alto. "We have information that Ladin Detective Agency is being investigated for the distribution of child pornography." She pushed the microphone up to Oates's face. "Can you verify that information?"

"Out!" said Oates.

Van Huis and I shambled over the litter into the reception office. Marg had turned away from the camera. Delia Dumas wore an inflated blond bouffant that didn't match her eyebrows and made her head look too big for her body. Over a white silk blouse she wore a blue blazer with a Channel 9 logo on the pocket. The cameraman stood behind her—very tall—running footage over the top of her head.

Oates put one hand on Delia's shoulder and the other hand on the lens of the camera and pushed them backwards.

"Don't touch the camera," said Delia, the syrup drained from her voice.

"Out!" said Van Huis. "This is a police investigation!"

Oates pushed the news crew back into the hall and pulled the door shut. Dumas and her cohort set up in the common area. The piece aired as a Five O'clock Investigative Report and as a lead feature on the *Eleven-O'clock News Final*. The newsies cut in file footage of me handcuffed and being lead into the Grand Rapids Turnkey after the Talon murder—I was released. They had a shot of Oates carrying a cardboard box out to Van Huis's van. The carton was diffused into a blurry dot. Dumas reported that the Kentwood Police would not comment and attributed her information to "informed sources."

Wendy filled me in on the details. I called to tell her that we weren't quite done with the clean-up and I planned to rack it on the sofa in the office. She didn't seem to mind that I wasn't going to make it home. The woman's a rock.

A GALE FORCE SHIT-STORM sounds exactly like a ringing telephone. I'd rolled off the sofa and fired up the coffee pot when I heard the first crack of thunder. Jeanne Peabody, the new claims supervisor at Pacific Casualty, sounded surprised to hear my voice. She said that Pacific Casualty would no longer be using contract investigative agencies.

"Jeanne," I said, "the story on the news was misguided and misinformed. I'll probably have to sue."

"I don't watch the news," she said, her voice chilly enough to freeze the tuxedo off a penguin. She hung up.

I folded my blanket and walked it out to my car. I found my windshield in sprinkles again. A chunk of broken concrete lounged in the passenger seat. The green dribbles on the asphalt autographed the mischief.

"Son-of-a-bitch," I said, disgusted but not particularly loud. A woman walking in the parking lot turned her head away and scurried through the gathering maze of cars to claim sanctuary at the entrance to the building. I dropped my blanket in the trunk and slammed the lid.

Brisk footsteps approached from behind. I raised both hands over my head and said, "Don't shoot, I'm only the piano player."

A familiar voice asked, "Where were you around two this morning?"

"Good morning to you, too, Shep," I said and turned around.

Detective Shephart, late of the major cases crew in Grand Rapids and, by news accounts, currently the Commander of the Metropolitan Task Force charged with solving a spate of hooker mutilation murders, approached, his face as pale and chiseled as an insription on a tombstone. Tall but thin and old at forty, his eyes had aged more translucent than blue. All the hair had skidded off the top of his head, while the remainder formed a laurel of gray-brown stubble above his ears and trailing down the nape of his neck. The dry cleaner had issued a fugitive warrant for his blue permanent-wrinkle suit. He'd buttoned his sweat stained collar and had cinched up his rumpled tie.

"Art, I need to know where you were." His breath smelled of a "blast of mint-freshness" but could not overpower the eau d'bar towel that lingered around him like a shroud.

"Right here," I said. "Slept on the sofa."

"Who with?"

"Nobody. It's a narrow sofa." I walked around to unlock the passenger door of my car.

"Did you see anyone? Talk to anyone? What time?"

I pulled the door open and glass nodules showered onto the blacktop. "Don't you want to ask me what happened here?"

"Somebody smashed your windshield," he said. He shrugged. "Like I give a shit."

"My sidearm is in the glove box," I said. I unlocked the glove box and stepped back. Reaching for a pistol just now would have been unwise, but with the windshield gone I couldn't leave it in the car. "I thought you might want to reach in there and get it yourself—save patting me down."

"Sure," he said. "Back the fuck up."

When I got back around the taillights he reached in and hauled out my Detonics. He smelled the barrel and then looked it over. He smiled. "You had my initials blued over."

"Yeah. You were so intent on making a trophy when you arrested me, I couldn't see your work going to waste. Now, it's sort of my trophy. What do you think?"

"Screw you," he said and scattered the contents of the glove box onto the seat to join the chunk of concrete and glass shards.

"No spare magazine in there," I said. "I picked up a couple and a box of ammo yesterday. They're in my desk."

"How about a knife or letter opener?"

"Nope. Once I shoot 'em I don't feel any need to read their mail."

"You're a funny guy, Art," said Shephart, deadpan. "But I know you used to carry a pocket knife."

"They still rag you about that down at the Turnkey?"

"Where's the knife?"

"In the pants pocket of my suit," I said.

"Is that what you put in the trunk?"

"You want to read me my rights? Take me downtown?"

"No," he said, "I'd rather have some answers." He stuffed my pistol into his hip pocket.

I dangled my key ring by the trunk key and held it out to Shephart. He stepped up, snapped them out of my hand and opened the trunk, weaving a little when he bent to look inside, he caught himself with a hand on the spare tire. Just a guess—he was in need of a shot of carburetor cleaner to get his motor running.

"You all right?" I asked.

He took a breath. "Fine," he said. He picked up the blanket, shook it, and then cast it aside to stir the rest of the rummage in my trunk. "Why do you have a blanket in your trunk?"

"Same reason I have a shovel, tire chains, and a bag of kitty litter," I said. "This is Michigan."

Shephart shut the trunk. "So, who saw you here last night?"

"Marg and Lorna."

"Who's Lorna?"

"A snout."

"They gonna be in this morning?" asked Shephart.

"We cleaned and straightened up the office until three-thirty or so. I don't expect them too early."

"You were all together until three-thirty in the morning?"

"That's correct, officer," I said. "C'mon in. I'll get you their phone numbers. I put some coffee on—ought to be ready by now."

Shephart's shoulders went round. "Coffee," he said. "Coffee'd be great."

We left the car and started up the steps. "Heard about your promotion," I said. "It was on the news."

"It's a Buddhist barbecue," he said. "Nobody with a career would touch it. Lucky for you I don't believe everything I see on the news."

"You think maybe I cut up hookers, but I draw the line at perverted books?"

"We searched your office after the Talon murder," said Shephart. "We didn't find any shit like that."

"Maybe I just expanded my business."

"That kind of shit's a hardwiring problem. It doesn't come on sudden-like."

I opened the door and held it for Shephart. "A vote of confidence," I said. "Maybe I should call you as a character witness."

"Do me a favor and don't mention my name."

"To what do I owe the honor of this visit?"

"Coffee first," he said. "Then tell me about this break-in. You keep business cards here?"

We stepped into the reception area. One of Marg's clients was talking to the answering machine and bailing out.

"Cream? Sugar?"

"Hot and black," he said.

I filled a couple of mugs from the rack and set them on my desk, which was—for the first time in recent memory—neat and organized. A big desk blotter covered the inscription. Shephart took my pistol out of his hip pocket and set it in the middle of the blotter.

"Next time, wag your own pistol in," he said. "You ain't quick enough to shade me." He picked up his cup and sat in the wing-back chair under the monitor I'd replaced the night before.

I picked up the pistol, put my hand over the ejection port, racked the slide to the rear, and locked it in place. Shephart froze mid-sip. A fat .45 caliber-two-hundred-grain-semi-jacketed-hollow-point bullet pressed itself into my left palm and I stood it on end in front of me. "They broke in night before last. About the only thing they didn't rifle was my business cards."

Shephart made a hard swallow and lowered his coffee. I punched the magazine out and laid it on the desk with the pistol.

"Jesus!" said Shephart. "I forgot that you carried one in the spout." He rocked to his left. I figured he must have been carrying his service piece on his right hip. His face got a little paler. After a sip of coffee he was sitting straight again. "Just what did they get into?"

"Everything. They trashed the place. Stole one file—still has me guessing."

"Why?"

"There's a copier in the investigators' room. All they had to do was make a copy and I'd never have known what was taken."

"So what'd they take?"

"Privileged," I said, "We've already been around that corner." I opened my top right-hand drawer and extracted a squeeze can of gun oil.

Shephard produced a clear plastic evidence bag from the inside breast pocket of his suit jacket and flopped it onto my desk. In the bag was one of my business cards, encrusted with a rust-brown blood stain.

"There's a million of those things circulating," I said. "I pass them out like beads at a Mardi Gras Parade."

"Woman found dead by a payphone on the river walk at two o'clock this A.M.," said Shephart. "The handset was hanging by the cord and she had this in her hand."

My telephone rang.

"You want to get that?" Shephart asked.

"Machine will get it," I said and held the Detonics upside down to oil the rails and the bulbous end of the barrel. "I don't know what to tell you."

"I thought you might explain what's written on the back," said Shephart. He flipped the bag over and showed me Scott Lambert's telephone number. "The number's a private line into some outfit called Light and Energy Applications."

I looked up. Shephart was working me with those fluoroscopic eyes cops have. I said, "Five foot one or two, thin, mid-forties, brown hair bobbed off about ear level?"

Shephart set his coffee down and hauled a pad and pen out of the side pocket of his coat. "Yeah."

"Oh, my God." I let the pistol and oil can clunk onto the desktop.

"Who was it? There was no purse or ID."

"I gave that card to Anne Jones."

Shephart wrote it down. "Who's Anne Jones?"

"Anne Frampton," I said. On the fourth or fifth ring the tape machine picked up. Nate Saxon, the owner of the biggest contract adjusting firm in the state—six offices and eighty adjusters—gave me the kiss-off.

"The artist?"

"Yeah."

"She know this Anne Jones?" asked Shephart.

"Anne Frampton is Anne Jones."

"Jesus," said Shephart. He rolled his eyes up and collapsed back into the wing-back chair with his pen and pad in his lap. "You sure?"

"Got a picture?" The description didn't match the harridan Anne lived with, but maybe she had some other playmates.

Shephart groped a picture out of the side pocket of his jacket and sailed it, spinning face down, onto my desk blotter.

Not that I wished anyone else dead: I just made a silent "please-God" prayer and turned over the color Polaroid head shot taken at the morgue. It was Anne—lips blue and eyes vacant.

"What a waste," I said. "It's Anne. She has a brother. I can give you his address and phone number. He'll know how to contact their mother."

"Thanks."

"What the hell happened?"

"Somebody stabbed her once, downward, behind the clavicle with a blade long enough to sever her aorta. She was dead when she hit the ground." Shephart worked me with the cop eyes some more. "Tell me about Light and Energy Applications," he said, like it was an afterthought.

"One thrust?"

Shephart looked up from his pad and demonstrated a downward thrust using his pen clinched in his fist as a prop. "Downward from the right, two inches from the neck, some kind of straight- bladed dirk. We can't get a casting because the doer rocked the blade side to side." He rowed the pen to demonstrate.

"Anne sure as hell wasn't a hooker," I said. "Were there any other lacerations?"

"No, but it was in the slasher's neighborhood. Even the Son of Sam worked on his marksmanship."

"This wasn't a psycho. A psycho likes to cut. He gets off on the screams, the terror, and the spray of blood. One thrust wouldn't do it for him. If he'd been interrupted, you'd have two bodies this morning instead of one. This wasn't your guy. This was an assassination."

"Maybe," said Shephart. "Chief says it's a Task Force case."

"He doesn't know who this is."

"My case," said Shephart, his eyes hot.

"Get real. This ain't your guy."

"I ask the questions. You tell me what you fucking know."

"Okay," I said and studied him. Under the ashen face lurked the remnants of fire. I'd known him for years, not always pleasantly. If a breath, a word, could burn off the cocoon of alcohol, I judged it unlikely we'd end up with a butterfly—more likely a moth that hung out in your closet and ate your sweaters.

"That's the stolen file," I told him. And then I told him the rest—including the parts about Lambert, about the lake shore, and how Lambert wanted the address but I wouldn't give it to him. I told him about the Andys, the trip to Brandonport, the guy with the broken neck, and how Dixon maybe did or didn't eat his gun. He wrote it all down, but the part he liked best was when I got to the ginger ale can with the cigar butt in it.

"See Van Huis over at Kentwood," I said.

Shephart snapped his pad shut, swilled his coffee, and bolted out of his chair. He left a "stay available" hanging in the air somewhere between Marg's desk and the front door.

I picked up the telephone, someone was on the line.

"Hello, hello," he said, "I didn't hear it ring."

It wasn't a familiar voice. He could have been one of Marg's client's. Maybe he needed time to rethink what he was going to say. I punched the button twice and got a dial tone.

I dialed up Light and Energy. Lambert had stepped out. Did I want to speak to Dunphy?

"This is Art Hardin," I said. "Please have Mr. Lambert call me."

She said that she had to have a subject to write down—that Mr. Lambert generally didn't answer open calls.

"You tell Scotty that if I don't hear from him right-most-rikki-tick I will definitely call back and tell whoever answers the phone exactly what this is about."

I let the handset slide back on the cradle. The telephone started ringing. I opened my drawer and put the gun oil away. By the time the Detonics was loaded and on my hip the answering machine picked up.

It was the fellow I had hung up on. Said he was the producer of the evening news and did I want to make a comment.

"How about this," I told the empty room. "You now head the short list of people who'd better pray I never get diagnosed with anything terminal."

I picked up the telephone. "This is Art Hardin. My lawyer will be contacting you. Why don't you just chat him up for a while?" I banged the phone back down.

"That was brilliant, Art," I said. "Now the bastard knows where you are." I picked up the handset and parked it in the middle of my desk blotter.

I stood up to go to the investigators' room and my pistol slid out of the waistband of my sweats and down the leg. I caught it before it hit the floor and laid it on the desk pointed at the telephone.

The Prestige Motors file—along with the rest of the files—was back where it belonged. I looked up Tracy's telephone number and went back to my desk. The handset was making a "neep, neep, neep," sound.

"Gonna be hard for Lambert to call you that way," I said and put the handset back in the cradle. I sat and drummed my fingers on the desktop while I stared at the telephone.

"Better call Tracy while you still have some short term memory," I said and dialed her up. I got an answering machine and instructions to leave a message after the tone.

"This is Art Hardin. You gotta quit smashing my windshield. I'll give you the first one because you were pissed, but last night is definitely it. Quit." I started to hang up but put the phone back to my face, "And fix your hydraulic lines. You're leaking green slop all over my parking lot."

I banged down the telephone, and it started ringing. I let the machine get it. Lambert. He was sorry about the misunderstanding with Dunphy...he'd talked to Wendy ... good job . . . just send the bill . . . no problem . . . he needed me to recover the computer discs when the cops were done with them. I picked up the telephone.

"Why don't you have Andy pick them up?"

"Art?"

"Yeah."

"Who's Andy?"

"At least two people," I said. "Maybe I haven't met them all yet."

"Art, you're losing me."

"I only took this job because I thought I could protect her. Why didn't you just leave her the hell alone?"

"Anne?"

"Joan of Arc!"

"Dunphy gave me your message. I went to meet Anne but it was a little strange. Maybe she'll cool off in a couple of days."

"She's dead," I told him. "She's laying on a slab in the morgue. That's as cool as they get."

I hung up, but that didn't seem to do it for me, so I banged the receiver onto the cradle four or five times, hard enough to ring the bell.

Still no joy.

I ripped the phone out of the wall and threw it into the wastebasket.

THE IDEA OF A HEART-TO-HEART conversation with Hank Dunphy suddenly held considerable charm. The errand got off to a slow start. I stashed a couple of spare magazines in my pockets and after some scouting and deliberation I settled on concealing my pistol in a Mickey-D's burger bag rescued from Marg's trash can.

A white Chevy Suburban wallowed in the shade at the back of the parking lot. The front end sported a flat black push-bar covering the grill and, painted on the side, a gold leaf "Cable News" sign, which left you wondering if they were collecting news or installing cable. When I pulled my car over to the dumpster a man in a "Cable News" ball cap and blue coveralls stepped out of the truck with a video camera. I never should have talked to the news director on the telephone.

Once I had the corner of my windshield loose—I had to kick it from the inside—the rest of it peeled out of the tracks like a big stick of gum. I tossed it in the dumpster and chased it with the chunk of concrete. What's newsworthy about that I don't know, but the man with the camera kept grinding away.

The crap Shephart had scattered around went back in the glove box, and I brushed the glass off the seat with the snowbrush the boys gave me for Christmas. My bag of McPistol went under the armrest. When I was younger, I always had a convertible. No windshield is a lot windier than no top.

The Suburban showed up in my mirror at the stop sign at Forty-fourth Street. I signaled a right turn. So did he.

Twenty years ago Forty-fourth Street had been the back road to the airport. Now it's a commercial strip that sprawls from the airport in the east to Jenison in the west. The traffic is usually crazy, but at lunch time it's psychotic.

"Never do anything in traffic that requires someone else to have brakes." Good advice when my father gave it to me, but advice I ignored to rocket through eastbound traffic into a slim opening, turning left into westbound traffic. The woman driving the car in my rearview mirror flashed me a well-deserved bird.

I got my eyes forward just in time for a panic stop. The traffic light was red at Kalamazoo. I stole another glance in the mirror. The cameraman had jumped out of the Suburban and run up to the corner to eyeball me until his partner could get the van up to the corner. I cut through the parking lots to turn north. At Thirty-sixth I cut back east—no more white Suburban, but a red Dodge sedan made the turn with me.

Just to be fastidious I turned north again at Breton and the Dodge came with me but laid way back. I slowed, but the Dodge wouldn't close up, so I went east at Twenty-eighth. At the Beltline I went north again; so did the Dodge.

The Beltline is a boulevard that skirts the eastern side of the Grand Rapids metropolitan area. It moves pretty good until about three o'clock when the commuters tie it up as they head for the northern suburbs. I burned a couple of yellow lights. The Dodge burned the reds to stay with me.

I took the left lane and honked on it as we approached Michigan Avenue. The Dodge had to come out or give me up. I watched the mirror. The Dodge pulled out and cranked on, and I veered into the left turn lane. The car in front of me didn't take the yellow arrow. I stopped and the Dodge was first in line behind me. The driver ducked his head like he was digging for a station on the radio but I made him anyway: Fidel/Andy.

I put my hand into the burger bag and dog-eyed him in the mirror. He kept his face tipped down. He was losing hair at the crown of his head. "That ain't no halo, Andy, ole buddy," I told him in the mirror.

They had worked hard to gaslight me, but a suicide at a stoplight would be hard to sell. He had to be an idiot not to know he was toasted. On the outside chance that he was still chilly I decided not to get out and screw my gun into his nose.

We got the green arrow and turned onto westbound Michigan Avenue. After we cleared the light, Fidel junior lagged behind until he had a couple of cover cars. As we went east, Michigan Avenue opened up from a quiet residential into a four-lane commercial strip.

Downtown Grand Rapids is located in the Grand River valley. Eastbound traffic gets a postcard-scenic view of Grand Rapids as Michigan Avenue rockets down a long steep hill into the legal and financial hub of the city.

At the top of the hill, across from the hospital, I pulled into a carwash. The Dodge took a parking meter on the downgrade, a half block past the carwash—just before some orange safety cones blocked the curb lane for a road crew laying fresh asphalt.

The attendant had a spray-wash wand in his hand. He was in his late teens wearing a rock groupie T-shirt, frayed cut-off jeans, and yellow rubber boots with black soles.

He told me, "You ain't got no windshield, man. We can't wash a car what ain't got no windshield."

"You wash cars here?"

"Well, yeah but . . ."

"Wash this one!"

"We can't be responsible for damage to your car, man. There's a big sign over there." He pointed to a large black and white block-lettered sign with a wide red border.

I said, "I'm pretty sure that my antenna and rearview mirrors are safe." I pushed the shift lever up to park, stepped out, and telescoped the antenna into the fender.

"I got to ask the manager, man." He shook his head.

"Good idea," I said. "Go get him."

"You got to pull it outta line."

I opened the door and took the burger bag off the seat. "Park it anywhere you want," I told him. "I got to use the rest room."

"Hey! What are you doing?" asked the attendant. He spread his arms. "Where are you going? You got to move this car." The lady in the car behind started on her horn.

"I'll be right back, pard. I got an urgent call of nature. The keys are in it." I gave him a nod, stepped through the back door of the carwash, and walked along the line of sudsers, waxers, and blow-dryers to the front door.

Fidel/Andy, already out of the Dodge, eased cautiously up the sidewalk toward the carwash. He wore black shorts, a blue floral Aloha shirt, and black felony flyers—high-top tennies with a red ball logo on the ankle. He had spent some time as a brushbeater. Hauling a heavy combat pack had given him legs so muscular that wearing trousers had rubbed the hair from the back of his calves. His shins were a mass of scars from the knee down.

He stopped, hauled a cigarette out of his shirt pocket and turned toward the car-wiping crew like he was turning his back to the wind. He took his time lighting up and stared at the cars and men over the top of his lighter. Finally he exhaled a cloud of smoke and strolled toward the back of the carwash.

When he passed, I went out the front door. Traffic on the street by the rear entrance to the carwash was backing up and punctuated with a lot of horns and squealing tires.

Fidel/Andy's Dodge wasn't locked. I climbed into the passenger seat. The automatic shoulder belt hummed down the track above the door and strapped me diagonally across the chest. In the glove box I found a cell-phone. The "low battery" light was on. I pushed redial.

"Intelligence Research Associates," a woman with a husky feline voice purred into the telephone.

"This is Andy," I said. "Let me talk to the boss."

"Mr. Cameran isn't in," she said. "I can take a message."

J. William Cameran. I knew him! Yet another retired FBI type. Smug. Aloof. At Michigan PI Council meetings he sat in the corner and pouted like a kid kept in at recess, but he never missed a meeting.

The J. Billster had embarrassed an industrial client out on the lake shore. The company found itself the subject of a lawsuit when a secretary discovered a camera he'd installed in the ladies' room. They fired him and hired me. I managed to ferret out their substance abusers without resorting to stupidity. J. William was not impressed. He went around and bitched to guys in the trade that I'd snaked his client.

"Just tell him that Andy called," I said.

"Andy who?"

"You know which Andy."

"No sir, I'm sorry, this is just his service. You're getting scratchy. I think your battery is low."

"No message," I said. "I'll call back. What's a good time?"

"He picks up his messages in the morning. Maybe you can catch him then."

"Thanks." I hung up.

The Dodge had a trunk popper. I pushed the button. Nothing happened. I jerked the glove box light loose and pulled off the positive lead. Another pull got me enough slack to reach the trunk button. I touched the hot lead to the negative soldered weld on the back of the button. The trunk clunked open.

I found my gym bag, the one taken in the burglary—loaded with my radios, video camera, and Kevlar vests. I slammed the trunk and punched nine-one-one on the cellphone.

"Grand Rapids Police," said the lady dispatcher. "What's the nature of your emergency?"

"My name is Art Hardin," I said. "My offices were broken into a couple of days ago. A man has my property in the trunk of a red Dodge parked on the hill on Michigan Avenue just west of the carwash. The car is just a couple of blocks up the hill from the police station."

"What's your name?"

"Art Hardin."

"Where are you calling from?"

"A cellphone. I'm standing on the sidewalk next to a red Dodge on the north side of Michigan Avenue."

"How do you know your property is in the car?"

"I saw it."

"What's the license number on the vehicle?"

I read it to her.

"Your battery is fading," she said. "Can you give it to me . . ." She was gone.

A patrol car passed eastbound on Michigan Avenue. I waved both arms and shouted. The car turned left into the back of the carwash. Fidel/Andy came out the front door of the car wash and walked over to the pay phone on the front wall of the building and appeared to drop coins in the slot. He sidestepped the length of the phone cord so that he could look down through the now empty tunnel of a carwash bay.

I climbed into the Dodge through the passenger side, slammed the glove box door after the cellphone, and hit the electric door locks. I had to shrug out of the auto-seatbelt to get into the back seat. Laying on the floor I got my McBang-Bang in both hands and rolled my eyes up to watch the side window above my head.

Love that new car smell, but the red Dodge soaked up rays fast. I blinked against the sweat that stung my eyes. Sweat dripped into my nostrils. I shook my head. Someone pulled on the driver's door and then cursed. I couldn't see a thing.

Keys jangled and then worked the door lock. The car sagged as someone climbed into the driver's seat, and I got a blast of cool air. Fidel/Andy banged the door shut. The seat belt hummed along its track and the engine cranked to life.

The words I had to say were easy: You're under arrest, I have a gun, put your palms flat on the ceiling and keep them there until the police arrive.

I couldn't see the words. My mind showed me a picture of Annie-fannie laid out on an autopsy table, gutted like a rabbit.

I sprang onto my knees, grabbed the seatbelt with my left hand, wound an extra turn around Fidel/Andy's neck and tugged hard. His hands shot up to claw at the strap of fabric. I put my lips next to his ear and whispered, "I've had just about enough of you."

IN THE PROFESSION OF ARMS, LIFE IS LIKE A ROW OF DOMINOES. Get angry, you make a mistake. Make a mistake, bad things happen. I got angry. Fidel/Andy head butted me, which split my lip and, as I found out later, broke my nose. From that point, bad things just sort of fell one upon the other.

I clubbed Fidel/Andy across the forehead with the Detonics. The blow drove his head into the driver's window, but it gave him some slack in the seatbelt I'd coiled around his neck, and I think he got a breath there.

Andy's eyes were open but the vacancy signs were on. Nonetheless he managed to get an arm around my head and flopped me into the front seat. Pulling me over the seat jammed his foot on the gas pedal, but it was my elbow that hit the shift lever. The tires squealed. We launched down the hill.

I hung tight to Fidel/Andy's seat belt—turning his face blue—and knocked the shift lever up with the pistol. Pulling on the belt, I got my head high enough to see over the dash. A ten-yard dump truck loaded with asphalt sat rooted to a red stoplight half way down the hill.

The Dodge made a series of jerks. Andy still had the gas nailed. A dull thud came from under the floorboard announcing the failure of the transmission, and we were freewheeling. The stoplight changed to green, but the truck was still showing brake lights. Andy let go of the seat belt and elbowed me in the chest.

I switched off the ignition and pulled out the keys. My back was on the front seat. I pulled my knees up to protect my chest. That's when I saw the double-edged fighting knife in Andy's left hand. I brought the Detonics up.

"You're under arrest," I told him. Given my split lip and the fact that my mouth had filled with blood, I'm not really sure what it sounded like, but it made a spray of blood that settled on my face and his shirt.

I heard the driver's door open and felt a rush of air. Fidel-Andy cut the seat belt where it crossed his chest, from the top down toward his body. The knife—very sharp—parted the seat belt, the aloha shirt, and probably some of Andy.

The seat belt whipped loose from his neck, and he turned toward me with the dagger raised to strike. I clicked the safety off the pistol, got it at an up angle over my chest and squeezed off. Deafening. Gunpowder stung my forehead.

The driver's window exploded as the door swung wide. Andy disappeared. I got my feet off the ceiling and knees on the floor. The asphalt truck had started a low gear lurch into the intersection. Jerking on the steering wheel did no good; it was locked in place. I dived onto the brake pedal with my hands. Antilock brakes caused the pedal to vibrate and I resigned myself to the crash, but the Dodge stopped with only a jolt. I hauled myself up off the floor. The nose of the Dodge had wedged itself between the mud flaps of the asphalt truck. It rose and then fell as it peeled loose from the tandem rear wheels.

Out the rear window I could see Fidel/Andy stumbling to his feet and clutching his chest, but the real attention grabber was the white news truck bearing down on the back of the Dodge. The push bar in front of the truck's grill rose as the driver nailed the gas in place of the brakes. I unassed the Dodge.

Due to a certain lack of grace brought on by haste, I ended up sitting on the street next to the open driver's door. The news truck hit the Dodge— he never did find the brakes—and the doorjamb caught my left shoulder. One of the cops said I spun like a top but I only remember going around once. The door of the Dodge came at me in a blur, but only fanned me, as the Suburban drove the Dodge into the asphalt truck. I finished the three-sixty in time to see Fidel/Andy hobbling to the curb.

I turned my head again and found that I was sitting next to the driver's door of the news truck. I pulled myself to my feet by the mirror bracket—had a difficult time getting my left hand over my head—and stepped onto the running board to peer into Suburban and see if the news idiots were all right.

The driver, wearing his seatbelt, sat with his chest against the steering wheel. The cameraman sat strapped into the front passenger seat with his arms folded around his head.

The nose of the Dodge had been driven under the asphalt truck. The impact accordioned the rear of the Dodge and it stuck up in the air like a cat in heat—rear wheels off the ground. The dump truck dragged the Dodge off the front of the news truck as it continued into the intersection.

The Suburban driver sat back in his seat, looked at the retreating Dodge, and then at me. It was Deliveryman/Andy, of the "I-have-a-package-for-Art-Hardin" charade in my office. He squinted his eyes, twisted his head, and yelled, "Frank! The blokes on the running board!"

The cameraman unwrapped his arms from his head and looked over at me. Deliveryman/Andy pulled the shift lever into reverse. I tried the door but it was jammed or locked.

The cameraman bent over to retrieve something from the floor. Deliveryman/Andy lay down sideways in the seat. The camera man came up with a cannon—a twelve-gauge shotgun, business end looking as big as a garbage can. The tires squealed. The truck lurched in reverse. I slipped off the running board. The driver's window erupted in a shower of glass.

The push bar of the Suburban had been bent in the middle and driven back into the grill. The radiator trailed steam as the news truck backed up. The air brakes on the asphalt truck gushed, the dump truck stopped. The rear wheels of the Suburban screamed and smoked, tearing in my direction again.

I ran for the Dodge and, with a hand on the bashed back end, scrambled onto the scrap of the roof that still protruded from the back of the dump truck. Steam poured over the front of the Suburban, obscuring the windshield. I took a double-tap on the spot where the cameraman and his shotgun should have been.

The Suburban veered to my right. I got one more shot into the windshield on the driver's side, a passing shot. The passenger window started down and the barrel of the shotgun came out. I popped two into the door as the truck passed.

My right foot felt an ice water jolt that turned scalding hot as asphalt oozed out the tailgate of the dump truck and engulfed my right deck shoe. I jumped to the ground—my shoe stayed—and peeled the sock off as a Grand Rapids Police car roared past in pursuit of the white Suburban.

I retched a mouthful of blood onto the street and stood studying the glob, with my hands on my knees, while I inventoried my teeth with my tongue and found the split in my upper lip.

The driver of the dump truck charged up to me trailing profanity. His overalls were orange, his face red and shaded by a grease-stained ball cap. He had the stub of a fat unlit cigar screwed into the side of his face. He said, "What the fuck is going on?"

I straightened up and looked at my blood smeared fingers. Moving my eyes from my fingers to the driver. All the f-words would have hurt too much, so I said, "Shit!"

The asphalt truck driver looked at my hand and then at my gun. He wheeled and showed me the soles of his work boots as he ran for the cab of his truck. Which was just as well—I couldn't get any air through my nose and my face felt inflated—I wasn't up to explaining much.

The diesel engine of the dump truck ejected two coal black jets of exhaust as the driver tried to pull off the Dodge. The trickle of asphalt gave way to an avalanche. The dump truck dragged the Dodge slowly down the street under a spreading, steaming black mass. No more red could be seen.

The gas tank on the Dodge let go. *Ca-rumph*. And I'm sitting again, in the middle of a hail of flaming asphalt pellets peppering the street. The Dodge came loose from the back of the truck. I buried my head in my arms but had to come out to bat hot particles off my arms and legs. My sweatshirt was on fire. I pulled it off. I could smell scorching hair. I slapped my head. Flames danced on what was left of the load of asphalt in the truck's rear dump-trailer.

The white Suburban blew the light at Pearl, spinning a minivan that had entered the intersection. At Monroe it turned left into the curb lane, on the oncoming side of the street, and threw out the anchor. I wondered if Deliveryman/Andy knew that he was right across the street from police headquarters.

As the police cruiser made the corner the Suburban sprang into reverse and T-boned it sideways into the middle of the intersection, then fled south down Monroe in the oncoming lane. Traffic peeled open like a banana.

The passenger door of the cruiser opened, and the officer cranked off two rounds from his shotgun before traffic closed back around the Suburban. Police officers flooded from the doors of the hall of justice—some in uniform, others not—with their weapons at the ready but could not fire because of the traffic.

The dump truck, engulfed in black smoke, stopped and the driver leapt from the cab with his cap crammed to his face. He pulled the pin on the flaming trailer and ran back to climb into the cab. He gunned the engine and pulled out, leaving the trailer to drop down on the dolly. The brake hoses stretched and snapped like rubber bands, and the flaming trailer started to creep, unguided, down the hill until the air had bled off and the brakes locked up.

"You only get six with that midget," said Fidel/Andy from behind me.

The voice sounded close. I took two quick steps forward before I turned. His shirt was sliced, exposing the metal plate in the front of a Kevlar vest and a long transverse gouge bisecting a powder burn. He lunged toward me with his arm swinging the knife in an arc at the level of my neck. I pumped my last round into the plate in his vest.

A witness on the street told the police that I shot him "casually." I don't know if that's true. I do admit to a certain amount of amusement with the *ka-tank* the 200-grain hollow-point made as it flattened itself into a nickel sized lump and delivered up three hundred-thirty foot-pounds of muzzle energy.

"Bad guess, asshole," I told him as he made a backward plunge to the street the way kids flop into a snow bank to make an angel. I noticed he had a serious road rash on his left arm and leg. "You're under arrest.

I asked, "Who do you work for?"

His lips moved, but he didn't make any sound. A good thing. In Michigan that kind of language in public can net you a tall fine or a short stay in the crowbar Hilton—not that it measured much against the fact that the local police had just penciled him and his crew onto their short list of things to do immediately.

He rolled up on his knees and struggled to his feet. "Now, he said, "You're *screwed!*" The "screwed" part came off a little breathless, but he had a joyous face.

I smiled too—at least I think I smiled, it hurt my face—and punched out the empty magazine. It clattered onto the street. The witness said that I grumbled something at Fidel—thank God he was sure about the "You're under arrest" part.

I took a spare magazine out of my pocket and shook it at Fidel/Andy. His face dialed up, "Oh-shit" and he started to turn back up the hill. I slammed the magazine into the pistol. By the time I thumbed the slide stop and the slide slammed into battery, he was making long strides up the hill toward the auto wash. I took a double-tap on his broad flat back. Vests generally don't have a plate in the back but the Kevlar strands will usually take the spin out of a hollow point and not allow it to penetrate. Fidel/Andy made a forward somersault onto his fanny.

I bent over and spit another glob of blood onto the street. My left shoulder hurt, my eyes were swelling shut, and the sole of my right foot was burning. Fidel/Andy struggled to his feet. I took a series of quick steps—the pavement was hot from the sun—and stopped, holding my right leg bent at the knee.

"Stop," I told him. "You're under arrest. If you take off again, I'll take your knees out." I wiped the sweat that stung my eyes—another mistake. My nose let go in a gush of blood. When I straightened up Andy had staggered farther up the hill.

A weaving walk was the best pursuit I could manage. Andy had gotten enough distance to make a tight shot undependable. He stopped and bent over, clutching his chest. A red burn had blossomed on his neck, probably from the seat belt. He retched some blood. It looked like a good idea, so I did it, too. When I raised my pistol, he was off again. I lurched after him. Something big and blue crashed me onto the street.

To my left I heard a big Chevy motor winding up, followed by a hell of a bang. A swarm of lead whooshed, passing above me. I turned my head to the left. I was on my back with something heavy on top of me.

The white Suburban careened past and up to the curb on the wrong side of the street. Fidel/Andy hobbled up to it and climbed in the back door on the driver's side.

An arm in a blue sleeve extended a fat nine past the front of my face. The air came alive with sirens. The fat nine barked to life. Up the hill tires screeched. Cars with sirens passed in a rush. The steady "tack-tack-tack" of an M60 machine gun opened up in short bursts—somebody was getting hosed by an expert gardener. A helicopter passed overhead. The noise faded over the hill.

I turned my face back up. My eyes had swelled down to slits. All I could make out was a bushy guardsman's moustache twitching around the words, "You're under arrest."

NEVER NEED YOUR NOSE SET. I don't want to talk about it. When we were finished they gave me a face-mask ice pack, handcuffed me to a gurney, and wheeled me into a cubicle of green curtains. Staff sadists stopped by one by one. Like Ebenezer Scrooge on Christmas Eve, I could not escape my visitors.

The first was the ghost of "sweet Jesus deliver me." He dressed my burned foot. As preparation he scrubbed it in a basin of hot soapy water with a good stiff brush—thanks a lot—and used a hoof pick to pry loose the big pieces.

Next came a demon with an angelic face—a wraith in white. She told me I had a stress fracture of the left clavicle and installed a kind of backwards brassier brace that kept me sitting straight, even though I was lying down.

Tiny Tim showed up clad in green scrubs and leaning on a noisy cart instead of a crutch. Wearing latex gloves and a surgical mask he "just popped" a couple of stitches in my lip. "No need for additional anaesthetic." God bless us, every one—no goose for him.

After a few moments of peace I heard someone stroll into the cubicle and stand around making groaning noises. I retaliated with rude silence. They pulled up a chair. I lifted the mask to see who it was. Jacob Marley, done up as Detective Bart Shephart, wearing yesterday's shave and a battered coat over a knit shirt with a raveled collar. By way of a sympathetic greeting he said, "Hardin, you look like shit."

I eased the ice pack down on my face. "That's not a point I'm qualified to argue with you, Shep," I said.

"They have to shave off your moustache to sew up your lip?"

Anyone else, I would have said, "Sure," and let it go at that. But Shephart's a detective and should have noticed.

"I shaved it off before I talked to you at my office."

"Didn't notice," he said, deadpan.

I said, "There's a lot of that going around." It's hard to be catty with an idiot.

"So you think I'm an idiot?"

Mind readers are worse than idiots. They catch you lying.   "I don't think you're an idiot," I told him. "I think you drink too much."

"I never drink on the job."

"Yes, you do."

"A beer with lunch doesn't count."

My guess is that Detective Shephart needed a slug of gin to slow his hands to the point that he could light that first cigarette while he sat on the edge of his bed. "A beer for lunch is drinking on the job," I said.

"I can handle it."

"You're an alcoholic."

"I can quit any time I want."

"Drinking causes problems in your personal and professional life."

"Maybe," he said.

"Maybe you're a problem drinker. Quit."

"I didn't come here for a lecture," he said.

"Too bad. The novocain's wearing off. Lecturing helps me share the pain."

"Your pal, Scott Lambert?" said Shephart. "He's the doer. He's in custody, and he's taking you with him."

"Lambert was a client. Maybe he did it. I didn't help him."

"Hank Dunphy? You know who he is?"

"Works for Scott Lambert," I said.

"Says you set up the meet between Lambert and Anne Frampton."

"He's lying," I said. I didn't look up, but I heard Shephart moving in his chair. "If you're going to arrest me, read me my rights."

"You're already in custody."

"Discharging a firearm in the city limits."

"Prosecutor is talking conspiracy to commit murder."

"Prosecutor has his dick in his hand," I said.

"Prosecutor has Lambert by the ass," said Shephart. "The soda can in your office had Lambert's prints on it. And he's a secretor, the cigar butt in the can was his. Anne Frampton had some of his hair in her hand."

"He broke into my office to steal the report? That makes us conspirators?"

"Maybe you did it yourself to cover your tracks."

"Right. Then I spread around a load of kiddie porn to throw you off the scent."

More foot shuffling and silence. After a moment Shephart said, "Prosecutor wants you off the street. He'll run it up the pole to see if the jury salutes."

"He'll get egg on his face."

"You think he cares?"

"I think he likes a good box score." I said. "Why complicate a canned shoot on Lambert?"

"Exactly," said Shephart. "You can be a witness. You gotta get on board before the train pulls out."

"He knows how to write a subpoena. I already told you everything I know."

"He's had you on the stand before. You play to the jury. They like you. Or maybe you take the fifth."

I pushed up on one elbow—big mistake, hurt like hell—took the ice pack off my face and said, "So he sends you to snake in here like a pal and threaten me."

Shephart looked down at his scuffed brown wing tips. "More like a Rabbi," he said. "I'm the only one you'll talk to."

"I wish I hadn't," I said. My eyes throbbed. I lay back down and eased the ice pack back on my face. "Doesn't this seem a little easy? Lambert isn't stupid. He's a scientist. Maybe he leaves a clue, but a neon sign? Christ's sake, come on."

"The jailhouse is full of geniuses."

"What about the guys I shot it out with on Michigan Avenue?"

"Covering his trail," said Shephart. "You got no reason to protect him now."

"Pete Finney," I said. "You got any more questions, he's my attorney."

Shephart stood up. I heard the chair slide.

"Tell 'em I need something for pain," I said.

"You need a guard on this door," he said. "I'll see what I can do." Shephart made it sound like an apology.

"Shep, I can't even sit up. I sure as hell am not going to stage the great escape."

"Not to keep you in," he said. "To keep them out. We found the Suburban at the bottom of the gravel pit up on Plainfield and the Beltline. Found a guy in it. Blue coveralls, not the guy with the beard."

"Frank," I said. "He drown deep-sixing the truck?"

"Shot twice," said Shephart, his voice grim. "You know this guy?" I heard his pen click.

"Don't know him. The driver of the Suburban yelled his name. Maybe one of your guys got him."

"Our guys don't shoot .45 hollow points."

"I'm sure the prosecutor is thrilled."

"Two of ours got hurt. The prosecutor has reports from three different officers who say you were defending yourself."

"So that's three cops he don't call to the stand."

"Look, even the guys that don't like you respect what you did."

"Yeah, if I'd done it right nobody would have got hurt."

"See, that's the thing, Art. You think you're Jesus Christ, and everybody else is stupid. And you're a hot dog. That's why the guys don't like you."

"I thought it was because I was private heat."

He laughed. "Course not! Anyway, you did call us first. You tried to arrest them. You stood and fired against the draw, even after you were banged up."

He told me the rest—about spinning like a top and about the witnesses on the street. And how Fidel/Andy and his pals hosed the news helicopter to make their escape. It was all on the news. The prosecutor's office was withholding comment pending the investigation.

"We don't get the news here," I said.

"Yeah."

"More than you should have told me."

"Yeah," said Shephart. He left.

A nurse came in and gave me a shot. I never felt the needle come out.

. . .

I recognized the voice of Matty Svenson, Special Agent, FBI, but not much else when I opened my eyes. I was in a bed—handcuffed to the rail—and in a private room. An IV dripped into my left arm. The band-aid in the crook of my right arm testified to a blood draw—I'd missed that as well. The ice pack was gone. I had a metal strap pasted over the bridge of my nose. Matty said I looked like shit. I guess some things had not changed.

Matty smelled better then Shep—Gardenia, I think.

I blinked to get her in focus. She had hair down to her collar with a little flip and dressed like a lawyer—navy business suit with a white knit shell and an a-line skirt.

"That's what Bart Shephart said this morning."

"Yesterday," she said.

"What a difference a day makes. I'm working my way up the ladder. Tomorrow I get the CIA?"

Matty made a face. "You awake?" she said. "I need you to be awake."

"Gimme a minute."

"You want coffee?"

"I want the puddle pan."

"I'll get the coffee," she said. She rattled her knuckles on the door and it opened as if it were spring loaded.

In less than thirty seconds a Valkyrie in white rode in, a brown plastic carafe in her hand. She wore her light brown hair braided and coiled on the back of her head like a yarmulke, held in place with a yellow wire butterfly perched on a hairpin. A yellow ribbon had been stationed on her lapel. She measured my work in a beaker and poured it into the toilet.

"You're lucky," she said. "I'll be back."

I didn't like the look in her eye and it's hard to figure "lucky" against being handcuffed to a hospital bed.

Mattyy traded places with her and brought a large 7-11 coffee with her. No bag. I looked from the coffee cup to her face.

"What?" she said. "You want a latté from Starbucks?"

"Too fast," I said. "How many guys you got outside that door?"

"Enough." She handed me the cup. "Drink your coffee."

"Too hot. I'm awake. What's up?"

She picked up a portfolio from the chair beside the bed and unclipped a photo from a stack of papers. "This the man you saw in Brandonport?"

Fidel/Andy.

"I took the picture," I said. "Did you get a good print off the camera?"

"This the man you shot at on Michigan Avenue?"

I counted on my fingers. "Four times. I didn't miss. He was wearing a vest."

"El Guitmo," she said. "A terrorist."

"Speaks English like you and me," I said.

"Really," she said, deadpan.

"And?"

"And, Uncle Sam needs your service, Colonel."

"Sorry, I'm retired and I have another rather pressing engagement just now."

"Maybe this is more important," she said. "I have to talk to my boss, and he has to talk to his."

"I'm lying in a hospital bed."

"Perfect, if you want the job."

"Sure," I said. "What's the job?"

"Bait," she said.

. . .

Gretta—good name for a Valkyrie—turned out to be a sweet soul. She took the dressing off my foot while she explained that the doctor had decided to let the burn air out.

I told her that I hadn't heard from my wife. She said that she couldn't carry messages for prisoners, but that my attorney was in the hall. Maybe he could help.

She left and Carl Norton walked in. I called him Pete, but I was studying my foot—beet red with a blister just under the knot of my ankle.

"Beastly sorry," he said, feigning Pete's British accent, "but Squire Finney has been summoned to other matters."

Squire Norton was black and a picture of sartorial splendor, his suit Italian, his shirt linen—a dandy down to his waistcoat, french cuffs, and the diamond stickpin in his tie. He'd shaved a full head of hair in favor of a fashionably shiny pate. Bespectacled in gold self-dimming aviator glasses, he had affected a goatee trimmed too short to pinch but waxed into immobility.

"Private practice suits you," I said. "The last time we met it was polyester and permanent press."

He said, "Crime pays, very well, every day, and usually in cash."

"Can I afford you?"

"I doubt it. I don't think you're a criminal. Pete asked me to call because he has taken the Lambert case. The prosecutor is offering a deal—he wants you as a witness for the prosecution."

Carl Norton had run for County Prosecutor while working as an assistant prosecutor. Things had been amiable in the press, but Carl lost the election and found himself relegated to shoplifting and drunk-driving cases. He quit and went into the criminal defense business.

"Do tell," I said.

"You plead guilty to attempted possession of child pornography and he scores you a walk on the Lambert case."

"He wants his cake and thinks he can eat it too."

"He's an optimist," said Norton. "He knows you don't get what you don't ask for."

I held out the plastic thunder jug. "Tell him to rub this and see if a genie pops out."

Carl smiled and looked away. I planted the jug back on the tray table.

"Supposed to be a lamp," he said, and turned back. "And every time he rubs your lamp the damnedest genies pop out—civil rights lawyers, old meat-eating dinosaurs from the Justice Department, and armed goons from federal agencies nobody has heard of show up dressed like undertakers. He wants to use the kiddie porn charge like a crucifix to fend off the creatures of the night."

"The guys I shot it out with broke into my office and planted that crap, and probably the evidence against Lambert."

"Much too big a bite for a jury," said Carl. He folded his hands in his lap. "Better to let it all come down to possession."

"They found it in my office."

"Just so," he said. "To be in possession of anything, you have to be able to exercise control of the disposition of the objects or property. Pete tells me you can prove that you were out of town until the morning the break-in was reported."

"People get busted all the time for pot and paraphernalia other people left in their cars," I said.

"They didn't leave it in an automobile that you were apprehended driving."

"Thin," I said.

"But substantial," he said. "In this case I viewed the contraband. Two hundred and eighty-seven copies of the same magazine—all but seven of which remain in shrink-wrap packages—hardly seems like a personal reading collection. Especially since every one of them belongs to the post office."

"You're putting me on?"

"If you like, but in this joke the post office keeps a certified inventory. The inventory indicates that the items found in your office were on hand at the close of business Saturday, two days before they were recovered from your office and while you were out of town."

"How did someone get evidence out of a federal facility?"

"Not our problem. The contraband wasn't being held as evidence, anyway. It's used in postal sting operations."

"The Post Office? I don't believe it."

"Doesn't matter. What matters is that I know and I can prove it. If the prosecutor knew he would have to tell me. I don't have to tell him." Squire Norton showed me a full arcade of baking soda fresh teeth. "I owe him one."

"Come on," I said. "You know. He has to know."

Carl made a round mouth and arches of his eyebrows, "Oh," he said, "that would be bad . . . wouldn't it?"

"I don't think his dislike for me would override his caution or his respect for the law."

Norton had "not if he thought he was going to get caught" written on his face. But instead he said, "You're probably right, so you should be thinking of your defense in the death of the Frampton woman. He'll take Lambert first and then come after you. Separate trials."

"Expensive."

"For you," said Norton. "I need a ten-thousand dollar retainer. That doesn't make your bail, and it doesn't last past your arraignment. I'll need a complete statement of your net worth."

"What kind of fish do you think I am?"

"For this you'd better be a tuna," Carl said, with a Cheshire smile. "A fish with a lot of meat."

"So, basically my choices are a) give all my money to the state, in fines and restitution—and go to jail, or b) give you all my money and don't go to jail."

"You could still go to jail," he said, nonchalant, like a cruise on the SS Jailhouse was a fringe benefit. He studied my face dimly, brows knitted behind the wire rims of his photo-gray glasses, and shrugged. "Maybe not as long."

"I thought I was being held on discharging a firearm."

"Just so. But if we get you arraigned on that charge and make bail, we'll just force the prosecutor into action on the other charges. As long as you're already in custody, he has other *fish* to fry. Right now, all he wants is to hear the results of our meeting."

"Tell him I declined your services," I said.

Carl twisted his head and leaned back.

"For now," I said and tried to mimic Carl's cat face.

Norton laughed. He shook a finger. "I always hated it when your name appeared as the defense investigator."

"I need to think about it," I said, trying for the sound of sweet innocence. I showed him my open palms. "They keep me shot full of pain killers. I need to let my head clear."

Carl Norton stood up, peeled a business card out of his pocket secretary, and handed it to me. It was the cheesy one. The card with no gold leaf, the kiss-off card that lawyers give to people they don't want—or don't expect—to call back. He walked out and I could hear him laughing in the hallway.

I DREAMED OF A GOAT-FACED MAN wearing a striped top hat. He gave me the finger—the index finger. He said, "Uncle Sam wants you." I woke up still handcuffed to the bed frame.

Two guards had been posted outside the door. They never looked in. I could have been hanging from the light fixture. They wouldn't have known. They passed their time with gossip until I went to sleep.

As often as I adjusted my position, the handcuffs woke me. I learned that, "So and so was a screw-up." And later, "Somebody else got promoted on their face when they should have been out on their ass." Now the voices in the hall were gone.

Someone wearing heavy shoes with cleats on the heels clanked up the hallway toward my door. The room was dim with that oblique morning light. Nautical twilight. The time when things happened before Uncle Sam discarded me, before his armed minions became creatures of the night.

Nurses wore crepe soles that squished and squeaked on the buffed tile floors. In any case, it was not yet time for soupy oatmeal and burnt toast.

The door handle cranked hard and noisily. I raised my right arm and let it lay across the pillow—pulling on the head rail to preload my right hand—and watched through one eye, open a slit.

She was six feet tall, had severely short hair, and wore a jail guard's uniform. She flopped a large brown envelope—felt like a boat anchor—on my chest and loomed over me, taking the handcuff off my left wrist.

"You're out of here," she said, and disconnected the cuffs from the bed rail. She hammered her heels out of the room, her trousers straining to contain a wide backside, and took the handcuffs with her.

I found my property in the envelope—wallet, car keys, and pistol, with the spare magazines, including the one I dumped on the street. A check for eighty-two dollars and fourteen cents drawn on Kent County covered the cash I'd had on my person when they wheeled me into the emergency room.

I was still holding the envelope, staring amazed at the pistol, when Gretta breezed in the door carrying a paper bag and turned on the lights. She wore a lime green pants-suit uniform, a white ribbon affixed to the lapel, and her hair done up in a tight bun with a white dove soaring at the end of her hair pin. Gretta dropped the bag onto the bed tray and bent over to examine the IV needle in my arm.

"I'm not in the jail wing," I said.

"Haven't been since you got the shot of Demerol and took the long nap," she said, her dour face focused on her work. She zipped the tape off my arm. "Sheriff wouldn't allow the off-duty city policemen to guard the door in the jail ward." She pressed a wad of cotton in place with her thumb. "Guards filed a grievance with their union—said the city cops took their overtime. Sheriff said you didn't warrant a guard." She removed the needle. "Somebody from the city patrolmen's association mentioned off-duty county shields not getting any deference in the city, and here you are. How many private rooms do you think they have in the jail ward? Hold that," she said.

I pressed the cotton in place with my fingers. "Hadn't thought about it. I hope I don't have to argue with my insurance company over the room."

"Somebody decided to pay, or you wouldn't be here," she said. She cut off a piece of tape and strapped the cotton ball to my arm.

Gretta stashed the tape and scissors in the pocket of her uniform and picked the chart from the end of my bed. She made some entries and scowled. "You haven't had a bowel movement."

"I was just leaving."

"Still," she said, her face serious.

"Give me your number, you'll be the first to know."

Gretta corralled her smile down to tight lips and a tilt of her head. "I have to take the chart to the desk. I'll be back. You should get dressed."

My clothes were in the paper bag Gretta left on the bed tray. They'd been washed and folded. Holes burned in the shirt matched the red sores on my chest and stomach. Only one shoe and one sock. Just as well. My right foot was still airing out, the drained blister having left a flap of loose white skin.

I limped into the bathroom and found a monster lurking in the mirror. A shiny metal brace pasted to his face underlined eyes camouflaged in shades of brown, blue, and green. Two black stitches zipped his lip together. His cheeks were a bramble of grizzled stubble.

On the sink I found a toothbrush and tiny tube of toothpaste in a clear plastic wrapper. I brushed the monster's teeth. It made him happy, but he still looked like shit.

"You shouldn't be walking on that foot without a bandage," said Gretta as she came back in the room. She had me sit on the bed while she applied a gauze bandage with a hard sole like a shoe—to my right foot.

"Take these with you," she said, and dropped a wad of the gauze shoes in the sack she'd used to bring my clothes. "Don't be walking around until that burn heals." She showed me a wad of gauze gloves. "Use these to change the dressing. Use them once and throw them away. If the dressing is dirty, change it. If it's wet, change it. If you're bored, change it. Until you see your doctor, keep that foot clean and dry, and don't be picking at it, hear?"

"Yes, ma'am."

"I'll help you put that brace back on."

"My shoulder's bruised," I told her. "The brace hurts."

"You shouldn't be leaving the hospital," she said. She helped me shrug into the brace like she hadn't heard my complaint. "You have to stop at the nurses' station to sign a release. I suppose it's for the best. The guards left this morning."

Gretta walked to the door and pulled in a wheelchair. A fat, battered, brown wooden cane hung from the back rest. "The morning paper said you killed that man they found in the gravel pit," she said, and pushed the chair up to the bed. "How do you live with that, Mr. Hardin?"

"Gretta, I thank God for every sweet breath I draw."

"I'll never understand men like you," she said. "How can you talk about God?"

"Are you a religious woman, Gretta?"

"Yes," she said, "and I try to serve God in his mercy."

"And you have been sweet and gentle with me," I said. "And I thank you for that." I rolled my eyes up to her face without raising my head, and waited for her to meet my gaze. "The man died the way he lived," I told her. "He and his friends did their level best to kill me. But I'm not the man who lost a friend and left him to rot in a gravel pit."

"The cane was donated by the hospital volunteers," she said. "Bring it back when you're steady on your feet."

• • •

My son, Ben, met me at the door as Gretta wheeled me out. He had his hair under a ball cap and stood with his arms folded over a black T-shirt emblazoned with a red "Nine Inch Nails." Wendy's old Cadillac sat parked in the drive with the passenger door standing open.

"You look terrible," he said.

"That's an improvement," I said. "Yesterday, I looked like shit." The sun warmed my face. The air, free of the antiseptic smell of the hospital, made my lungs feel light.

Shoot-from-the-lip Ben, ever fast with a quip, said, "You don't look good, Dad." He pushed the chair up to the door of the Caddy. A tan envelope lay on the passenger seat. I put the cane on the floor of the back seat.

"What's that?"

"Lady came by and left that while I was waiting for you to come down. Said her name was Matty. Said you'd know her."

A white label on the front had been addressed to a "Col. A. Hardin," with my service number. I threw it on the dash, got out of the chair, and climbed into the car—Ben not quite sure if or how he should help.

"It's all right, son," I told him. "All the parts work. I'm just a little banged up."

Ben pushed the door shut, walked around, and climbed into the driver's seat. "So who was the blond lady?" He started the engine.

"Matty Svenson from the FBI," I said. "I was hoping for another exciting ride in the Camero."

"Danny had to take Mom down to Lansing today. Ma said it would be easier for you to get in and out of this one. Why's an FBI lady giving you military orders?"

I opened the envelope. It contained two sets of orders, one ordering me from the Retired Reserve to the Individual Ready Reserve, the second assigning me to Annual Active Duty Training as a Liaison Officer with "Law Enforcement Agencies." The third item, a white card: DA Form 2818, a concealed weapons permit—listed a civilian weapon, mine. The signatures were grand, in black ink, and illegible. I had the distinct impression that if I blew on this stuff twice, the envelope and its contents would burst into flame.

"I'm going to do some military liaison work with the civil authorities while I'm off my feed," I said. "What's the grand attraction in Lansing?"

"The State Police want to revoke Mom's detective license. You know, because of the stuff they found in your office. They came out and searched the house. Ma is hot. She's meeting Pete Finney in Lansing."

"Jesus Christ!" I said, and smacked my hand on the dash. It hurt my shoulder. "What did they take out of the house?"

Devilment washed over Ben's face. "Just Danny's *Playboy* magazines, but they brought them back. Ma threw them out." Serious again, he said, "They wanted to take the guns but Pete was there with some kind of writ so they couldn't, and he didn't let them go through Mom's files, either. Cops had a big shit fit. They put some stick-on seals on the gun safe and Mom's filing cabinet. Pete says they have to 'show cause' or something like that, down at the courthouse."

Ben pulled out on the street. I flipped down the visor, made like I was checking my face in the vanity mirror, and watched the street through the rear window. A black Chevrolet Blazer pulled out after us.

"You guys are missing school," I said. I flipped the sun visor up.

"Danny's on a three-day suspension. I'm going in after I drop you at the office."

"What the hell happened?"

"Some guys after school said dumb stuff," said Ben.

"They said something so he got in a fight?"

"Weren't no fight, Dad. He just thumped 'em."

"Doesn't sound like Daniel."

"They started pulling on his pants—said to show 'em how he posed for pictures."

"Good God." I shook my head and it hurt my nose. "Daniel all right?"

"Cut his knuckle on a guy's braces. He had to get a stitch. The other guys—he just shined his shoes on their backsides."

"So how come Daniel's suspended?"

"'Zero Tolerance,' Dad. If you get in a fight you get suspended." Ben turned left onto Michigan Avenue.

"That's a crock. I'll discuss it with the principal."

"Ma already chewed him out. You could hear it down the hall."

"At least you didn't get in trouble."

"No," said Ben. "I hit the social worker, but that was at the sheriff's office. I guess they got more tolerance."

"What?"

"After they searched the house we had to go down to the sheriff's office. Some twinky social worker kept asking sick questions. He kept getting behind me, rubbing my shoulders and saying it was okay to tell him this sick stuff he kept making up."

"You should have just walked out—told the deputies the guy was touching you."

"I did," said Ben. "They said I had to talk to him. Ma went in and told him to keep his hands to himself."

"And?"

"He was all innocent. I told him not to touch me. So the next thing, he's behind me saying sick stuff, and playing with my hair. That's when I elbowed him."

"What happened?"

"Deputies came in and picked him up. They said we could go home. Ma went to the desk and filed a complaint."

I closed my eyes but changed my mind about rubbing my forehead. I flipped down the visor.

"Black Blazer went straight at the light," said Ben.

"Just take me to the house," I said.

"Ma said I had to take you to the office," Ben said. "She sent a bag of clothes. It's in the trunk. She said she'd call when she got back from Lansing."

I flipped up the visor.

• • •

At the office, I took the steps two at a time—the bag in one hand and the cane in the other—and stopped halfway up to wave at Ben. He wasn't having any. I had to jog up the rest of the steps before he'd leave.

160

In my absence someone had elongated the stairway down to the first floor. I took the stairs one at time leaning on the rail. At the bottom of the steps I leaned on the cane to get over to the office door.

Marg sat at her desk, her hands folded on a clean desktop. She'd had her hair cut into a shag with bangs and wore a lilac blouse with a Russian collar over a blue pleated skirt. When she saw me, she closed her eyes.

I flopped on the sofa across from her desk. "Hair's nice," I said. "Didn't know you had ears."

She shifted her eyes to look at me without turning her head. "I didn't expect you in."

"Things kind of slow?"

"I'm waiting for a client to pick up his books."

"Plans?"

"I'm working on my resume," she said.

"You still have one client," I said. "One that appreciates your loyalty and thinks you do a damn fine job."

"State police were here this morning," she said. "They took the license off the wall and left an envelope on your desk for for your pocket I.D."

"I'll call Pete Finney," I said.

"Finney called to say he couldn't represent you because he took the Lambert case."

"I'm not charged with anything. They gave me back my sidearm and threw me out of the hospital this morning."

"I wish Pete was here," she said. Marg stared at the Ladin Associates sign painted on the window with a wistful face. Misty eyed, she said, "Pete, my husband."

"I knew who you meant," I said. I gave her the envelope Matty had left me.

Marg looked at the label and then at me. She pulled the orders out. "I never thought I'd be glad to see things like these again. They always meant we had to move and start over, with strangers in a new place."

"This time they mean we're going to get to the bottom of this. And the smug bastard that took our license down is coming back to put it where he found it."

"Actually, he was pretty decent about it," said Marg.

"Too bad," I said. I winked—it hurt. "That's going to take all the fun out of it."

Marg smiled and shook her head. She put the orders back in the envelope. "Botch the job and they'll claim they never heard of us."

"Comforting that some things don't change," I said.

"Pete would make them put it in the frame and hang it up," she said.

I wrestled myself off the sofa and patted Marg's desktop as I limped past on my way to my office. I'd be glad just to get the license back. Peter A. Ladin definitely would not have let them off that easy.

I found my desk blotter pushed aside to reveal the graffiti carved in my desktop. The frame, the nail, and the wall hanger lay neatly lined up below the inscription. A business card paper-clipped to the envelope for my pocket ID read—Archer A. Flynt, Office of the State Attorney General. Maybe this was going to be more fun than I thought.

The telephone had been rescued from the trash and placed back on my desk, not much worse for the wear. I pulled on the wall cord. It was stuck. I leaned over to look. A new wall plate had been installed and the cord connected. I picked up the handset and got a dial tone.

"Marg? You had the telephone repaired?"

"Was it broken?"

"Really," I said.

"I didn't expect you to be in," she said.

I sat, thinking about it, and decided that there was nothing to do but take it for a test run.

Pete Finney was out or had told his secretary not to forward my telephone calls. She wouldn't transfer me to his voice mail. Finally, she agreed to take a note—"Pete, I have been released without charges, A. Hardin." She said, "Mr. Finney doesn't always pick up his messages."

"You just put them in the trash?"

"If he doesn't pick them up."

"This concerns the Lambert case," I said. "Pete would think this was important information—if he knew. But, of course he won't. If you follow me? I have no real expectation that Peter Finney, Esquire, will ever be apprized of this note or its contents."

"What did you say your name was?"

I gave her the message again, and made a mental note never to pay Pete's tab late.

Lorna Kemp breezed in wearing yellow shorts, a white shell, and a French braid in her blond hair. From my office door she stared at me, her mouth momentarily open before she said, "Oh, my God."

"Only hurts when I laugh."

"You shaved off your moustache," she said.

"Damn fine investigator," I said. "Notice anything else?"

She tilted her head to one side and then the other. "Nope."

"I've been getting some complaints lately."

"I think those sweats have had it," said Lorna. "Maybe some cheap sunglasses—the wraparound kind, and a shave. What do you think?"

"How about you give me the bag from the sofa, and about ten minutes. We need to have a powwow."

"Matty Svenson called me at my flat," said Lorna. "She wouldn't talk to me on the telephone. I had to meet her at a bench in Calder Plaza. I brought my stuff." She turned to retrieve the bag from the sofa. In the front office I heard her say, "Sure, I'll tell him."

I heard the front door fall shut, but not in time to look up into the monitor to see who it was. Lorna stepped in and dropped my paper bag on the wing-back chair. She thumbed over her shoulder and said, "Detective Shephart said for you to wait for him. He went down the hall." She left and pulled the door shut behind her.

My spare glasses were on top of the pile in the bag. I put them on. Pain. I pulled off my sweats and dropped them in the waste can along with the back brace. Wendy had sent jeans, a belt, and a knit shirt with a collar, but no socks. I guess she was in a hurry.

I dropped the bag on the floor and sat on the wingback chair to navigate my burned foot into the jeans. Marg told someone they would have to wait a moment.

The door exploded open and bounced off the wall. Leonard Jones, casual in a blue blazer and gray slacks, stormed in with a K-bar knife in his hand and cold certainty on his face.

He said, "Tell me one reason why I shouldn't kill you right now."

"BECAUSE I DIDN'T KILL YOUR SISTER," I said. "And because you're an operator. You don't do things out of personal malice. And you don't do things without adequate planning."

I bent down to pull up my trousers. Leonard stepped up and held the tip of the k-bar knife in the divot behind my jaw, under my ear.

"What makes you think I haven't planned this out?"

"If you had, I'd already be dead," I said. "You wouldn't have a Walther pointed at the back of your head. And you'd know that a police detective was about to walk in the front door."

"Tell me who killed Annie," he said. He didn't look back.

Lorna racked the hammer on the Walther. "Wasn't Art," she said.

Leonard didn't react, if you count not cutting my throat while I pulled up my trousers.

"Right now the case against Scott Lambert looks pretty good," I said.

"Little anchors?" said Lorna.

"Smiley faces are in the wash."

The front door swept open.

"Detective Shephart!" Marg said, like he was deaf. "Art has a visitor."

I picked up my trash can and held it out to Leonard. "Hi Shep," I said, and locked eyes with Leonard. "Leonard Jones, Anne Frampton's brother, stopped by."

Leonard dropped the knife in the can and I arranged the trash to cover it. Lorna turned, concealing the Walther, and walked to the investigators' room.

Shephart walked in cinching up his tie under a day-old five o'clock shadow. "You still look like shit," he said.

"Leonard, this is Detective Shephart," I said.

"We talked on the telephone," said Shephart. Shephart offered his hand and Leonard took it.

"Pleasure to meet you," said Leonard. He took his hand back.

I took the paper bag off the chair, limped back to my side of the desk, and started my belt through the loops of my trousers.

"What brings you to town?" said Shephart.

Leonard deflated into the wingback chair, his shoulders round and his face distraught. "Annie was released. The Frampton woman refused to take custody or make any arrangements. I have been seeing to things. Mom won't . . ."

Shephart took the chair across the desk from me, blinked, and took a long breath.

"There doesn't appear to be a will or any insurance," said Leonard. "The Frampton woman doesn't return my calls. I had to hire an attorney." Leonard's chin sunk to his chest and his hand went to his eyes.

"Can we get some coffee in here," I yelled, and threaded my holster onto my belt.

"I've got a client," said Marg.

"I got it," Lorna announced from the investigators' room.

"My mother. . ." said Leonard. He paused, squared his shoulders, and sat at attention—both spit-shined black loafers flat on the floor. He rubbed his hands together. "My mother won't allow Annie to be buried next to Dad. The couple that owns the plot next to ours lives here, in Kentwood. I've been talking to them."

Lorna stepped into the office with a cup of coffee in each hand. She parked them, one apiece, in front of Leonard and Shephart. "Drink it black, right?" she said.

"Just right," I said.

She looked at me and said, "Brewing another pot."

"Black's fine," said Leonard. He palmed the cup to feel the heat and sat back on the chair, leaving the cup on the desk.

"Certainly Anne left enough of her work to cover her expenses," said Lorna.

Leonard shook his head. "Frampton woman is holding a public art auction and estate sale Saturday. She says that Anne owed her a lot of money. My attorney says we'll have to sue."

Shephart sipped his coffee gingerly and set it down. "You were discussing the case when I walked in."

"Seems like the case against Scott Lambert is pretty solid," I said.

"I need to remind you both—Mr. Lambert may have been charged, but he has *not* been tried. The man is out on bail and presumed to be innocent."

"Except you thought he was guilty enough to arrest and charge," said Lorna.

Shephart wagged his head, took a pack of cigarettes from his pocket, and shook out a smoke, unfiltered. He tamped it on the desk and I pushed the ash tray over to him.

"Mr. Jones, may I call you Leonard?" said Shephart.

"Sure." Leonard folded his hands and stared at Shephart.

Shephart let the cigarette dangle from his lips while he searched his pockets. I showed him my lighter. He nodded his head. I smiled and beckoned with my fingers. He made a snort and slid the pack across the table to me.

"Three days," I said, and lit up.

"Good time to quit," said Shephart. "You could be a problem smoker."

I put the lighter on the pack and slid it back to him.

Shephart picked up the lighter but took the cigarette out of his mouth. "Leonard," he said, "I'm sorry for your loss. Your sister was a respected artist. She was a great loss to the community."

I looked at Lorna. She made an astonished face back at me. Three complete sentences bereft of any allusion to carnal gymnastics—a whole new facet to a very rough jewel, this Detective Shephart.

"It would be a terrible disappointment to her memory," said Shephart, "if you made a terrible mistake—did something to put yourself in the courthouse instead of the man charged with this terrible crime." He lit his cigarette.

Leonard stood. "Detective, when we spoke on the telephone, you promised to keep me informed." He offered his hand.

Shephart dropped his cigarette in the ashtray, stood, and took Leonard's hand. "Absolutely, I have your number."

"Good," said Leonard, "I have my sister's estate to see to, but when I'm done, I trust you will save me making my own inquiries." He gave Shephart's hand a last pump and let it go.

Shephart smiled, "Yes sir, I have your number."

When he got his hand back he plumbed a business card out of his wallet and gave it to Leonard. "If you have any questions, call any time. If I'm not in, I'll get the message."

Leonard saluted him with the card and walked out. Shephart sat and took a long pull on his cigarette.

"Shep—"

Shephart showed me an index finger and turned his head to listen for the front door to close. The door opened and fell shut. Shephart leaned back in his chair to look around the corner of the door and then turned back. "Bastard's strong as an ox. What is it with you old military types?"

"Has to do with knowing what your job is, and risking your life to do it for people who give you no respect and basically haven't got a clue."

Shephart shrugged, nodded, and took a drag on his cigarette. The telephone rang. In a stream of smoke Shephart exhaled, "For you I got a clue."

"Pete Finney on line one," Marg announced from her desk.

I picked up the phone. "Pete, I thought I was persona non grata." I stubbed the cigarette out and straightened the burned end—still had half a smoke left.

"You were, until this morning," said Pete. "I got a revised witness list. You're not on it. They're calling Detective Van Huis to introduce the physical evidence."

"Play hell laying the ground work," I said and snagged the cup of coffee that Leonard Jones had left untouched. Lorna gave me a wave and headed back to the investigator's room.

"They'll use Detective Shephart," Finney said.

"Sitting right here. Want to talk to him?" I took a gulp of coffee and swallowed.

"Not on your life. What I want is for you to take the case as the defense investigator."

"Can't," I said.

"Client insists."

"Some state dick from the Attorney General's office"—I opened my top desk drawer and took the card out—"Archer Flynt, came in here this morning and took my license off the wall."

"Not from the licensing agency?"

"Nope, that's why I called," I said

"I'll look into it," said Pete. "And along that line, Wendy and I were in Lansing today for a hearing on her license."

"My son told me."

"We have a 'show cause' hearing on the search warrant for her files in two weeks. The licensing bureau agreed to postpone their hearing until then, but you need to talk to Wendy."

"Talked to Carl Norton," I said.

"Well. Arthur. You understand?"

"Damn good man," I said. "Has some insights concerning the merits of the search warrant you mentioned."

"Not that you can mention, just now?"

"Absolutely."

"I want to talk to you before I telephone him," said Pete.

Shephart started to rise, a question on his face. I shrugged and shook my head. He settled back into his chair and worked on his coffee and cigarette.

"Carl says the prosecutor will charge me after the Lambert trial."

"Only if Lambert is found guilty," Pete said. "In any case, that wouldn't be for some time. I do think that I would be able to represent you by then—barring something unforeseeable."

"Yeah," I said, "Carl mentioned mortgaging my soul and selling my children into slavery."

"All the more reason to work on a win in the Lambert case."

"Not much I can do without a license. And I'd have to overcome my lack of faith in Lambert's innocence."

"I have to assume that was for the detective's consumption."

"You could always hire me as your in-house investigator."

"I don't think my partners would go along," said Finney. He laughed. "They see you as a dependable source of income."

"That leaves Archer Flynt and the Attorney General's office," I said and swirled my half cup of coffee into a maelstrom.

"I'll look into it," said Finney. "And do telephone on the other matter. The sooner the better." He hung up.

I set the telephone back in the cradle. "I'm impressed. You were particularly decent to Mr. Jones." I took a slug of Leonard's coffee.

"I don't want you winding him up," said Shephart, leaning toward me. "Anything happens to Scott Lambert and I'm back on the missing persons desk until our local nutcase takes another victim."

"You don't think Scott Lambert is killing hookers?"

"I think his mother still cuts up his meat."

"You don't think he killed Anne Frampton?"

"Oh, he's good for that one," Shephart said. He leaned back in his chair, his hands in his lap. "He's taking the fall. I couldn't stop it if I stood under him with a net."

"Case is that solid?"

"The DNA in the cigar butt and from the hair follicles found in the Frampton woman's hand match Scott Lambert. He's lucky there's no death penalty in this state. The day he keels over dead, I'm declared a hero, the prosecutor a genius, and the guys doing the hookers can walk."

"Guys?" I picked up my half-a-cigarette and pulled it straight between my fingers.

"Guys!" Shephart picked up my lighter.

"There must be some other DNA samples," I said.

"Plenty. They're hookers." He clicked the lighter twice and a flame danced up. "Semen in every orifice—from multiple donors. Except the Frampton woman. Nothing." He slipped his thumb off the pedal, and the flame went out. "I like a local pimp for a couple of the women. Then there's the nutcase. And maybe a copy cat."

"The prosecutor is smarter than that," I said and put the half cigarette in my lips.

"Lambert is O positive. He matches in five cases."

"So am I," I said.

"Me too," said Shephart. "And most of the people we'd see if we looked out the window."

"DNA analysis?" I beckoned for the lighter.

"Gets complicated, time consuming, and expensive when you have to sort out multiple donors. Also subjective." Shephart thumbed the flame adjustment on the lighter.

"Prosecutor will let Lambert spend the money," I said. "And take the benefit of the doubt when the experts start to argue."

"Lambert's taking the fall," Shephart said. "And your prospects don't look good." He slid the lighter across to me.

"So you drove all the way out here to gloat?"

"I'm looking for the same thing I was looking for when I met you in the parking lot."

"A cup of coffee?" I flicked the lighter twice but got no flame.

"The knife. In the report—about your little donnybrook up on Michigan Avenue."

I stared at Shephart and his matter-of-fact face. "I'm still looking at some exposure here."

Shephart's face didn't change. "Guy came at you on the street with a knife. We have a witness."

"So ask him," I said. I examined the lighter. Shephart had turned the flame all the way down.

"Guy don't know from a knife."

"So do a picture drop."

"Maybe you have some suggestions," said Shephart.

"Cheese cutter, plastic picnic knife, and, ah, maybe a commando knife."

"I got a cheese cutter and a plastic picnic knife at the house," Shephart said. "What's a commando knife?"

"Straight bladed dirk about eight inches long." I showed him the distance between my fingers.

"Sounds familiar."

"Maybe that's because there's a lot of them," I said. "A guy named Brian Hemmings—the Frampton's houseman—down in South Haven had one just like it." I slid the flame adjustment to about halfway, flicked loose less than an inch of flame, and turned my head sideways to save my nose while I lit up. "The guy your witness mentioned was on my flight to Brandonport."

"I don't suppose you've noticed any other cutlery laying about," said Shephart.

I picked up my waste can, rattled it, and parked it on the desk in front of Shephart. "Belongs to Leonard Jones. It's a Marine survival knife. Single edge."

"How?" Shephart shrugged. "What?"

"I haven't touched it," I said. "You want to test it or not?"

• • •

Lorna stepped in the door, dropped her work on my blotter, and said, "Marg and I are going out to a late lunch. Can we bring you anything?"

"You said something about meeting Matty Svenson."

"Marg's in kind of a hurry," said Lorna. "We can talk when I get back."

Marg loomed in the door behind Lorna. She closed her eyes and made one negative wag of her head.

"Sure," I said. "Where are you going?"

"Kentwood Station for the buffet," said Marg. "It's dark and quiet. I've had all the excitement I can handle today."

"If they do a burger, bring me one of those. Or surprise me." I locked eyes with Lorna. "No unsweetened iced tea, thank you."

Mischief wafted across Lorna's face. "Exercise would be good for you." They left.

Lorna had totaled out her time sheet. Thirty-seven hours by Thursday—Marg would be thrilled she had saved us the overtime. Lorna has also totaled out her expense record.

Investigation is communication. Lorna's a good investigator and has excellent language skills. Mostly, I just reviewed her work, wrote a summary, and attached billing memos. The job took less than an hour.

I leaned on the cane and made the trek to the restroom. When I got back, I found a foil wrapped ham and cheese grinder waiting on my desk next to lemonade in a plastic cup. Nurse Gretta could wait for the good news.

Lorna walked in and took the straight backed chair across the desk from me. "Matty told me to get the hell away from you if I wanted to start my job with the DEA in the fall," she said.

"Life goes on," I said. "We agreed at the beginning that you were just filling in until fall."

"If I walked away now—"

"It's not a question of loyalty," I said. "I don't have a license."

"Someone carved 'die bitch' in my windshield," said Lorna. She leaned toward me and put her hands on the desktop. "I'm not going to walk away from this one, or the next one. If I do, I may as well go and drop my application at Burger Shack."

"I think you can do better than that," I said, and unwrapped my sandwich. "What do I owe you for this? All I have is a check from the Sheriff's Department."

"You owe me a chance to be there when we kick sand in their faces."

"You're young," I said, "and life is long. This may not be what you want to do."

"We've had this discussion before. I took the right decision for the wrong reason. But—"

I showed her my hand. "You're an adult." I waved the hand once and put it away. "We need background work on the crew from South Haven. Brian Hemmings for one."

"And Shelly Frampton," she said.

"And Leonard Jones," I said, "but Detective Shephart is on that trail."

"I don't believe for a minute that he would have hurt his sister," she said and leaned back in her chair.

"Leonard Jones is an operator," I said. "I need to know if we can trust him. He's an ace at sand-kicking."

"Like you spoke to my roommates?"

I nodded.

"Cool," said Lorna. She sprung from the chair. "I'm on it in the morning."

"I'll ask Wendy to put you on her payroll. She can bill Lambert for your time. You need to be working for a licensed agency to keep your concealed carry permit valid. Until then, you want to keep a low profile—maybe keep the pistol in your trunk."

"Sure," she said.

"No. I mean really." I stripped the paper off the straw and stabbed it through the lid. Lorna walked out. I took a drink of what turned out to be unsweetened lemonade. I had to hold it in my mouth with my hand to keep from doing a spit take on my desk. I labored through a swallow and said, "Auk, Jesus."

From the front office I heard Lorna say, "I like it tart." The closing of the front door cut off the sound of her laughter.

· · ·

I called the house a couple of times. No answer. I left a message. It seemed like Wendy had to be back since I'd talked to Pete Finney in the early afternoon. I filled in time—changed the bandage on my foot—until the light outside my office window had faded.

The front door opened and I looked up to the monitor. Wendy struggled in carrying two suitcases. I stood, set the cane aside, and walked around the desk. "God, am I glad to see you."

Wendy set the luggage in the doorway between us. She wore tan sweats and had her hair wrapped in a knot on the top of her head. Her eyes were puffy and hot with rage.

"Don't touch me," she said.

"What?"

"Do you have any idea what we've been through?"

"I talked to Ben. I talked to Pete Finney." I shrugged. "I was in the hospital."

"Oh, yeah. I called. You were asleep. Goddamn it!" Tears started down the edge of her nose. "They dragged us through shit. And where were you? Asleep! You were asleep, you asshole."

"I asked for something. I thought they gave it to me because I was in pain."

"It's always all about you. You made this mess with the crap you had in your office."

"Just a minute! Thirty-three years! Tell me what you believe."

"I saw. They showed me. God, it was so sick!"

"Get out," I said—calm and surreal—like I heard someone else say it. "Leave the bags and get out."

She left. The room swam. I held onto the desk, hand over hand, to get back to my chair. I racked a round into the chamber of my old friend and punched the magazine out.

"GO AHEAD," SAID A MAN WITH A HOARSE VOICE. "Save me a lot of work." He leaned in the door, hovering over the luggage that Wendy had left, and showed me the business end of the twelve gauge shotgun. "Wouldn't have missed this for the world," he said. "You ruined my singing voice and broke three of my ribs."

"I had a busy day," I said. "Don't take this personal, but . . ." I shrugged.

He reddened. "That's right, piss me off." Using his right hand to cover me with the shotgun he flipped the baggage behind him with his left. "Frosting on the cake."

He wore a white T-shirt and black cut-off jeans. The Velcro tabs of a ballistic vest showed through the fabric of the shirt.

Fidel/Andy. He'd shaved his beard and his head. A narrow three-inch bruise tattooed his right eye into an expression of continued surprise. Road raspberries held high season on his left arm and leg. I looked up to the monitor. The front door to the office stood open, blocked by the janitor's gray canvas trash cart.

"El Guitmo," I said.

"Who?" He stepped through the door and got both hands on the street sweeper.

"El Guitmo—famous international terrorist."

He laughed. "Too cute by half. Somebody from the Bureau tell you that?"

"Matty Svenson."

He shook his head.

"Special Agent."

"Whatever." He pointed the shotgun at my pistol and shoveled the muzzle toward my head twice. "Busy, busy," he said. "In the mouth. Improves the aim."

"You know," I said, and tried to make it sound like a revelation, "you can still come in. Tell them what you know. Hell, they'd probably give you a medal—save the Bureau the trouble and embarrassment of a prosecution."

"They really didn't tell you shit, did they?"

I let the pistol fall onto the desktop.

"What are you doing?" he croaked, and looked from the pistol back to my face.

"Like to leave a note. Mind?"

"Keep it personal," he said. "Too bad you don't have a computer. I do suicide notes that bring a tear to the eye."

I took Lorna's expense report and turned it to the blank side. "I'm a street detective," I said. I picked up my red editing pen.

"Shame," he said. "We could have left a lot of dirty pictures on your hard drive—you never would have skated the pornography charge."

"Where did you get that crap?"

"You wouldn't believe me if I told you. Write."

I looked at him and said, "Post Office."

"Right you are." He tilted his head to one side. "You should thank us for that. You had friends. They wanted to take you out without having to kill you."

I wrote a couple of words and lay the pen down.

"Write."

I picked up the pen. "Who was it wanted to do me the favor?"

"What's it to you?"

"I'm planning to haunt the bastard," I said.

He laughed. "Old bureau type named Cameran. He had a friend who was a postal inspector."

"Intelligence Research Associates?"

"He said you snaked his client and thought planting the books was hilarious."

I wrote another word and looked up. "What's this to him?"

"He's doing the patent complaint for some battery outfit."

"You, too?"

"Write," he said.

I started another word.

"Just business," he said.

"They said you were a terrorist."

"These days everybody is a terrorist. Makes the job easier. Besides, who told you terror wasn't a business?"

"Guess I'm old school," I said. "Enlighten me."

"Religion is politics. Politics is business. It's all the same. It's about who's the boss. The boss gets the tight women and the fresh cuts of meat."

"But you do the dirty work," I said. "What do you get, besides used?"

"Who's to say what's dirty work? Moses terrorized the Egyptians. Was that religion or politics? The angels of God slaughtered infants in their cribs. It's the winner who decides what's criminal and what's sacred. I'm just a little cog on a big wheel. The job pays good and I like the rush."

"Must be a very large and shiny wheel."

"A cartel. One that likes energy business the way it is."

I scratched out a couple of words. "World's changing."

"World'll change when the cartel changes it."

I set the pen down.

"Look," he said. "You bought this shotgun at Meijers this afternoon. It'll do the job just fine."

"You bang up someone just to look like me?"

"Used sunglasses and some bandages. We did a driver's license. Cops'll never look past the paperwork."

"Clever," I said. I showed him an open palm. "Question. One professional to another."

"As long as you're writing."

I picked up the pen. "You kill the Frampton woman?"

"Nope."

I started another sentence. "C'mon, it was all too damn neat—the break-in, the cigar butt, the hair in the Frampton woman's hand."

"I was taking care of Dixon—gave him diarrhea of the brain before he

176

developed diarrhea of the mouth. Man should never forget who his friends are."

"Okay, we—you and me—were out of town."

"Bitch killed the Frampton woman."

"Bitch worked for you?"

"Naa. Was a freebie. We billed for it—don't tell anybody." He laughed and then shrugged. "We had to plant the hair on the body." He made it sound like an excuse.

"Bitch have a name?"

"How the hell would I know?"

I made a period, moved to the bottom of the note, wrote a big "A" and stopped. I looked at the now bald and beardless Fidel/Andy and arched my eyebrows.

He sighed. "Guy who came to scope your office. He was there and ready to do the job. He set it up. Sent the Frampton woman a gift certificate for an expensive dinner good only one day—her birthday."

I said, "Andy?"

"Everybody's Andy."

"Except Frank."

"Frank was Andy," he said. "Now he's John Doe."

I finished my signature, pushed the note toward him, but left my palm firmly planted and spread across the text. He pulled at the corner but I held fast.

"Old bitch. Language was terrible. 'Mother this, fuck that.' Frampton woman picked up the telephone. 'Bitch, faggot, dyke'—pow, dead artist. Gimme the mother-fucking note."

I let go of the paper. Fidel/Andy glanced from the note back at me with his eyebrows holding hands.

He said, "What the fuck is this? Asshole!"

"Mary had a little lamb," I said and snatched the Detonics. I pulled the muzzle up looking for the front sight.

Loud rapid cracks came from the front office. Fidel/Andy lurched toward me, his face astonished. The shotgun erupted and took my curtain through the window. On the monitor I saw Wendy through a haze of smoke, standing with her .380 in both hands. Fidel/Andy racked the shotgun.

I found my front sight. "And tied it to the heater," I said taking the slack out of the trigger. Fidel/Andy, spinning left, was already in profile. I put the sight on his ear. Squeezed. A pink fog shrouded his head.

The shotgun barked. The monitor exploded. Fidel/Andy piled onto the floor like a puppet with its strings cut, his right hand flexing on the comb and trigger of the shotgun. Stepping around the desk I snapped the magazine into the Detonics and hit the slide stop.

"Every time it turned around it burned its little seater," I told him, but I don't think he heard me. He had a nickel-sized hole through his right ear. The left side of his head spackled my office door and his brains hung in the air like a fine mist.

I stood on his hand to break it loose and kicked the cannon across the office carpet. Wendy stared at the pistol in her right hand, her left hand holding her mouth. Her face blanched, from behind her hand she said, "I emptied it and he just stood there." Her purse and my shave kit lay discarded at her feet.

A thunder and rumble came from the stairwell. Through the office window I saw Matty Svenson—clad in a black jacket emblazoned with FBI in white letters, black slacks, and her blond hair pulled back in a ponytail—leading a herd of black-clad, helmeted agents down the stairs with carbines at the ready.

I thumbed up the safety on the Detonics and planted it on Marg's desk, took the .380 out of Wendy's hands, and skittered it next to the Detonics. Taking Wendy's hands in both of mine, I raised our hands over our heads and backed Wendy out the office door, pushing the canvas cart before us.

"What? Stop!" Wendy said. "What are you doing? Oh, God!"

Disgust pinched Wendy's face. "Don't touch me." Wendy turned her face away. "You're covered in blood."

Wendy struggled. I held her hands. An agent with a helmet and a Kevlar mask over a woman's face covered us with an MP5 and said, "Freeze or you're dead!"

Matty brushed by us into the office with two other black-clad agents. Other agents took up covered positions, kneeling at corners, and aiming their weapons down the hallway and up the stairs. Outside, tires squealed and a clatter of automatic gunfire—punctuated with shotgun blasts—rose in the parking lot.

Matty looked up from the fat nine she had pointed at the pile of meat in my office doorway. The agent covering me and Wendy put the MP5 to her shoulder and leaned into the weapon. Tires squawked in the parking lot and vehicles collided. Buzz bursts from MP5's were answered with the steady tack-tack-tack of an M60.

Two agents from inside my office burst from the office door with Matty stepping on their heels. "They're with us," Matty said to the agent covering Wendy and me. "Go, go, go!"

I released Wendy's hands. She pushed off of me and looked at her hands. Horror pressed her cheeks hollow. At the top of the stairs agents crashed the door open but froze in the doorway. I heard the sound of what they saw. *Toop. Toop.*

"Oh, shit!" Astonishment washed down Matty's face. I dived onto Wendy, smothering her to the floor. Some agents bounded down the stairs, others made a pile on the red tile entrance way. I clutched Wendy's head to my chest and turned my head to the wall.

Two explosions ripped through the parking lot. Ceiling tiles cascaded to the floor. Dust hung in the air. I backed off of Wendy. She got to her knees and crawled away to vomit on the floor.

Matty stood in the hallway, her jacket covered with a fine gray dust. Her pistol dangled at her side. She stared at me. She said, "My God! What?"

"Forty millimeter rifle grenades," I said.

Matty wheeled and charged up the stairs to exit the building with the other agents. I stepped over to Wendy to help her to her feet. Her face and sweatshirt were smeared red and pink with small white flecks. She made her way to the restroom, alternately leaning on, and pushing off, the wall.

I looked at my shirt, found it spattered with blood and brains, and pulled it over my head. I inspected the front of my undershirt for holes, found none, and pulled it off to use as a towel.

In the office I dropped the shirts into Marg's trash can. The smell of smoke, cordite, and scorched flesh wafted in through my exploded office window. Sirens, some approaching and others fading into the distance, deadened the sounds of cursing and discharging fire extinguishers in the parking lot.

I threw one of the suitcases Wendy brought onto the sofa, found a shirt and a pair of jeans, and put them inside the door to the ladies' room for Wendy. In the men's room I rinsed off, but discovered I needed to wash my hair. The water ran red as it swirled down the drain.

In the hallway I found black-clad FBI agents standing on office chairs to reinstall ceiling tiles. Wendy had kicked my shirt and jeans out of the ladies' room. An agent carried my exploded office monitor up the stairs, two more wrestled my office door up the stairs behind him. Men in blue coveralls had the late "El Guitmo" zipped into a black body bag and parked on a gurney waiting for the stairway to clear.

Matty stood at Marg's desk. She folded her arms when she saw me. The telephone rang. I limped in to answer it.

Through my office doorway I saw my desk and the wingback chair had been moved by agents rolling up the carpeting. Matty put her hand on the telephone. She said, "Art, we have to get a lid on this."

"Telephone works in my office, too," I said. The telephone rang again.

"We fixed it," said Matty. "The room mike is in the telephone, it runs off your service current."

"You recorded it all?"

"I can't say," said Matty. The telephone rang.

"You *heard*."

"Art, I stopped listening when your wife came in."

"*C'mon!*"

"We heard. Not me. We thought it was the cleaning service. We ran the plate on the truck."

The answering machine took the call. "Arthur, this is Pete Finney. Sorry to ring you up so late. It's important that we speak."

"My wife is in the restroom," I said. "Get a lid on that. Tell her where the crap they found in here really came from."

"Arthur, if you are there . . . I rang your house. This really is most important."

Matty nodded and took her hand off the telephone.

"Pete," I said. "I just stepped in when I heard your voice. Mind if I put you on the speaker while I tidy up?"

"If you like."

"What's up?"

"A couple of things. First, I've just spoken with Scott Lambert. He says he'll take you on as his security director. If he does that you would be able to work the case."

"He wants to pick up my office rent and staff?"

"Perhaps you could work out of his space."

"If he's paying the rent this *will* be his space," I said.

"Well, all right then," said Pete. "You were harboring some doubts earlier."

"None," I said. "You're working late."

"There has been a bit of a mix-up. Scott was arrested at the airport tonight. He had a borrowed passport. They have revoked his bond."

• • •

Wendy sulked in the passenger seat, her arms folded over the shoulder belt and crushing her bosom. My shirt came down to her knees. She'd rolled the legs of my jeans up to her calves. I backed out and threaded her old Cadillac through a maze of four-door sedans and around the flat-bed car hauler winching the second of two exploded and burned FBI vehicles.

Armed and black-liveried FBI agents guarded the parking lot and ignored our departure. Kentwood patrol cars lined the street and had been parked with their emergency lights left rolling. Detective Van Huis's fake-woody minivan sat parked on the lawn between the sidewalk and the curb. At the intersection a Kentwood patrol officer directed traffic with a burning road flare in his hand. He flagged me to a stop.

Van Huis knocked on my window. I let it down.

"What the hell is going on here, Art?"

"Feds cornered a terrorist in my office," I said.

"Yeah, and then what? They won't tell us shit."

"You gotta talk to them, Jerry," I said.

"Follow me down to my office," he said.

"Am I under arrest?"

"No."

I shook my head. "I gotta go."

"Fine," he said. "You're under arrest." Van Huis waved his hand and we were looking up the muzzles of weapons in the hands of several Kentwood police officers stationed around the car.

"Then I'm allowed a phone call," I said. "And I call the feds."

"This is bullshit," said Van Huis.

A knot of black-clad agents started up the street from the office parking lot.

"Jerry, come and see me in the morning. I'll be in the office," I said.

Van Huis stood up and looked toward the office. In the rearview mirror I could see the knot of agents spreading out, their MP5's at port arms. One of them yelled, "Is there a problem here, officer?"

I said, "They're not going to let us have this argument in the middle of the street, here. Or even at our level, Jerry. Your chief is going to have to bitch at somebody from Justice. For God's sake, come and see me in the morning."

Van Huis waved off the Kentwood patrolmen. "You ain't there in the morning, you're a fugitive," said Van Huis. He yelled at the officer with the road flare, "Get this one out of here."

"We can't go to the house," said Wendy, cold, like she was discussing the bus schedule.

The officer stopped traffic and motioned us out. I turned left toward the city. "Probably right." I said. I watched the mirror. No vehicles were allowed to come out after me.

"You can't come to the house," she said. "I promised the licensing bureau that you would not have anything to do with my daily operations or be at my office until after the hearing on my license."

"I think we have that straightened out."

"Matty, the FBI Agent—your friend—said that the details of this case were 'confidential.' She said this was an open case and that she wouldn't be able to testify on my behalf."

I turned right onto the next residential street and parked at the curb. I leaned on the car to get back to the trunk and set my suitcases in the street. At the open driver's door I took my cane off the floor in the back and dropped the keys on the seat. "Go home," I said.

"Art!" she said. "What are you doing? You can't walk."

I shut the door, stuffed the two-suiter under my left arm, and got the handle of the suitcase with my left hand. My shoulder should have hurt. It didn't. I leaned on the cane and started back up to the main drag a step at a time.

At the corner Wendy pulled to the curb, on the wrong side of the street, and ran the window down. "At least let me take you to a motel," she said.

"You don't want to be hanging around with me," I said. Carrying the two-suiter under my arm wasn't working. I set the bags down and got them both by the handle. A station wagon turned onto the street and squealed to a stop. The driver cursed out the window.

"You're not safe out here," said Wendy.

"You're not safe if you're with me," I said.

"You fucking bitch," yelled the driver of the station wagon. "Move that goddamn car!"

I dropped the bags and walked over to the driver's window of the stationwagon. "Excuse me, sir," I said, and hooked the cane around the driver's neck to pull his head out to where we could be eye to eye—he was maybe nineteen, and liquored up. "Perhaps there's another way to resolve this matter. Sir?"

He squeaked out an answer. "I could just go around."

"My man," I said. "You have far to go to get home?"

"Down the street." He rolled his gaze around my face with horror in his eyes. "A couple houses."

"Good. When I let go of you, you put your head on the seat and rest until we are gone. If you don't, I'm going to hurt you."

I hobbled over, picked up the bags and returned to the driver's window of the wagon. "How's it going?"

"I'm resting."

"My man. I have to tell the lady that you apologized for the language."

"I'm sorry."

I put the bags in the back seat of the Cadillac, took the shotgun seat, and pulled the door shut. "He's had a bit to drink," I said. "Says he's sorry for the language and is just going to rest there for a bit until we are gone."

Wendy drove. Streets came and went. Stoplights were streaks of red and green. I tried to imagine my life without Wendy. Nothing came to mind.

THE SIGN READS "EXIT TO JUPITER" and keeps getting stolen. Wendy made the turn, took the Jupiter Street bridge across the Grand River, and turned east onto Rouge River Drive. She picked the Anchor Inn, north and east of the city.

The Anchor Inn is a Ma-and-Pa-Kettle motel consisting of a string of ground floor rooms with a gravel drive. The rates are cheap, but not cheap enough for me to stay for long.

Wendy said, "I'll get the room."

I watched through the window. She used her beloved credit card and there'd be hell to pay for that. Back in the car, she drove to the last unit, handed me the key, and said, "I'll help you get the bags."

"Not a problem," I said.

"C'mon," she said. "We'll make it in one trip."

I unlocked the door, stumbled in, and threw the cane on the bed. Wendy set down the two-suiter, pushed the door shut, and leaned her back against it. "I'm staying," she said.

"There's only one bed." I switched on the lights, revealing knotty pine walls and a splatter painted ceiling. The double bed, draped in a red spread, filled most of the room.

"We'll make do," said Wendy.

In my mind I had a picture of her sitting and staring wistfully out this window instead of one at the house. "Suit yourself," I said, and pulled the curtains closed. "You want to use the shower?" I swung the suitcase onto the bed, flopped the lid open, and tossed the Detonics and Wendy's Maverick .380 on the spread.

"Just let me call the house," said Wendy. "There's a spare magazine in my purse."

I set Wendy's purse on the bedside table next to the telephone and racked a fresh magazine in the Detonics. She dialed the house. I hit the bathroom—commode and a white metal shower stall—for a pit-stop before Wendy tied up the room. "Your dad's okay," said Wendy. "I'm here with him. Take this telephone number . . . I want you to drive Ben to school in the morning . . . So, don't pull in the lot . . . And if I'm not back, I want you to pick him up at the bus stop."

I hobbled out and hung my cane on the doorknob. Wendy brushed by. In the bathroom the faucet handles squeaked and the pipes hammered as Wendy turned on the shower. I snapped on the TV. The cable was out, and I dialed the desk. They knew; that's why we got a discount. For entertainment I sat on the bed and changed the bandage on my foot.

Wendy settled on the bed next to me, smelling scrubbed and wearing one of my white T-shirts—her nipples and panty lines imprinted in the thin fabric. She rubbed her palm on my cheek and then rested two fingers on my lip.

"They shave your moustache for the stitches?"

"Sure," I said.

"The stitches are ready to come out," she said. "Hand me my purse."

She wrestled her glasses from the purse and a pair of cuticle scissors from a black zippered case. Pushing me closer to the light, she tilted her head back to study my lip through the bottom half of her glasses. I looked down to watch her fingers but my eyes settled on her breasts.

Wendy smiled. "Got something on your mind?" She pulled on one of the stitches and snipped.

"You need to get a couple guys with a video camera on Hank Dunphy," I said.

"Done. Anything else?" She pulled on the second stitch and snipped.

"Lorna Kemp," I said.

Wendy's hands dropped into her lap. Her eyes wide, she said "Really?"

"She needs to be on your payroll, to keep her carry permit valid."

Wendy dropped the stitches in the ashtray. "Sure," she said, "I'll only have a license for a couple weeks anyway."

I closed the lid on the suitcase, stationed it in front of the door, and moved the chair from the bedside table to the foot of the bed. Sitting on the chair, I rested my feet on the suitcase and settled my pistol onto my lap.

Wendy crawled across the bed and stood behind me. She rubbed my cheek, resting her other hand on my shoulder. "You can shave now," she said.

"Thought I'd grow a beard," I said. "I need something to hold up the nose brace."

"I talked to my doctor."

"It's an allergy?"

"It's menopause." Wendy's voice broke. She covered it with a chuckle and added, "I'm getting old, Darlin.'"

I'm sorry? Wrong answer! Don't worry?—borders on stupid. Wendy gripped my shoulders, massaged one circle with her thumbs, and heaved a ragged sigh that I felt shift the hair combed over the bald spot at the back of my head.

I went with, "I don't think of us as old."

"We're not kids anymore, Art."

"Sure we are," I said. "That's what my dad calls us—'the kids.'"

"He's ninety-three."

"On his third wife and plays golf twice a week."

"Miniature golf," said Wendy.

"Only has to carry one club that way," I said. "Says golf is all about the putting game, anyway."

"And the point is?"

"The point is we are too young to focus on the putting game, too young for free coffee at Mickey D's, and too young for Social Security."

"They sent me an AARP card," said Wendy, her voice not amused.

"And we're too young for the 'senior discounts.'"

Wendy kissed my bald spot.

"We're at a awkward age," I said. "It's like being six years old on a hot summer day. You're too young to decide to water the grass and too old to rollerskate naked in the lawn sprinkler."

Wendy whacked the bald spot with her fingers, rested her hand back on my shoulder, and said, "The doctor said I might get a little cranky."

"Not so's I've noticed," I said.

"I didn't mean what I said."

I patted her hand. Wendy didn't drink. Only anger gave light to her unvarnished thoughts. "I know," I said. "You came back and saved my life. What else could I ask for?"

Wendy slipped her hand off my shoulder. I heard a rustle of clothing, and pink nylon panties dropped into my lap.

I went to bed.

• • •

Cool and overcast, the morning delivered up rain that hung in the air like mist. In the parking lot behind my office, news vans had replaced the government sedans.

Wendy pulled up to the stairwell.

"Glad I shaved," I said. "I'm not hauling my luggage into the office in front of these news crews."

"I'll be back for you tonight."

Delia Dumas bailed out of the *Live News at Five* van. Her umbrella, with red and white panels, snapped open like it had been on a static line. Today was mauve blazer and yellow blouse day. A morning breeze tugged at the bumbershoot, but Delia's hair held its ground.

I buttoned my gray pinstriped suit coat and straightened my tie. Rounding the front of the Cadillac, I made a point not to make eye contact with Delia. Wendy lowered her window.

"Aren't you forgetting something?" Wendy said.

"All I've got is a check," I said, and reached for my wallet. "It's only eighty-four dollars, but I think it will cover what you put on your card."

Wendy closed her eyes and arched her eyebrows. "You've got me," Wendy said. She opened her eyes. "And I want a kiss."

I bent over, put my hand on Wendy's shoulder, and gave her a buzz. Delia's cameraman—his camera in a clear plastic shroud—made it news. Print photographers added flash.

When I stood up, Delia had her hand mike in my face. "Mr. Hardin, can you tell us what happened here last night?"

"No." I turned and lumbered toward the stairs.

"The FBI has released a statement," she said.

I said, "The FBI has an office downtown."

"Who was 'El Guitmo?' Why would the FBI confront an international terrorist at your office?"

The driver's door to the Cadillac opened. Wendy, still in my jeans and dress shirt, launched. She grabbed the microphone and pulled it up to her face.

She said, "Where do you get off calling anyone a terrorist? You said he was a 'reliable source,' when he was spreading filth about my husband. You're the terrorist."

The print guys got their cameras busy. Delia's cameraman swung his camera to Wendy. Two other news crews picked up the stroke. I made good my escape.

"You put his lies on the news" said Wendy. "You ruined our lives. There wouldn't be terrorists if people like you refused to do their bidding."

From the top of the stairs I heard Wendy pull her car door shut. I turned to see the crowd of newsies part as she pulled the Caddy into reverse. I ducked in the door, grabbed the hand rail, and hopped down the steps on my good foot.

Through the office window I could see Marg at work at her desk, which was parked on the bare concrete floor—the FBI having ripped up the carpet and taken it away as "evidence." I tried the office door and found it locked. The herd of newsies was already on the stairs. Marg looked up from her work as I jangled my keys to twist the lock.

Still long steps away the chorus of voices began as I pushed the door open, "Mr. Hardin! Mr Hardin! Mr. Hardin!" I pulled the door after me and locked it.

Marg arched one eyebrow under her new shag hairdo. She wore a red blouse with puff sleeves and had a client's books open for entries. She looked over the half-glasses perched on the end of her nose and said, "Redecorating?"

The newshounds knocked at the door. I ignored them.

"Got a visit from the notorious 'El Guitmo' last night."

"Headline was bigger than the story," she said. Something about an international terrorist killed in a clash with federal agents—no real details."

Delia Dumas pecked at the window with a coin. I looked up. Her lips were moving. Her cameraman cranked away over her shoulder.

"I should have listened when you said we needed blinds on that window," I said, and started into my office.

"I'll remind you when we redecorate," said Marg. As I passed her desk Marg pushed a registered letter my direction.

"County Gun Board," she said. "Came this morning."

My cane made hollow thunks on the bare cement floor. I hung it on the edge of my desk and flopped into my chair to peel open the envelope. I was summoned to a hearing of the Gun Board on Thursday next and cautioned not to carry a concealed weapon "if you no longer have a valid detective's license."

From my top desk drawer I extracted the brown envelope of orders Matty had left with my son, folded it into thirds, and stashed it in the breast pocket of my suit jacket. The front door opened and out of habit I looked up to where the monitor should have been hanging and saw the cable and power cord dangling from the ceiling.

"Excuse me," said the voice of Detective Van Huis, his tone gruff. "No, you can wait outside. Back up! The lady wants to lock the door."

I shrugged out of my suit jacket and hung it on the back of my chair. When I turned back, Van Huis flopped the morning paper onto my desk. I read the banner headline, TERRORIST DEAD, and the tag line—STALKED KENTWOOD P.I.

"What the hell is this?" he said.

"Don't know," I said. "I haven't read the paper."

"What the hell happened? Feds won't say shit!"

I picked up the paper and turned it around.

"How come your window's boarded up?"

"I'm being stalked by terrorists."

"Where's your carpet? Where's your office door? Where's that damn monitor I have to duck to sit in this chair?"

"Gone."

"Why?"

"Ask the feds."

"I'm asking you."

I picked up my telephone, sat it in the middle of the desk, and spoke to it, "Specifically, Detective Van Huis, I have nothing to add to what the FBI has released for publication."

Van Huis leaned forward, and with his palms on the desk, yelled at the telephone. "I want to know what the explosions in the parking lot were. I want to know why we recovered your janitor's stolen van shot full of holes and burned to a hulk." He looked at me and added in a normal voice, "Well?"

189

"I was inside, I don't know." I shrugged. "The explosions were loud. I heard a lot of shooting. I don't know about the van. I was here. I talked with you in the street last night. Are you telling me that my janitor is stalking me?"

"All right," said Van Huis. "I can play this, too. You don't have a detective license. You don't have any business walking around with that pistol on your hip."

"This is private property, and I am now the Security Director for Light and Energy Applications."

"I catch you on the street wearing that pistol and I am going to run you in. I don't care about your weasel-ass attorney or how many feds pop out of the woodwork."

The telephone rang. Marg picked it up. "Security, Light and Energy Applications," she said.

I always knew she was listening.

"Yes, he's in," she said. "Just a moment please." She announced from her desk, "Pete Finney on line one."

"It's my pet weasel," I said. "You want to talk to him?"

"Just tell him you're going to need bail."

"If I go out there unarmed and get killed, who are you going to get your answers from?"

"Art," Van Huis said, "I'm a policeman. I'm going to try to see that you don't get killed—even if you won't help me." He turned to walk out of the office.

"Jerry," I said. He looked over his shoulder. "Thank you."

Van Huis nodded and stepped through the door.

"Forgot your paper," I said.

"Already read it."

I picked up the telephone. "Pete, I'm glad you called. Something's come up that we need to talk about. It concerns the Lambert case."

"Good," said Finney. "Scott Lambert is the reason I called. I need you to join me for a conference with Mr. Lambert this morning. Can you be at the county jail in an hour?"

"Are you at your office?"

"Yes, I have a couple of small matters to clear up."

"Great, I need a ride," I said.

"I have a motion with Judge Barton this afternoon."

"Back up!" I heard Van Huis growl from the door to the hallway. "No.

You can't wait in the office. Clear the doorway."

"I'll fend for myself when we're done," I told him. "From the sound of the local police, I may not need a ride back."

"We might find that advantageous. Scott was set upon by a gang of hooligans in the jail last night."

● ● ●

"All very interesting, Arthur," said Finney—made it sound like "Awtha," minds his r's in the courtroom, though—"but it's hearsay. And then the prosecutor asks why this man cannot be called as a witness and you answer, 'I am ever so sorry sir, but someone blew his head off.'"

Finney nailed the brakes and swerved right to avoid a left turner. "Heathen," he said.

"Had his signal on, Pete."

"Wouldn't be a problem if Americans drove on the proper side of the street."

"No, I guess then he'd have been turning right." I hooked up my seat belt.

"Exactly," said Pete. "But we have to deal with things such as they are. In Mr. Lambert's case, he had an ugly scene with the deceased just prior to her violent demise and the authorities recovered his hair from her hand."

"He was set up and the hair was planted."

Pete looked in the mirror. "Bloody carnival parade!" We've two of those news vans and a string of autos following us."

"People hoping that I'll tell them what the feds won't."

"I read the story this morning. Odd they would say the man was killed in a 'clash with federal agents.'"

"Why's that?"

"They are usually very particular about calling them Special Agents."

"You read like a lawyer," I said.

Pete turned his face to me. A wry smile wafted over his lawyer's mask and dissipated like smoke. Pete's half century had begun to bulge in his suit, and show up gray in his bristle thicket eyebrows and carefully trimmed beard.

He didn't ask the question. He turned back to the business of driving and said, "We need the man who witnessed the murder of Ms. Frampton and soaked Lambert's hair in her blood so it would stick to her palm."

"Not like we can just snap off a subpoena," I said. "But Hank Dunphy's

191

available and he is in this up to his armpits."

"It was Mr. Dunphy's passport and ticket Scott Lambert tendered when he was apprehended at the airport. The jury wouldn't believe Mr. Dunphy if he personally confessed to the murder on the stand."

"They never check my passport," I said.

"Mr. Lambert used the passport as identification at the boarding counter."

"They don't look even vaguely alike."

"Scott charged up to the counter at the last minute and put his thumb over the picture," said Finney, exhaling the words as if he were confessing his own stupidity.

"He should have just walked away."

"The police were at hand."

"Like they knew he was coming?"

"Probably," said Finney. "He has had to forfeit his bond."

"Guess it wasn't the bond agent that ratted him out."

"Mr. Lambert posted a half-million in cash."

I levered the electric window switch of Pete's brand new silver Lincoln. Nothing happened. "Something wrong with the window?"

"Sorry, locked out—kids, you know. I can put the air on if you like."

"I thought I'd have a smoke before we got to the jail."

"Really rather you didn't," said Pete. "We can loiter in the parking lot while we put your pistol in the boot."

"I left it at the office," I said and made a pat inventory of my pockets. "Doesn't matter, I don't have any smokes. So what's this about Lambert getting the shit kicked out of him?"

Finney put the blower on. "Chingos," he said. "What do you know about them?"

"What I read in the paper," I said, "some Hispanic gang, supposed to be linked to the Mexican Mafia. I don't know as that's true."

"They dusted him up. I don't know how bad. They want twenty thousand dollars for protection."

"Bad idea," I said. "Any amount of money paid to them would just turn out to be a down payment. Have them put Scott in 'punk city.'"

"Fred Timmer is the assistant prosecutor on this. I talked to him about segregation, but he passed the matter off to the sheriff. He said that the operative policy was that Mr. Lambert would have to identify his attackers."

• • •

Fred Timmer—six foot, but narrow at the shoulders and pigeon chested—stalked about the hallway outside the interview room wearing a tan polyester suit and carrying a cardboard index file tucked under his arm. Seeing me, he heated up until the red in his thermometer showed in his face.

"Listen, Hardin," he said, "you should be in this jail, not walking around the hallways."

"Mr. Hardin is the Security Director for Light and Energy Applications," said Finney. "He will be working on Mr. Lambert's behalf."

"Please tell me you'll put him on the stand," said Timmer.

"You may ask anything you like, so long as you have foundation."

"I have questions about his morals and the reliability of his testimony."

"That's up to the jury," said Finney. "I may need to confer with you after we have spoken with Mr. Lambert."

"I'll be here," said Timmer, his face serpentine.

Lambert, wearing green jail scrubs, sat with his right hand cuffed to a metal ring bolted to the table. Both of his eyes had been blackened, his left open only a slit revealing a yellow iris awash in a sea of red. His left upper lip bulged, swollen so large that his lips would not come together on the right. A gauze patch covered his right cheek.

"They beat the shit out of me. I'm passing blood." said Lambert, adding a pf sound to his esses and revealing a gap in his teeth.

Pete dropped his satchel on the floor and turned on his heel, his eyes electric. He rapped on the interview room door with his fist. The door came open and he said, "Have you seen Mr. Lambert?"

"Want to confer already?"

"My client has been savaged."

"This is the jail," said Timmer. "It's full of criminals and perverts. It's where they belong," he added in a louder voice. In a conversational tone he went on, "We have lodged our displeasure with the sheriff." And louder again, he said, "But things happen, don't they?"

"Is that a threat?" said Finney, his tone even and inquisitive.

"Not at all," said Timmer, his mouth full of innocence.

Finney pulled the door shut and stepped over the bench on our side of the table.

"He said if I plead guilty," said Lambert, lisping the t's around his missing teeth, "that I could be alone in a safe cell."

Finney sat, dug a yellow pad out of his satchel, and smacked it on the table like he was killing a bug. "He talked to you?" Finney plumbed a pen out of his pocket. "I can't believe it! The man has lost his mind!"

"Not exactly," said Lambert. "He was in the room when they brought me in. The guard let him out and he said it. You know, from the hallway through the door before it closed. Like he was talking to the guard."

Finney scratched notes. Without looking up he said, "I understand that you need only identify your attackers to be placed in segregation."

"I told them who did it," said Lambert, sitting straight and making his eyes as wide as he could. "They put me back in the cell with them and this is what they did." He peeled the bandage off his cheek and revealed a deep cigarette burn. "Said it meant I was their bitch. If I didn't pay, they'd pass me around."

"You can't pay them," said Finney.

"Then tell that bastard in the hallway he has a deal. These guys are going to kill me."

Pete put his pen away. "Big prostate, small bladder," said Finney, "I should have stopped by the restroom before we came up." He walked to the door and knocked to get out.

When the door closed behind him I said, "Well, we're a matched set."

"Not hardly," said Lambert. "You got to defend yourself. I can't do anything. There's too many. They're all over me. If I could get a bunk I'd be afraid to sleep."

"Pete's right. This isn't a good idea. It's just the first of many larger payments."

Lambert shook his head.

"Fine," I said. I wanted to rub my face but knew better. "Who, how, when, and where?"

"Hank Dunphy."

Hank Dunphy? Are you nuts? I let him finish.

"You met him at the airport. He'll bring the money to your office. Twenty thousand in tens and twenties. Then tonight, at ten o'clock, you take it to Milwaukee Street, by the zoo. There's a pedestrian tunnel under the expressway. Wear a Detroit Red Wing T-shirt and ball cap. Look for a man in a Detroit Lions T-shirt."

"I think you need to look long and hard at Mr. Dunphy."

Lambert waved his free hand. "I know you had a misunderstanding, but

Hank Dunphy is very loyal. We were at BuzzBee Batteries in the R&D department together."

Pointless. "Scott, I'll do what you ask, but you have to listen to Pete. In the meantime I have a lead on the person who killed Anne Frampton."

"Who was it?"

I shook my head. "I was told that it was a woman."

"Anne was a lesbian."

"You knew?"

"Certainly."

"Why on earth did you ask me to find her?" I tried to conceal my anger.

Lambert looked away. "I had to find her. We did a physics project together in college. BuzzBee Batteries is challenging my patents. They said I developed the technology while I worked for them and stole it. Anne knew the truth."

"She had a sculpture. Looks like a ship sailing out of a brick wall. When the light hits it, a sea captain appears."

Lambert snapped his head toward me and made the happiest smashed face I have ever seen. "*The Dutchman?* You saw it?"

"It's on the mantel at the Frampton estate."

"That's all I need. I asked Anne about it, but the woman she was with got angry and started shoving me."

"She use a voice synthesizer?"

"She didn't say anything. She just shoved me and threw plates of food. They escorted me out of the restaurant. Christ, I thought I'd been invited."

"Hank Dunphy sent you there?"

"Wasn't his fault. Somebody called and said they were from your office."

"That wasn't the deal, was it? I was to give her your telephone number. Period."

"You can't understand how important this is. Programmable machines the size of molecules and absolute conductivity at ambient temperatures."

"I bought one of your cameras," I said. "Amazing."

"The science is light years in front of the engineering. This year I can print batteries onto greeting cards. In five years I'll be able to paint a battery onto an automobile like a primer coat. The finish coat will be photoelectric. You can guess the rest."

"I just like the idea of changing the color of my car with a switch," I said. "But somebody with a lot of money has bought some very heavy hitters..."

The door opened. Finney's voice came from the hallway. "Mr. Hardin, we need you to come out here."

I shuffled out to stand in the open door. My foot had much improved but wearing only one shoe gave me an odd gait. I found Pete in the company of Timmer and two armed deputies. Pete stood with his hands folded, looking at the floor. The deputies looked bored. One of them had his handcuffs out.

He said, "Are you Arthur Hardin?"

I looked at Finney. He would not raise his eyes to meet mine. "Don't tell me, let me guess," I said. Timmer's face went stupid, which in his case I believe passed for smug.

The deputy said, "I have a warrant for your arrest."

"Finney, your client should take the plea or he's fucked," said Assistant Prosecutor Fred Timmer, in a loud voice. The deputy took my arm and tugged, the interview room door fell shut.

Timmer, a head taller than Pete Finney, never saw it coming. Pete seized him by the lapels and shoved. Timmer thumped onto the wall and slid down onto his fanny, exposing red and green plaid socks above his brown tasseled loafers. Papers exploded from his cardboard index file in a flurry of legal snow.

The deputies turned from me and seized Finney by the arms.

"Why don't you try thumb screws," said Finney, his face red and eyebrows welded together. "It's not enough you've had the man beaten senseless?"

Timmer looked up from his seat on the floor, his mouth working on the syllables of non words until he arrived at, "Ass, ass, ass . . . assault? And battery!"

"Bloody inquisition!" said Finney. "I'll have your bar card shellacked to my dust bin!"

Timmer's face remained stunned. "I could have you arrested!"

"What is it for me?" said Finney. "The rack?"

"We had nothing to do with what happened to Lambert."

"You're using the circumstances to your advantage."

"We have no control over how your client is lodged," said Timmer, gathering the papers from his lap and the floor.

"You remain an officer of the court," said Finney. "Turning a blind eye is no less culpable. Mr. Lambert tells me he is passing blood."

"He has been examined," said Timmer, stuffing papers into his cardboard file.

The deputies let go of Finney and he straightened his suit. "I should like to have him seen again."

Timmer climbed to his feet. "That's up to the sheriff. I'm prepared to overlook this accidental collision. But Hardin is wanted on an open warrant."

"Mr. Hardin had no open warrants," said Finney. "I checked before asking him to work on the case."

"He'll have one shortly," said Timmer. "I just signed the charges, possession of child pornography."

I shook my head. "Talk to Matty Svenson."

"The charges are written under state statutes," said Timmer.

"Oh, I wasn't talking to you," I said.

• • •

They spent forty-five minutes wadding my suit into a paper sack and deciding whether the metal brace on my nose was a weapon. They issued me a set of jail scrubs, but refused to return my cane and opted to have a trustee push me about in a wheelchair.

The guard called him Manny. His dark auburn hair stood out from his head in all directions. A scar raced down his forehead, divided his left eyebrow, and leapt past his eye to his cheek where it skidded to a stop just short of a threadbare moustache. At five feet ten he probably weighed a spare one-thirty. He said I should call him Flaco.

"What's the 'Manny' stand for?"

"Manuel, as in Manuel Austin," he said. "You got any smokes, man?"

"We got the same tailor," I said. "No pockets."

He pushed me down the hall, past a stairwell, toward a large maple veneer door attended by a uniformed guard and a sign made from a file folder. The sign—hand lettered in black felt tip marker—read, "Arraignments."

"Guess it don't matter," he said. "They said you was going to the jail ward at county general. You don't got to buy a bed."

"Austin?" I said. "You from Texas? What?"

"Baja, man. Lots of Anglo names there. Even some blue-eyed-blond chiquitas. You be right at home, eh?"

"No habla," I said.

"No sweat, man. Everybody speaks money."

A guard twisted a key into the door and pulled it open.

"You get in there, don't be making no noise," said Flaco. "Piss off the judge and your bail go up."

The room, darkly paneled and brightly lit, featured a wooden table, a straight-backed chair, and a video camera on a tripod aimed at the chair. A small microphone had been duct-taped to a soft drink can on the table. Against the wall a television was stationed on a cart.

Half a dozen men in green jail scrubs, belly chained together in a file, lined the back wall of the eighteen-by-twenty room. One guard briefed us. "When your case is called, sit in the chair, look at the camera, and speak in a normal voice." The other turned on the television.

The picture rolled. Judge Mathews, Judge Mathews, Judge Mathews, I knew him from American Society for Industrial Security meetings, where he'd revealed that he wore Bermuda shorts and an Aloha shirt under his robes.

"It'll stop when it warms up," said the guard.

I sat through a drunk driver, a dropsy case—man dropped drugs on the ground as he was approached by a police officer—and a grand theft auto. The picture was still rolling when they called my case: possession of child pornography for distribution. I could feel a half ton of eyes on my back as Flaco pushed me up to the table.

"Approach," said the voice of Pete Finney.

Unseen, Fred Timmer said, "The rights of the people of the State of Michigan cannot be vindicated in the Federal venue."

"William Meredith, United States Attorney's Office," said a voice.

"This is highly irregular," said Judge Mathews, Mathews, Mathews.

"We can save the Court a good deal of time, Your Honor," said Finney.

"I object," said Timmer.

"I'm prepared to file a brief," said Meredith. "But given the sensitive nature of the ongoing investigation we would ask the court for some leeway, Your Honor."

Mathews lowered his chin, spread his arms like Christ on the cross, and said, "Approach." Covering the microphone with his hand he closed his eyes and slowly nodded his head to his right, spoke to his left, and then shooed the lawyers from the bench like flies from a picnic lunch.

"Mr. Timmer," said Judge Mathews.

"Based on the evidence at hand," said Timmer.

"Starts with a 'W,' Mr. Timmer," said Mathews.

"I see no reason to withdraw the charges," said Timmer.

"Adjourned," said Judge Mathews. He struck his gavel.

"Your honor, my client is in custody," said Finney.

"Release the accused, Mr. Timmer," said the judge.

"Your Honor," said Timmer, "if we can just reconvene and take a plea, I would be glad to discuss bail."

Judge Mathews turned his head to the right and said, "Long date."

Off screen a lady's voice said, "Yes, Your Honor."

Timmer said, "Your Honor—"

Judge Mathews gaveled. "Contempt. Let's explore the idea, Mr. Timmer. What was it you were going to say?"

"Mr. Hardin will be released immediately," said Timmer.

Judge Mathews struck again. "Fifty dollars. See the clerk. Next case, please."

Hoots and stomps filled the room. The question came in a chorus. "Who's your attorney?"

"Pete Finney. He's in the book," I told them as Flaco wheeled me away from the table. The door opened and the guard from outside the door stepped into the room, his face a question mark as he looked around the room and then at Flaco.

"This man been released, man—no shit," said Flaco. "I got to take him to the desk." The guard nodded and Flaco rolled me out the door.

The door closed and we were alone in the hallway, an administrative section of the jail. "Dude, you are too cool," said Flaco. I lurched back in the chair as Flaco broke into a dead run. "This is a shame—no shit, man—but the Chingos got to say hello."

A foot short of the stairway he let go of the chair. "Ola, motherfucker."

I caught the hand rail and swung out of the chair as it bucked down the first step. The chair crashed down the stairs. Flaco backed up and looked up and down the hall. No one. He shrugged and took a sharpened tooth brush with a duct-tape handle out of his shoe.

"Think about it, Manny," I said. I extended my left hand palm down. "Think about why my hand is so steady."

"Maybe because you are stupid," he said, curling his lip.

I stepped out of my one shoe and put it on my left hand. Pulling my shirt over my head, I wrapped it around my left arm and wrist. "Think something else," I said.

"I think somebody already kicked your ass, and all that beef don't scare me."

"Yeah? Keep thinking. I'll be right with you." I started up the steps.

"I think you walk real good for a man I got to push around in a wheel-chair," he said. "And I think I already done what I was told." He backed away several steps and then ran.

"Good thinking, Flaco."

●　●　●

The barred gate closed behind me. The gray metal door in front of me slid to the right and revealed Matty Svenson waiting with her arms folded over a denim jacket that mostly covered a black turtle neck sweater. She wore gray slacks and had rolled the sleeves of the jacket up to her forearms.

"Slumming?"

"Trying to fit in," she said. "How am I doing?"

"Great. Nobody'll notice you."

"So the guys that just left weren't hitting on me?"

I walked over to the window. The guard—unseen through a one-way window—pushed a form out the window for me to sign.

"They offer you a can of Spam and a box of crackers?" I signed the form and it snapped back in the window like a frog's tongue.

"Mentioned a pizza and a six pack," she said.

"Must be rutting season." An envelope with my tie and belt came out. They'd issued me yet another check for the sheriff's check they confiscated.

We threaded our way through a maze of people with sullen faces seated on the wooden benches to the hallway and out the revolving door into the sun and a sweet breeze. Matty produced a pair of sunglasses and a set of car keys.

"The blue one," she said.

"Four door sedan, black walls, and a spotlight," I said. "We got 'em fooled now."

"This belongs to a friend of yours."

"Yeah, Uncle Sam."

"J. William Cameran," she said. "He's currently sitting in the fifth floor lock-up at the federal building and sweating out the answers to some very hard questions."

I climbed into the shotgun seat. A passing white pick up tooted as it passed and Matty waved.

"They with you?"

"They wish," said Matty. She pulled her door shut and twisted the keys into the ignition.

"What are we doing in the J. Billster's ride?"

"I'm searching it."

"Got any cigarettes?"

"J. William doesn't allow smoking in his vehicle." Matty produced an unopened pack of smokes from the pocket of her denim jacket. "Pall Malls all right?" She dropped them onto the seat between us.

I hammered the silver end of the pack on the dash. "There's a chalky undertaste to the mousse here," I said. "I'm up to my armpits in Bureau people. Former agents, informants, and whatever your Mr. El Guitmo was—he wasn't a stranger."

"Paranoia, Art. You read too many paperback novels."

"I go to the post office all the time," I said, and zipped open the cellophane wrapper. "I'm so paranoid I actually look at the posters. A guy who looked like Fidel Castro kind of sticks in your mind." I peeled open the silver foil corner of the pack and shook out a smoke. "I don't think he'd have much shelf-life on the street. And 'El Guitmo?'" I lit up and savored the sweet smoke. "Give me a break."

"Spur of the moment," said Matty. "I thought it was pretty good."

"You didn't need me to quiz him. What were you doing, waiting for him to tidy up?"

Matty turned north out of the lot and drove in silence with her cheek twitching over a tight jaw and her knuckles white on the wheel. At Michigan Avenue she turned right and said, "I told you I wasn't listening to the audio."

"Right."

Matty snapped on the radio and got a pig-and-whistle band, drumming and drilling at *After the Morning*. "I was in the weeds," she said. "I had to relieve myself. Your wife was going in and out. The van belonged to the janitor—we ran the plate. I can't just hang it out the door like the guys."

"They hang it out the door? That's disgusting."

Matty turned south onto the Beltline. "You know what I mean. When I got back to the van your window exploded."

"Sorry you missed it," I said, and pulled open the ashtray—it was full of parking change. I flicked my ash into the coins. "He ratted you out."

"I can't tell you anything," she said.

"Your 'El Guitmo' was under so long he went native?" I shook out a cigarette and offered it.

"We thought he was dead," said Matty. She punched in the dash lighter and took the smoke. "Ebola in West Africa. We didn't ask for the body."

I said, "You thought he was reincarnated?"

"He used someone else's contact code."

"He played you?"

"He played Cameran," she said.

"So now you're covering for Cameran."

"I'm a Special Agent, not a prosecutor. Cameran's an asshole." The lighter popped up. "On his best case—the only one that went to jail was his informant. When he retired, he opened Intelligence Research Associates and tried to run it from his desk at the Bureau." She pulled the lighter out of the dash and lit her smoke. "We had to load his crap in a box and change the door code."

"So they are going to cover for him?"

"Probably," she exhaled in a cloud, "if he can give us the rest of the crew. We can't really ask you to continue."

"What do I do? Post a want-ad: 'Art Hardin, All-ey, all-ey in free.'"

"If you think you can still contribute," she said, and looked at me, adding a smile with a flutter of eyelashes, "I won't need to ask you to return your orders." She turned into my office parking lot and stopped in front of the steps.

I stepped out and took my cane off the floor in the back seat. "I was looking forward to the check."

"Don't hold your breath."

"Keep these?" I said and showed her the red pack of cigarettes.

She snatched them out of my hand. "Not on your life," she said.

• • •

I found Detective Archer A. Flynt with his backside parked in my wingback chair. He didn't stand up when I walked into my office, and I had to step over his feet to get around the desk to my chair.

"Let's dispense with the pleasantries," he said, leaning forward and resting his elbows on the knees of his gray wool suit.

"Okay," I said, and leaned my cane on the edge of my desk. "Just hang my license back on the wall and get the hell out of here." I plopped into my chair. "How's that?"

"Won't get it," he said, raising his eyebrows and wrinkling the forehead under his gray flattop haircut. "I was in the courthouse this morning. I want the names of the people you paid off and how much you paid them."

"Nobody and not a dime. Anything else?"

"Did you ever give money to Detective Gerald Van Huis?"

"He came over to take a vandalism report. I gave him a soda."

"Five dollars?"

"No."

"Five hundred dollars?"

"Nope."

"Five thousand dollars?"

I shook my head.

"You're lying," he said and sat back in the chair.

"You're insane."

Flynt reached into the breast pocket of his jacket, produced an evidence bag containing a book of raffle tickets, and flopped it onto my desk, then stared at me over fists folded in front of his face.

"They pay you for this?" I said. "You get a paycheck every week?" I laughed.

"You lied. I can prove it." He sat straight in his chair. "It's all I need."

"I like you, Flynt. You've got style. You're a fucking idiot, but you got loads of style."

"I've got your license," he said and stashed the evidence bag in his pocket.

"You don't have my license. You've got a piece of paper."

"I want your pocket ID."

"Can't have it," I said.

"You have to surrender it."

"Bring someone from the licensing bureau and I'll give it to them."

"They report to us."

"I report to them," I said.

"Put it in the envelope I left and I'll mail it."

"Pete Finney. That's my attorney. Go see him—and for God's sake, don't leave out the raffle tickets."

Flynt rocketed to his feet. Looming over my desk, he lifted his side of my desk off the floor. "No Goddam pervert is walking around with a detective's ID in his pocket," he said, teeth bared and sinews standing out from his neck.

"You're absolutely right," I said.

Flynt's face fell blank and his mouth dropped open. That's when the plywood came off my window and someone outside yelled, "Hey, Hardin, I got a present for you."

A **FAT AND FIFTYISH LEPRECHAUN** in a lime-green "Monkey Wards'" polyester suit leaned over and stuck his head in the window. What remained of his hair resembled cotton batten glued behind his ears. He said, "Ahh, my name is Billy Clements."

I heard the boot impact Billy's backside. He let out a scream and thrust his hands out like Superman. Detective Flynt released the edge of my desk and caught Billy. The impact backed Flynt up a couple of steps, but he kept his feet. Billy clutched Flynt—one arm over Flynt's shoulder, the other around his midsection—until he found his feet.

"Detective Archer A. Flynt, State Attorney General's Office," I said and waited for Flynt's startled eyes to meet mine, "this is Billy Clements, Sales Manager, Prestige Import Automobiles."

"I . . . I don't work at Prestige Imports anymore," said Billy as Flynt pushed him away. "Strictly Station Wagons, Inc." on Alpine just before Ann Street. Billy flicked out a business card like a switchblade. "Drives like a car instead of a truck."

Flynt stared at the card and then at me. Billy sheathed his business card.

Ken Ayers, decked out in full scooter trash, sat in the window dangling his feet over my credenza. "Oh, shit" was written on his face, but he made a single wave of his hand and said, "Hi."

Flynt scowled at me and said, "What?"

I rocked my chair back. "Poker," I said. "You want to sit in?"

Flynt focused narrow eyes on Ken and then me. "They came in the window?"

"Army buddies," I said. "Sometimes a little too playful." I fished a deck of cards out of my top desk drawer and tossed it on my blotter. "Nickel, dime, quarter. Low card in the hole is wild. What do you say? Want to sit in?"

"I want your pocket ID," said Flynt.

"I'm not going to give it to you. You don't have the authority to ask for it."

"We'll keep it unofficial," said Flynt. "Maybe you can get it back later."

"Leave the license you took off the wall."

"I'll see you in court."

"I'll see you personally hang the license back where you found it. In the meantime, you're on private property. Good afternoon, Detective."

"Suit yourself," said Flynt. "You should cooperate. Things could work out."

Whatever was on my face, I don't know. Flynt shook his head and left.

"So go ahead," said Ken Ayers, sliding off the window sill to step onto the credenza.

Looking sheepish, Billy backed a step toward the door. "I did it," he said. "I'm sorry. I broke your windshield. Twice."

With a hand on the sill, Ken stepped off the credenza. "I thought you were nuts until I heard that part about the hydraulic leak. Tracy was steady bitching about that leak. It's the power steering pump. I've replaced the line twice. Damn thing still leaks. Howard Butler made good old Billy here buy my old lady's Jag or go to jail. With that and the money from the bank, she squared up with the dealership." He batted the dust off his black leather vest with both hands.

"I want to pay for the damage," said Billy. He took an envelope from his jacket and stepped just close enough to drop it on the desk with a shaking hand.

"It's ah . . . it's ah, three hundred dollars," said Billy. "It's ah, all I got—my four-oh-one-kay and the market the way it is, you know—Butler wanted cash."

I picked up the envelope and dropped it in my drawer with the deck of cards. "The car's still in the impound," I said. "I'll have it towed down to the shop. All you have to cover is my deductible and the tow. I'll send you a copy of the bill."

Ken said, "I'm sure a slick, sophisticated gentleman like Billy here would be glad to let you drive his car while yours is in the shop."

"Sure," said Billy, his face draining as he reached into his pants pocket. He jingled loose a small ring with two keys and set them on the desk. "There's a spare set in a magnetic box in the bumper."

"Great," I said. "Which one is it?"

They both looked at me, incredulous, and said in unison, "The white Jaguar."

"Cool," I said, and felt a smile bump up against the nose brace.

"I just need a ride," said Billy.

Ken put his hand to his forehead, closed his eyes, and said, "I'm starting to get a picture of you wagging your wrinkled weenie at my wife."

Billy fled.

Ken laughed and shook his head as Billy tore open the door, banged a shoulder on the door jam, and spun into the hall. "You were square with my wife," said Ken. He leaned on my desk. "Now we're even. I ought to kick your ass just for GP's, but it looks like somebody took care of that."

"You read the newspaper?"

"Nah, I got shit to do. Just tell me where I can find the dude and I'll go shake his hand."

"In the fridge, down at the county morgue."

Ken stood straight. "Oh," he said. He sat in the wingback chair. "Your old lady whack him out?" He crossed his ankles and stretched out his legs. "Trade you even up—sight unseen."

"State secret," I said. I opened the file drawer in my desk, scooped the folders to the front, and nested my telephone in the back of the drawer. "Maybe we can do some business."

Ken clasped his hands behind his head and leaned back in the chair. "Hardin, you're a trip," he said.

I pushed the drawer shut. "Tell me about the Chingos."

"Punks," he said. He laughed. "Tracy's still pissed. I wouldn't drop by for dinner anytime soon."

"And the Chingos?"

"Grifters mostly. How's this come out to be business for me?"

"Think of yourself as a consultant."

Ken folded his arms—a practiced move that made his biceps bulge—his drooping moustache making a comic frown of a serious face. "What's it pay?"

"What it's worth," I said. "So far the Chingos are punks and grifters. I can get that from the newspaper."

"Guy named 'Loo-wheess' is the president." Ken tilted his head to the right, "I don't know his last name. Street name is 'Poco Loco' because he is a crazy weasel-ass little fuck. Likes to say the Chingos are Mexican Mafia, but I think that's bullshit."

"Why?"

"Chingos are too fat. Mexican Mafia is hungry. They'd eat through these guys like mice in the cupboard; leave 'em laying in the gutter in their skivvies."

"How did they get fat?"

Grifters—like I said—con games, everything from 'I found a wallet in the street' to telemarketing charity scams. They run crooked dice and card games, whores, and protection in the Mexican stores down on Grandville. If you're a wetback you see the Chingos for green cards, driver's licenses, and social security cards. They even got legit businesses. A couple of tanning parlors to launder money, some palm reading joints, and Luis owns the Rabbit on Wealthy Street."

"The college hangout?"

"Was. Now it's a titty bar. How am I doing?"

"Couple yards," I said.

Marg knocked and leaned around the doorframe wearing a blouse best described as a mauve silk T-shirt. "Hate to interrupt all this male bonding," she said, "but I have an appointment with the cable company. If you're leaving through the window I'll lock the door."

"This is hardly worth my time," said Ken. "You can lock the door after me."

I sorted two fresh Franklins from the envelope Billy Clements had surrendered and pushed them across the desk.

"Jesus Christ," said Ken, "I'm paying myself."

"I can have Marg cut you a check."

Ken snatched the bills. "I do my business cash," he said.

He walked out.

Marg shut off the light in the front office. I heard her lock the door. Just as well—without my monitor I couldn't see who walked in. Ken was at the window pushing the plywood back in place and bitching.

"Hardin, I could have traded murder one down to drunk and disorderly with that," he said.

I leaned back in my chair and folded my hands in my lap. "Still can," I told him. "It ain't like the prosecutor has been my best bud lately."

Ken moved the wood aside and bent down to look me in the face. "So what the hell are you doing?"

"Background stuff," I said. "I have a client up to his ass in Chingo alligators and I need to drain the swamp."

"That Lambert guy?"

"Thought you didn't read the newspaper."

"It was on the tube."

"He's taking a cruise of the SS Kent County. The Chingos want big money not to kick his ass, again."

"That's their kind of gig."

"I don't like their kind of music," I said. "You can't buy any singles. I think all they're selling is albums."

"Maybe you need a different disc jockey."

"Maybe a couple."

Ken moved the lumber aside and sat in the windowsill. "Tell me about it," he said.

My telephone started ringing, muffled in the desk drawer. "I need a couple of guys to play lullabies. Every night Lambert gets a good night's sleep, the job pays a grand."

"Each," said Ken. "In cash."

"Done," I said.

"Won't work," said Ken, shaking his head.

"You said the Chingos were punks." My telephone kept crying about being stuffed in the drawer.

"We can handle the music for the cruise, but the natives in the village'll get to beating their drums and doing a fucking war dance. Could get ugly all over the island unless you parley with the chief and get his mind right."

The answering machine took the call, Wendy's voice said, "Pick up if you're there."

"I'll get his mind right," I said.

"I want to be there," said Ken. "This I got to see."

"Suit yourself," I said. "When can you line up the DJ's?"

"Call me," said Wendy. She hung up.

"I'll call ya," said Ken.

"Not on this phone."

Ken slid his fanny back and squatted outside the window. "You got my number," he said, "use a payphone." My telephone started to jingle and vibrate in my drawer again. Ken lined up the plywood with the window opening and wedged it into the bottom rail. Over the top of the wood he said, "Cash—no bullshit, man."

"Bullshit and no cash," I said.

Ken banged the panel into place.

The telephone rang as I took it out of the drawer and set it on the desk. I figured it was the FBI testing the line but when the answering machine picked up I heard Hank Dunphy's voice.

". . . Light and Energy Applications. I'll keep this brief. There's no need to return the call. We've had to forfeit Mr. Lambert's considerable bail. As a result we will not be able to pay your invoices. Mr. Lambert was under considerable duress when he offered you employment with this firm, and considering the fact that his current situation takes him out of the corporate loop, I am afraid that it is left to me to inform you that you will not be employed by Light and Energy in any capacity. Under no circumstances will the Board of Directors agree to submit corporate assets to the extortionate demands of criminals. Should you require any clarification on these matters, please contact our attorneys at Traxmire, Tulley, and—"

I snapped up the telephone, "Dunphy? Are you fucking nuts?"

"Mr. Hardin?"

"F and A howdy, you dumb bastard! You think I don't know you're in this up to your armpits?"

"Whatever do you mean?"

"I mean it's time to come to Jesus. You call Pete Finney, you tell him everything. Then you call the FBI and beg them to hide you."

"Is that a threat, Mr. Hardin?"

"That's the best advice you're going to get today. As of just now, when you left the message, you exhausted your usefulness to the cartel and that raggedy-assed battery outfit you've been shilling for."

"That's absurd."

"Nobody left you a message for Scott to meet with Anne Frampton. Why were the detectives waiting at the airport for Scott to show up with your ticket and passport?"

"The former is ridiculous and the latter is a question you need to ask Mr. Lambert."

"The former is a fact. You made my airline reservations. You're the only one who could have sicked the Fidel Castro-looking dude on me. He missed me. But I didn't miss him. And before we had to sweep up his brains he told me what was on his mind. Including your involvement in the plan to murder the Frampton woman."

"I'm not going to listen to any—"

"For God's sake, Dunphy, you're burned, you're busted, and you're expendable! Get your toothbrush, go down to the federal building, and pound on the FBI's door until they let you in."

The receiver crashed in my ear. I clicked the telephone until I got a dial tone and pecked out a number I knew all to well. Pete Finney was in his office, and his secretary was no longer blocking my calls. I told him about the call from Dunphy and wrapped up the story with, "I think we just crashed and burned."

"Arthur, you really must let me do the talking," Pete said. "Talk to me, and I will talk to them."

"He was just leaving a message."

"Mr. Dunphy left the door open. He may not have meant to, but he invited you to contact his counsel."

"Traxmire, Tully, and somebody. I cut him off."

"I talk to them every day," Pete said. "Hugh Traxmire and I are golf partners."

"So you knew this was coming?"

"Not a word. I am surprised. Nonetheless, Mr. Lambert remains the majority stock holder, and the patents are in his name. There really is no question as to his authority, but his current situation does make it difficult for him to act."

"What if Lambert is dead or permanently unconscious?"

"He was sent to the hospital to be examined after the fiasco at the jail."

"I'm not sure that's going to make a big difference. The Chingos made a run at me in a hallway in the admin section of the jail."

"This is where I defer to you, Arthur," said Pete.

• • •

I twisted the steel peg key into the driver's door—no key hole in the passenger door—and the convertible top popped loose from the windshield and the windows started down. I jumped back.

Two ladies sat watching me from the front seat of a pale blue minivan. At the back of the lot a Chevy Blazer with darkly tinted windows started up. The sky threatened in shades of steel gray and a moist edge softened the breeze. I twisted the key again and watched the top disappear into the "boot."

I climbed into the white Jag and fired it up. The ladies waved and laughed. I waved back even though I had no idea who they were. When I turned north on Breton, sprinkles were on the windshield, I couldn't find the wipers, and the black Blazer was still with me.

I took Breton to Lake Drive, pushing the speed limit in the hope that I was driving out of a squall. At Wealthy I turned left onto the red brick pavers where the Jag was invisible behind up-turned noses and raised pinkie fingers. The Blazer turned into the Onion Crock restaurant, prob-ably for some of their fantastic onion soup that comes topped with melt-ed cheese that runs down the sides of the bowl. Two blocks east the pavers gave way to blacktop.

The Rabbit, a two-story white stucco cube with parking at the side and rear, toed the sidewalk on the north side of the street. A hard-rocking Prince number rattled the inward sloping front windows, which had been *de rigueur* for the building's first incarnation as a neighborhood market. Gang signs had been keyed into the flat black paint that now covered the windows. The double front doors each displayed a sign. The one in English read, "Entrance at side door."

Just half past three, and the lot brimmed with a democratic mix of Beamers and battered pick-up trucks. I pulled up to the "Valet Parking" sign and an olive-skinned young man with a black pompadour, ruffled white shirt, and tuxedo trousers with a cummerbund ran to open the dri-ver's door, holding an umbrella over both of us. I gave him the keys.

"No," he said, "you just give me the green key. That's the valet key."

"What's the difference?"

"The green key doesn't open the trunk, sir."

"Cool," I said. "You know how to put the top up?"

He smiled. "Sure," he said.

"Good, do that." I peeled off the green key and reached into my pocket.

"That's okay, sir," he said. He took the key and gave me a poker chip with a number on it. "Maybe you want to take care of me when I bring the car back."

"Car belongs to an acquaintance," I said. I gave him one of Billy's steel engraved portraits of Grant. "Don't park it in the neighborhood."

"Count on me," he said. He smiled as he took the fifty. "I'll wipe the seats."

I took my cane off the back seat—the package shelf was upholstered to look like a seat, just no room for legs—and made a show of leaning on it as I made my way through the door.

A cocktail of stale beer and cigarette smoke hung in the air. "Ten dollars," said the doorman—five feet ten and about fifteen stone as the Brits would have it. He was liveried pretty much the same as the valet driver, except that he wore a satin bow tie to match his cummerbund and the sleeves of his shirt had been removed at the shoulder. The veins of his biceps and forearms stood out like forking road maps to the iron pile where he'd built the massive arms that sleeves could no longer contain.

Tattooed hash marks marched down his neck into his shirt collar. The thin skin of his arms was mostly blue with jailhouse graffiti including an ornate "Chingo" under a death's head with a dagger on his right bicep. He racked a six-cell flashlight under his left arm and thrust out his right hand. "I got change," he said. In his left hand he held a wad of bills as thick as the Detroit Yellow pages.

"I didn't come to see the girls," I said. "I have business with Luis."

"Ten dollars," he said. "I don't know no Luis."

"Poco Loco," I said. His eyes snapped to my face. "You know who I mean. This is business."

"How you hear that name?"

"Flaco. At the jail. He had a message."

The doorman laughed. "He the one that kicked your ass?"

"You got to be kidding. He ran away—showed me so much of the bottom of his shoes I thought he was kneeling and praying."

The doorman nodded a disgusted face. "Boss is busy. He don't want to talk to you."

"How do you know?" I said. "You didn't ask him."

"The boss is busy, he don't want to talk to nobody."

"How do you know he's busy?"

"When he ain't busy he'll come downstairs."

"Fine," I said, "I'll have a beer and wait."

"Ten bucks."

I felt my face curl up a smile—a little pressure on the nose brace, but it didn't hurt anymore. I gave him Billy's last half yard. He made a show of counting out four tens in change which he offered to me folded in half and tucked between his first two fingers. I held them in front of his face and fanned out three tens.

He smiled and shrugged. "Maybe you dropped it on the floor."

"Turn your hand over," I said. "I think you'll find it under your thumb."

He turned his hand, the bill lay tucked into his palm with his thumb. "A little joke," he said. He handed me the bill.

A woman with pencil-sharp silicone breasts and a sequinned G-string writhed out a hip-hop number against a brass pole mounted on a mirrored stage. Dancers in nylon panties danced on tables and dry humped the laps of seated customers.

Leading with my cane, I sidestepped though the maze of tables and made my way to the bar. The bartender looked at me and nodded while he loaded a tray with long necks. I picked up a matchbook from an ashtray on the bar. The cover featured a rabbit in a tuxedo and top hat with a cane. On the inside a question lurked behind the matches, "PRIVATE PARTY?" There was a telephone number.

Shafts of red light, reflected from a disco ball, cut through a foot-thick tide of cigarette smoke that washed the ceiling. I ordered a Corona with a wedge of lime and got four singles in change for the doorman's ten spot. The house was packed. Too many to count. I set out in a slow search for a door that led to a stairwell.

A lap dancer screamed, slapped a customer, and climbed off his lap. Backing up she yelled, "Rudy!" Pointing an accusing finger on the end of an extended arm, she added, "The bastard stole my tips."

The customer stood up. Dressed in a flannel shirt and jeans, he wore a backwoods-bush beard over a weathered face. He was six feet tall and well over two hundred pounds. He said, "I caught the bitch trying to lift my wallet!"

The doorman with the arms turned out to be Rudy. He said, "Time to go, man."

The customer picked a looping right fist off the table and laid it on the side of Rudy's head.

Rudy let his head ride out the punch. He smiled. "Big mistake, man." Rudy drove the butt of his flashlight into the big man's solar plexus.

The customer bent forward, clutching his middle with both arms. Rudy spun him toward the door and planted his foot in the big man's backside. The crowd applauded. I found the stairway through a curtain at the far end of the bar.

AT THE TOP OF THE STAIRS I found a curtain in place of a door. The office amounted to a raveled rug, a battered desk, and a stanchion fan in the corner of a stockroom. I told Luis, Poco Loco, "Your guys are punks!"

He sat rocking in his chair, hands limp on the desktop—humming or groaning—wearing photo gray glasses. Maybe in his late twenties, he had a full head of curly black hair and a pencil moustache like a tango dancer. I couldn't tell if his eyes were open. If he'd noticed me he didn't let on.

The sweet smell of cut burley hung in the air. Cases of cigarettes stood, stacked in long dark rows, among truck-load quantities of computers, projection televisions, and video game players still in shipping cartons. The wooden floor vibrated with the hard rock beat from downstairs.

The quantity of goods wasn't as amazing as the fact that it had all come up a steep narrow stairwell and would have to go down the same way. I entertained the notion of the floor giving way to the music and the customers finding themselves under a piñata cascade of swag.

Luis's attire needed a passport to get to the dry-cleaner. His suit—the jacket hung from the back of his chair—was custom cut from black pinstriped wool and Italian silk. French cuffs finished his tailored white linen shirt. A dragon, hand painted in gold, stood rampant on his red silk tie. His wristwatch and jewelry were worth more than his thugs had demanded from my client. Maybe the attraction of extortion was simply the fact that you didn't have to haul it up and down the stairs.

I rapped my cane on Luis's vacant desktop and yelled, "Aye!"

The receiver jumped off his telephone and clattered onto the desk. A woman let out a muffled yip under the desk. Luis bolted straight in his chair and snapped his head toward me. "The fuck?" he said. He put his hands under the desk and pushed.

I said, "You know where the restroom is?"

Luis didn't get his nickname from diminutive size. He was as wide as I was and probably as tall, if he stood up—which I didn't think he'd do just now.

He said, "Get the fuck outta here."

I set my beer on his desk, the wedge of lime still sticking out the top. "That's no way to talk to a paying customer who's just looking for the pisser."

Luis picked up the telephone handset and stabbed the disconnect twice with his finger. He studied me with a mean face until his eyes went wide and he pushed the chair back to look under the desk. "Just a minute," he said, and then into the telephone, "No, not you. Send Rudy up here." Luis banged the phone down and looked at me. "Guy's coming," he said.

I let it pass.

"He'll get you what you need," he said.

"Rudy?" I heard hurried heavy footsteps on the stairs.

"Yeah."

"Met him downstairs," I said. "He's a good guy?"

"The best. You think you're fucked up now? Give it a minute."

I stacked my hands on top of my cane. Rudy slashed the curtain aside with his flashlight and filled the doorway. "Rudy, my man," I said, "I was just telling your boss about the fast count you tried to give at the door."

Rudy made a sheepish smile, looked at Luis, and shrugged.

Luis said, "Get him. The fuck. Out of here."

Rudy smiled and let his head tilt to one side. "I tole ya he was busy, man."

"And break something he walks on," said Luis. "That should keep him off the stairs."

Rudy stepped toward me with his left foot, his flashlight cocked in both hands like a long ball hitter stepping into a three-and-two count heater. I drove the tip of the cane into the toes of his left foot hard enough to make the floor thump like I'd dropped an anvil. His face blanched stark white as he piled onto the floor and abandoned the flashlight in favor of his foot.

The woman under the desk screamed and the desk bumped up. My beer went airborne. I caught it with my left hand and set it back on the desk.

Luis's hands pushed under the desk. "Just fucking stay there," he said. "You don't want to see nothing out here." He leaned to his right. I heard a desk drawer sliding open.

Rudy roared like a bear and started off the floor. I flipped the cane, curved end down, and laid a nine-iron drive on Rudy's right knee. I heard a wooden snap. Rudy crashed onto the floor, held his knee, and screamed. The end of the cane skittered across the floor, leaving a splintered point which I turned and hooked under the knot in Luis's tie.

"Better be a taco," I told Luis. He showed me his open palms. "The whole drawer," I said. "Set it on top of the desk." He did. It wasn't a taco. It was a chrome Astra .25 engraved with scrolls and filigree, nestled in about three inches of twenties, fifties, and hundreds.

Rudy grabbed my ankle. I whacked his patty. Luis reached for the Astra and I smashed the drawer on the back stroke. Luis snatched his hand back as the drawer exploded in a flurry of currency.

The woman under the desk yelled, "Hey, what's going on?"

Luis told the woman to shut up while he made an astonished face and counted his fingers.

"I gotta do my set," she said.

"You're with me. Somebody will fill in," said Luis.

"They'll get my tips."

Luis handed some bills under the desk. He looked up. His face red, but voice calm, he said, "Who the fuck are you?"

I sorted the Astra out of the wreckage of the drawer with the splintered end of the cane and covered it with my business card. Luis reached—slow and ginger—took the card with two fingers and rocked back in his chair.

"Arthur Hardin," he said. "Peter A. Ladin Investigative Associates." He smiled. "You don't mind if I keep this?"

"No," I said. "You might want to give me a call—maybe come and pay me a visit."

A woman's hand crept from under the desk to gather currency within reach. I nudged bills closer with my foot.

Luis mugged his face with his hand. "What the fuck do you want?"

"You offered to do some business. I came to talk about it."

He shook his head and shrugged.

"Scott Lambert," I said. "He's in the county jail. Your guys beat the shit out of him—said he had to front the Chingos twenty grand or they'd make it a double header."

"I don't know what you're talking about. Who are these—what you say—Chingos?"

"That's what I wanted to know," I said. "So I asked around. On the street. And everybody says the Chingos are punks."

"I don't know from Chingos," said Luis, his knuckles white, hands gripping the arms of his chair.

"Take Rudy, for instance," I said. "Got Chingo written all over him and lying in a pile here. I mean, things don't look good. I don't know if the Chingos got the horsepower to deliver or not. You see what I'm saying?"

"Well, they tuned up the guy you told me about." Luis made a sympathetic face. "Maybe," he said, and waved a beggar's open palm at me. "And this is just advice, one businessman to another. Maybe, you should pay these guys. He shrugged, "Y'know. Whoever they are."

"No, they tune him up again, the Chingos don't get paid."

"Maybe this guy you told me about don't like that arrangement."

"Don't matter. He gets any more lumps, he's taking a plea. The goose with the golden eggs is doing twenty-five to life and ain't got cigarette change, much less twenty grand a week."

Luis slipped off his glasses and bit on the end of one of the legs. He made narrow eyes and then chopped the leg at me. "I guess you know if he has a deal tomorrow. I don't know these guys, but I think they're looking to get paid if they deliver."

"Tomorrow, if we got a deal," I said. He should have chided me not to miss a payment. He didn't.

He slipped the glasses back on, and said, "Now I got a question."

"Sure."

"How did you think you'd get out of here?"

I picked up the Astra. Rudy made a shaky attempt to rise and I broke what was left of my cane across the top of his head and told him, "Goodnight, Rudy."

"Punks or not," said Luis, "that ain't going to get you out of here."

I popped the magazine out of the Astra, thumbed a .25 caliber rimfire out on the desk, and hauled the Detonics off my hip. Dropping the tiny round down the .45 caliber barrel of my Detonics, I held the pistol next to my ear and rattled it.

"Right you are," I said. "Too small for a big job." I whipped the muzzle at Luis. The .25 caliber bullet bopped him on the forehead and fell into his lap.

"I got two plans," I said. Plan Number One is I shove this hog leg up your ass and high-step you down the stairwell while you tell everybody everything is cool. Or—Plan Number Two—you finish your business with your lady friend and I swill my beer while I walk out of here." I drew a bead on his nose, thumbed the hammer, and asked, "How about it, Luis? You a little crazy or a lot stupid?"

Luis nodded, and made the evil eyes of a patient man. He looked under the desk and said, "C'mon honey, you got a lot of money to earn."

• • •

Billy had a car phone. I called Wendy collect. "Got a ride, Hon," I said. "You don't have to pick me up."

"I called," said Wendy.

"I know."

"You know? Why didn't you pick up the phone?"

"I was in the middle of something."

"Something more important than me?"

"Nothing is more important than you," I said. "The telephone was in the drawer, and I had scooter thug sitting in my window."

"Flowers," she said, "or you don't get to see the tape."

"Talk to me."

"Dunphy met with two guys. I didn't recognize either one. One of them, a blond guy, seemed to be calling the shots. Dunphy gave the other guy a white plastic bag."

"Blond guy?" I said. "You can do better than that." I looked in the mirror. The black Chevy Blazer hung two cars back.

"He had big blue eyes and tight buns," said Wendy.

"You can show me the tape when I get home," I said. "I'm headed for the office to check for messages and see if Lorna has left her reports. I don't think I'll be late."

"I've heard that before," said Wendy.

"Things happen."

"Don't let any bad things happen," she said. "I love you."

"I love you, too," I said, and hung up. I wiped my eye with the heel of my hand. There seemed to be a vacuum in my chest I couldn't fill with air. Guess I should have had more for lunch than the wedge of lime.

The Blazer made the turn onto Lake Drive with me. I turned right into a bowling alley parking lot, scooted behind the building, and parked the Jag behind a dumpster. When the Blazer pulled up I was already out of the car, leaning on the door with my arms folded to conceal the fact that I had my pistol in my hand.

The passenger window of the Blazer buzzed down and Matty Svenson's voice said, "Nice ride."

"A little flashy for street work," I said.

"Who's Tracy Ayers?"

"The lady who sold the car to Billy Clements. Billy lent me the car until mine is out of the shop. Title transfer probably isn't on the teletype yet."

Matty stepped out wearing a trace of lipstick and her blond hair tied in a knot at the back of her head. A Kevlar vest flattened her figure under a black-hooded sweatshirt. She wore matching black sweatpants and a nylon windbreaker.

"You can park the heat, Colonel. What's up?"

I slipped the weapon back on my hip. "I need some flash money. Needs to look like about twenty grand."

"Your client was going to provide that," she said, and produced a red pack of cigarettes. She shook one loose and held the pack out to me.

"He's in the house-of-many-slamming-doors and his second in command, Hank Dunphy, came up lame." I took the cigarette and drilled it into the corner of my mouth. "Dunphy said he wasn't picking up my invoices and the plan to make me Security Director was in the toilet."

"Communication problem?"

"Way more than that," I said. "One of Wendy's people shot some film of him meeting with two guys and handing over a package."

"Refresh my memory," said Matty. "Who is Dunphy?" She bit a smoke out of the pack and put the pack away.

"Hank Dunphy, the plant manager at Light and Energy Applications in Ada."

She lit her smoke. "Who'd he make the meet with?"

"Don't know yet, gotta see the film. If I were you, I'd police him up." I beckoned with a finger and Matty handed me her cigarette. While I used the hot end to kindle mine, I said, "You need to ask him the hard questions before he has one of those fatal accidents that have been going around."

Matty took her cigarette back and took a hungry toke. She savored the smoke and looked thoughtful. When she exhaled she said, "If you were me, you'd need probable cause."

I shrugged. "So just lean on him a little."

"I have to talk to my supervisor," said Matty. "Since the shit hit the fan at your office I need permission to take my clothes to the dry cleaner. I don't get to hang around taverns."

"Strictly business."

Matty laughed and tossed her head.

"My client is an innocent man. I'm trying to keep him healthy. The Rabbit belongs to the Chingos, some guy named Luis—I don't have a last name but his street name is Poco Loco. Chingos beat Lambert—"

"I know the story," said Matty. She flicked the ashes off her cigarette.

"You know he's not guilty," I said. "I need the flash money."

Matty folded her arms, which brushed open her jacket. She had her Baretta in a black canvas hip rig. "I'll ask, but I don't see it."

"Put Lambert in protective custody. Feed him some pizza in a cheap hotel."

Matty shook her head. "State case, and the prosecutor is already asking too many questions. Getting you loose cost favors that could get me assigned to screening packages in the mailroom."

"What the hell did you tell him?"

"I told him that if he turned you loose, your life span probably wouldn't exceed the statute of limitations."

"Funny."

"Wasn't a joke," said Matty. "He didn't laugh."

"I need something done about the pornography charges."

"Cameran gave up his license and he's out of the club. The postal inspector was fired for cause."

"Something public," I said. "My wife is a detective. People lie to her. It's hard for her to believe your explanation since you won't testify to the story for the licensing board."

"Policy, Art," she said, "You know I can't do that. I could get fired for what I told her."

"Not good enough. My kids are going through hell at school and my youngest son decked some county social worker."

"I'm sorry about that," she said, looking me straight in the eye. "Just the same, this is hardball. You want to play softball, get a job as an insurance adjuster. If you need a marriage counselor, you don't get off by laying that problem at my door. You got yourself into this case long before I got involved."

"Hardball?" I said, I could feel the blood rush to my face and pound in my ears. "I got your hardball . . ." In extra innings I was going to say but Matty raised her hands in surrender.

She said nothing but made a small round hole of her mouth and blew a narrow stream of smoke while she looked at her shoes. When she looked up she said, "We'll do better. I don't know what yet."

"And if I get waxed you'll send flowers."

"Not officially," she said, and laid a discerning gaze on what remained of her cigarette. Her nails, usually pointed and polished, were clipped as short as mine and devoid of even a clear lacquer. She took a final drag and ground the butt out with her running shoe. "There's two more," she said without looking up.

"Two more what?"

"Two more guys—we know who they are. Cameran gave them up."

"Bring 'em in."

"They're off the farm," she said. "That's the problem with rented loyalties." She climbed back into the Blazer. Through the still open window she said, "They'll come for you. Let us take them." The window went up and the Blazer pulled out.

I threw what was left of my cigarette after the Blazer and yelled, "Be my guest!"

• • •

The Blazer followed me back to the office. The two ladies in the blue minivan pulled out of the lot as I parked the Jag. In the office I found that Marg had left for the day.

Lorna Kemp sat perched on the edge of Marg's desk like a kid on a swing and looked very pleased with herself. She wore a white shell and tan slacks, both decorated with random black smudges. She said, "The records were in the basement of the volunteer fire station," and handed me a fat sheaf of papers.

"The short version," I said.

"Shelly Frampton died fifty-seven years ago," she said.

"Not possible."

Lorna waggled a finger. "Top sheet," she said.

It was a death certificate. Shelly Frampton, aged thirty-one months, had perished in an automobile accident. "Different Shelly Frampton," I said.

"That's what I thought," said Lorna, "and that's before children were routinely assigned Social Security numbers. So I went to county birth records to verify the parents. I found out I had the right Shelly and that she was a twin."

"She had a sister?"

"Brother," said Lorna. "Look at the arrest report for the day we were down there."

"Oh, my God," I said. The name of the person on the arrest report was Sheldon Frampton. "I never would have guessed."

"A lot of people were fooled," said Lorna. "Including Sheldon, until he was sixteen."

Whatever was on my face made Lorna laugh.

"No, really," she said. "The doctor on the death certificate, Lionel Jaymuny—I found him."

"Christ, he'd have to be ninety."

"Ninety-one. He's in the Methodist home. He told me the story—I mean sort of—between catnaps."

"How the hell did you do that?"

"He's a registered voter."

I flopped on the sofa, looked at my burned foot—it was filthy—and dropped the papers in my lap. "So, tell me the story."

"Once upon a time, before seats belts, kiddie chairs, and airbags, a family pick-up truck slid off an icy road and hit a pole. Father was killed. Shelly was in her mother's lap and crushed against the dash. Sheldon had been standing on the seat and went through the windshield. His larynx was crushed and he was cut up, including his private parts. Mother survived, but needed chemicals to deal with the fact that the little girl died in her lap."

"Jesus," I said. "How bad was it?"

Lorna bent her head down and rounded her shoulders. She stuck her hand out and shook it feebly as if it rested on the top of a cane. In an old man's voice she said, "That's none of your business, Missy. You just need to know that we done right by that youngster. Don't matter what happened. It was the best thing we could do."

"They raised Sheldon as Shelly?"

Lorna straightened up and shrugged. "Mother did. Home schooled and loaded with hormones. When Sheldon was sixteen, his mother took a bath with an electric hairdryer. Sheldon was made a ward of the court and found out that what was in his pants was kind of hit and miss."

"Oh, God," I said and started working my pockets looking for a smoke. I didn't find any. Lorna said she was fresh out.

"From that point Sheldon was Sheldon. He finished high school at a state facility and when he was eighteen he found out that he was a rich man. He went to MSU and got a degree in veterinary science, but wasn't much of a party animal. He got arrested for assaulting a prostitute and was voluntarily committed.

"In two years Sheldon was Shelly again and amiable enough as long as she took the prescribed medication. Shelly went back to MSU as an assistant professor and kind of a celebrity, active in the gay community. Shelly and Anne Jones met and hit it off."

"Yeah," I said, "Shelly was still hitting the day we met her."

"Anne tried to drop the charges but the complaining witness was the sheriff's deputy. The papers you've got there indicate that Sheldon pled 'no contest,' paid a fine, and was sentenced to an anger management program."

"All right," I said, "what we need here is for you to put Anne and Shelly together at the penthouse restaurant in the Amway Grand the night that Anne was murdered. They'll remember because Anne got in a row with Scott Lambert that night. Maybe there's a security video. Lambert was escorted out of the building."

"I need to go home and clean up," said Lorna. "Tomorrow all right?"

"Sure, and there's a couple more things. I need the low-down on the houseman at the Frampton estate, and call Leonard Jones and tell him he can help by having his lawyer file whatever is necessary to stop the sale of Anne's sculpture, *The Dutchman*. Tell him it's in the main house of the Frampton estate—in the parlor—on the mantel, over the fireplace."

"I need an expense check," said Lorna.

She took the thirty-nine dollars I had in my pocket and left. I yelled for her to buy some cigarettes as she was going out the door. She laughed and said she already had some.

I locked up. Outside I found the sky clear and the air cool. I left the top up and started the Jag with the first key out of my pocket—the one with the green tab. I had half a tank of "petrol," a good thing considering the fact that Lorna swung with all my cash.

A mile down Forty-fourth Street a Kentwood police cruiser cut me off. I slid off the shoulder trying not to bend Billy's ride. Detective Van Huis bailed out of the passenger door of the cruiser with a snubby .38 in his hand. In the rearview mirror a dark brown plain wrapper slid to a stop, blocking the back of the Jag. Detective Flynt exploded out the driver's door with a fat nine in his hand.

Someone yelled, "Throw the keys out the window!"

I stuck my hands out the window and dropped the key.

"Are there any firearms in the vehicle?"

"Got one on my hip," I said.

"Get out of the car and lay on the ground."

I yelled, "Not happening! I just got this suit out of the dry cleaner, and you guys know damn good and well who I am."

On the far side of the cruiser someone racked a shotgun just as Matty pulled up in the black Blazer. The passenger door of the Jag opened and a man in a gray permanent-wrinkle suit crouched around the edge of the door opening and pointed a Glock .40 caliber pistol at me. "You're under arrest for carrying a concealed weapon," he said.

"I have a permit in my pocket," I said. "May I get it out?" He nodded and I gave him the DA 2818. He looked at it and made a face like a cat considering a hamster in a plastic ball.

"What the fuck is this?" he said.

"Who the fuck are you?" I said, trying to sound breezy and sincerely inquisitive, but it came off smug and accusatory.

"A police officer," he said. "Get out of the car."

Matty yelled, "Hold it right there! What the hell are you doing?" She had her FBI windbreaker on and her credentials in her hand.

I ended up in the back of the Kentwood Cruiser. They left my pistol on the roof of the Jag and stood around yelling at each other and pointing fingers at their own badges. That's when I saw the white van that had pulled onto the shoulder about fifty yards back. The cargo door on the passenger side slid open and the heavy barrel of an M60 with a folded bipod came out. I pounded on the window and yelled. Detective Flynt gave me an evil face but looked where I was pointing.

I HIT THE FLOOR and got a shower of glass as the windows of the cruiser exploded. "You can shoot back anytime now," I said to the floor of the police cruiser. Nothing. "Hell, just show 'em those badges." The second burst from the M60 cut through the seatbacks of the cruiser and hammered into the dash before I heard the .40 caliber bark an answer, syncopated yips of 9mm followed, and the church mouse sneeze of Van Huis's detective special. I decided that spreading flat against the floor had it all over rolling into a ball.

I heard the van accelerate and the M60 lift its leg on the front of the cruiser. The tires exhaled, and the cruiser banged down on its knees. The handguns fell silent, doors slammed, and two vehicles scratched out in pursuit of the van.

I rolled my eyes around, trying to direct my hearing without moving my head. An approaching siren grew louder. I flexed the muscles in my arms and legs—nothing felt numb or wet. Pebbles of safety glass cascaded off my back as I eased onto my knees.

The backseat of the cruiser was devoid of door handles. I reached through the air where the window had been, opened the door from the outside, and shook glass from my suit as I walked back to the Jag. Traffic had resumed and motorists rubbernecked the cruiser. People yelled as they passed. Horns honked. I ignored them. A whiff of cordite hung in the air.

The Jag had emerged unscathed. I did my best Eddie Izzard; "Dashed decent of the chap on the stutter gun." My pistol and DA 2818 had been cast onto the driver's seat, but the key was nowhere in sight. I stuck my hands in my pockets to consider the situation as a Kentwood Fire Rescue truck pulled up with its rollers on.

Billy Clements had said I'd find a spare set of keys in a magnetic box in one of the bumpers. I was thinking how much I really didn't want to lie on the ground and look for it when a med-tech ran past me to look into the shot-up cruiser and I realized that the steel peg in my pocket was the key with the black shank. I hadn't been searched, just sort of sent to my room so the adults could argue.

The med-tech looked at me and then back into the cruiser. He wore yellow turnout pants with suspenders and a white shirt but had left his hat with his jacket in the truck. He opened the back door of the cruiser. Glass pebbles splashed onto the street.

"You see what happened to the guy that was in here?" he said, his face incredulous. In his late twenties, he wore his full head of sandy hair cut in a flattop except for the back, which he'd let grow long enough that he'd had to tuck it down the collar of his shirt. "They said there was a guy in here."

"I opened the door from the outside," I said. "The window was gone."

He walked toward me, surveying me as he came. "You were in there?"

I nodded.

"What happened?"

"Drive-by shooting," I said.

"I was a Navy medic assigned to the Marines," he said, and pointed at the cruiser. "Somebody stitched that up with a machine gun."

I laughed.

"No, really," he said.

"The pun," I said. "You were a medic . . . and they stitched . . ."

"Yeah," he said. He smiled and shook his head. "Well. I mean. Why'd they do that?"

"Detective Van Huis went after them. I expect he'll ask."

"We got the call from a state police dispatcher," he said and made it sound like a question.

"Van Huis and a patrol officer left with a couple of state cops," I said, "their car being under the weather and all."

"So, you're all right? I can look you over."

I pointed to my nose brace and said, "No, I think I've had all the medical attention I can stand for a while. I think I'll just go home and quit hanging around policemen."

I reached through the window of the Jag, picked up my pistol and put it on my hip. The med-tech watched me from the corner of his eye, his face doubtful.

"I'm a detective," I said.

"Not from Kentwood," he said.

"Private."

"Cool," he said. He fondled the Jag with a hungry gaze. "You have any openings—you know, like part-time?"

"Yeah," I said, "I need someone to take beatings for me and occasionally sit in the back of police cars."

"That's okay," he said and started back to his truck. "My old Dodge gets me around just fine."

• • •

Rusty met me at the door and leapt straight up in the air—all four feet off the floor. I caught him in my arms. He rubbed his neck on my face and ran his fat red tongue over my cheek and across my ear. It knocked the brace on my face loose and a rainbow of colors burned out of my sinuses into my eye sockets.

"Damn! Dog!" I set him down and caught the now whirling house by the handrail on the stairs. I inspected my nose with tentative fingers and found it still intact. Dancing a circle, Rusty stepped on my foot. "Geeze, dog! Whose side are you on?"

"He's been searching the house for you for three days," said Ben. "He got up on the bed and dug through the comforter and the pillows looking for you. Mom had to put your coat on the floor before he'd lie down and go to sleep."

Wendy met me at the top of the stairs. I pushed the brace back in place with one hand while I hugged with the other. She wore one of my knock-around flannel shirts over a sleeveless white sweater and red slacks.

"The roast is ready to come out," she said.

"See?" I said. "Right on time."

"I waited half an hour before I put the meat in."

"You're a better man than I," I said.

Wendy whacked me on the shoulder.

"Ow! What the dog missed, you caught up with."

"Serves you right for not being home," Wendy said.

"You weren't supposed to consort with the likes of me."

She squeezed me and said, "I like to consort with you."

I kissed her on the side of her head; it was all I could reach. "If they find out I came here, you're in big trouble."

Wendy rubbed my back and said, "Nope." I let her go and she headed for the oven. Pulling on her oven mitts, she said, "The guy they've had parked at the end of the drive knocked on the door after you called. He said the hearing was canceled and we could take the tape off the gun safe and my file cabinets."

"What brought that on?"

"He said he didn't know. They just told him to give me the message and clock out because he was on overtime."

"You didn't tell me about the surveillance," I said.

Wendy pulled the roaster pan out of the oven and set it on the counter. "Given everything that's happened I would have needed my people if the state police hadn't been out there."

I stepped up the last stair. The table was set for three.

"Where's Daniel?"

"Burger flipping," said Ben. "He's working the dinner shift 'til close." He walked up to check my face. "Looks better—sort of a uniform yellow brown. You look like an albino raccoon."

I should have roped a headlock on him and issued the Dutch rub. A couple of years ago I might have, but now he was as tall as I am, and the dog had already worked me over.

"Cuts down on the glare," I said. "I'm saving a fortune on sunglasses." I shrugged out of my suit jacket and hung it in the closet. "Why don't you cue up that tape your mother has for me?"

"I gotta find a place to save my game," said Ben. He had a role playing game on the TV.

"Tape's on the end table," said Wendy. She looked at me. "I need you to slice this."

I took my pistol off my hip and set it on top of the refrigerator. Rusty followed me, lock-step, into the kitchen. Wendy hung up her mitts and laid a platter on the island counter next to the roaster pan. I washed my hands in the sink and found the carving set.

"Get out of the kitchen, dog," said Wendy, and waited for him to move so she could open the refrigerator for the milk.

Rusty walked around the end of the counter, made a u-turn, and sat at my feet. I forked the roast out of the pan—a pork roast Wendy had rubbed with sage and cooked in a nest of potatoes, carrots, and fat slices of onion with a little garlic salt—and set it on the platter. Rusty studied my moves with bright, expectant eyes and about an inch of pink tongue lolling from his open mouth.

"Okay, here it is, Pop," said Ben. The TV set showed Hank Dunphy, ersatz fiduciary for Light and Energy Applications, climbing into a silver Mercedes SL with a shoebox under his arm. In the lower right of the screen the time rolled continuously—10:15 A.M.

I sliced a steaming sliver off the end of the roast and pushed it aside with the fork. Rusty reeled in his tongue and danced his front paws on the linoleum.

"He only begs because you encourage him," said Wendy.

"I am the soul of canine discipline," I said. "Your guys shoot this out of a car?"

"Rented a van," said Wendy.

I winked at Rusty and mouthed, "Too hot." He wiped his nose with his tongue.

The next shot was Dunphy walking into the Old Kent Bank branch on Twenty-eighth Street in Grand Rapids. The trip had taken twenty-two minutes.

Wendy took the roaster pan and spooned the potatoes and carrots into a serving bowl. I made half-inch slices of roast. The scene on the TV wiped, nine minutes had passed, and Dunphy was exiting the bank with a fat white plastic bag the size of a football, rolled up and tucked under his arm.

"You want to fast forward this?" said Ben. "He just goes to lunch."

"Let it run," said Wendy. She mixed cornstarch in a cup of water for gravy.

Dunphy wheeled his Mercedes into Popeye's Chicken on South Division Ave. Rusty's nose did the boogie-woogie around the end of his face. I flipped him the sliver I'd let cool. Dunphy backed his car into a space at the rear of the building. The surveillance vehicle had obviously pulled into the drive-thru line.

"Risky," I said.

"You. Are. Feeding. The. Dog." said Wendy.

"Little piece of fat," I said.

"What's risky?" said Ben.

"Pulling into the drive-thru line," I said. Rusty wiped his muzzle, his tongue as big a dishrag. "If the subject pulls out, you're stuck and your surveillance is over." I cut another small sliver. Two men walked up to Dunphy's car.

"Right there," said Wendy. "The guy in the windbreaker gets the shoebox and the guy in the suit gets the bag. I hope you know who they are, because this surveillance tied up two of my people and cost Lambert over a thousand dollars."

"Cheap at twice the price," I said. "The guy in the windbreaker made an appearance at my office the day I left for Brandonport—done up like a deliveryman—and said he had a package for me. I saw him again when I got back. He drove the 'cable truck' the cops found in the gravel quarry. I think he's on the FBI's short list of things to do.

"The guy in the suit is a fellow by the name of Luis. I don't know his last name, but he's the leader of the Chingos. I'm told his street name is Poco Loco."

"What's a Chingo?" said Ben.

"Street gang," I said. I flipped Rusty the sliver. Wendy picked up the platter.

"Let's eat while we still have some roast," she said.

• • •

After dinner Ben re-embarked on his video odyssey, Wendy fixed a plate for Daniel, and Rusty tidied up the scraps. I retired to the bathroom, made a pile of my clothes, and filled the bathtub—an oversized fiberglass number with waterjets.

With the jets on full whoosh, I reclined in the hot water with a wet washcloth on my eyes—the nose brace had come completely unstuck—and replayed the surveillance video in my mind. Deliveryman/Andy had done the talking, finger pointing, and instructing—made Dunphy sit in the car while he loomed over him in the open door.

Luis, in the same suit I'd seen him wearing at The Rabbit, had taken the white plastic bag and made an insolent face. Deliveryman/Andy had leaned into Luis's space and made slow instructions—maybe threats—

around an index finger hovering scarce inches from Luis's nose.

Deliveryman/Andy had slammed the door of the Mercedes, made some last pronouncement, and walked off with Luis, the shoebox under his arm. They had departed in a pale green sedan—a disappointment—I had expected a little more style from Luis. Wendy's operative had zoomed tight on the license plate: Wisconsin, MKT . . . something, I'd jotted the number into my notepad.

The bathroom door opened and closed. The lights went out.

"I thought I'd find you here," said Wendy.

"Everybody has to be somewhere," I said and lifted the washcloth off one eye. Moonlight frosted the room with a silver glow. Wendy stood beside the tub in her robe.

"Where are you?"

"Hoping for an out-of-body experience," I said. I rinsed the cloth, folded it, and put it back on my eyes.

"Why's that?"

"Because the fit inside this body has a few pinches, just now."

I heard Wendy's robe hit the floor and felt her step into the tub, a foot on either side of my hips. She whispered, "Let's check the fit in this body."

. . .

I don't know if Dunphy had more lumps than I did, but his were fresher. He sat, catatonic, on my office sofa. His hand clutched the handle of the briefcase. Blood dripped from his wrist onto the upholstery.

Marg sat at her desk, her eyes mostly whites and her face pale. She shook her head at me as I opened the door.

Dunphy wore sunglasses and the same suit I'd seen in the surveillance film. His collar loose and his tie at half mast, he turned his face toward me. The left side of his face was purple and a half-size larger than the right. His lip was torn but had stopped bleeding. The left sleeve of his tan cashmere suit coat bore a rust-brown stain from the elbow to the wrist, probably from wiping his lip. I couldn't see his eyes.

I asked him, "Why did you come here, Hank?"

He said, "I'm sorry." His hand began to tremble on the handle of the briefcase.

"The briefcase," Marg squeaked.

I slipped my hand around his and tightened his finger against the handle. "Don't do it; you won't have to be sorry."

"They have my wife and daughter."

I looked him straight in the sunglasses and told him, "Ten seconds after this goes off, they'll kill 'em."

"No," he said.

"Think about it," I said. "Once you do this—give them what they want—they'll have no use for your family."

The telephone rang.

Marg picked it up. "Peter A. Ladin Agency." Her voice would have sounded calm to anyone who didn't know her. "No, Mr. Hardin isn't in yet . . . He called. He had to stop at the courthouse. . . . Maybe an hour or so. . . . Would you like to leave a number? . . . Certainly."

Marg shook her head, her mouth not quite closed.

I told Marg, "Just go. And pull the fire alarm on the way out."

"No," said Dunphy.

I squeezed his hand. He winced.

"He's out there," said Dunphy, his voice an octave high and strained through glass shards. "He's watching. He can set this off."

I eased up.

"If she leaves, he'll set it off. If there's a fire alarm, he'll set it off. If he knows you're here, that's it."

"I had to have walked right by him," I said.

"I wasn't sure when you walked in," said Dunphy, "not until you spoke. When we met, you had a moustache. They said you had a brace on your face, and walked with a cane."

"Is there a trigger in the handle?"

"There's a piece of fishing leader . . . it goes," Dunphy swallowed, "from my thumb . . . through a hole in the briefcase. It's on a spring. If I pull out, it goes off. If I let it go slack, it goes off."

I inspected the handle. They had installed the line into Dunphy's palm with a fishhook sunk into the base of his thumb.

I looked at Marg. "You can go to the far end of the building. Get up to the ground level."

"If I don't answer the telephone, they might set it off," she said.

"I'm taking Hank into my office," I said, and nodded toward the open doorway. Dunphy eased off the sofa, my hand still clutching his hand to the handle of the briefcase.

"They said I had one foot in prison and the other in the grave," said Dunphy. "Said if I did this they'd provide for my family. If I didn't, they'd just kill us."

Marg pushed a pink message slip at me as we passed her. She took the telephone and climbed under her desk. The message was from Detective Van Huis: "Call me."

I sat Dunphy in my desk chair, the briefcase on the desk, and picked up the telephone. I pecked out the number for the direct line into Van Huis's desk.

"Van Huis, Kentwood Detectives," he said.

"Hardin," I said. "This is important."

"Not anymore," he said. "Wrote my report this morning and some fed came in with the chief and took it—made me sign some paper—if I mention the incident they'll send me to Allenwood to play shuffleboard with Mob guys." He hung up.

I dialed back. Van Huis had it in the middle the first ring. "Better not be Hardin," he said.

"Listen," I said. "This is important."

"Lose this number."

"I've got a man with a bomb in my office."

"Dispatch," Van Huis said, his voice muffled—maybe his hand over the phone. "Richie, get me dispatch on your line." His voice louder, he said, "All right, Art. Talk to me."

"Got a man outside with a radio detonator," I said. "You roll up like gangbusters and this thing goes off. I'm going to put you on the speaker." I clicked on the speaker and hung up the telephone.

"I'm recording this line," said Van Huis. "Tell me about the package."

"It's in a briefcase tethered to the arm of Hank Dunphy."

"What's it made out of?"

"It looked like sticks of clay or putty," said Dunphy, "smelled sweet like candy, marzipan."

"Probably Semtex," I said.

Van Huis asked, "How much?"

"Weighs like a phone book," said Dunphy, sweat beading on his now blanched-white forehead. "Get out to my house. They've got my family."

"We're talking a smoking hole in the ground," I said.

"Someone is on the way," said Van Huis. "I'm going to talk to the man with the bomb. What's your name?"

"Hank Dunphy. I live on Rosebud Court in Ada. They have my wife and daughter. It's a Tudor, the only one on the cul-de-sac."

"How many men are in the house?"

"Three. They were in the den—in the back of the house off the pool. There's a sliding glass door."

"What are they driving?"

"They don't have a car," said Dunphy. He closed his eyes and seemed to fight for his balance in the chair. I put my free hand on his shoulder. "They used the car they came in to bring me here."

"Tell me about the car."

"It's green. A sedan."

"Taurus?" I asked.

Dunphy turned his face to me. "Yes, I think."

"Look for a Taurus with Wisconsin plates," I said. I thumbed open my notepad and read him the number.

Dunphy exhaled a word, barely a whisper, "How?"

I said, "I'm a detective. I know things, Hank. I know Scott Lambert was framed and you helped. Why don't you tell us now? Before we all die and you can't tell us—and you have to face eternity with the lie on your lips."

"I gave them the soda can with Scott's cigar butt in it," said Dunphy. "I gave them hair from Scott's hairbrush, from the restroom in his office."

"Who?" said Van Huis.

"The men who made the bomb. They broke into Hardin's office and left the soda can. I don't know what they did with the hair."

The office door opened.

"What was in the shoe box you gave them yesterday?" I said.

"Oh, my God," said Dunphy.

A man holding a fire department badge in his hand walked into my office. He was lean and athletic despite stark white hair and a furrowed face. He wore a white shirt, the sleeves rolled up past his elbows, and blue work trousers.

"What was in the box, Hank?"

Dunphy didn't answer. He looked at the fireman.

"Mike Fulton," said the fireman, "I'm not a bomb guy, but—"

"Engineering samples and data CD's," Dunphy said.

"—I was in ordinance disposal before I retired from the military. I know about plastic."

"Mike, this is Van Huis," said the speaker telephone. "You don't have to stay. We've got someone from GRPD on the way."

"Jesus, Jerry," said Fulton, "I'm here, let me take a look at this." He slipped on a pair of reading glasses and bent to examine the briefcase.

Dunphy's hand began to tremble. I firmed my grip. "Just try to relax your fingers," I said. "I've got a good hold."

Fulton produced a box knife from his pants pocket and sliced through the side of the briefcase, from end to end, along the edge next to the handle. Setting the box cutter aside, he hauled out a palm sized hand mirror and a pencil. With the rubber end of the pencil he lifted up the slit and peeked into the case using light reflected with the hand mirror.

"Definitely a bomb," said Fulton. "Plastic with an electrically fired blasting cap. There's a deadman's switch and a radio receiver."

"Can you leave it and vacate the building?" said Van Huis.

The telephone rang in the front office.

"If this amount of plastic detonates," said Fulton, "Flo Jo couldn't run fast enough."

"Get it off the man's arm and evacuate the building," said Van Huis.

"He'll set it off," said Dunphy, his whole arm shaking.

"I've got a little girl on line two who wants to talk to her daddy," Marg announced.

"What do you want to do, Jerry?" I said. "For Dunphy to talk I have to put you on hold."

"Let him talk," said Van Huis.

Fulton lifted open the slice with his fingers, sliding the pencil into the opening like he was threading a needle. I handed Dunphy the telephone and punched line two.

"Hi, baby. . . . Yes, it's your daddy. . . . No, I didn't share the cookie dough. The man isn't here yet."

Fulton looked at me and whispered, "A bull dog clip."

I gave him one from my drawer.

"It doesn't hurt my hand, Baby. . . . It's a pretend game."

Fulton clipped it to the wire leader where it passed through the briefcase.

"Amy! Amy! . . . Why is my wife screaming? . . . you bastard! . . . Yes. . . . Yes, stop it. . . . Yes, Hardin is here."

Hank Dunphy revealed himself to be a man who could evacuate a building with stunning alacrity. No sooner had Mike Fulton—full time fireman and retired military bomb disposer—clamped off and cut the trigger wire, than good ole Hank was gone like last week's paycheck.

I called after him on the stairs, "Hank, you forgot your briefcase!" He didn't look back. I bounded after him, trundling the briefcase in front of me like a tea caddy.

"Excuse me," I told a pair of matrons as they stepped aside to make way. "Man forgot his briefcase." They had a shopping bag full of Campbell's Soup labels for the office down the hall from mine and could not conceal their disgust for Hank and I playing tag on the stairs.

"I should say," said the lady in the black straw hat with matching bag.

"Well, I never," said her friend, demure in a white blouse and brown pleated skirt.

"Hold this, toots, and tell me what you never," I couldn't give it to her, even though she did put her hands out—I had to catch the door with my shoulder before it fell completely shut. When I got out onto the porch

Dunphy was already in the middle of the lot and dodging parked cars like they were trying to tackle him. A dozen steps and half as many seconds would put Dunphy in the middle of an open field and I could lob him the "Hail Mary."

Flashing brakelights caught the corner of my eye. The green Taurus crept down the apron toward the street, surrounded by FBI agents in black windbreakers, Matty among them. She wore a black skirt and hose. A sling carried her left arm. She pointed her Beretta at the driver's window with her right.

"Stop! Turn off the ignition! You're under arrest!" they all chanted in madrigal, while the Taurus slowly plowed agents into the street.

I abandoned Dunphy—wasn't really his briefcase anyway—and scooted down the stairs to run after the Taurus. Through the rear window I could see the driver holding the detonator in view—threatening with it in his right hand.

I ran along the passenger side of the vehicle, past agents who took me in their sights, their faces first angry, then ashen. I dived onto the hood and held the briefcase to the windshield.

"Pop it now, asshole!" I yelled and peeked over the case to look the driver in the eyes. Jack Anders. I wish I had been surprised. He never saw me. His eyes fixed on the briefcase and his face became mostly open mouth. He bailed out of the driver's door and ran.

Left to its own devices, the Taurus rolled into the street with me still on the hood. Lucky for me, the ride carried me wide of the of gunfire directed at the fleeing Jack Anders.

Jack slowed to a quickmarch, then stopped. He turned to face the gaggle formation of agents with his arms spread and showing his empty palms. The firing stopped. Jack wore a tan windbreaker unzipped over a white knit shirt. A half-dozen small cones of fabric stood out from his shirt, each with a small hole at the tip. A cloud of astonishment wafted across his face as his eyes engaged each of his pursuers. He glanced at his shirt and wiped it flat with his hand, red circles spread around the holes. He turned and, making precise steps, walked into the street like a mime descending an imaginary stairway.

The curb on the far side of the street stopped the Taurus. I left the briefcase racked on the windshield and slid off the hood to try the passenger door. Locked. The driver's door stood open. I ran around and threw the shift lever into park without climbing in, the detonator—a garage door opener—lay on the passenger seat.

A yellow taxi rounded the corner. The driver seemed to be studying something in his right hand. I waved my hands and yelled. If he looked up, I didn't wait to see. I ran for the circle of agents who stood staring down their gunsights into the vacant eyes of the pile of meat that had been Jack Anders.

Behind me brakes locked up and tires squawked. An angry voice called after me, "What the fuck are you doing?" Matty looked up and fixed me in flaming arrow eyes.

"That was stupid," she said. "What the hell did you think you were doing?"

"I didn't think he would pop the bomb if it was in his lap," I said, in favor of what I was thinking: *Trying to improve on your circular firing squad strategy, Matty!* "Why'd you shoot him?"

"Because he had the detonator," said a Washington dinosaur agent, who probably knew J. Edgar personally. He had at least a decade on me and a full head of gray hair with a laser-straight part on the left and hair swept back on the right. The only one without a FBI stenciled jacket, he wore a charcoal suit over a pinstriped blue shirt with a red tie on a lithe and lean body. He holstered a chrome .357 and walked off.

I said, "Who was that?"

"Your best friend," Matty said.

"I shouldn't tell him the detonator was on the passenger seat?"

"Go ahead and roll him over," Matty said to nobody in particular. She gave me a sidelong glance, "No. I wouldn't mention that."

"Hey, Mack," said an angry voice. I turned to see the taxi driver. An extra day of whiskers put more hair on his face than on his head. A hammock of soiled yellow T-shirt captured a belly that fell over his belt like an apron. "You can't just stop your car and leave it in the street."

A battered pick-up truck loaded with lawn equipment rounded the corner. Its front bumper dived for the pavement and tires squealed, but it still tagged the back bumper of the taxi cab.

"Why not?" I said. "You did."

"Oh, shit," said the cabby as he turned and speed waddled for his vehicle. "Jesus Christ, what else?"

"There's a bomb in the Taurus," I told him. He cut a hard right and headed for the open field behind my office.

"So, who is this?" said Matty. She holstered her weapon.

"Cab driver," I said.

"On the ground," said Matty, definitely not amused.

"On the ground is what remains of Jacob Anderson, AKA Jack Anders," I said. "He worked for the late Mr. Dixon—was doing an undercover at Light and Energy Applications in Wisconsin when he disappeared. I found him in Brandonport, wearing a ski mask and pointing a revolver at my head."

"Why didn't you report him to the police?"

"He convinced me that it was my fault."

Matty showed me narrow eyes and tight lips.

"I guess you had to be there," I said.

"I've got something for you in the car." Matty started for the parking lot.

"Bust a flipper?"

"Dislocated shoulder," she said. "Your playmates hosed the tires on the Blazer and it rolled like a red rubber ball."

"So you didn't get them?"

"Not something I can discuss," she said.

A man decked out like the Michelin man, rolling one heavily padded leg around the other, carried Dunphy's briefcase toward a sandbagged steel tub loaded on a trailer. A county rescue truck squeaked to a stop near the steps to my office. Two FBI agents walked by—bookends for Hank Dunphy, his hands cuffed behind him. They marched him to the rescue truck. He implored all who could hear to send help to his wife and daughter.

I asked, "Somebody is doing that, right?"

"He tried to blow you up," said Matty.

"Sins of the father."

"Your best friend is on the way to catch up with the SWAT team we sent while you were still in the office with Dunphy," said Matty.

"So who is this man who is supposed to be my best friend?"

"Did he ask you any questions?"

"No, ma'am."

"Return the favor," Matty said. "He flew in last night, and if we roll up the third man in twenty-four hours he'll be able to walk on the Potomac with a bag of congressional funding under each arm."

"The guy you just ventilated wasn't Jacob Anderson?"

"No, but he does make two down and one to go." She unlocked the door of a tan government sedan and nodded at the passenger door. I pulled the door shut after me and Matty told me to look under the seat. I fished out a green and white football-shaped leatherette shoe bag with a black cord handle. Inside, four packets of hundred dollar bills in bank wrappers made twenty thousand dollars. It didn't make much of a pile.

"I don't suppose this really matters now," I said. "Dunphy admitted the plan to frame Scott Lambert."

"I wouldn't look for Lambert to be on the street any time soon," said Matty. "You can count on Dunphy to clam up as soon as he stops begging for help. The prosecutor will be playing heavy defense. He took Lambert for a half million in cash and twiddled his thumbs while Lambert took a beating."

"Guess I better count this," I said.

"Count it or don't," said Matty. "I don't care. There's a receipt. You don't sign the receipt, the money stays here. Sign it, and I want to see the money once a day. You lose any of the money and the Bureau will be all over you like ants on a jelly bean."

I started counting cadence for Franklin and Matty started working her pockets. She searched her purse.

"Out of smokes?" I asked.

Matty patted the shoulder of the arm in the sling. "The patch," she said. "Damn thing itches like mad and I'm still looking for a cigarette."

"What brought this on?"

"The doctor who set my shoulder."

"You didn't fall for that, did you?" I said. "They'd tell you to quit smoking to cure a hangnail."

"I was injured in the line of duty. The bastard wrote it on my chart."

"Christ," I said, "the world is turning to shit. Now I gotta buy my own cigarettes." I finished counting the bills, signed the receipt, and left Matty sucking her thumb.

• • •

Marg sat at her desk posting a ledger with her "leave me the hell alone" half glasses perched on the end of her nose. As I opened the door she said, "Am I going to blow up, or can I get some work done?"

I patted the top of my head and said, "You kind of flattened out your hairdo while you were under the desk."

Marg drilled a finger into a pink message slip. "The landlord called and said he'd let us out of our lease and return our deposit if we were out of here by the end of the month."

"Not happening," I said. "I'll give him a call."

"No need," Marg said. "They'll have a door on your office and measure for carpet today."

I skulked past Marg, locked the money in the equipment closet, and retreated to my desk. Marg went out the front door and down the hall. I heard every step. Searching my desk for smokes produced no joy, so I rifled my suit. In the hanky pocket of my suit coat I found a note from Wendy that read, "I said cruel things. I didn't mean them. Sorry—I love you."

"'Methinks the lady doth protest too much,'" I said to my empty office. I snatched up the telephone, but found my hand shaking. I could hear myself ranting at Wendy, "You wanted to believe them. You said what you thought. You wanted to be, 'poor Wendy.' You spent months looking out the window watching our marriage dissolve into the night. Now it could be my fault. 'Poor Wendy. Art was such an asshole. How could she have known.'" I banged the handset back in the cradle.

I'd passed two party stores before I thought to stop for smokes. The next opportunity was the strip mall on Breton. The window of the "Buck-a-Piece" store displayed Detroit Red Wing Stanley Cup T-shirts. They didn't have any Red Wing hats, so I went with a white golf hat and a Red Wings bumper sticker—probably work just fine in the dark tunnel where I was told to deliver the money. A roll of duct tape and a heavy rubber mallet with a wooden handle ran the tab up to a fin.

The cashier at the drugstore said that cigarettes were four and-a-half a pack.

"Cigars?" I said.

"Aisle seven on the left," she told me.

I found a "special," buy one get one free and stopped at the greeting card aisle on the way back. How come the cards never say what's on your mind? "I love you, but I feel like a stranger in our house . . . in our bed . . . loved not wisely but too well," and lines about casting away pearls of great value—but that shoe had been on the other foot.

"Maybe it still is," I told the rack of cards and felt air rush into the void in my chest that I had been fighting for days. I read them all. It took an hour, maybe longer. I don't know. Long enough for the store dick to get cross eyed trying to watch out of the corner of his eye while he tried to appear really interested in disposable douches.

I settled on a card with a little girl and boy on the cover. They wore "dress up" clothes from an attic trunk in the background; him in suspenders with an old pipe, her with a string of pearls, a scarf, and an acre of hat. Inside it read, "When you're young at heart/Life is forever new."

I don't know what it cost. It needed another line—I sat in the car with my pen poised to strike. Nothing came to mind. I turned on the radio to find inspiration from some minstrel but got the news instead.

Lead story: A gas explosion destroyed a home in Ada. A woman was dead, a little girl in intensive care. Names withheld. Then sports, weather, and a little humor to wrap up: Two members of a local motorcycle club had been arrested after getting liquored up and dumping a trash receptacle into the lap of the desk sergeant at the Grand Rapids Police Department.

I stashed the card in the breast pocket of my jacket and drove back to the office. A man in a blue serge suit sat on my sofa and passed the breeze with Marg. As I opened the door he waved. His forehead lasted all the way to the crown of his head. The rest of his brown hair lay brushed back from his face along the sides of his head and formed fender skirts over his ears.

"I didn't know if I should wait," the man said in Ken Ayers's voice.

"Harley Davidson on the big board now?" I said.

Ken climbed off the sofa trenching his shirt collar with a finger. "Yeah. Maybe. Hell, I don't know."

"I know," said Marg, "and I'm not telling either one of you."

Ken followed me into my office and took the wingback chair. I opened the closet and unzipped the bag that Matty had given me.

"You missed all the fun," said Ken.

"Had all the fun I could stand this morning," I said and liberated a packet of Franklins.

Marg stepped into the doorway and pointed at the wall behind my desk. The agency license was back in the frame and covering the unfaded paint square that had marked its absence.

"That cop that was here when Billy Clements came by to lend you his car?" said Ken.

"Archer Flynt," I said.

"Yeah," said Ken. "He walked in and flopped that piece of paper on Marg's desk."

"I told him that wasn't where he found it," said Marg.

"Man, you shoulda seen his puss," said Ken. "Marg reached in her drawer and gave him the frame. You woulda thought she fixed him a shit sandwich."

"Sorry I missed it," I said.

"Wait," Ken waved a hand and laughed. "He comes in, bangs it up on the wall, and turns around—Marg is standing in the doorway and makes him hang it straight."

Marg aimed a finger at me and said, "And you make sure it stays there."

"Yes, ma'am," I said. Marg went back to her desk. I dropped the bundle of currency in Ken's lap on the way to my chair. Ken riffled the end pack of Franklins under a tent of approving eyebrows. I rocked my chair back and stacked my heels on the corner of my desktop.

Ken stuffed the fifty yards into the breast pocket of his suit coat and said, "What's the plan, boss?"

I let my head fall to one side and passed my hand over the top of my head.

"A weave, man," said Ken. "I sent it out to be dry cleaned."

"I was afraid you went Wall Street on me."

"This is what I wear to court."

I folded my hands on my chest, fingers interlaced, and said, "Heard any gossip lately?"

"Friends of mine had lunch with your client," said Ken.

"Gourmet?"

"Fried bologna and macaroni with a breath of cheese sauce."

"I know that place," I said. "I was there yesterday but they canceled my reservation."

"Heard you had lunch at The Rabbit."

"Earthy ambiance, but I'd hardly call a wedge of lime lunch."

"I heard somebody was serving hickory," said Ken.

"Special order," I said. "How was my client when your friends talked to him?"

"Scared shitless when they sat next to him," said Ken. He laughed. "But they said your client found a bunk and had a quiet night."

"Fancy that."

"Ain't nobody going to have a quiet night if we don't take care of business," said Ken.

I put my feet on the floor, hauled a can of oil out of my desk drawer, and lubed the rails of my lead launcher. "Guess we ought to go for a ride," I said.

• • •

The revolving sign atop The Rabbit was already lit—turning relentlessly in the evening twilight like a radar antenna, searching for customers long on libido and short on prospects.

"You got to be shittin' me," said Ken.

"Nope," I said. "That's where we're going."

"I can't think of anything Luis would like better than a big chunk of your ass."

"How about a big chunk of my ass and twenty thousand dollars?"

"Well?" said Ken with a twist of his head, "Yeah."

I pulled up to the curb two blocks short of The Rabbit and dug the matchbook out of my pocket. On Billy Clements's car phone I dialed the "private party" number.

Half a dozen rings and the bartender answered. "Rabbit," he yelled into my ear. The din of the crowd and a quarter's worth of "Smoke on the Water" nearly drowned him out.

"I'm looking for a private party," I yelled back into the telephone.

A smile usurped the doubt from Ken's face. He said, "Much better idea."

"Hang on a sec," said the bartender. I heard a clunk, he must have set the handset on the bar. Half way through "Magic Carpet Ride" Luis interrupted Steppenwolf.

"Private party starts at a thousand dollars," he said.

"Art Hardin," I said.

Ken did a double take.

"Fuck you want, asshole?" said Luis.

"Thought I'd stop by for a beer."

"Stop by any time you want, man. Your friend Rudy's here. He was just sayin' how much he'd like to see you. Maybe buy you a beer. Shoot the shit."

"Scott Lambert got a good night's sleep."

"What's it to me?" Luis said.

"Twenty thousand dollars," I said. "Thought I'd just bring it by."

Ken searched the glove box and worried his gaze around the car. I nodded at the "Buck-a-Piece" bag on the package shelf.

"Just a minute," said Luis. The telephone clicked onto hold and I got salsa music while Ken snatched the bag into the front seat.

Luis picked up the line. The background noise was gone. "You can bring me all the money you want, but if you got business with somebody maybe you better do that first."

"Just seems like a waste of time," I said.

"You forget where you supposed to go?"

"Hampton Street?" I said. "The tunnel under the expressway."

"Maybe it was Milwaukee Street," he said. "Maybe there's a secret handshake you got to remember."

"Nah. Detroit Red Wings T-shirt and hat."

Ken pulled the rubber mallet out of the bag and looked at me with his face screwed into a question mark. I nodded. He dropped the mallet on the floor and plumbed his hand through the contents of the bag.

"Well? See! You got it figured, man. Go and do your business, and ah— come by here, and ah. . . . Rudy have a nice cold beer waiting for you."

"Corona with a wedge of lime," I said.

Luis banged the phone in my ear.

I started the Jag, pulled into traffic, and took the first right. At the alley I turned left. Most of a block down I found an empty cement slab behind a plumbing shop and backed in.

I had an excellent view of The Rabbit—the brightly lit parking lot as well as the side and back doors.

"There ain't no money in here," Ken said into the bag.

"Let me see it," I said.

Ken shrugged and handed the bag to me with concern hung from his eyebrows like a curtain.

I looked into the bag and then stuck my hand in to search around. The tape, the hat, the shirt, and the bumper sticker were all there.

"Ain't this a bitch," I said. "I must have told the dumb bastard a fib."

26

Matty, in her plain sedan—followed by a blacked-out Suburban—bucked and lurched down the rutted alley past Ken and me while we were still parked behind the plumbing shop. Ken allowed as how he thought they were the police. I let him lecture me on the subtleties of identifying unmarked police vehicles. Half a cigar later Rudy—leaning on a cane and wearing a hip-to-ankle air cast—along with the bartender, the car valet, and a couple of guys I'd not seen before, departed in a couple of cherried-out mid-sixties Chevys that climbed up off the ground like camels departing on a caravan.

I backed the Jag up to the delivery door of The Rabbit and we walked around to the side door. A dancer in a sequined G-string and a cocktail length white rabbit fur coat worked the door, a tall black dancer with a Nigerian hairdo and dangling gold lightning-bolt earrings stood behind the bar, and the Bee Gees were "Stayin' Alive." Luis leaned on the bar. When he saw us, he closed his eyes and turned his head away.

"The haps, Luis?" I said. The odor of hops and cigarette smoke hung in the air. On the stage a very nearly flat-chested blond—wearing Dale Evans hat and white leather chaps over Hanes Her Way—rowed her hands in rhythm to her thrusting hips, riding an imagined pony through knee deep, dry ice fog.

"Fuck you doing here, man?"

"My car broke down a couple of blocks over," I said. "I figured, you know? I'm here. I give you the bag."

Luis bent his head down and rubbed his forehead. When he looked up he said, "Who the fuck is this?"

Ken folded his hands in front of him and squared his shoulders.

"An associate," I said. "I got your bag here. This is a tough town, you know—a half-dozen guys beat the shit out of you and then demand a lot of money so it don't happen again."

"He's a cop," said Luis.

Ken curled a lip and narrowed one eye.

"You're going to hurt his feelings," I said.

"Mimi," Luis called out to a brunette with dark eyes and flowing hair hawking lap dances. She looked up from the customer she was leaning over. Luis nodded at Ken.

Braless under a baby doll top with a G-string and fish net stockings, Mimi walked up to Ken, threw her arms around him under his suit coat, and writhed her body against his. She turned her face up to his and said, "I got the lap dance if you got time, Sugar."

Ken smiled down at her and said, "Later, doll. I'll be sure to ask for you."

Mimi ran her hand over Ken's backside as she walked away. She looked at Luis and shook her head.

Luis said, "Fine. Too bad about your car." He looked at the bartender. "Give these guys a Corona with a wedge of lime."

"Panther piss," said Ken. "Gimme a Bud."

"Whatever," said Luis. "I'll call you a cab."

I held the bag out to him. "Shit, just take this. You delivered."

Luis backed up and showed me his empty palms. "I don't know what you got in that bag. I don't have anything to do with what you got in that bag. You got to go somewhere, take a cab."

"They keep records. The drivers have a log. Something—God forbid—goes wrong, the cops will be all over you."

"A lot of people who come here take a cab home," said Luis.

"They have some trouble, it's nothing to me, man."

"The cops are looking at me hard," I said. "Say they find me and some of your associates end up in the emergency room."

"Look, everything is cool, man," said Luis. "I understand you got some doubts. It's cool. No sweat, man. You'll see."

The bartender delivered the longnecks. I laid the bag on the bar.

"This belongs to your boss," I said.

The bartender reached for the bag. Luis grabbed the bag and shoved it at me. I took it.

"I'll give you a ride," said Luis.

"You sure, man?" I said. "You want to go where I'm going?"

"Yeah," said Luis. "I want you the fuck out of here."

I looked at the bartender and smiled, "He wants to go with me. That's important, because I don't ever want to take anybody someplace they don't wanna go."

The bartender looked at me sideways and then shook her head. She walked off to the other end of the bar. Ken picked up his beer and took a long tilt.

"I'll drop you off," said Luis. "A block, maybe—you can walk the rest. You'll be safe. You got your associate."

"Lead on," I said.

"Ain't you gonna drink your beer?"

I shrugged. "Rudy's gonna buy me one when we get back."

Luis's face got mean and satisfied. Ken swilled the rest of his longneck and set it on the bar.

"Car's in the back," said Luis. "C'mon." He led us through the curtain past the stairwell.

"All right," I said to the back of Luis's head, "we're out of sight. You can have what's in the bag now."

Luis spun around and chopped a finger at me. "Look, I've had it—"

And *WHAP!* That's when he got it. I smacked Luis between the peepers with the rubber mallet. He was all wrinkled forehead and kaleidoscope eyes, but not the only one surprised. The head of the mallet bounded from his forehead and flew off the handle. He deflated into a pile. I stood staring at the empty wooden handle in my hand.

"The fuck you bring me for?" said Ken.

"Ya know, Ken," I said, "you just can't buy shit for a buck these days." I swapped the wooden handle for the roll of duct tape. Luis mumbled something in Spanish I didn't *habla*. I rolled him over and taped his elbows together behind his back, then his ankles. I told Ken, "You said you wanted to be here," and sat Luis up to run turns of tape securing his hands and wrists to his body, tore off the tape, and said, "besides, I need you to carry him up the stairs to his office." I taped Luis's mouth.

"Why do I always get tapped for the grunt work?" said Ken.

He pulled Luis to his feet and draped him over his shoulder like a carpet. On the stairs, "Jesus Christ, somebody wants to move a freezer—call Ken. Fucking piano—I told her not to buy that goddam thing."

I opened the back door and yelled, "Yeah, okay, I'm coming—let's go." I pulled the door closed, picked up Luis's glasses, and trudged up the stairs. Luis sat flopped in his chair. Ken surveyed the row of cigarettes—about a third of the cases gone since my last visit—and the electronic equipment.

A large red circle swelled on Luis's forehead. His eyes were wild and his sinuses had emptied across the tape, down to his chin. He snuffled and strained through the flow, flaring his nostrils to gain his breath. I pulled the tape loose and he gasped a breath.

He said, "Fuc—"

I put the tape back in place.

"You know, Luis," I told him, "I'm willing to bet there's a box of tissues in this desk." I found them in the top right-hand drawer, pulled out a wad, and wiped his tape and chin. Folding once, I held the wad over his nose. "C'mon, honk. No reason to be embarrassed, I raised three kids."

He blew. I wiped and dropped the wad in the wastebasket. I studied his forehead, whistled, and shook my head, "That's gonna leave a mark."

Ken shifted through the cases of computers, making a short stack on the floor.

"I have a couple of questions," I said. "I wasn't going to do this. I planned to take you to the hospital and show you a little girl. Her house blew up and killed her mother. She's horribly burned and struggling for every breath. But that would be cruel and unusual. And maybe you want to help me anyway.

"You and your friend met with Hank Dunphy behind a fast food restaurant on Division Avenue. You took a bag full of money from Dunphy. Except I don't think you liked the man you drove there in the green Taurus."

Ken sat on the pile of boxes he'd made and folded his hands in his lap. Luis's eyes darted, refusing to look at me, his face astonished under the gray strip that covered his mouth.

I leaned my backside on the desk, put my finger in Luis's face, and pushed my face into his space. "I don't think you like him because he talked to you just like this."

Luis locked hot and angry eyes with mine.

"You didn't like it then and you don't like it now. That man you don't like blew up a house with a woman and a little girl in it. I want you to tell me where to find him. I know you know. I know you've been providing vehicles, little odd jobs, and probably meals and housing. He pays good but he doesn't respect you. You put up with that because the money is good. But what you don't know is that he is a mercenary—a terrorist—and when he is done with you, he will kill you. He left one of his associates to rot in a stone quarry—a guy who'd been loyal but became a liability when he got hurt. When this man you don't like is done here, you will be a liability."

I watched Luis close his eyes.

I said, "Nod your head if you want to talk to me."

Luis nodded. I pulled the tape loose.

Luis leaned toward me. He said, "Live fast, Anglo, life is short."

I put the tape back on and patted it. "Right. Well, that would have been too easy. Let's see what's in the bag."

Holding the bag open in both hands, I rolled my eyes up to Luis without raising my head. His eyes went wide. I said, "Humm? This?" I reached in the bag. Sweat ran down Luis's forehead and over the red goose egg above his eyes. "No, not this, not yet."

I set the bag in my lap. "You know, I had planned to play "the hammer of truth game" with you. You know, fix your hand to the top of the desk and ask you a bunch of questions I already know the answer to. When you lie I hammer your hand. When I get to the question I don't know the answer, you flinch if you're going to lie and I just keep pounding away until I get a straight answer—except you got a hard head and I bought a cheap hammer, so we got to improvise.

I opened the bag and looked in. "Oh, yes—indeed," I said and seized an object in the bag. Luis bolted to his feet. I planted a foot in the middle of his chest and shoved him back in the chair. "Think of this as a trip to the dentist," I said.

I took the bumper sticker out of the bag and displayed it in both hands. "See, Detroit Red Wings. I know that's familiar."

I watched his eye dart around the room.

Luis said, "Ahh humm a hum-hum."

"Oh, I know, you're thinking, 'What can that lunatic do with a bumper sticker?'" I studied it and then showed it to him edge on. "Very sharp if you move it fast. Don't you just hate paper cuts?" I showed him the backing. "Or maybe you peel off the backing and use it to pull out hairs. How do women do that? Wax, I mean." I hunched my shoulders and shook my head. "Gives me the shivers."

"Humph-hoo," said Luis.

"You know," said Ken, "I don't think his mind's getting right."

"Yeah," I said. "I think he'd rather be with his friends."

I took the hat out of the bag, peeled the backing off the bumper sticker, and applied it to the hat. "What do you think, Luis?" I put the hat on my head. "In the dark tunnel where I was told to deliver the money—where your associates are waiting to cave in my skull—think this will work?"

Luis's eyes took on a cold stare. I took the shirt out of the bag, rolled it up like I was dressing an infant, and looked at Luis through the head hole.

"Haa-haa-humph, hum."

"Don't worry. I bought an extra-extra large." I pulled it over his head and down his torso. I put the hat on his head. "What do you think, Ken?"

"Looks just like you."

Luis's eyes went wide, and his cheeks belled out from the scream held back by the gray strip across his mouth. He convulsed against his bindings, his feet running against the tape that held them together.

"I don't want to hear it, Luis," I said. "You could have helped. Now we're down to, 'What comes around goes around.' Ken, if you will do the honors, please."

Luis did not cooperate and earned a short straight right to the side of the head from Ken. "Don't make me hit you again," Ken told him. "I'm starting to like it."

I eased the edge of the curtain aside. Lights in the back room had been turned on. The bartender sorted empty longnecks into cardboard cases she'd spread out on the floor. She left and returned twice. I could hear Ken groaning. The lights went out and we eased down the stairwell and out the back door.

I guess people who own Jag rag-tops don't travel with much luggage. I had to put the top up before we could close the trunk lid over Luis. In any case he didn't make the task an easy one and needed a couple of body blows before we could fold him into an amenable shape.

We pulled out. Luis banged around in the boot. "Noisy bastard," I said.

"I think they're supposed to be dead when you put them in the trunk."

"I bow to your experience."

"How the hell should I know?" said Ken. "There ain't no trunk on a Harley."

We'd turned north onto Division when the red and blue rollers came on behind us. I looked in the mirror. Matty.

"Oh, shit!" said Ken. He shot a hand into his pocket and threw the bundle of fifties in my lap. "Tell them that's yours."

"Nothing to worry about," I said.

"Good, you can pay me tomorrow."

"If you insist," I said.

"Tell 'em I'm a hitchhiker," said Ken. "If they let me slide, I can get your bail posted."

I turned into the parking lot of a dry cleaning shop and stepped out of the car. Matty shut off the rollers and met me at the rear bumper. The Suburban pulled in behind her and killed its headlights.

"Art, you put a man in the trunk of your car."

"Two-seater, Matty." I shrugged and tried for the sound of confused innocence. "The package shelf is upholstered like a seat, but—"

"Open the trunk, Art."

I fumbled the key out of my pocket. My nameless best friend—the one newly flown in from Washington—stepped up between us.

"Luis Montalvo?" he said making the question sound like a statement. He unfolded a pair of glasses and hung them on his face.

"Luis," I said. "Street name Poco Loco, but that's all I have."

"He ready to talk?" my nameless friend asked.

"Ready as he is going to get," I said.

Matty looked from me to the man from Washington and back. I opened the trunk. The light came on. Luis lunged and struggled to yell against the tape. His eyes, beseeching, darted from my nameless friend to Matty. When no one moved to help him he lay very still and closed his eyes.

"This is it, Luis," I said. "Your shot. Don't blow it. Your blond-haired pal and his friends. Where are they holed up?" I pulled the tape loose.

He told.

• • •

"Sometimes all you can do is pray," is a cliché that has never provided me with much comfort. I much prefer my grandmother's oft-proffered, "The Lord helps those who help themselves."

"No one leaves or makes a phone call," said my nameless Washington benefactor—by way of inviting me and Ken to accompany the surveillance team. His third man being my witness to the Anne Frampton murder, I held little faith in his administrations, given the "extreme prejudice" with which Fidel/Andy and Jacob Anderson/Andy had come to justice.

"Tahiti Tanning," Luis had been in a hurry to tell them, before being sent to share separate cells with Hank Dunphy in the fifth floor at the federal building. "In the upstairs apartment—four or five guys."

As the night progressed Luis and good ole Hank set about informing on one another. By morning Luis proved to be the rat with the longest whiskers and won the "material witness" cheese- eating contest. State and federal charges against Hank Dunphy took days to compile, but among them was conspiracy to murder for hire. The bag of cash he'd given Luis was to purchase a "suicide" for Scott Lambert.

Ken slept loudly on the floor of the surveillance van, taking up most of the spare "foot space" and using his rolled-up suit jacket as a pillow. The van, a five-ton cargo box, had been done up as a telephone truck complete with boom and cherry picker. Inside, three technicians worked video, sound, and infrared consoles behind walls covered with black foam sound-absorbing insulation. Matty and I shared the precious little floor space not taken up by my itinerant hitchhiker's slumber.

At ten o'clock infrared cameras revealed three heat signatures—people— moving about the apartment above the tanning parlor, which had not a single customer despite tax returns that claimed monthly gross sales of ten to twelve thousand dollars.

Around eleven the clerk—a teenager with school books—turned out the lights and locked the door. Two additional people had arrived at the apartment by a quarter after one. By three-thirty the warrants, police, and fire department were in place. Forty minutes passed with no movement from the "heat signatures" inside, and an FBI SWAT team took the doors down.

On the back stairs one of the heat signatures presented itself as a hundred-and-twenty-pound mastiff with a spiked collar and a case of the ass. The boys in black counseled it with an MP5. The remaining occupants, roused by the gun fire, proved to be better armed than dressed and died in their undershorts.

An M-60, two forty-millimeter grenade launchers, a half-dozen LAWS rockets, and nine pounds of plastic explosive were recovered. All in all, a fine night's work, particularly if the third man—deliveryman/Andy—had been among the suspects dealt with. He was not, and upon that revelation one more cliché reared its ugly head: "The shit hit the fan."

"WHAT IS IT WITH YOU PEOPLE and all this dog shooting? Jesus Christ!" I said, as I stepped down from the surveillance van into the cool morning dampness. My nameless friend loomed over Matty, talking, moving his hands around the big picture and using the leg of his glasses to make the fine points.

"Ruby Ridge—you shot the kid's dog. Waco, same horseshit. What did you think would happen? Come to my house. Shoot my dog. You'll think Sherman's march to the sea was a tea dance."

"Excuse me?" he said—no arch in the eyebrows, no raise in the voice— his face the placid plowed field of Godhood and focused solely on me.

I took the moment to unwrap a cigar, clamp it between my bicuspids, and light it up. When his attention was spent and eyes swung back to Matty I said, "You just walked on your own banana, and it's your fault."

He snapped his eyes back to me and said, "Fault's hardly the point."

"Fault will be important when you park your ass at your desk to write your report," I told him. "Somehow I don't see you wrapping it up with, 'Thanks to my trigger happy cowboys—'"

"That's about enough—"

"The third man would be enough," I said. "And you don't have him. And you don't have anyone to ask where he's at."

Matty closed her eyes and gave one negative wag of her head. My anonymous friend folded his glasses and swept them into his coat pocket.

He said, "I bow to your superior technique."

Matty's chin hit her chest.

"Pepper gas would have taken out the dog. The yip might have woken them up but it wouldn't have sent them grappling for their firearms."

"We don't train that way," he said.

"And that vindicates you in what way?"

"The agent could have been shot while he was spraying the dog."

"Gas works on people," I said.

"Gas is a tactic we frequently employ."

"When you want to set the place on fire."

"That's never the intent," he said.

"I'm sorry," I said. "I don't find that answer credible."

"Thank you for your comment and criticism, Mr. Hardin," he said—more like a growl—his lips revealing a lot of teeth. He turned. Walking away, he offered, "Should you have something constructive to add, I'm sure Agent Svensen would be pleased to discuss it with you."

"Okay, Matty," I said, "you want to make it a hat trick?"

My friend stopped. Without turning around he said, "You know where he is?"

I looked at my watch—a quarter after five. "Just now, I haven't the foggiest notion." I took a drag on my cigar but it had gone out for want of attention. Turning, I leaned close to the side of the surveillance van to block the wind and lit my smoke. My nameless best friend turned about, his face a wry smile. I turned and exhaled a stream of smoke containing the words, "I know where he'll be at about ten o'clock this morning."

"Have another one of those?" he asked.

I plumbed the package out of my pocket and shook one loose. He took it. Matty tugged at my sleeve.

"Hey," she said, and took one when I turned the pack to her.

I offered her my pocket lighter. She waved it off and stashed the cigar in her purse.

"When I get home," she said. "If I ever get home."

"Don't inhale it," I said.

"I worked my way through law school as a Miami-Dade patrol officer," she said.

Our Washington visitor took my offer of the light, lit the cigar, and blew a stream of smoke on the hot end so that it glowed cherry red. "God, that's awful," he said.

"Same aged Chinese newsprint they used for the firecrackers we shot off as kids," I said.

"Agent Svenson, would you see to it that our guest, Mr. Ayers, is provided with transportation."

"Yes, sir," she said. Matty shot me a hot glance and stashed the cigar in the pocket of her windbreaker as she turned to walk to the back of the van.

"What is it you want?" he asked.

I told him, "I want to know what's going on."

He put the cigar to his mouth to take a toke, but thought better of it and held the cigar out to cast a discerning eye on the short brown shaft while he said, "It's all in front of you. And you're a professional. I'm surprised you care."

"Hey, I'm flattered," I said. "Pretend I'm stupid."

"A man of the nineteen-sixties would ask what he could do for his country."

"Taking your refuge, wrapped in the flag?"

He smiled and said, "Where do I find the man I'm looking for?"

"So we're back to, 'What's this about?'"

"Scott Lambert."

"You're right, I had that one," I said. "Lambert holds several patents which are a sea-change in energy technology. BuzzBee battery is contesting his patents, but I doubt they have the money to front the operation we have been looking at."

"They were acquired by a Middle Eastern energy consortium. BuzzBee Battery Inc. now consists of twenty-two people occupying an office space in Hackensack, New Jersey. Their manufacturing facilities and research and development laboratories were sold off. BuzzBee batteries are now manufactured by a jobber in Indonesia and distributed, for a fee, through a discount store chain. The remaining staff in Hackensack doesn't have the authority to run a petty cash fund and probably has no knowledge of the ongoing litigation."

"The Middle East? As in oil?"

My friend nodded and took a drag on the cigar.

"Sounds like a fairy tale to me."

He watched me, smoke escaping his mouth around the cigar. Taking it out of his mouth and using it as a pointer he said, "If you read the newspapers you know that the Middle East provides only thirty percent of our oil energy needs." He flicked the ash off the end of his smoke. "What the newspapers don't tell you is that there's a whole generation of young men who grew up quite comfortably in the Middle East. They are now traveled, educated, and from families of dwindling fortune and no prospects."

"The people running against Lambert were not Middle Eastern types."

"Pogo," he said.

"Poco Loco?"

"No. Pogo with a gee."

"Is that an acronym?"

"Comic strip."

I asked, "So, who's Andy?"

"ANDI, is an acronym. Allied Nations Defense Intelligence—a private consulting firm that operates from a post box in Jakarta. Their assets are, for the most part, abandoned or fugitive American and British agency types."

"Mercenaries?"

"We have been reaching out since nine-eleven, looking for sources whose placement was more important than their character. Until now their work has been clean, quick, and efficient, but at some point they decided to use our special relationship as a cover to run against U.S. interests."

"Great story," I told him. "The post box in Jakarta was a nice touch."

"I assure you."

"Oh, I have little doubt. But that doesn't explain what happened to me and Dixon. The IRS screwed Dixon."

My friend shrugged, "Dixon had tax problems long before this matter."

"The IRS screwed Dixon on cue."

"A coincidence."

"The post office provided the crap that was planted in my office."

"The way Cameran tells the story, you've been crowding his client list for years. The pornography was provided by a misguided friend."

"Cameran knew who Andy was."

"Cameran thought he was working a legitimate case for BuzzBee Battery."

"He thought working a legitimate case involved breaking and entering and planting evidence?"

"Cameran's retired, not an employee of any Federal Agency."

"Sheep-dipped?"

"No, he's really retired."

"So, that's your story and your sticking to it."

"Basically."

"Probably work," I said. "But it doesn't explain why you are here. Personally, I mean. And doesn't explain why you bothered to haul me out of the crapper."

"My work is," he said and pursed his lips, closing his eyes to search the inside of his head for a word. "Oversight." He looked at me almost casually and said, "Dixon caught on to the fact that ANDI had been doubled back on us and wrote a report that was more accurately filed than read. Since he was a retired federal officer, an account of his suicide landed on my desk and I found the report. At that point we received your photo of a man we had stopped looking for because we thought he was dead."

"Seemed like an excellent patsy?"

"With Dixon's report and the shoot-out with the local police, here, the cat was pretty much out of the bag. Nothing to do but tidy up. To use your parlance, I hauled you out of the crapper and hosed you off because it was convenient"

"Now that I believe," I said and clamped my molars on the end of my cigar. After all my work he still wasn't surly—guess that's why he was in charge of "oversight." I exhaled the last palatable toke on my cigar. "The man you're looking for," I said, "is the only witness to a murder that my client has been charged with."

"That sword could cut both ways."

"I need him alive."

"Fine. You take 'em," he said. He dropped his smoke on the ground and stepped on it. "But if he gets away from you, he won't get away from me."

• • •

To say that Bart Shephart *lived* somewhere is a dreadful stretch of the language. What he does is collide with the end of the day in a third floor walk-up above a hardware store near the corner of Alpine and Leonard.

At a quarter to seven I tried the telephone—no answer. I bought him a twenty-ounce coffee at a party store, climbed the steep outside stairwell to his "loft," and pounded on the door until his neighbors started yelling "shut up" out their windows. I found a key on the molding above the door.

Yelling in the door yielded more ugly responses from the neighbors. I stepped into a living room decorated in the ancient forgotten warehouse motif—the room being taken up with dusty moving cartons taped shut. A battered recliner attended a TV with a tin-foil-and-coat hanger antenna. Scattered about the room was the truly definitive collection of empty Kessler's bottles—ranging from pints to half gallons.

In the bathroom I followed a path through towels and clothing to the commode where I poured off the top two and a half inches of coffee. In the medicine cabinet I found a pint of Kessler's mouthwash and filled the coffee cup. Bart lay in his bed with his back to me, under a brown army blanket among about four loads of laundry. I shook him.

"Bart, Bart, wake up, Bart." I started him rolling toward me. He came awake with a five shot Smith hammerless ace-bandaged to his right hand. I grabbed the weapon by the frame and cylinder and managed to save the cup of coffee from the swipe of Bart's left paw. "Stop it," I told him, trying for a calm voice. "It's me, Art—Art Hardin."

"Are you fucking nuts?" he said and blinked his eyelids over bloodshot pools that looked like X-rays of chicken embryos. "I could have killed you. How the hell did you get in?"

"I used the key you leave over the door for the housekeeper. I thought you'd like to talk to a man who witnessed the Frampton killing."

I left Bart the coffee and went down to the car to call Lorna Kemp. The line clicked two or three times as the call was forwarded. Lorna had it before the third ring. In the background I could hear Leonard Jones ask in a sleepy voice, "Did you get it?"

She told me that Brian Hemmings was a registered nurse and had been fired from the state hospital where Sheldon Frampton had been committed. No one was volunteering explanations for the firing.

"Leonard Jones's attorney wasn't able to get the restraining order," said Lorna. "They're probably going to auction *The Dutchman* this morning."

"All right," I said. "I'm bringing Detective Shephart. There's a good chance that a man who witnessed Anne's murder will be there. I need you to meet me at the auction."

"What time?" she yawned.

"Auction starts at ten," I said. "Why don't you stop and see if Leonard Jones can give us a hand?"

"Sure," she said.

After forty minutes Shephart came down, having performed a minor miracle. He'd found a clean shirt, a gray suit, and a red tie. Of the two of us, he looked the less rumpled.

"I'm not an alcoholic," he said to break the silence after an hour on the road.

"Hair of the dog is all," I said. "Anything ever come of the knife I gave you in my office?"

"Came back from the lab a zero—fish guts and smoked ham. Where in the hell are we going?"

"South Haven," I said. "To an art auction at the Frampton estate."

Detective Shephart nodded off, then growled and gnashed his teeth for the rest of the ride. We found the iron gates swept open. Clouds gathering in the west over the lake promised rain later in the day. A yellow canvas tent big enough for a revival meeting had been set up on the lawn in front of the main house. News vans with tall satellite antenna booms crowded the inside of the fence line.

Cars lined both sides of the highway, including several ominously plain sedans. Parking inside the gate cost half a yard. If I hadn't been on Lambert's nickel, I'd have been some of the riffraff that turned away. Brian Hemmings collected the money and issued me a snotty face. I parked the Jag on a tennis court among a flock of high dollar sedans and liveried chauffeurs polishing limousines.

Detective Shephart hit the porta-potty and I picked up a white numbered paddle to bid. The catalog was eighteen pages and printed in color on slick paper. *The Dutchman* was item twenty-two. We had ten minutes.

"All right," said Shephart, buttoning his suit coat. "Where is this guy? I'm on my own time and I haven't had much of that lately."

"See, there's the thing," I said. "He's on the FBI's short list of things to do. So it's not like he is going to be anxious to talk to us."

"He might not be here," said Shephart, making an accusing face.

"He's here. The FBI rolled up his crew this morning."

"We should be looking for him at the airport."

"If he can get away with some artwork sold here today, he wins." I showed Shephart the picture of *The Dutchman*. "If he doesn't, he has nowhere to go."

"He could have sent someone else."

"Possible," I said. "I hope not."

Leonard Jones and Lorna Kemp walked up trying to look all business, despite that certain glow which hung over them. Leonard wore a tan herringbone sport coat over khaki pants and blue shirt open at the collar. Lorna was clad in a black shell over white denim slacks, with a dash of very red lipstick and her blond hair tied at the back of her head with a black velvet ribbon.

Shephart exchanged a handshake with Leonard. Lorna folded her arms against a cool breeze off the lake.

"Warmer inside the tent," I said.

"As long as those dogs aren't loose in there," she said. "Who are we looking for?"

"Remember the day I left for Brandonport?"

Lorna nodded once.

"The guy who said he had a package for me."

"Blond guy with the brown delivery jacket and lump under his left arm. The one that opened the door with his hanky."

"That's the one," I said. "He bragged to one of his associates that he'd seen the murder. Said the doer was a woman."

Lorna shifted her eyes to look at the house.

"Only maybe," I said, "I brought the booking photo you submitted with your report."

Leonard said, "You mean—"

"We don't know that," I said, "And—"

"He shouldn't be here," said Shephart.

Shephart and Jones shared a glower.

"He's a beard for Lorna," I said. "She's seen the man we're looking for and can probably get close without spooking him. If he does spook, Leonard has the beef to hold him."

"Civilians," said Shephart.

"The street is full of plain wrappers which means the tent's full of feds. For now they've agreed to let us make the apprehension, but I think that's only because we can finger him."

"Just so you know," said Shephart, "I'm on a 'frolic of my own.' If this goes to hell, nobody sues the city."

"Fair enough," I said. I looked at Leonard and Lorna. They nodded in agreement. We split up and headed for the tent.

We found standing room only, with a beef trust of brown shoes loitering near the doors and trying to look like art connoisseurs. Ladies in designer suits wearing the remnants of small furry animals filled most of the chairs. Here and there portly middle-aged men sat testing the tensile limits of expensive suits and studying the catalog. The air hung sweet with cologne, albeit tempered with a dash of moth crystals.

In the center aisle near the podium someone had parked a wheelchair with a lump of old codger in it. An oxygen bottle fixed to the chair snaked a clear plastic tube to a face lost under a winter hat pulled down to cover the ears and all but a shag of gray hair at the collar. A brown knit shawl—folded to a triangle—rolled languidly off both sides of a humped back, but failed to hang low enough to conceal a urine collection bag hung from the armrest.

Leonard and Lorna took the far side. Shephart and I took the near. Lorna looked over to me when she made it to the rear corner on her side and gave one negative twist of her head. I hadn't seen our man either. Matty sat in the first row and had abandoned her FBI windbreaker for a cable-knit yellow cardigan with a rolled collar. My nameless benefactor from Washington had coiled up on the last chair on the left side of the center aisle, a bidder's paddle hovering over his fist like the hood of a cobra.

Klieg lights illuminated the stage. Sheldon Frampton stepped up to the podium—provincial in old tweed with patches at the elbow and cradling a meerschaum pipe—with his hair silver gray, parted high on the left, and brushed straight back from his face. He had affected bushy eyebrows and a grizzled guardsman's moustache.

Sheldon patted the microphone with his fingers and looked pleased at the noise it made. He settled the pipe into his pocket and produced his voice synthesizer.

"I-can-not-tell-you. How-pleased-I-am. That-you-have-come. To-day. Anne-so-loved-her-work. She-lives-on. In-each-piece. You-may-take-home."

After a titter of polite applause Sheldon took a seat at the edge of the stage, the man with the gavel stepped up, and several cell phones leapt to ears from purses and pockets.

The sheer volume of money in the world often astounds me. I can remember a trip up the intracoastal in Miami. For a long stretch the yachts never shrunk to less than a hundred feet. The same sense of awe fell upon me as the items succumbed to the gavel. Casual waves of paddles and languid nods of the head signaled bids called at hundred-thousand dollar intervals.

The auctioneer—all nostrils, a pinky finger, and an affected highbrow accent—said, "Item twenty-two. An early work of Ms. Frampton's. Quite frankly a decorator piece with a rather amusing photo-active aspect. I would like to start the bidding at fifty thousand dollars."

No one stirred. I searched the crowd like a shipwrecked sailor looking for a raft. Nothing. My friend from Washington made an evil face at me. The auctioneer stepped away from the mike and bent close to Frampton for a whispered conference. When he returned to the microphone he said, "Very well, twenty-five thousand."

After a pregnant silence the man from Washington flashed his paddle.

"Twenty-five, may I have thirty?"

I showed my paddle.

"Thirty, yes—now thirty-five."

Matty bid.

"Thirty-five, thirty-five. Last call at thirty-five." The auctioneer picked up his gavel, which was really a fat walnut wedge that lacked a handle.

Matty looked like she was going to poop in her chair.

"Forty," said a woman in a green suit with gold buttons and some kind of red fur for a collar—her face hidden under the brim of a white felt hat.

"Forty-five."

Being my caliber, I bid.

"Forty-five, forty-five, now at fifty."

The codger in the wheelchair flashed a paddle.

"Fifty."

An attendant in a white uniform shirt and pants stood up from beside the old man. He wore a freshly cut flattop and a walrus moustache, both nut brown. He pushed the paddle down and shook his head at the auctioneer.

"Just keep that in your lap, Mr. Farragutt," he whispered. "Miss Molly only left it for you to hold, while she went to the dunny."

The man with the gavel pointed at the old man in the chair. "Fifty-thousand."

The attendant showed the auctioneer a shrug and his open palms.

"Fifty-thousand—once. Fifty-thou . . ."

"Fifty-five." The man from Washington.

"Sixty." The woman in the green suit.

I said, "Sixty-five." And showed my paddle.

Shephart whispered toward my ear, "Are you nuts?"

"I like it," I said.

Matty bid seventy.

The old man started to raise the paddle from his lap. The attendant thrust it down with both hands. The crowd made a nervous titter.

"One hundred thousand dollars," said a clear strong male voice halfway up on the right. The paddle appeared over the right shoulder of a man whose blond hair formed a wreath around a bare flesh yarmulke.

Why hadn't I seen him? For that matter, why hadn't I seen the attendant in the ice cream suit? I side-stepped along the back row of chairs and had to nudge Shephart with my shoulder to get him started.

"*The Dutchman*, I have one hundred-thousand dollars. One hundred and ten?"

The man from Washington held up his paddle.

"One hundred and ten thousand," said the gavel master, his face astonished. "Can I have one-twenty."

Shephart nodded for me to go up the middle while he went for the side aisle. The man from Washington got to his feet and the brown shoes slouching at the doors came to attention.

"One hundred and ten thousand. *The Dutchman*. Can I have one hundred and fifteen?" He pointed the gavel at the woman in green. She shook her head. "One hundred ten thousand dollars once."

The old man's paddle launched from his lap. He laughed, "*Heach, heach*." Sounded like a child drawing carpenter's twine through a hole in a shirt cardboard.

The gavelist stared at the attendant. "One hundred and fifteen thousand dollars. Can I have one-twenty?"

I closed in on my quarry. As I drew even with his row of chairs he looked at me—a glass eye and a bulbous red nose. Definitely not my man Andy. He held up his paddle.

"*The Dutchman*. One hundred twenty-thousand dollars."

I stood three feet from the attendant. He should have looked relieved. He didn't. He looked pissed and that is when I knew. Andy had dyed and cut his hair. I shook my head at Shephart.

The auctioneer said, "Excuse me, gentlemen."

I looked up to the stage and said, "I am so sorry. My dog has wandered off." I looked around the crowd. "A little Pomeranian, if you've seen him. He's such a scamp. Ko-ko, Ko-ko, Ko-ko." I whistled twice.

"If you please, sir."

I smiled. "Sorry. I'll . . . just be in the back here."

The gavelmeister cleared his throat. Andy turned to look at him. I laid a half nelson on Deliveryman/Andy and dragged him around the wheel-chair, toward the stage. People exploded from their chairs and flew side-ways like snow as the brown shoes plowed toward me and Andy.

I tilted my head to the side to defend my nose. I told him, "For God's sake man, don't fight, don't go for a weapon. They're here from Washington and looking to send you back as luggage."

"Get stuffed," he said.

The world suddenly consisted of hands and guns. I heard a thunder of retreating feet and screaming women. About a thousand angry men yelled, "You're under arrest," and added a variety of obscenities concern-ing heritage, body parts, and a least one mention of sheep. We careened toward the stage and fell into a pile.

Someone pulled me to my feet. Turned out to be Bart Shephart. The gaggle of agents unpiled, jerking and dragging Deliveryman/Andy toward the door. Sheldon Frampton sat bemused in his chair at the edge of the stage. The auctioneer had fled and taken *The Dutchman* with him.

"Wait," said the man from Washington.

The agents stopped like a power failure. They shoved their prize into a sitting position on the edge of the stage. Handguns on the ends of arms stuck in his face like a hound with a muzzle full of porcupine quills.

"Ask him," said my nameless benefactor.

I moved my head until I could make eye contact through the crowd. "You saw the murder of Anne Frampton?"

"Right enough. Didn't do the job myself, mind you, but I did plant the tuft of hair in her hand."

I pointed at Sheldon Frampton, "Was it him?"

Andy passed Sheldon a casual glance. "Nope, it was a woman. Kind of an older nag."

I fished the photocopied booking picture of Shelly Frampton out of my breast pocket and passed it between the growls and grumbles from the agents I had to nudge aside. Deliveryman/Andy took it and turned it to the light, pushing the paper out to arm's length and squinting his eyes.

"Not a good picture," he said, "But 'at's her, right enough."

"Sure?"

"Never forget. One stroke—real talent, she had. Women pushing men out of all the trades these days. Still jealous of the old bat's style, I am. The Frampton woman read her out, in right short fashion." He folded the paper and chopped it at me. "She didn't say a word. Just set to her work like Old Saint Nick and was off. Didn't stop to look. Didn't need to."

Deliveryman/Andy moved to hand the paper back but thought better of it and lay it on the stage. He said, "About time isn't it, Andy?"

I heard the sound behind me. *Poowing*. The sweet metallic chime of the safety handle disengaging from a hand grenade. The veterans in the crowd were already a blur, the old man was out of the chair—no longer old and no longer a man, but a lithe twenty-something brunette with dark eyes and an Uzi.

I had already taken two steps and dove into the chairs when I heard the grenade hit the stage. It didn't have time to bounce. I'd wrapped my arms around my head for protection and they muffled the sound and concussion of the detonation. Suddenly dark, klieg lights rained onto the stage. The podium somersaulted down the center aisle.

Outside, short rips from the Uzi punctuated the sounds of running feet, cursing, screaming, and intermittent handgun fire. I looked at my hands, rubbed my arms, and pushed the padded folding metal chairs off of me as I sat up.

Detective Shephart lay with his face in the turf at the base of the stage. Sheldon Frampton's feet stuck in the air on the far side of the stage, pant legs wrinkled to the knees exposing hairless legs, wool socks and oxfords. Leonard and Lorna rose from the ground at the rear of the tent, and two last agents scampered from among the chairs and out the door.

I knelt next to Shephart and touched his neck with two fingers, looking for a pulse. He batted my hand away.

"Goddam it, Hardin," he said without looking up. "This was my day off."

"Are you all right?"

Shephart pushed himself up to his knees, sat on the stage, and brushed the turf off his suit. "Blast went over me, but some goddam moose stepped on me. Where's Frampton?"

"On the other side of the stage. Looks like he just sat there and watched it happen."

"Or didn't know what was happening," said Shephart.

Leonard and Lorna, hand-in-hand, walked toward us—Leonard nonplussed, but calm in contrast to Lorna's wide eyes and unsteady gait.

"Hardin, you're as good as your word," said Leonard. "You got 'em, but I didn't expect justice to be this quick."

One of Sheldon's legs kicked and slid along the edge of the stage until it fell out of sight. I scooted around to the back of the stage. Sheldon's face and hands were peppered with measle spots. His hand worried a thin footlong shard of wood—a piece of the podium—protruding from his chest, which rose and fell with his labored breath. I pulled his hand away from the shard.

"Leave it be, for now," I told him, holding his hand as it shook. "If you pull it out, your lung could collapse or you could bleed to death."

He swallowed and his lips moved. I rummaged his coat pocket for the voice synthesizer and pressed it to his throat.

"What-what-hap-pened?" Sheldon's eyes searched. "I-can-not-see."

"I'll get an ambulance," said Lorna. She patted Leonard's shoulder. "Stay here." She hurried off.

"Mr. Frampton," said Shephart. "I'm a police officer. You are badly injured. We have summoned help. While we wait I need to talk to you. A man is in jail for a murder that he did not commit. Your statement could correct a horrible injustice."

"My-rights."

"If you recover, this statement won't be used against you."

"Shel-ly," said Frampton. "Shel-ly-did-it. Poor-Anne."

"For God's sake, Frampton," said Leonard, with a break in his voice. "Why?"

"I-loved-them-both. Anne-and-Shelly. My-fault. I-grabbed-the-wheel. Mother-told-me."

"Anne Frampton?" said Shephart.

"Shel-ly-loved-her-too. A-fraid-she-would-leave. Anne-could-talk-so-mean," said Frampton. He closed his eyes and his head fell to the side.

I patted the hand I was holding. "Hang on, Sheldon. Help is coming."

"Was-hard-for-Shel-ly," said Frampton without opening his eyes or turning his head. "Her-life. So-hard. Lived-with-aw-ful. De-cis-sions. She-did-not-want. She-did-not-make."

Sheldon opened his eyes and turned his face to Shephart—squinting and blinking as if the light had returned. With his free hand he patted Shephart's bent knee.

"Shel-ly-is-gone. She-told-me. Be-fore-she-left. She-was-sor-ry." He closed his eyes. Tears plowed the furrows under his eyes and he made a sigh that turned to a cough. Blood ran from the corner of his mouth. "She-told-me. Not-to-be-lone-ly. Not-to-be-sad. She-said. Some-times. You-just-have-to. Start-over."

Mr. and Mrs. Deliveryman/Andy—God knows who they were—left in the black wagon. Sheldon got the white wagon with the lights on it. Brian

Hemmings rode with him. I left Leonard and Lorna sitting in Annie-fannie's studio—clinging to life and one another—-watching the wind and rain drive the waves from Lake Michigan to expend themselves on the shore.

The man from Washington departed without comment. Matty left a note in the Jag. "I'll be at my desk in the morning. Bring the money. There's a form you have to sign."

I dropped Bart Shephart at the Detective Bureau and headed for my office. My car had been dropped off with a new windshield in place. The keys were supposed to be under the mat, but the doors were locked. What the hell, the Jag needed one more ride.

I pulled off the blacktop at the end of the lake and looked across the water to my house. The sun lay dim and low in the clouds that threatened from the west. For now, the lake rested without a ripple. Lights from the house reached across the water in reflected streaks to point my way home.

The card I'd bought for Wendy lay heavy in my pocket—the little boy and girl on the cover. I took it out and read aloud, "When you're young at heart/Life is forever new." I took out my pen and wrote, "Let us begin, again."